GW00859202

Rebecca's Redemption

Book One

Erin Heitzmann

AuthorHouse™
1663 Liberty Drive
Bloomington, IN 47403
www.authorhouse.com
Phone: 1-800-839-8640

First published by AuthorHouse 7/28/2009

ISBN: 978-1-4490-0277-0 (e)
ISBN: 978-1-4490-0275-6 (sc)

Printed in the United States of America
Bloomington, Indiana

This book is printed on acid-free paper.

Chapter 1

Rebecca Halloway sat with pristine grace on the piano bench, her clear, emerald eyes dancing across the room toward Moira Bronlee who was seated at the organ. The two women were concluding the evening church service with a round of hymns, while the pastor sang along with the rest of the congregation. There was a jovial spirit in the quaint white building, and Rebecca thought it was the perfect conclusion for their week long revival celebration. The lively music continued long after the parishioners had wandered down to the basement in search of food, with Rebecca launching into a new hymn to see if Moira could keep up. Her bright eyes lit across the room to meet the steadfast gaze of the old woman, her soul reveling in the beautiful music, as well as in the spirited talent of her friend. Finally, with a chortle of defeat, Moira flung her hands into the air.

"I can't go on!" she conceded with a wry smile. "These old fingers have lost their stamina I'm afraid."

Rebecca laughed lightly and continued to play, her fingers dancing over the ivory keys, while she asked, "Are you staying for the dessert social, Moira?"

"I'll be staying," the old woman said, "but I'm not sure how social I'll be feeling."

Rebecca giggled, knowing that even in her grumpy state Moira was a love. She had been a fixture in the Church by the Sea since Rebecca had been an infant, and Moira was as dear to her as her own grandmother had been.

"Shall we go down then?" the woman asked, pushing herself to her feet with a grimace.

"Not tonight, Moira," Rebecca smiled. "I think I'll pass on the socializing and take the long way home to savor the evening instead."

"You'd best not set your mind on that, young lady," Moira cautioned with a stern scowl. "There'll be men about tonight with all those ships in port..."

Rebecca gave a nonchalant toss of her head, having heard the cautious words of warning several times before. Although she had never felt threatened by the sailors who often meandered about the city, still she took great care not to draw unnecessary attention to herself. Portsmouth was a prominent hub for the massive British ships fighting the war with Napoleon Bonaparte's France, and when the sailors were granted shore leave, they spent most of their time imbibing in rum and drink in the various taverns scattered throughout town. Rebecca needn't have heeded the warning on this night, for she had seen on more than one occasion the effects of rum on otherwise genteel men.

Rebecca stood to her feet and moved to embrace the old woman. "I will be careful, Moira," she whispered, holding on to her dear friend a bit longer than usual. "And I'm going to take the path along the shore...I won't even catch sight of one of those fearsome sailors. Eat a slice of pie for me," she added before turning to leave.

Moira watched Rebecca slip out the door, her short, auburn hair forming natural tendrils about her face in the moist air of the English coast. The old woman fretted over the girl as if she were her own and worried about her relentlessly, for she knew the girl was oblivious to the dangers that surrounded her living in a town such as Portsmouth. Many in the church's congregation shared Moira's concern for Rebecca's naïve manner, for she was much adored by all who knew her. Now, as the old woman watched Rebecca wander down the path, she was tempted to follow after her, wanting to make sure no harm befell the girl, but instead she turned with a sigh to climb down the narrow steps of the sanctuary, her arthritic joints in no mood for a stroll.

Rebecca walked out into the cool evening breeze, reveling in her memories of the revival service. She considered the Church by the Sea her second home, and the parishioners the extended family that had been dearer to her than her own had been, for she seldom saw relations on either her mother or her father's side of the family. Her mother was of Irish decent, and her father was an Englishman, but having both been called into the service of the Lord as young adults, the family had spent time in Africa, France and Spain for most of Rebecca's young, childhood years, allowing little time to consort with cousins, aunts, uncles and grandparents. The Halloways had returned to England shortly before Rebecca's sixteenth birthday, and now, nearing adulthood, she was feeling the Lord calling her into the ministry as well, just as He had called her parents so many years before, her father as a doctor, and her mother as a school teacher. Having witnessed their faithful ministry to others with selfless abandon, she was a fresh sapling with roots that were firmly embedded in richly tilled soil. Rebecca had always known in the deepest depths of her soul that her only true happiness would be found in serving God, and having just recently celebrated her eighteenth birthday, she was preparing to return to the coast of Africa once again, this time as a young woman, and alone.

Rebecca left the safety of the church to meander down the path toward the shoreline, humming to herself the melodies of the hymns she and Moira had played that evening. The waves of the Atlantic Ocean were lapping at the moist sand, leaving no evidence of those who had passed by, while the sounds of the reveler's mirth were carried across the wind to her ears. At times like these she was grateful that she and her parents lived on the outskirts of Portsmouth, putting them a good distance away from the boisterous activities of both the lonely sailors, and those who chose to consort with them. Rebecca had seldom felt comfortable in the presence of young men, considering them instead a needless distraction from her calling, and so she avoided all who pursued her with romantic interests in mind. Moira needn't have voiced her concern on this night, Rebecca thought ruefully, for she was vigilant to keep a safe distance between herself and any male presence who might express an interest in something other than just a casual acquaintance. Rebecca smiled to herself at the thought of the old woman, and her unrelenting efforts to see Rebecca married and on her way to motherhood. A soft giggle escaped her as she continued on her way, intent on avoiding the rocks embedded in the craggy pathway.

Several feet ahead of where she walked, a group of unruly and overly imbibed sailors tussled at the water's edge. They had long ago been tossed from the taverns because of their raucous behavior, and now they sat in a drunken stupor on the beach making lewd comments to those who unknowingly wandered nearby. It wasn't long before one of them caught a distant glimpse of Rebecca from where he lounged on the damp sands of the shoreline.

"Well, have a look over there boys," he slurred, "...a wee lassie out for a stroll. What say we have a little fun?"

The men glanced towards Rebecca, their eyes filled with malicious intent, as they began to scatter into the leafy foliage of the brush lest she see them.

"Hey," slurred another. "Let's take her back to the ship with us. Seems a shame to partake of her pleasures for only one night!"

The others began to snicker in the darkness where they lingered, hidden from the girl's sight, while they waited for her to draw near.

Rebecca grew weary of the jagged rocks embedded in the ground, and was grateful when she finally arrived at a broad expanse of sandy terrain, where she was determined to remain for as long as she was able to in the hopes that she would avoid a nasty fall. She was distracted by her pensive musing, and oblivious to the four drunken men who lurked in the shadows, plotting to abduct her and steal her away to their ship. She continued to meander along the path until she was startled out of her reverie by the sound of rustling in the nearby trees. Rebecca glanced up in surprise, only to find a strange man teetering on the path in front of her, a disheveled midshipman's uniform loosely slung over his shoulders and his breath heavy laden and reeking with the odor of rum.

"Hullo, miss," he slurred, his lewd gaze raking over her small form.

Rebecca took a precautionary step backward, her heart pounding at the unexpected sight of the bedraggled stranger. "Oh! Excuse me..." she stammered, making a deliberate move to step around him.

Without warning she watched the sailor lunge toward her and she crouched low to the ground, her heart catching in her throat in fear. Turning to make an attempt to flee from his menacing grasp, she was stunned to see herself surrounded by strange men, but before Rebecca could utter a cry for help, she was struck on the side of the head with a blow that sent her reeling to her knees. She remained there for an instant, a look of bewildered terror in her eyes, before she slid listlessly into the brush. A loud gasp of air escaped her when she hit the ground, where the damp sand muffled the sound of her groans. She was too dazed to resist the men who gathered her into their clutches, and soon felt her consciousness waning, as the sailor's took hold of her arms to drag her haphazardly toward a dinghy resting near the water's edge. Rebecca was aware for only a brief moment that she was being tossed about on the waves before she slipped into unconsciousness, as the darkness enveloped her at last.

It was the smell that first assaulted her senses when she began to stir, and she struggled to open her eyes only to realize that she was in total darkness. A wave of nausea overcame her with unexpected force and she struggled against the urge to expel the contents of her belly. Unable to quell the sensation, she turned to release the bile rising in her throat, gasping in alarm when her hand fell upon the lifeless limb of the cold body lying next to her, unmoving and still. Her head throbbed with any sort of movement she made and she clenched her jaw tightly, determined to keep from crying out at the sharp stabs of pain that coursed through her with each violent spasm of her stomach. When she had finished vomiting, she turned back and tried to orient herself to the unfamiliar surroundings. Reaching out with her hands, she was dismayed to find that she was surrounded by bodies, some twitching with sporadic tremors and others not moving at all. She could hear the low groans of misery arise from the shadowed forms when they began to stir around her, while the stench of musty air soon grew unbearable. With a start she realized she was in the belly of one of the many frigates that had been moored in the harbor, and she knew without a doubt that her first priority would be to disguise herself as one of the men lest they discover there was a woman in their midst. Blinded by the darkness, she again reached for the motionless form of the man beside her. She struggled to maneuver his heavy body in an attempt to slide his tunic over his head. A moan escaped him when she tugged at his flaccid limbs, but to her great relief, he did not awaken, and she hurried to steal the shirt from his limp frame. In one, swift motion she slipped her dress down over her shoulders, quenching the bile that again rose in her throat at the putrid smell of the clothing she pulled over her head. The man's trousers came off much easier, for they had already worked their way nearly down to his knees. She slipped them on in haste and struggled to stand to her feet, where she teetered precariously before attempting to move. Once safely hidden beneath the clothing, she tore a strip of the cotton undergarments she had worn to bind around her head, while she twisted her dress into a tight bundle, hoping to discard of it as soon as she was able to. She then drug herself across the sea of bodies, some mumbling, others cursing, and still others saying nothing at all as she crawled over the top of them. She stumbled blindly across the expanse of the floor and followed the wall with her hands until she felt a door give way. Squinting against the bright light of day, she climbed up to the deck, where she was quick to blend in with men working there. None paid her any mind at all as she set about coiling the lengths of rope strewn about, keeping her face lowered and hidden from sight, while she began to utter desperate prayers for deliverance from this nightmare she had awakened to.

Chapter 2

THE DAYS READILY dissolved into nights while Rebecca struggled to keep up with the crew in their tasks aboard the *Defiance*, a large frigate under the command of Captain Thomas Cromwell. She soon lost all track of time and it began to seem like ages since she had last seen sight of land. Though her heart was breaking with homesickness, she gave thanks to God each day for keeping her identity hidden from the men. None took notice of her as she went about her days in silence, praying and hoping that her deliverance would be quick in coming.

It wasn't long before Rebecca began to realize that the men aboard the Defiance were an unruly bunch, and their captain was even more incorrigible, but what else was to be expected aboard a ship called Defiance, she thought. During the daylight hours, Captain Charles Cromwell remained secluded in his stateroom, drinking himself into an angry stupor. By night he was usually passed out and the men became loud and belligerent, while the officers remained hidden in the safety of their quarters, unwilling to place themselves in harm's way by attempting to maintain order among the obnoxious crew. Rebecca, ever cautious until the very end, kept herself safe by slipping into a small storage closet during these times, protected from and oblivious to the bloody fights that too often broke out among the undisciplined lot.

Almost as abundant as the fighting was the insubordination, and floggings occurred with great frequency aboard the Defiance, as did even more severe punishments that Rebecca made a desperate attempt to hide herself from. She was relieved that the men did not concern themselves with her presence, and realized they had become much accustomed to the unfamiliar faces of young stowaways. They had little cause to concern themselves with her, for she never uttered a word, and she was vigilant to stay hidden away as much as she was able to lest she draw unwanted attention to herself. She prayed without ceasing for a chance to escape the Defiance, and having not seen land since she had been abducted, she prayed that it would be soon. She had been formulating a plan of escape since being taken captive, and was determined to disembark with the crew at their first port call, with the hopes of stowing away on another vessel bound for Portsmouth, her beloved home.

Rebecca's opportunity for escape came sooner than she had anticipated, when one afternoon while enjoying the warmth of the sun on her back, she overheard a group of men making plans for their mooring in Cadiz, a large port city on the southern coast of Portugal. Tilting her head toward the direction of their conversation, she wondered if this was the deliverance she had been praying for. She listened with a keen ear while they spoke of the taverns, the women, and the rum awaiting them in Cadiz, but even after several minutes, they had not yet disclosed when the frigate would arrive at her destination. No matter, Rebecca resolved, she was determined to be ready to take her leave of this vessel as soon as the opportunity presented itself.

It was just four days later that shoreline of Cadiz was in sight, and Rebecca was breathless with excitement at the thought of boarding a ship headed back to England. Although it was almost two full days before the massive Defiance sailed into port, and then a half a day longer for the captain to dismiss the crew to their shore leave, Rebecca waited with resolute patience, certain that her moment of deliverance had come at last. She remained on deck while the ship dropped anchor, watching and waiting for the bustling activity on the frigate to subside until she was finally able to steal onto the last dinghy taking men ashore.

Once aboard the dinghy, Rebecca kept her head lowered for the short trip to shore, being careful to keep her eyes averted from the glances of the men who sailed with her. She breathed a giddy sigh of relief when she felt the welcome scrape of solid ground beneath her, as the skiff slid onto the sand in the shallow waters of Cadiz. Hastening over the side, she paid no attention to the water that sloshed at her legs, her only thoughts consumed with putting as much distance as possible between herself and the men of the Defiance. She carried nothing with her, having had nothing save for the dress she had worn when she had been abducted from Portsmouth. Her only possessions now were the clothes she wore on her back, and her memories of home which had never ceased to linger in her heart.

Rebecca thought it strange being on land again after having been at sea for three long months, and it left her feeling a bit nauseous. She stood for a moment, hoping to still her swaying legs before she began to wind her way through the throngs of people lingering about the town. She gazed at the myriad of colorful ships floating in the harbor while she wandered near the water's edge, taking care to stay close to where the frigates were moored in the hopes of overhearing which among them would be sailing back to England. She kept her eyes and ears open as she strolled past the taverns, hoping to come across a group of rum laden sailors bragging of their travels at sea…of where they had come from, and of where they were sailing to. Glancing around, she soon found an overgrown clump of foliage, and she tucked herself away in the thickets to keep herself concealed from the eyes of the men lurking about.

It wasn't long until Rebecca heard someone speaking of her beloved Portsmouth, and with a cautious breath she peeked out from behind the brush. She saw that the voices belonged to men who were tanned and muscular, staggering about in their drunkenness while they mumbled with slurred words of their ship, *Redemption*, and of how, come the morrow, they would be sailing back to England.

Rebecca stifled a gasp of elation when she heard mention of the word redemption, and thought surely it must be a sign from God that the frigate they sailed on was to be her deliverance. Too long had she been delayed she thought, in her plans to minister to the lost, and now finally, after three trying months at sea, she would be returned to her home where she would resume her life where it had been so unexpectedly interrupted.

Rebecca glanced again at where the men lingered before nestling back into her hiding spot lest she be seen, and she waited with nervous anticipation until the men had finished their pints of rum. Only when she saw them staggering toward the path that would lead them to the water's edge did she dare to venture out from behind her sanctuary to follow after them, being careful not to get too close while they stumbled toward the skiff that she hoped would return them to their ship. She slipped in behind them and meandered along as if in a stupor, trying her best to appear intoxicated with drink…a feeling she had never before experienced in her sheltered life as a missionary's daughter.

Nearing the water's edge, Rebecca was relieved to see that the young sailor waiting in the small dinghy didn't even pause to give notice to the men tumbling into the boat. It was obvious to her that he was irate at having to put up with the raucous crew and wanted only to be relieved of his post for the evening.

"Come on, then!" the young man shouted. "I haven't got all bloody night!"

The few moments it took to get all of the staggering bodies into the skiff felt like hours to Rebecca, but before long the small boat began to bob about on the waves, as the irate sailor began to row against the surge to deliver the boisterous group to their ship. Rebecca kept her gaze peeled in the darkness as the brightness of the moon faded for a time behind a heavy cloud. When they drew nearer to the shadowed frigate listing on the water, the cloud dissipated, and the bright moon illuminated the name *Redemption* resting regally on the luminescent waves. Its name, reflected clearly in the water, brought tears to Rebecca's eyes, and she covered her mouth to feign a cough lest her emotions give way to the sobs that hovered in her throat. Rebecca gazed in awe at the beautiful sight and gave thanks to God for providing this vessel to return her to her home. She cast a quick glance at the faces peering down from the railing and was stunned to see a rope ladder being flung over the side of the massive ship. Rebecca doubted she would ever manage to drag herself up the precarious rungs, until she watched through an expression of awestruck wonder as the intoxicated sailors tossed themselves haphazardly onto the ladder to begin the long crawl towards the railing, swinging to and fro in the air as they went. Swallowing her apprehension, she prepared to make an attempt to climb aboard, and it was fortunate for her that the men were in such a drunken state, for her clumsy efforts passed unnoticed by those who watched from above.

Rebecca breathed a sigh of relief when her feet landed on the solid deck of the Redemption, and she moved with haste away from the clusters of men who lingered nearby before allowing herself the liberty to glance around at the unfamiliar surroundings. She was surprised to see that the frigate somewhat resembled the Defiance, only the Redemption appeared to be much larger. It would be easy to remain hidden from the crew on this ship, she realized, and she again offered thanks to God for His mercy at leading her to the vessel which was sure to return her to England. With little effort she blended into the crew who chose to remain on deck, and few paid her any mind at all when she set out to find an unoccupied space in which to hide herself away for the remainder of the night.

The crew aboard the Redemption seemed much more orderly than those aboard the Defiance, for their captain, William Jameson, ran a tight ship, and harsh discipline of the men was rarely practiced, or necessary. It was evident to Rebecca as time went on that the crew respected their captain, and the camaraderie among the men was a welcome distraction after witnessing the violent outbursts all too common on the Defiance. In no time at all Rebecca began to feel safe aboard the Redemption and mingled with ease among the hard working men who went about their day-to-day tasks with high-spirited vigor. She remained unsure as to when the captain planned to sail for Portsmouth but was content to wait until that moment came. To help pass the time she worked in the galley along side Eddy, the ship's cook, a considerate man who seemed to her to be all of twenty years. He was kind to Rebecca, believing her to be a young boy…a mute stowaway in need of a safe haven and desperate enough to seek one aboard the Redemption. Rebecca, in an effort to keep her identity hidden from the crew, never uttered a word to him, but she soon discovered that his endless chatter more than made up for her silence. They spent most of their days together side by side, working to feed the hungry crew, until nightfall, when she would slip away to the rear of the frigate in an effort to seek some much needed solitude, while the men enjoyed their free time below deck in the crew's quarters. Her most enjoyable moments were spent lying beneath the stars and whispering through the chilled air of evening to the Lord of the wonderful adventures she would have when her prayers for deliverance had finally been answered. And then, when the darkness of night enveloped her in its lonely embrace and she could no longer keep her eyes open, she would make her way to the small storage compartment which she had claimed as her berth and drift comfortably off to sleep, unnoticed by all who considered the Redemption their home.

Several of the officers on the ship soon became familiar to her, and her favorite among them was a lieutenant by the name of Paul Burgess. He had the most considerate manner with his men, and it was easy to see that he held their respect and admiration as well. The other lieutenants seemed to be more reserved and aloof, maintaining an officer's air of superiority, and although they didn't intermingle with the ship hands, they did not treat them maliciously as some of the officers on the Defiance had taken pleasure in doing. Rebecca enjoyed watching the interactions of the ship's crew, but especially those involving Mr. Burgess, for it was obvious to her that he held the loyalties of his men. Rebecca considered him young in comparison to most of the other officers onboard the Redemption and she found herself gazing often at his kind face, with his dark eyes that lit up when he was acting in jest, and a ready smile for even her on occasion. She found her thoughts turning to home less and less and soon settled into a contented complacency aboard the frigate, confident that God's plan for her life would soon resume its course.

Chapter 3

THERE HAD BEEN little relief from the blistering sun for the past several weeks and tempers on the Redemption were running short. The frigate had been caught up in the doldrums, the lack of a breeze casting an oppressive mood over the crew as well as the captain. They had been at sea now for well over two months, and all were growing weary of the relentless boredom. After the midday inspection the captain ordered a round of rum to boost the men's spirits and Rebecca could hear their glad shouts from the galley, where she and Eddy were preparing the noon-day meal. She wandered to the doorway to steal a quick look through the bright sunlight, curious to see what the commotion was all about.

Eddy heard the whoops of delight as well and glanced over his shoulder to say, "It'll be a loud night tonight with the rum starting so early, I can guarantee you that!"

Rebecca cast a wry grin his way and nodded her head, turning to peer again through the portal when the squeals of surprise and shouts of laughter reached her ears. She caught a glimpse through a cluster of men who were spraying one another with water, and soon spotted Lieutenant Burgess in the center of their circle, no doubt trying to cool himself from the penetrating rays of the sweltering sun.

"Well look at that," Eddy grinned, grabbing her up by the arm to drag her towards the corridor. "Looks like we won't have to suffer this infernal heat after all!"

Rebecca slipped free of his grasp, preferring instead to remain in the safety of the small room, but with a quick shake of his head he pushed her toward the deck to join in on the carousing.

"Come on now," he laughed. "I won't be leaving you behind!"

Rebecca continued to struggle as he pulled her along behind him and into the circle of men. She was dismayed to see them peeling off their wet clothing, and was quick to shut her eyes against the sight of their nakedness. In her embarrassment she turned away and made another attempt to break free of Eddy's grasp. With a stunned gasp of surprise, she felt cold water coursing down her back, while burly arms reached to draw her into the throng of sinewy, wet bodies.

"No, please...let me go!" she whispered to Eddy, her eyes darkened with alarm, but he was already lost to the exhilaration of the moment and remained unaware of her pleading. Rebecca thrashed about in her efforts to break free of the hold the men had on her as the water sloshed among them, but still she was tugged further and further into the rambunctious melee. A low moan escaped her when she felt her tunic being torn loose from her shoulders, and with relentless determination she clawed at those that restrained her, desperate to make an escape from the precarious situation.

Glancing through the crowd in horrified confusion, she soon became aware of a strong pair of hands twisting her around, until with a gasp of surprise, she found herself face to face with Lieutenant Burgess. She grappled against his grip on her as he laughed and jostled her about, again teasingly making an attempt to loose the clothing from her shoulders. She heard him shouting encouragement to the men who wrestled with one another nearby, and they too, joined him in his efforts to pull the clothing from her body. In a desperate panic, she struggled once more to break free of their circle, and pushed with desperation at the hands that held her in a vise-like grip, determined to keep her identity hidden from them all.

Lieutenant Burgess wondered why the lad resisted with such vehemence, certain he must be as miserably hot as the rest of them, and in a loud voice he said, "Come on, man! You can't be afraid of a little water...a bath would do you well!"

Rebecca wrapped her arms around herself, hoping to dissuade the men from their intentions, but they were not to be deterred. By now the entire group was caught up in the high spirited adventure, and they laughed and pushed her about as Lieutenant Burgess took hold of her wrists and attempted to force her arms behind her back. Rebecca was terrified by the determination of the crowd, but helpless to overcome their strength. With a grimace of desolation, she watched the officer reach anew to grasp the muslin tunic covering her small frame, and with great dismay, Rebecca again heard the stitching begin to give way. She uttered a piercing cry and made one last, deliberate attempt to free herself. Spinning around to face the lieutenant, she thrust her knee up and into his belly with as much energy as she could muster. She heard him gasp in surprise at the force of the impact, and felt his hands drop from her shoulders, leaving Rebecca looking on with a bewildered expression of relief, while the young officer double over in pain, his breath catching with great, ragged gasps in his throat.

Lieutenant Burgess felt the air being pushed from his lungs with the impact of the blow. He was stunned by the lad's actions more than anything, for he knew that the punishment for assaulting an officer such as himself would be severe. It took a moment for him to catch his breath, but even in his great discomfort he was aware of the eerie silence that fell over the crew gathered on deck.

The men were dumfounded by what they had just seen, and turned to glare at the lad with vicious contempt, he being the one who had dared to strike out at their most revered officer. Before Rebecca realized what was happening they were piling on top of her, striking out in blind fury, while their fists pummeled every exposed area of her body.

Rebecca crumpled to her knees beneath the weight of them, trying to fend off the blows of the cursing mob before she slid with a cry of defeat to the ground. She gasped for air from where she lay, crushed on the deck of the frigate, and what little air she drew was filled with the scent of sweat and blood. Her last thoughts before the blows drove her into darkness were of her father and mother, and the possibility that perhaps she would never see them, nor her beloved homeland again.

Lieutenant Burgess was quick to regain his composure and stood to his feet.

"Stand back there!" he shouted, trying desperately to peel the insidious crew away from the boy. He had no doubt that they would kill him if given the chance, and he wanted to deal with the situation in his own manner. "Stand back I said!"

His screams were soon heard above the din, and he watched while the men stepped away from the lad's crumpled body. He glanced down and began to nudge at the listless form with his foot, trying to stir him to consciousness, but to no avail.

"Lock him in the hold," he growled to his petty officer. "I'll deal with his insolence when he regains consciousness."

Petty Officer Andrews reached down to grasp the tunic clinging precariously to the limp body and began to drag the young stowaway to the hold in the belly of the ship. He saw that the boy remained motionless and silent, and he doubted this one would survive the night. Pushing the heavy door open, he drug him into the darkness and left him lying on the cold floor, where he saw the bruises beginning to stain the pale skin, while the blood dried in a crusted layer over the boy's face. "Pity," he mumbled. "And so young..."

Several hours later Rebecca began to stir and she struggled to open her eyes against the swollen lids that held them shut. Reaching up with a tentative hand, she felt the welts of the bruises beneath the dried blood. Any attempt at moving brought waves of pain coursing through her limbs, and it was then that she remembered the attack on the deck of the Redemption. She was relieved that the men had not killed her, in spite of the agonizing throbbing in her head. With a sigh of weariness, she gave in to the aching fatigue that overcame her, and again drifted off into unconsciousness. She slept for several hours, never fully waking, but only stirring on occasion due to the pain that wracked her frail body.

Petty Officer Andrews returned to the deck after a hearty meal of mutton and boiled potatoes. Yawning in his contentment, he moved to resume his position on watch. He was aware of someone approaching, and was surprised to see that it was Lieutenant Burgess. "Good evening, sir," he said with a smart salute.

"Good evening, Mr. Andrews," the officer replied. "Has the boy awakened yet?"

"No, sir...hasn't stirred a bit that I can tell."

"Well be sure to call me when he regains consciousness," he ordered. "We have unfinished business to attend to."

The petty officer waited until the lieutenant returned to the quarterdeck before he again retreated below to observe the battered body lying in the hold, still not expecting to find any signs of life, and almost thinking it would be better if the lad never regained consciousness at all.

On the second day after the beating Rebecca was able to open her eyes a bit and saw that she was in a holding cell of some sort, with a stout door surrounding a small opening covered with bars. She gazed about the dimly lit area and wondered if she was alone, or if she shared the room with others. "Hello?" she called out in a tentative manner.

Hearing nothing, she attempted to raise herself from the floor and found that she could make out voices in the distance, but none that she recognized. She soon caught sight of a wooden bowl that had been placed near her, and hoped it might have a bit of water in it with which to wash her face. She struggled to pull herself close enough to reach it, and when she did she found that it was filled with dried porridge that someone had left for her to eat. With a defeated cry she dropped back onto the unyielding ground and cried out in her anguish to be free of the pain that permeated through to her very bones. She soon drifted back to sleep, for later she was awakened by the sound of the rusty hinges on the door as someone pushed it open. Rebecca dared not look to see who entered for fear they would once again be stirred to wrath and resume their beating. Instead, she remained still with her eyes closed until she felt a foot nudging her with trepidation.

"Are you still alive, or did they do you in?" she heard a voice mutter, as if not really expecting to hear an answer.

Rebecca lay unmoving, too frightened to respond. She grimaced when she felt someone attempting to roll her onto her back, and moaned at the pain that again coursed through her. Opening her eyes, she glanced up to see a wizened but kindly old face staring down at her.

"Lord have mercy!" the petty officer exclaimed when he caught a glimpse of the boy's battered appearance.

Rebecca struggled to escape his piercing gaze, ashamed of what she must look like. She made a feeble attempt to sit up, causing the ragged tunic to slip from her shoulders, exposing that which she had been relentless to conceal for so long. Grabbing at the torn clothing in shame, she lowered her head and began to weep in her despair.

Petty Officer Andrews stared in stunned disbelief at the sight, finally aware of what Rebecca had been so desperate to hide since she had been abducted. The shock he felt in discovering that there was a young woman on board soon gave way to pity, but the petty officer remained silent while he watched her hasten to adjust the tattered garment in the hopes of covering her bruised nakedness. In his great discomfort he turned without speaking and departed, closing the door with a solid clang behind him. He lingered behind the closed door for some time, rendered speechless by the secret that had been revealed, while he contemplated what to do with the newfound passenger that had just been discovered.

Rebecca continued to weep long after the petty officer had departed for fear of what was to come, knowing in her heart that death was preferable to losing the innocence she had so long held dear. The last sliver of remaining light faded away and she leaned against the cold wall in weary despair. The words of scripture that had always sustained her in the past sprang with sudden clarity to her mind, and she began to recite them in a reverent voice. *"Lord, let me not fear the reproach of men, nor be terrified by their insults, for the moth will eat them up like a garment, and the worm will devour them like wool. Be my everlasting righteousness, and grant my salvation through all generations."*

She began to sing then in a low voice the hymns that spoke of the Lord's redeeming love and mercy, until she became aware of His peace descending on her heart, like a soothing balm to anoint her wounded spirit. She continued in her worship for what seemed to her like hours, and when she could no longer keep her eyes open she slid back onto the floor with a sigh, slipping into a restless slumber as the pain faded into darkness along with her concerns for the morrow.

Rebecca was awakened a short time later by the creaking of the door as it was pushed open once again. She watched the old man enter carrying a large bucket of hot, soapy water. He set it down beside her and said, "I'll leave you to go at this alone if you wish, but I can help some if need be."

Rebecca peered up at him in a wary silence, unsure of how to respond. She wondered if he had alerted his captain to her presence, and shuddered at the thought of having to face the man. She continued to gaze at him through swollen lids while a myriad of thoughts coursed through her mind, until she saw him give a shrug of his shoulders and turn to leave.

"I thank you," she whispered to his retreating form.

He turned back when he heard her voice and regarded her with a curious gaze, for it was obvious to him that she was uncomfortable with his presence. No doubt she would be, he considered, after the beating she had suffered at the hands of the crew. He couldn't help but wonder how she had come to be on the Redemption in the first place, and knowing that she most likely distrusted his intentions at this precise moment, he avoided drilling her with questions and instead gave a quick nod and proceeded to leave the room.

Rebecca watched him depart, and waited until the door was pulled firmly shut behind him before she reached into the metal pail and brought out a cloth heavy with the scent of lye. It felt soothing on her bruised skin, and when she rinsed the rag in the steaming bucket, the water turned crimson from the dried blood that had covered her flesh. She was able to scrub only her face and neck before the pain became too unbearable, and she soon lay back down to relieve the agonizing ache in her limbs. A short while later Rebecca woke with a start, hearing a voice speaking to her, but from where she could not determine.

"Are you awake, miss?"

Rebecca realized she must have drifted off to sleep, for the room was again cast in the dim shadow of darkness and the silence above deck was more noticeable. In her fear she remained silent, her heart pounding in her chest as she heard the door being pushed open once more. Rebecca peered into the darkness until the familiar face of Petty Officer Andrews appeared again before her. She saw that he held a steaming bowl in his hands, and when he set it near her, she could smell the aroma of a hearty stew. She glanced at him with a look surprise on her face, and found herself suddenly speechless and humbled by his kindness, while she made a feeble attempt to sit up.

He knelt down beside her and moved the bowl close to where she sat propped against the wall. "Come on now," he said, helping her to shift into a more comfortable position, and wincing with guilt when he heard her catch her breath from the pain the movement brought upon her. "I'd best bring the doctor to have a look at you," he remarked, concerned that the men may have broken some of her bones.

"No please, don't, sir," Rebecca begged, with tears threatening to spill from her eyes.

He stared down at her and felt remorse for the sight that beheld him. Her face was discolored by dark bruises and he was certain her salty tears stung as they slid down over her torn flesh, yet he was taken aback by the steadfast and imploring gaze she maintained upon him while he towered above her. "I'll have to inform the captain of your presence eventually you know," he reminded her.

"Yes, but please, can it wait just a bit longer?" she plead.

Mr. Andrews contemplated her request for several moments before nodding his head in resignation, knowing all too well that Captain Jameson would not be pleased in discovering there was a woman on board his frigate.

"Do you need help eating that?" he asked, nodding at the bowl of stew he had placed next to her.

"No, sir..." she replied, "but thank you for bringing it to me."

He gave her a slight smile before turning to leave, unsure of how to respond to the frail, young lady. His heart was heavy with the knowledge that he would have to divulge her secret to his commander, for he knew the captain's discipline was sure to be swift and severe.

Rebecca whispered a prayer of thanks for the kindness of the man and the provision of the food before she began to eat. The hot stew was soothing to her stomach, and in no time at all she had emptied the bowl. With a soft sigh of content, she set it aside and turned to find a more comfortable spot on the hard ground. She shivered as she tried to curl into a corner in the hopes of conserving her body's dissipating heat, and when she finally drifted off to sleep, her dreams returned her to the beloved shores of her home and into the loving arms of her family.

"Good morning, miss," the petty officer called before opening the door to the hold, making an effort to announce his arrival.

Rebecca pushed herself upright, her head throbbing painfully with the abrupt movement. She glanced at a blanket that fell from her shoulders and wondered for a brief moment who had placed it over her. "Hello," she called out.

The door to the hold creaked open and Mr. Andrews entered, carrying another bucket of water and a steaming bowl of porridge. He glanced across the room to where she sat and was startled by the pallor of her skin, despite the ominous, purple bruises which lingered. "Your looking better it seems," he forced in a cheerful tone, hoping the expression on his face didn't belie the comment he had just made.

Rebecca nodded her head, trying to smile through the tears that again brimmed in her eyes. She had never found herself in such a helpless state before and she was overcome both with pain, as well as with gratitude at his thoughtful consideration of the circumstance she had found herself in.

"What is it?" he asked with alarm.

"Nothing, sir..." she whispered. "I'm just so grateful for your kindness towards me."

He gave her a curious look, surprised that she would consider his paltry actions worthy of accolade.

"Forgive me for being so bold, sir, but may I ask your name?" she inquired in a timid voice.

"Petty Officer Andrews," he said, adding no fanfare to his introduction.

Rebecca nodded through a slight smile and said, "It's very nice to make your acquaintance, Mr. Andrews."

He averted his gaze in his discomfort, unaccustomed to the presence of young women, and especially young women displaying any sort of sentiment. "You'd best eat that porridge before it gets cold," he said in an abrupt manner, turning to leave her to her breakfast.

"Mr. Andrews," she called, "thank you...for everything, sir."

He held his hand up in acknowledgement of her words of gratitude, but did not turn to face her.

"Sir?" she called again.

He stopped then, and twisted around to meet her gaze.

"I think I'm ready to speak with your captain," she said, making an effort to appear brave, though her face held only trepidation.

He stared at her for a moment, wishing he could allow her to keep her secret concealed from Captain Jameson, for he knew that a certain punishment awaited for her unauthorized presence aboard the Redemption, and he was hesitant to see any further harm come to her, especially so soon after the horrific beating she had suffered on the deck. The petty officer was aware though, that Lieutenant Burgess intended to settle scores with the girl, for he knew that the officer still believed her to be a young boy. With a sigh of realization, he knew that this moment would have to come to pass one way or another. "Alright," he replied. "I'll arrange for you to see him then, if you think you're ready."

She stared after his retreating form, thanking him once again before she began to eat the hot gruel that he had brought, and when she had finished she began to pray with fervent desperation from the words of scripture written on her heart.

"Lord, guard my life and rescue me; let me not be put to shame, for I take refuge in you. May integrity and uprightness protect me, for my hope is in you."

Mr. Andrews was reluctant to arrange for the meeting between the girl and Captain Jameson so soon, thinking maybe it best if he wait until she had fully recovered from her injuries. He was overcome with guilt at the thought of what was to come, but knew well that if it was discovered that he had assisted in concealing her identity, he would see a flogging as well. Without further thought of delay, he made his way to the deck, where he found Lieutenant Burgess leaning against the railing in a casual manner while he observed the men who worked there. Thinking perhaps his senior officer might offer a suggestion of how to inform the captain of their unexpected stowaway, he made his way towards where he lingered, a cautious air of hesitance about him. "Sir, may I have a word with you?"

"Of course, Mr. Andrews," the lieutenant replied. "What is it?"

"Do you think we could speak in private, sir?"

"Certainly," he said with a curt nod. "Let's go to my quarters."

As they made their way through the throngs of men, Mr. Andrews felt his stomach begin to churn with raw nerves. They soon reached the young lieutenant's berth, and Mr. Burgess was quick to offer the petty officer a chair.

"Thank you, sir," he said, feeling much too nervous to sit, but not wanting to appear rude he lowered himself onto the wooden seat.

"Now, what is it you need to speak to me about, Mr. Andrews?" he asked, taking a seat across from the petty officer.

"Well, sir," he began, "I don't rightly know how to tell you this, but the young lad we have down below?" He faltered for a moment and waited for the officer to digest the words. "It would appear...well...turns out he's not a boy, sir."

The lieutenant studied the old man for several minutes and then asked, "What are you saying, Mr. Andrews?"

"What I mean is, that's not a boy we're holding down there, sir…it's a woman."

The officer stood with sudden abruptness, knocking his chair over backwards while he stared at his petty officer with a look of bewildered confusion.

"What do you mean it's a woman?" he demanded. "Where did she come from?"

"I don't know, sir," Mr. Andrews replied. "All I know is she's been here all along…we just didn't know it…until now that is. I reckon that's why she attacked you the way she did…you know, when you were trying to take her clothes off and such."

Lieutenant Burgess stared at the man in stunned disbelief, while he recalled with a sick feeling growing in the pit of his stomach the horrific beating the girl had taken, no doubt for the simple reason of trying to protect her identity. He paused to consider the implications of telling Captain Jameson of her presence, knowing full well that the captain had little tolerance for women, and especially women who happened onboard his frigate unannounced. He began to pace the floor of his small quarters thinking of how best to broach the subject with his commanding officer, until he came to an abrupt halt in the middle of the room and asked, "Has the captain been informed of her presence?"

"Why no, sir," Mr. Andrews replied. "I thought you ought to be the first to know. Thought maybe you might know how to say it better 'n me…"

"Yes, I see. He will want to be informed as soon as possible no doubt…" he mused, while continuing to pace, muttering under his breath at having to be the one to deliver this disturbing news to his captain.

"Where is the girl now, Mr. Andrews?" he asked.

"She's still below, sir, in the hold."

"Very well…I will inform Captain Jameson of the situation. Be prepared to bring the girl to his stateroom if I should send for you."

"Aye-aye, sir," the petty officer replied, turning to leave.

Lieutenant Burgess breathed a weary sigh before making his way to Captain Jameson's quarters, in no mood to face the wrath of his commanding officer that was sure to follow. The captain's call to enter led the hesitant lieutenant into the stately berth.

"Yes, Mr. Burgess, what is it?" the captain inquired upon seeing the nervous glance emanating from the face of his young officer.

"Sir, a situation has arisen that I was only recently made aware of…do you have the time to discuss it now, or shall I return at a later hour?"

"Now is as good a time as any, Mr. Burgess," he replied, his curiosity piqued by the uneasy manner of the young man.

Lieutenant Burgess hesitated, having hoped that the captain would be preoccupied with more important matters and unable to hear the disturbing news that he had come to deliver. Captain Jameson waited expectantly for him to speak, while the officer struggled to find the words that would evoke the least amount of wrath from his captain. Lieutenant Burgess finally cleared his throat and began to explain in a tentative voice, "Do you recall, sir, the young crewman who assaulted me on deck this past week?"

"The lad in the hold?" he asked. "Yes, I remember. Did he awaken yet? There is certainly a flogging to be delivered if that is still your choice of punishment, although most would prefer to see the insolent boy hanged."

"No, no…I don't think we ought to hang this one," he murmured.

"A flogging it will be then. You will want to dispense the lashes yourself, no doubt."

"No, a flogging wouldn't be appropriated either, I'm afraid," he mumbled.

"Well what then?" he demanded. "The boy has to be punished."

"Well, sir…it turns out the boy is not who we thought him to be."

"Oh? And who did we think him to be, Mr. Burgess?" he snapped, finding himself growing irritated by the lieutenant's hemming and hawing.

"A *boy*, sir."

The captain stared at the young officer for several moments, unable to comprehend what it was he was trying to say until he finally erupted in frustration. "For pity's sake, Mr. Burgess, stop speaking in riddles and tell me what it is that you are so miserably hinting at!"

"It would appear that we have a woman onboard, sir," he explained with haste.

"A what?"

"A woman."

"What do you mean there's a woman onboard?" the captain snapped. "How on earth would a woman have made her way onto my frigate?"

"I'm not sure, sir. I just know that she's here, and she's in the hold."

Captain Jameson cursed forcefully under his breath and muttered, "Well get rid of her!"

Lieutenant Burgess stared at him, unsure if he had correctly understood the words spoken by the captain. "Get rid of her, sir?" he asked.

"Yes, get rid of her! I will not tolerate a woman onboard my ship, and especially one who is here by such deceitful means."

Lieutenant Burgess cleared his throat and asked, "How do you presume one gets rid of a woman, Captain?"

"Throw her overboard where she belongs…sneaking onto my frigate...she deserves no less! In fact, I ought to see her flogged by the fleet first and then tossed into the waves. Teach her a good lesson, it would!"

Mr. Burgess cleared his throat once again, taking great pains not to see the wrath of Captain Jameson directed towards himself. "Do you suppose, sir, we ought to speak with her first? Let her offer an explanation if she has one, and then get rid of her?"

Captain Jameson glared at the young officer with such hostile contempt that the young man took a precautionary step backwards. "There is no explanation good enough to warrant a woman stowing away on a ship doing service in a time of war… or any ship for that matter!"

"Yes, I realize that, sir…however, in this situation, I only think it fair that-"

"Fair has nothing to do with it," he barked. He stood to his feet and began to pace about the room, his brow creased in angry contemplation. After several moments he growled, "Very well...since you think it so important that we be fair, I will see her. Have her brought to my quarters immediately, and let's be done with this."

Mr. Burgess gave a smart salute and made a hasty retreat, lest the captain continue on with his tirade. He felt a momentary pang of compassion for the girl who would soon face the wrath of his angry commander, before dispelling the notion with the recollection that it was she who had committed the infraction, and deserved no less than what she had coming.

Mr. Andrews returned to the hold where the girl was being confined to inform her of the imminent meeting with Captain Jameson. As he approached, he heard her voice whispering in a melodic tone, and he wondered for a moment who it was that she spoke with. He pressed his ear to the door to listen for a moment, and a tender smile spread across his face when he realized that she was uttering prayers, though not in the manner he was accustomed to hearing prayers spoken. Even through the thick, wooden walls he could hear the lack of formality, replaced instead with a passion that consumed her voice as she plead with God for her very life. The certainty of the captain's fury surfaced once again, and as the smile faded from his countenance, he considered how best to conceal his worries from her. He thought maybe it best if he leave her to her meditations until it was time to take her the captain's stateroom, but decided instead that he'd rather deal with the matter sooner than later. He offered a light tap before entering to announce his arrival.

Rebecca gave him a tentative smile when he entered, and listened with a rapt gaze while he explained that she would most likely be brought before the captain and Lieutenant Burgess that very evening. She felt her stomach begin to knot in fear and grimaced at the discomfort, while she begged the Lord to give her the perseverance required to face the two men.

The petty officer became aware of the apprehension that crept into her eyes and said in a remorseful tone, "If there were any way to help you through this I would you know..."

"Thank you, Mr. Andrews," she replied, a sigh of weariness escaping her, "but I'll have to get through this on my own I'm afraid."

He offered to take her up to the deck to sit in the sun for a few moments, in the hopes of allowing her some fresh air, for the pallor that lingered worried him. He was certain her nerves must be in a jumble with the knowledge that she would soon have to face Captain Jameson, and he was relieved when she accepted his offer without argument. He saw her grimace in pain while she struggle to stand and he was quick to offer her his hand, pulling her upright with gentle ease. He watched as she swayed on her feet, the color draining from her face, and he waited near her until she had regained her composure. Seeing that she was ready, he turned to climb the stairs, aware of her quiet presence following behind him. He led her up the narrow corridor and onto the deck at the rear of the frigate to a tranquil and unoccupied area shaded from the evening sun.

"This'll be a good spot for you," he said, pointing to a small, wooden bench. "No one will bother you here, I'll make sure of it," he added.

Rebecca sank down with a grateful smile and sighed in contentment at feeling the fresh breeze on her face once again. She was comforted to see that Mr. Andrews remained nearby, coiling the ropes strewn across the broad expanse of the deck.

The petty officer glanced up at her often from where he worked, thinking if she were frightened, it was not obvious. He allowed her to rest undisturbed where she sat until the time came to present her to Captain Jameson. He hoped it would be a good while before he had to disturb her, but not even an hour had passed before Lieutenant Burgess appeared before him.

"Mr. Andrews," he began, "Captain Jameson will speak with the girl now."

Lieutenant Burgess saw Rebecca then, propped against the wall of the frigate. His face registered shock at her battered appearance and he was taken aback when she opened her eyes to look at him. The apprehension on her features was obvious, and in his discomfort he turned and walked away, leaving Petty Officer Andrews staring after him in surprise.

Rebecca glanced at the old man, who gave her an encouraging smile of reassurance and helped her stand to her feet. Her heart began to pound in her chest when she realized the time had come to plead for her life with the man who commanded the vessel she had stowed away on. She did not speak while she followed the petty officer down the narrow stairwell to the captain's quarters, but instead gazed at him in panic when they arrived at the portal.

Petty Officer Andrews turned to study the girl and was quick to note the dread which shadowed her features. "We can wait a moment if you need one," he said, wishing he could grant the frail, young, lady reprieve from the captain's wrath.

Rebecca took a deep breath bringing on a sharp stab of pain. She winced at the discomfort but quickly tried to regain some sense of composure. "It's alright, sir," she whispered. "I'd just as soon get this over with."

Mr. Andrews gave a quick nod and tapped on the dark, foreboding door of the captain's stateroom, just as anxious to see the matter settled as the girl was.

"Come," a deep voice called from inside.

The petty officer lifted the latch and stepped aside, allowing Rebecca to enter.

"That will be all, Mr. Andrews," Lieutenant Burgess said. "Thank you."

Rebecca stared at the retreating form of the petty officer, her only remaining hope of safety obliterated by the soft clang of the latching door. A sigh of despair slipped from her lips when she realized that he would not be staying with her, and she stood frozen in place, glancing with anxious eyes at the two men. She could see the captain standing near the window, his back turned towards her, while Lieutenant Burgess gave her a calculated look of indifference from where he sat across the room. She remained speechless, at a loss for words.

"Who are you and what are you doing on my ship?" the captain asked with a growl, not bothering to turn around to face her.

Rebecca remained silent, unsure of how to answer his abrupt question. Did he want the long version she wondered, giddy with fear, or the short and sweet? She nearly burst into a fit of nervous laughter at the thought, but was stopped short when the captain spun around to face her, and she could see that even from across the room his presence was darkly ominous and foreboding. She found herself mesmerized by his face, which was etched with deep lines cutting through leathery, tanned skin, giving evidence to his many years spent at sea. She continued to observe him with a steadfast gaze, contemplating how best to explain her unauthorized presence aboard his frigate.

Captain Jameson was stunned by the young woman's battered and bruised form and was quick to turn away from the sight of her lest she see the repulsion so evident on his face. His young officer had failed to forewarn him of the girl's wretched appearance, and he made an attempt to regain his composure before turning back to face her once again.

"Well, what do you have to say for yourself?" Lieutenant Burgess demanded, irritated by the girl's reluctance to explain her presence to the captain.

Rebecca's breath came in ragged gasps while she regarded the men glaring at her with such obvious contempt. Her knees began to buckle in fear and she leaned against the door in an attempt to steady herself, making a conscious effort to slow her breathing in order to answer their questions without succumbing to the wrenching sobs hovering in her throat.

"I'm from Portsmouth, sir," she murmured, not knowing where else to begin describing the incident that had changed her life.

"I don't care where you're from," the captain shouted. "I want to know what you're doing on my ship! How long have you been taking advantage of my transport and stealing from my larders?"

"Captain," she whispered, "I can assure you, I haven't been taking advantage of your transport…nor your larders."

He approached her then, angered by her indifference, but stopped short when he saw her shirk back against the unyielding door in alarm. He began to pace around the room without breaking his gaze on her contrite figure, acutely aware of her eyes transfixed on his face while she made another feeble attempt to speak.

"I came on board in Cadiz, sir," she began. "I'm only trying to get back home to Portsmouth. I overheard one of your ship's crew saying you were sailing there."

"Well not for several months we're not," he spat. "We *are* in the middle of a war, if you haven't realized it by now!"

Lieutenant Burgess remained silent, observing the frail, bruised girl making a valiant effort to hold her ground against the fury of the captain. He soon turned his gaze to Captain

Jameson who continued to tread the floor in agitation, no doubt considering the limited prospects of ridding himself of the girl.

"A woman onboard my frigate," he muttered before spinning on his heel to glare at her. "I've half a mind to throw you overboard!"

Rebecca remained rooted in place, her heart thumping erratically in her chest, as Captain Jameson crossed the room in two angry strides to tower over her.

"You will disembark when we reach the next port, where you will find another way to get to England, as I am not the one who is willing to take you there. Until then, you will remain confined to the hold. That is all," he growled, more to Lieutenant Burgess than to Rebecca, as he gave a quick flick of his wrist to dismiss them both.

"Captain!" Rebecca called out, her voice louder than she had intended it to be. "Please, let me at least continue to work on the Redemption. I'm willing to earn my transport to Portsmouth if you'll allow it, sir."

He turned around to meet her pleading gaze. "What worth are you to me?" he scoffed. "You are but a frivolous girl among hundreds of men! You are not welcome aboard this ship, and I will bear no responsibility for your deceitful actions. You have taken advantage of both me, and my crew with your unauthorized presence."

Rebecca winced at his angry words and watched as he made another attempt to depart, while Lieutenant Burgess moved towards her to return her to the hold. She again spoke forcefully, with the desperation of one determined to see her home and her loved ones once again. "I have not taken advantage of you, sir, nor have I intended to. I've been working with the cook in the galley ever since I came on board and I beg you to allow me to continue."

Captain Jameson, unaccustomed to such blatantly impertinent behavior, spun back on his heel and stormed towards her. "I don't care what your intentions were," he shouted. "If you do not remain silent in this matter, I will see you flogged for your insolence!"

Rebecca paled at his words but held her tongue, while he loomed over her for several moments as if daring her to speak again. His large hands were clenched into angry fists, and she realized how easy it would be for him to squeeze the breath of life right out of her if he were inclined to do so. Dropping her gaze in reverent submission, she prayed only for a quick escape.

"Now get her out of here before I do something I might regret later," Captain Jameson growled.

Mr. Burgess gave the captain a smart salute and nodded his head. Rebecca, needing no further prompting to leave, hurried into the corridor, where she paused to regain some semblance of composure before making her way up the narrow stairwell, weary despair etched into every aspect of her being. Lieutenant Burgess followed behind her, and was grateful to see Mr. Andrews waiting for the girl on deck. "Return her to the hold," he said in a terse voice. "She is to remain confined there until we moor in Lisbon," he said.

"Aye-aye, sir," Mr. Andrews replied, taking Rebecca by the arm and leading her back to the dank confines of the hold. "I'm sorry, Missy," he remarked with a hint of sadness. "I wish it would have turned out better for you."

Rebecca stumbled inside, too distraught for words. She leaned against the cold wall and slid to the floor, oblivious to the pain that lingered in her body. She glanced up at Mr. Andrews before he left and said, "Thank you for your efforts to help me, Mr. Andrews. I truly do appreciate your kindness."

Rebecca watched him depart and waited until she heard the lock clang into place before allowing herself to weep without restraint. She felt resentful towards the captain and his officer, and prayed in a fervent voice that the Lord would forgive her. *"Search my heart O God, and give ear unto my cry...cleanse me from my wicked thoughts, and lead me in the way of your everlasting righteousness. I beseech You to help me find favor with Captain*

Jameson, Lord...I believe you have not allowed this situation to have occurred for naught. And thank you for the presence of Mr. Andrews. Please bless him for his kindness towards me, and allow me to minister to him in the way that you would have me."

Rebecca began to feel a small semblance of hope after she had prayed and she determined in her heart to make the best of the situation she had found herself in. With a weary sigh, she nestled down into the corner and slipped off into a dreamless slumber, her shivering limbs going unnoticed in the damp chill of the night.

The days passed with agonizing monotony for Rebecca in the dank hold, but Petty Officer Andrews was faithful to deliver fresh, hot food to her, as well as water for bathing. On occasion, he would steal her up to the deck in the evening for a bit of fresh air, while the rest of the crew was enjoying the merriment down below. She was grateful for these moments, and always quick to express her deepest gratitude to the man. Mr. Andrews in turn, was becoming quite fond of Rebecca, thinking of her as the daughter he knew he would never have. He affectionately called her 'Missy' for lack of a better name and Rebecca, so moved by his kindness, did not correct him. He never asked her where she came from, not wanting to upset her, and she never volunteered the information, not wanting to bore him. The men had gotten wind that a woman was on board but the captain made it clear to them that any man who dared go near her would suffer severe consequences. Lieutenant Burgess on the other hand, needn't have heard the warning, for he made every effort to avoid Rebecca, wishing to have nothing to do with her and remaining only anxious to see her depart.

Chapter 4

THE BEGINNING OF Rebecca's second week in confinement dawned gloomy and cold. The damp air cut through her bones like glass and she huddled beneath the only blanket she had been given. Mr. Andrews had tried to provide her with warmer clothing, but those that she wore hung loosely on her petite frame. She yawned through a brisk shiver and stood to stretch her legs when a loud commotion erupted on deck. She could not make out any words, just the shouts of the crew's frantic voices. Suddenly and without warning, a massive explosion rocked the Redemption, throwing Rebecca to the ground. She tilted her head upwards, desperate to hear something other than the garbled and panicked shouts of the crew. Another explosion soon followed the first, and then another. Each blast seemed to rock the ship with more force than the last and Rebecca was growing alarmed. She glanced up in surprise when the door to the hold burst open, sending Petty Officer Andrews rushing into the room to pull her to her feet.

"Are you alright, Missy?" he asked, looking her over in alarm.

Before she could answer him, he had seized her by the arm and was dragging her out of the hold and up toward the deck. "It's not safe for you down here," he shouted over the noise of the battle taking place above. Rebecca remained silent in her startled confusion, and was quick to shield her eyes against the bright light of day as they burst forth from the darkened stairwell. Mr. Andrews hurried Rebecca across the short expanse of deck to hide her away in a small storage closet.

"Stay in there now, do you hear?"

Rebecca only stared, still too stunned to speak, as he pulled the door shut with a resounding slam. Petty Officer Andrews dashed off to assist his shipmates in defending the Redemption against the attack by the massive French frigate that had come upon them, while Rebecca struggled to keep her footing against the reeling of the vessel. It wasn't long before Rebecca realized that she could hear the horrendous commotion more clearly from the tiny closet, and she shuddered at the sound of the men's desperate cries for help. She approached the door with a cautious step, relief washing over her when she realized that it had been left unlocked. Forgetting the words of warning from Mr. Andrews, she opened the door wide enough to catch a glimpse of the melee.

Rebecca was horrified to see bloodied bodies strewn about the frigate, some lifeless and still, and yet a large number of others writhing in agony. Without giving thought to her own safety, she stepped out onto the deck of the Redemption in an attempt to attend to the wounded. Within just a few feet of the closet she had so recently vacated, she came upon a man with a large, deep gash on his thigh. Blood was seeping through the shred of muslin cloth that remained intact, giving evidence to the severity of his injury, and she was quick to kneel over him in order to apply a firm pressure to his leg, speaking in a soft voice while she tried to still his tumultuous writhing. She glanced around in the hopes of finding the ship's surgeon, but saw no one who appeared as if they were able, or willing, to help her. Biting at the hem of her tunic, she was able to free an edge of the muslin, and she quickly tore off a strip of the cloth to fashion a large pressure dressing around the man's leg. After securing it in place, she stood to determine her next patient. Rebecca was overwhelmed by the multitude of wounded men lying about, and she searched again to locate the ship's surgeon. She soon caught a glimpse of a man wearing an apron splatter with blood and leaning over a body lying near the stairwell.

"Sir! Are you the doctor on this vessel?" she shouted across to him.

"Yes, and you'd best stay out of my way," he warned in a curt manner, not even bothering to look up. The captain had informed him of the young woman's presence, and although he was intrigued by the news, he had no desire to turn his attentions to her needless whining at that precise moment. "There are dying men here, miss," he growled. "Do not distract me with your petty concerns."

"I have no petty concerns, sir, but I do have the ability to help you," she assured. "Where do you keep your supplies?"

He glanced up for a moment to find her confident gaze peering down at him. A sense of urgency pervaded the air between them, and without further thought he answered, "Third door from the bow on the starboard side. Take what you need."

Rebecca, unfamiliar with the language of seamanship, darted off to find the room he spoke of. She was able to locate the room without too much difficulty, but everything in it was strewn about in chaotic disarray. She began to sift through the supplies scattered about and soon found what it was that she needed. Stuffing the pockets of her tunic with suture thread, needles, cotton rags and tincture of witch hazel, she hurried back to the deck, where the explosions continued to wreak havoc on the massive frigate and the crew struggled to maintain their hold amidst the enemy's attack. Stepping cautiously through the battlefield, she lowered herself to attend to a man propped against a barrel, dazed and bleeding from a jagged gash to his head.

"Hello," she smiled, hoping her eyes reflected more calm than she was feeling at the moment. "I'm here to help you, if that's alright?"

The man's bewildered gaze drifted over Rebecca's features, which were suddenly encompassed by a luminous halo created by an obscure beam of sunlight, which for an instant, penetrated the copious layer of clouds. He remained silent and contemplative, as if perhaps he were dead and catching his first glimpse of an angel. Rebecca gave him a gracious smile in answer to his silence.

"All right then," she whispered, listening with an attentive ear when he finally began to mutter words that were indiscernible to her. With a competent hand she began to wipe the blood from his face in her preparations to suture his wound. She had expected the poor fellow to writhe in pain with the suturing, but instead he barely flinched during the entire procedure. His inquisitive gaze never left her features as she worked, and at last, when she had finished, she left him with a tender pat on the shoulder and hurried onto the next casualty, a young man without any visible signs of life. Reaching out for the wounded midshipman, she took his wrist in her hand, praying that she would find the telltale hint of a beating heart. With a startled gasp she felt the man's hand close around her own in a firm embrace, his eyes opening wide to plead for help, though the only sound which came from his lips was the gurgling of air mingled with froth-tinged blood as his body fought to prevail over the ominous grip of death. She knelt down beside him on the deck and asked, "Sir, may I pray with you?"

He nodded his head, tears flowing from his eyes as the realization of his imminent mortality became clear in his mind. Rebecca began praying with an impassioned voice for the salvation of the man's soul and he soon joined her in beseeching the Lord's forgiveness for his transgressions. When they had finished, Rebecca glanced around to find Mr. Andrews who was struggling nearby in an attempt to move the dead towards the center of the frigate and away from the where the men fought to secure their ship.

"Mr. Andrews!" she called out.

He spun around in surprise, wondering why she had ventured out in the heat of the battle. "I told you to stay put!" he shouted when he approached her.

"The men need my help," she said, motioning to the wounded strewn about.

"No...you need to get back in the closet! It's not safe out here!"

She shook her head and beckoned him instead to come to where the dying sailor lay. "Stay with him," she whispered. "His time on this earth won't be long now, and no man should die alone."

He watched her turn and hurry away, oblivious to the dangers lurking around her. A low moan from the man lying on the deck stirred him to attention, and he knelt to speak comforting words to his ship mate, until after just a short time he became aware of the man's soul passing from the realm of the living into that of the dead, while a look of peace lingered on his lifeless face. The petty officer slid the eyelids shut to hide the glassy stare of the fallen one and began to drag his still warm body toward the others that had been gathered on the deck of the frigate.

Captain Jameson stood assessing the damage to his ship from the quarterdeck while the battle continued to rage. The fatigue on the faces of his crew was evident even from a distance, and the bodies mutilated and torn a grim reminder of the horrific casualties of war. The attack on the Redemption had been sudden and severe, and already the frigate was in shambles. As he glanced about at the chaotic activity below, he caught sight of the girl working with frantic desperation over the body of an injured man who was writhing in pain. He stared at her in bewildered disbelief, both at her audacity to disobey his order to remain in the hold, as well as by her reckless determination to place herself in the midst of the fighting in order to come to the aid his men. From where he stood, he could see that she was speaking to the injured sailor with words that were indiscernible to him from so great a distance, but apparently consoling to her patient, while she struggled to tighten a tourniquet around the bloodied stump where a leg had once been. Captain Jameson continued to study her through the haze of smoke which hovered in the air, and he found himself intrigued by her resolve to initiate a rescue attempt for men she did not even know, in spite of the danger it posed to herself. He observed her determined efforts for several moments more, until finally she stood and began to drag her patient away from the men who hurried to clear the dead from the deck. With a startled gasp, he saw that she was covered with blood, and he wondered if she had been injured somehow during the battle. He saw her stop then, her gaze distant as it slid over the mass of carnage strewn about the deck, while a shadow of weary exhaustion covered her features. She lifted a hand to her forehead, as if in overwhelmed resignation, before continuing her valiant attempt to pull the wounded man towards the safety of the sick berth.

"Captain Jameson," Lieutenant Burgess called out. "The Redemption is secured, sir."

Captain Jameson turned for a brief moment, distracted by the sound of the lieutenant's voice, but relieved to hear that the battle had ended. He acknowledge his officer, who seemed oblivious to the girl's presence below, and when he turned back to observe his captive stowaway, he was disappointed to find that she had disappeared from his sight. Turning to attend to the needs of his officers, he stepped with a weary grimace through the decimated wreckage of the Redemption, in no mood to dole out accolades to the insubordinate heroine.

Rebecca felt as though the night would never end. She worked tirelessly in the small confines of the sick berth with

Dr. Ammons, who on occasion would glance across the room to study her, but the two did not speak above and beyond what was necessary to care for the wounded. She was exhausted after the long hours spent tending to the injured, but only when she was certain that the last of the men had been cared for did she staggered down the narrow steps to the hold. The door had been left ajar in their hasty retreat, and she didn't bother to close it behind her when she entered. Instead, cold and tired, she crumpled into the darkened corner of the room and slipped into a dreamless sleep. A short time later Petty Officer Andrews slipped his head in to make sure Rebecca had made it back safely. He breathed a great sigh of relief when he caught a glimpse of her small form huddled in the corner, and he covered her with the blanket that was lying on the floor near where she lay. Satisfied to see that she had returned unharmed, he turned and left so as not to disturb her rest.

Rebecca slept for several hours before the sound of the morning's activity stirred her from her slumber. Sitting up, she was startled to find herself covered with dried blood. The soiled tunic brought back the gruesome memories of the day before, and she wondered about the condition of the wounded crew. Glancing over to the door of the hold she was surprised to find that it stood open, and she rose to her feet to peer out into the darkened corridor. Seeing no one about, she ventured through the portal to go in search of fresh water so she could scrub the crusted blood from her body. She had expected to find Mr. Andrews working somewhere nearby, but he was nowhere in sight. She continued past the few men lingering on deck in her search for the man, but soon grew uncomfortable by their questioning stares.

"Are you alright, miss?" a burly man asked with a concerned look on his face.

"Yes, thank you," she replied. "But would you please tell me where I might find a bucket of clean water?"

"What need have you of water?" an irate voice demanded from behind her, "and what are you doing roaming about on deck? Captain's orders state you are to remain confined to the hold."

She twirled around to find herself face to face with Lieutenant Burgess. He stepped back in alarm when he saw her blood stained tunic and exclaimed in a loud voice to the midshipman standing nearby, "Mr. Robbins, get Dr. Ammons!"

"No, no," she stammered. "I'm just....I was....it's not my blood sir. I'm not injured, I just need to get cleaned up a bit."

He stared at her in confusion for several moments, waiting for her to explain herself.

"May I please find a bucket, sir? I could really use some clean water." she said again.

"No," he snapped. "What ever you have need of, you will wait for it in the hold where you belong. Water will be brought to you there."

Nodding in acknowledgement of his order, she turned to go back down the narrow steps to the dark confines of her cell.

"Wait!" he called.

She turned back to glance at the young officer.

"Who let you out of the hold?" he demanded, his eyes narrowed in suspicion.

Rebecca paused to consider the potential consequences to Mr. Andrews for releasing her from her confinement. She was not about to see the man punished for wanting to keep her safe, and whether or not it was his intention to leave the door ajar after her return last night, it was she who had made the decision to leave the hold this morning.

"I let myself out, Mr. Burgess."

"Well who unlocked the door?"

"I'd rather not say, sir," she answered in a reluctant voice.

Lieutenant Burgess stared at her for a moment in dumfounded silence.

"You'd rather not say," he repeated under his breath, almost as if mocking her. "You will tell me who released you," he growled, "or you will regret it."

Rebecca eyed him warily, her eyes large with apprehension, but never-the-less she held her tongue.

Mr. Burgess' face began to flush with anger as he waited for her to speak. Seeing that she was apparently just as obstinate as she was foolish he said, "Well I'm certain the captain will force it out of you then."

He stormed away, his fists clenched in agitated frustration. When he realized she did not follow him, he reeled back and shouted, "You! Come with me!"

"Please," she asked, "may I clean myself up a bit first?"

Rebecca was hesitant to face Captain Jameson in her current state, remembering that his last impression of her had not been favorable.

"No!" the officer bellowed. "We are going to deal with your insubordination immediately. The captain's orders are clear. You are to be confined to the hold until we can be free of you, and whoever disobeys that order will be punished."

The two of them continued on in silence until they reached Captain Jameson's stateroom. Rebecca felt a sudden knot of fear growing in her belly as Lieutenant Burgess rapped on the foreboding door, and she took a deep breath to calm her nerves at the sound of the captain's voice calling for them to enter. Her last confrontation with Captain Jameson had not been pleasant and she doubted this one would fare any better. Holding her breath, she watched Lieutenant Burgess reach around her to unlatch the door and she gave him a cautious glance as she stepped around his ominous form. He seemed to grow irate with her apprehensive gaze upon him and without further ado, he motioned with an exaggerated air for her to proceed into the captain's stateroom. Rebecca was quick to note the shadow of alarm that crossed Captain Jameson's face when he glanced up to see who had entered, but she remained silent and guarded before him, a contrite expression lingering upon her face. Captain Jameson and Rebecca Halloway contemplated one another for several terse moments until the captain finally addressed his young officer, his eyes remaining on Rebecca's face.

"What seems to be the trouble, Mr. Burgess?"

"Sir," he began, "I found her wandering about on deck just now and she refuses to tell me who has released her from the hold."

"I wasn't wandering, Mr. Burgess," Rebecca corrected in a soft voice, "I was simply searching for a bucket to gather some water so that I might clean myself up a bit."

"Well someone has released you from the hold," he shot back. "The door does have a lock on it."

"It was left open for me last night, out of simple concern for my safety, and I didn't think to close it when I returned," she said. "I'm afraid the fault lies with me, and no one else."

"The fault lies with whoever unlocked the door in the first place, and I demand that you tell me who it was!"

"It is I who am to blame, sir."

"*You* do not have a key," the lieutenant corrected, with sarcastic clarity.

"Never-the-less, I ventured beyond the confines of the hold on my own volition."

The captain regarded their exchange with intrigue. He thought that the girl's demeanor was admirable for a young lady, even though it was obvious to him that she frustrated his officer. Judging from her appearance, it looked as though she had worked through the night, leaving Captain Jameson at a loss as to how to handle the situation. He was hesitant to mete out punishment to the brave heroine who had so recently endeavored with such diligence to come to the aid of his crew, yet he knew that he had an obligation to reprimand her for her insolence towards his officer, as well as towards her apparent disobedience of his order. Having never been faced with having to chastise a young lady before, he remained silent while he considered his options. He saw that both the girl and Lieutenant Burgess stared at him with expectant faces, no doubt waiting for him to offer some semblance of a verdict.

"Captain," Rebecca said in an attempt to explain herself, "I am aware that I have disobeyed your orders, sir, for which I am truly sorry, but I alone am at fault and shall accept whatever punishment you deem necessary."

Captain Jameson was amused by the young woman's tenacity and struggled to keep it concealed from her in his expression. "Disobeying a captain's order is punishable by death," he remarked with a casual air.

Lieutenant Burgess stared at the man, his mouth agape. The girl frustrated him to no end and while he wished her gone from the Redemption, he certainly did not wish her dead! Rebecca on the other hand, appeared startled and mumbled a contrite, "Oh..."

Captain Jameson waited for several moments, expecting a tearful outburst, but more so hoping to allow the girl some time to consider his words so as to provoke in her an attitude of submission.

"Well..." Rebecca murmured in a soft tone, her gaze steadfast and direct, "I think that's a bit severe, sir, but I am prepared to die if that is to be your decision."

She stood unwavering with a contrite spirit while she regarded Captain Jameson, her heart at peace, for she was confident that the Lord held the measure of her days in the palm of His hand and had ordained her steps long before she had even been born.

Captain Jameson remained in quiet observation of the girl, searching her face for some hint of fear or trepidation, but he found none. Instead, he saw a veil of peaceful radiance settling on the girl's countenance, and again found himself intrigued by her unusual character.

"Would you leave us alone for a moment, Mr. Burgess?" he said at last, noticing that his officer was looking a bit pale.

"Of course, sir," the officer replied, grateful to be dismissed.

Rebecca's gaze followed the retreating form of Lieutenant Burgess as he left, and then returned once again to the captain.

Captain Jameson stood and walked toward the window, staring in silence at the vast beauty beyond the glass of his stateroom, while he pondered with great curiosity the nature of this girl thrust so unexpectedly into his life. "Who *are* you?" he implored, turning to look at her.

Rebecca regretted having disrupted the man's life once again, and had hoped that she could remain unnoticed below deck until she was allowed to take her departure from this vessel, but seeing how this was not to be the case, she whispered truthfully, "I'm just a girl trying to find her way home, sir."

He began to move toward her then, his intrigue getting the better of him. "I saw you yesterday...tending to my men. Why did you do that?" he inquired.

"Your men were wounded, Captain, and they needed help. Anybody would have done the same, sir."

"You could have been killed," he replied.

"I realize that, sir, but never-the-less, your men needed help."

Captain Jameson was taken aback by her humble response, and continued to scrutinize her while she gazed at him with an intensity he was unaccustomed to. Most men trembled in his presence, and now, as she stood before him in her repentant state, he was unexpectedly struck by her vulnerability. While she exuded an attitude of fearlessness, he saw that she radiated humility, even when faced with the prospect of death. At that very moment he would have done everything within his power to see her returned unharmed to her family in Portsmouth.

"Well, I can assure you that most men would *not* have done the same. However, your conduct under the circumstances was exemplary, and will be noted in the ship's log."

Rebecca remained silent, unsure of what to say. She did wonder though, if displaying exemplary conduct nullified the fact that she had disobeyed a superior officer.

She felt a grin tugging at the corner of her mouth, until the voice of Captain Jameson stirred her once again to attentive submission.

"I think you'll be relieved to hear that we have been diverted from our original plans," he began. "We will sail to the Azores Islands in order to host the Admiral Charles Perry for a state dinner. I won't be putting you off the ship as early as was expected."

Rebecca contemplated his words for several moments before asking, "Won't you just bury me at sea, sir?"

Captain Jameson nearly laughed aloud when he realized with astonishment that the girl believed she was to suffer death as a punishment for her minor infraction, and yet she remained willing to die to protect the identity of a mere ship hand! He attempted to hide his amusement from her when he spoke.

"It is the captain's prerogative to decide the punishment to fit a crime," he stated, "and I find your crime not punishable by death."

Rebecca breathed a sigh of relief and exclaimed, "Thank you, sir...there's so much more I had hoped to accomplish yet!"

Captain Jameson struggled not to chuckle at her exuberance and instead cleared his throat and turned his back to her once again. "I suppose we could find you more comfortable quarters, as it appears you will be staying a bit longer than we had anticipated."

"There's no need for that, Captain," she assured. "I'm more than grateful for the space you have provided for me in the hold. However, if I may be so bold, sir, as to request your permission to work with the cook in the galley, so as to repay my debt to you for your kindness?"

He stared at her while she spoke, once again astounded by her humble spirit.

"A hard day's work doesn't intimidate me, sir," she continued. "After all, I wouldn't want it to appear as if I'm taking advantage of your hospitality."

To think she considers this hospitality, Captain Jameson mused. However, he did fear for her safety were she to move about the frigate unescorted, yet he didn't want to keep her confined like a prisoner in a cell. He considered the options which would keep her safe as well as content for the duration of her stay aboard the Redemption. "I will move you to the quarters next to mine," the captain said. "You may move about on deck as you wish, but I would prefer that you keep it minimal. My men are not an unruly bunch but neither are they afforded much time to spend in the presence of women, and I do not wish to tempt their self-control. There is no need for you to earn your keep, but if you would like you're free to work in the galley with the cook…if he will still have you, that is."

Rebecca gave him a grateful smile and said, "Thank you, sir. I only hope I might repay you for your kindness one day."

The captain, still unaccustomed to the presence of the young woman on board his frigate, was quick to excuse himself from the emotionally charged situation to make an attempt to find Lieutenant Burgess in the hopes of delegating to him the task of securing the girl in her new quarters. Pausing for a moment before departing, he turned to Rebecca once more to ask, "By the way…what is your name?"

Rebecca considered his words with a pensive expression. How long had it been, she pondered, since someone had called her by her given name, much less inquired as to what it was? "My name…" she murmured.

"You do have a name, don't you?" he chided, startling her back to attention.

"It's Rebecca, sir," she said. "Rebecca Halloway."

"I see," he said, thinking it was a fitting name for the girl. He turned again to go in search of his lieutenant.

Rebecca remained rooted to the floor watching Captain Jameson retreat into the corridor, her face a glimmer of sheer delight. It was difficult to conceal her gratitude at the Lord's mercy which was so evident to her in this situation, and she was quick to bow her head to offer a sincere prayer of thanks, while making a great effort to subdue her emotions. A short time later Captain Jameson returned to the stateroom, Lieutenant Burgess following close behind.

"Lieutenant Burgess will see you to your quarters now," he told her, adding as he turned to his young officer, "And find her some clean clothing if you would."

Turning on his heel, Lieutenant Burgess motioned for Rebecca to follow him. She glanced once again at Captain Jameson and thanked him for his generous leniency towards her. He nodded in acknowledgement while he watched her depart, trying to make sense of the odd, young lady bestowed on his frigate.

Rebecca followed behind Lieutenant Burgess as he led to her new quarters. She was aware the young man remained disgruntled by presence aboard the Redemption, but she determined she would make every effort to gain his approval until she was able to take her leave of the vessel. When they neared the berth the captain had assigned her to, Rebecca watched the young officer reach out to push the door open before stepping aside to peer down at her with wary suspicion.

Rebecca proceeded with a cautious step around the irate officer not saying anything, until finally out of guilt she could hold her tongue no longer. "Mr. Burgess," she murmured, "I do hope you'll accept my apology for assaulting you that day."

Lieutenant Burgess' expression went from guarded indifference to outright contempt and in a voice tight with rage he said, "Let me set one thing straight between us...I do not seek your apology, nor do I accept it. I believe you deserved every bit of that beating you took because of your deceitful actions and I should have demanded that you hang before you confessed to your lie. I don't know what form of manipulation you used on Captain Jameson, but I will not be wiled by your trickery! If you hope to make it off the Redemption alive, I would suggest that you remain in your quarters where you belong. What happens to you beyond this point does not concern me, nor will I make an attempt to acknowledge your presence for as long as you remain on this frigate."

He was incensed by her intrusion into his world and resented both the confusion and the lack of control he felt in her presence. His past experience with women had been minimal and those he had known had been fickle, impetuous, and weak, often attempting to bend men to their will with feigned innocence and charm. She had already demonstrated her ability at feigned charm to dissuade the mind of Captain Jameson, in spite of her willful disobedience of his order to remain confined in the hold. No, he determined, he much preferred the company of his unpretentious ship mates and his unencumbered life at sea, away from the emotional tendencies of the female gender.

Rebecca was unaccustomed to hearing such lengthy dialogue from the young officer and she shifted in her discomfort, unsure of how to respond and of how to mend the contention that lingered between them. "Well I just...I don't want you to...I truly *am* sorry, sir," she stammered through a soft expression of remorse.

She watched the lieutenant make an abrupt turn on his heel and disappear into the corridor, leaving her standing in his turbulent wake and wondering how to repair the damage she had wrought. She made a mental note to persevere in her prayers for this one, being confident that the Lord could mend even the deepest of resentments. Rebecca remained in the doorway of the tiny berth for some time, glancing about in perplexed dismay, when she realized she was still covered with dark, crusted blood. Again she set out in search of water, but before she had even stepped into the bright sunlight on deck she decided instead to go in search of Mr. Andrews, knowing he would offer a willing hand and welcome company.

The deck of the Redemption was always a hectic bustle of activity during the daylight hours while the crew worked to secure riggings, hoist sails, and scrub the deck until it shone in the bright sun, and this day was no different except now the crew was left with the task of repairing the damage wrought during the battle. As the captain had requested, Rebecca tried to be discreet as she negotiated a path through the horde of tanned, sinewy bodies. When she passed by the crew she saw that some glanced at her with wary apprehension, while others paid her no mind at all, so she was surprised when she heard a voice call out from behind her.

"Miss? Excuse me!"

Rebecca turned and saw the ship's doctor, his head peering at her from behind the doorway of what she recognized as the sick berth. She was pleased to see his familiar face once more and walked back to speak with him. "Hello again," she said.

"Hello again to you," he smiled. "Perhaps now that the circumstances allow for it, we might get better acquainted?"

"I would like that," she sighed, grateful to have found one who did not so blatantly abhor her presence.

He motioned for Rebecca to come inside and she found herself back in the once chaotic room she had run to in search of medical supplies. She noticed that all order had been restored in the tiny berth, while the medicinal smell which lingered brought back pleasant memories of her father's clinic in Portsmouth. A wave of homesickness struck without warning and she took several slow, deep breaths in an effort to suppress the sudden urge to cry.

"Is everything alright?" the doctor asked, a look of concern etched on his face.

Rebecca nodded through a tight smile, but remained hesitant to speak.

"I saw the efforts you made on behalf of my men," he continued. "Many of them survived only because of your swift interventions."

"I was more than happy to be of assistance, sir," she replied in a soft voice.

"You seem to be somewhat competent in medical matters..."

"My father is a doctor," she explained. "I've spent many hours working with him in is clinic."

He nodded his understanding and cast a scrutinizing gaze over the soiled clothing that she wore. "Have you been injured?" he asked in alarm.

Rebecca shook her head and laughed saying, "No, but I *am* in desperate need of a good scrubbing!"

"Well then, come with me," he replied, leading her to a small supply closet. He opened the door and motioned Rebecca inside. "This will allow for some privacy. Wait here while I gather what you're in need of."

Rebecca stepped into the small room and gazed around at the variety of potions, tinctures, and salves neatly aligned on the shelves. Within minutes the doctor had returned with a bucket of hot, sudsy water and a bundle of rags. Handing them to Rebecca he said, "You go ahead and get started. I'll find some clean clothing for you."

Rebecca accepted what he offered with a smile of gratitude, pulled the door shut tight and began to peel off the tunic and trousers she wore. The fading bruises on her arms reminded her of what she had been through, and of how quickly things could change. With an appreciative sigh she began to scrub her hands and her face first, the rough rag bringing a tingling sensation to her fair skin. By far the most challenging aspect of being a stowaway on a ship full of men had been keeping clean, she realized. At times she longed for a hot bath but would have been just as grateful for a simple plunge in the ocean. After a short time she heard a light tap on the door, signaling the doctor's return.

"I'll leave these clothes right out here. I hope they fit you well enough."

"Thank you," Rebecca called out to him.

She managed to bathe the rest of her body with thorough haste before reaching out to retrieve the clean clothing. It was fortunate for Rebecca that her years as the daughter of a missionary did not afford her the luxury of developing a taste for fancy garments she realized, for instead of wrinkling her nose in dismay at the rough, muslin attire, she smiled with delight at the thought of a fresh tunic to wear.

She pulled the muslin smock over her head and smelled the familiar scent of lye, making her feel cleaner than she had in months. The trousers she pulled on were much too large for her and Rebecca giggled to herself as she fashioned the waistband into a knot to keep them from sliding down over her narrow hips. Once dressed in the fresh garments, she gathered up her supplies along with her soiled tunic and left the closet in search of the doctor. She saw that he waited in the sick berth, and with a swift sweep of his arm he removed the bundle she carried to deposit the soiled heap in a waste bin near the doorway.

"Please, sit down," he said, beckoning her toward a chair in the center of the room. "I'm Dr. Charles Ammons," he said, "and I would like to officially thank you for your generous assistance yesterday."

"It's a pleasure to meet you, Dr. Ammons," she murmured. "I'm Rebecca Halloway and I'm grateful to have been of assistance to you, sir."

Doctor Ammons eyed her with a curious look and asked, "So you're the young stow-away I've heard rumors of...what business have you aboard the Redemption?"

Rebecca considered his words with care, wondering how best to respond to his question. "Well," she began, "I have recently contracted with your captain to earn my transport to Portsmouth."

He grinned at her tactful reply and said, "So that's the story, hmm? Well, since you're under 'contract', perhaps you might be interested in spending some of your time in the sick berth? You would be a great help to me when we come under attack."

"Oh yes, I would be very interested," she exclaimed, her eyes bright with enthusiasm.

"Then allow me to show you around a bit," he offered.

Nodding, she stood to her feet and followed him to the closet that she had vacated just moments earlier. She watched him open the door and gesture to the shelves filled with a variety of tinctures. "Do these look at all familiar to you?"

"Mm-hmm," she nodded at him. "My father stocks his cabinets in much the same way."

Dr. Ammons led Rebecca into the small room, directing her attention to the suture thread, needles, antiseptic potion, and clean cloths used for wound dressings. "Supplies are not always this readily available I'm afraid," he explained. "Oftentimes we're forced to use whatever we can get a hold of to bind a wound or close a stump."

"Yes," she grinned. "The muslin tunic in that trash bin over there worked wonders yesterday."

Dr. Ammons, charmed by her innocent and unpretentious nature, led her back towards the center of sick berth where she reclaimed her seat. She gazed with an inquisitive expression about the small confines of the room and soon caught sight of a shelf neatly lined with books just above the door. She strained to read their titles from where she sat, until Dr. Ammons, aware of her apparent interest said, "They're all medicinal journals I'm afraid."

Rebecca gave him a forlorn smile and said, "Sometimes I think I miss books more than anything since I've been away. Our home was always filled with a vast selection of authors, and my favorite evenings were spent with my mother and father, just…

reading together." She glanced away as if somehow saddened by the sudden memory.

Dr. Ammons determined at that moment in his mind to find her some sort of proper literature just as soon as he was able to.

Just then Petty Officer Andrews passed by and did a round about when he spotted Rebecca inside the doctor's quarters. "There you are!" he exclaimed with a hint of relief in his voice. "I've been searching the whole frigate for you...you're supposed to remain confined to the hold, remember?"

Rebecca was perceptive of his irritation and felt a stab of guilt at not having alerted him sooner to her whereabouts. Standing to her feet, she gave him a look of humble remorse and said, "I'm so sorry, Mr. Andrews. I'm afraid I've lost track of the time, and I should have come to find you much sooner than now. I do hope you'll forgive me."

"I don't want no apologies, Missy," he exclaimed, "all I want is to get you back to the hold before the captain sees you wandering about. Come along, and be quick about it now."

"It's alright, Mr. Andrews," Rebecca assured him. "I've been assigned to new quarters."

"By who?" he demanded.

"Captain Jameson himself, sir," she said.

A shadow of dread sprang to Mr. Andrew's face while he contemplated the harsh reprimand he would receive for having disobeyed Captain Jameson's orders.

Rebecca caught sight of his grimace of apprehension and made an attempt to put his fears at rest. "Don't worry, Mr. Andrews," she said, "my dealings with the captain had nothing to do with you...you really have nothing to be concerned about."

Petty Officer Andrews turned with a flippant wave of his hand and stormed away, cursing under his breath for having left the door to the hold open.

Rebecca turned to Dr. Ammons and said, "Would you excuse me please?"

"Of course," he assured with a quick nod. "We can speak more later."

"Thank you," Rebecca called over her shoulder, as she hurried to catch up with the petty officer.

"Mr. Andrews, wait...please! Let me explain!" she called.

"There's nothing to explain!" he shouted, not bothering to turn around, or slow his stride. "I let you out of the hold, plain and simple, and I'll be paying the price for my stupidity!"

"No, you won't," she said. "I took myself out of the hold, and I made certain the captain is aware that I alone am responsible for my actions."

He reeled about to face her, a look of anger flaring in his eyes. "You think what you want, Missy, but that's not the way it works on this frigate! Captain's orders get broken, somebody pays...and that somebody's going to be me," he said, spinning on his heel to storm away.

Rebecca stood silent, aghast with dejection. She was devastated at having brought this burden of dismay upon the petty officer, but even more so by his apparent resentment over what had transpired that day. He had been unselfishly kind towards her in her plight, and she in turn had been willing to defend him unto death rather than see the wrath of the captain fall upon him simply for demonstrating a concern for her safety. Now it was likely, she realized, that he would despise her just as much as the other men did. With a weary sigh Rebecca returned to her quarters, in no mood for further conversation with anybody. Her heart was heavy with the knowledge that she had disappointed her one, true friend aboard this vessel, and without further thought she slipped to her knees to offer prayers for reconciliation, and to beseech the Lord to deliver Mr. Andrews from the grave distress she had brought upon him.

Chapter 5

Rebecca enjoyed her new found freedom aboard the Redemption and kept her movements on deck to a minimum as the captain had requested. She had not yet seen Petty Officer Andrews since that fateful day nor had she approached Eddy since the truth of her identity had been revealed, and now the thought of coming face to face with the two men sent nervous flutters reeling through her belly. She decided to confront her apprehension at addressing the cook on a blustery morning just two days after her release from the hold, but as she wandered near the ship's galley she found her brave façade wavering. By the time she reached the narrow corridor she could scarcely breathe and she found herself rendered speechless with alarm. Rebecca caught a glimpse of Eddy's broad shoulders hunched over the stove when she stepped into the small room, and it was obvious to her that he hadn't heard her enter. Her face was contorted by a grimace of trepidation and she stood motionless and silent for what seemed to her like hours until the cook finally turned around and took notice of her contrite presence lingering in the doorway.

"What're you doing here?" he scowled.

"Eddy," she began. "I came to talk with you, and to help you here in the galley…if you'll still have me."

"I don't need your help anymore."

"But the captain said I could-"

"I don't care what the captain said," he muttered, "I don't need your help."

"Please, Eddy… it was so nice working with you before."

"There was no *before*. I don't know you…never have, never will."

"Eddy, it's just me…I'm the same person I was before all of this came to light, so nothing's really changed between us, has it?"

"Nothing's changed?" he scoffed. "How do you figure nothings changed?"

She studied him with a forlorn expression and crept closer to where he glowered, her heart pounding against her chest at the young man's belligerent contention. "Please, Eddy…just give it some time. I'm the same person I was two weeks ago."

"Oh?" he scoffed. "And who is that? The helpless stowaway I thought you were, or the conniving liar you turned out to be?"

Rebecca stood silent, desperate to come to the defense of her actions but knowing in the cook's present frame of mind it was unlikely he would hear her out.

"Go on then," he said, giving a flippant wave of his hand in the air as if to shoo her away. "I told you to leave."

"Eddy, please...just give me a chance. I'll do the cooking for you, the cleaning, or whatever you wish… and…and you don't even have to speak to me."

Rebecca hoped that the contention which had apparently developed between them would dissipate if given the time to resolve itself.

"I said no," he growled.

Rebecca persisted in the pursuit of her cause with a note of pleading in her voice as she continued to approach him with an unrelenting gaze. "Eddy, it can be just like it was before... trust me."

"Trust you?" he shouted. "You've been deceiving me all along. Why should I trust you now?"

"I didn't mean to deceive you, Eddy," she continued. "I was only concealing the truth in order to protect myself."

"So you didn't trust *me* then?" he scoffed.

"No," she sighed, "That's not it at all."

The tension in the small room was heavy and charged with emotion...anger emanating from the cook and desperation from the girl. Rebecca stepped closer and took hold of Eddy's arm, intent on persuading him to relent. "Please, at least allow me to clean the galley for you then, after you've already gone for the night."

He recoiled in disgust at her touch and shook her off with a violent thrust, sending Rebecca reeling helplessly backwards against his strength. The hem of her tunic caught itself on the metal edging of the counter and she twisted around in an attempt to catch herself before falling to the ground. With a grunt of surprise her face crashed into the unyielding wooden slab, sending blood spattering in all directions. She slid to the ground, the pain stealing the breath from her lungs.

Eddy towered over her, both triumph and revulsion radiating from his countenance at the sight of her defeated form slumped at his feet. "You want to clean the galley?" he sneered, giving an angry toss of his head toward the fresh blood splattered on the walls, "Start with that then." He stormed away from her, his anger searing her soul like heat from a flame.

Rebecca couldn't bring herself to look at him, the agony of his rejection inflicting much more pain than the havoc wrought upon her body, and she averted her gaze in humiliation, trying to slow the flow of blood streaming from the gash above her eye.

"When you've finished," he muttered from the narrow doorway, "get out of my galley."

Rebecca sat in stunned silence, unsure of whether to cry out in despair or throw something in anger. "Fruits of the spirit," she whispered aloud, hoping to thwart the resentment welling up within her. "Love, joy, peace, patience..." She paused for a moment to glance around at the sight of the blood stained walls and a sigh of defeated desolation escaped from her misshapen lips which had begun to swell in response to the injury. "Kindness, goodness, faithfulness...gentleness and...self-control," she finished, a single tear sliding down her bruised cheek. She continued to gaze about the room with a heavy heart until her eyes caught sight of the shape of a cross, fashioned in red with the essence of her blood, and with a determined heart she began to pour out her thoughts to the One who had sustained her through this journey thus far. She prayed long into the night, her fatigue eventually giving way to slumber as she lay on the dark floor of the galley, unresponsive to even the rodents which scurried near her head.

Rebecca slept fitfully, waking only when the sound of Eddy's voice stirred her to consciousness. She lifted her shoulders off the cold ground in surprise and wondered for a moment where she was, until the pain which coursed through her head brought the memories of the incident that occurred the evening before back with unrelenting clarity.

"What're you still doing here?" the cook grumbled. "I thought I told you to leave."

Rebecca gazed at him without wavering and said matter-of-factly, "You did tell me to leave, Eddy, but I decided to stay awhile so I could pray for you. I guess I must have fallen asleep."

"So you could pray for me?" he jeered. "I don't want you praying for me."

"Actually," she sighed. "I wasn't praying *for* you, I was praying about you. You know...well, no, I suppose you probably don't know, but there's a verse that speaks of God's love for us in the bible."

He watched in intrigued disbelief as she continued to study him. Without warning she raised her eyes heavenward, as if envisioning some captivating words of scripture written on an imaginary tablet suspended in mid air, and he heard her begin to speak, her voice soft but passionately confident.

"How precious to me are your thoughts, O God! How vast is the sum of them. Were I to count them they would outnumber the grains of sand."

Her soft gaze swept over the wary form of the cook and without hesitation she continued in a matter-of-fact tone. "You see, I got to thinking...that verse applies to you too, Eddy, and even though I don't like you very much right now, apparently God still does."

The corner of her bruised lip tugged upwards in an attempted smile, giving her a lopsided, topsy-turvy kind of look and she said, "Humph...imagine that." She gave a casual shake of her head, as if willing herself to believe that Eddy could actually be deemed worthy of God's love, while he stared at her a moment longer before turning to leave, his guilt finally taking hold of his conscience at last.

Rebecca hung back until he had disappeared from sight and then pushed herself to her feet, anxious to escape the small confines of the galley. Keeping her gaze lowered to the ground she endeavored to slip unnoticed past the curious glances of the men who mingled on deck, hopeful that none would take notice of her battered appearance. She wanted only to retreat to the safety of her berth, far away from the questioning demands of Dr. Ammons, at least until the bruised swelling of her face had gone down some.

Finally tucked beneath the comforting weight of her blankets, Rebecca slept soundly in spite of the noise of the days activities, awakening only to the sound of the rumbling of her stomach late in the evening. Pulling herself out from beneath the warmth of the covers, she reached up with a tentative hand to touch her face, intent on determining if she resembled her old self again. Instead of rising though, she heaved a discouraged sigh and fell back onto the bed, in no mood to answer questions as to the sorry state of her appearance, even though it meant sleeping through the night with an empty belly. When evening began to cast its dark shadow over the Redemption Rebecca finally summoned the courage to venture out onto the deck, the cool night air beckoning with its fragrant ocean scent. She crept up the narrow stairwell and made her way along the starboard side to the rear of the frigate, her favorite place to sit and gaze at the sky when the activities of the evening grew too boisterous for her sense of prudence. The stars shone bright against the cloudless black of night, complementing the soft lull of the waves lapping at the side of the Redemption. With a soft sigh of content she nestled down into the cotton blanket she carried with her, oblivious to the sounds of men long lost to the curse of rum echoing a faint whisper on the wind.

Eddy took refuge below to wallow in his guilt and remorse. Visions of the girl's battered and bruised appearance played a haunting rendition in his mind and he was in no mood for yet another encore. He had returned to the galley after leaving the girl in her despondent huddle, hoping to find that she still remained, but the small room was void of her presence. He saw that she had removed the blood that had been splattered on the cupboards, and the floor boards had been scrubbed as well. A wave of guilt washed over him anew and he retreated to the deck to work along side the midshipmen in the hot sun, intent on forcing thoughts of the girl from his mind. His silence during the remainder of the day spoke heavily of his self-reproach, though none were aware of it source. Never-the-less, the men allowed him the solitude he sought, but even now the burden continued to weigh heavily upon his shoulders.

"Hey there," one of the men shouted at him during a lull in the evening activities. "We need another man for a game of Whist. You in?"

Eddy shook his head and stood to his feet to lift his hand in a despondent farewell, wanting only to go in search of the girl and offer his reconciliation. He wandered up to the deck, where he could recall seeing the girl on so many occasions before her identity had been revealed, leaning in a listless fashion against the side of the frigate and staring through an impenetrable gaze out over the waves. As he drew near to where he expected to find her, his hands clenched in trepidation at the uncertainty of what he would say to the girl, yet in his determination to make amends he continued on his way without further concern of matters pertaining to conversation.

Rebecca heard the advancing footsteps before she could see who it was that drew near, and she contemplated where to hide herself. An inward groan escaped her when she realized her moment for escape had passed and she decided instead to remain where she was, praying that whoever approached would not take notice of her marred face. When the footsteps finally stopped before her she glanced up, surprised to find that it was only the cook who peered down at her. They contemplated one another for several terse moments, as if pondering the words which would best bridge the chasm that had formed between them, while Eddy was flooded yet again with remorse at the sight of the girl's bruised appearance.

"Even me, you say?" he mumbled at last.

"Um-hmmm," she nodded through an unwavering expression of confidence.

He toed at an imaginary splinter with nervous hesitation. "Well, if your god likes even me, then I suppose I could put up with you once in a while."

Rebecca gazed up at him. "Thank-you, Eddy," she whispered.

A sheepish grin tugged at the corner of his mouth as he turned to go, but pausing for a moment, he glanced back at her once more. "What's your name then?" he asked, a curious glint in his eye.

"Rebecca," she murmured.

"Rebecca," he repeated, the sheepish grin lingering on his face. "Good night then, Rebecca," he said with a slight nod of his head.

He took his leave to retreat toward his berth, expecting sleep to come quickly now that he had finally settled matters with his guilty conscience.

Rebecca remained on deck for a time to offer her deepest expression of appreciation to the Lord for bringing her the peace and resolution that she had so desperately sought between herself and the cook. She was grateful that she would be allowed to bide the remainder of her time aboard the Redemption in the sanctuary of the galley, and escape the mindless boredom that accompanied idle dawdling. When the lids of her eyes grew heavy with sleep, she stood to stretch her limbs before ambling along to retire in the comfort of her berth, where her thoughts faded with ease in the darkness of night.

Rebecca awoke from a dreamless slumber to the scent of rain in the air, the damp chill slithering through her small room like a serpent. She hesitated to leave the warmth of her cabin, but in the end decided that she best confront those who would take notice of her appearance and deal with the questions as they arose. She determined that her first stop would be the sick berth, where she knew Dr. Ammons would provide her with the comfort and solace that she sought, and she hoped then to attend to Eddy in the galley lest he forget the pact that had been forged between them the evening before. Stepping out into the frigid drizzle she came face-to-face with Lieutenant Burgess, who stared at her for a moment while something resembling concern lit across his features.

"What happened to you?" he demanded, the look of concern too quickly replaced with irritated consternation.

"Nothing, sir," she stammered, having hoped for a little more time to prepare her story.

He continued to scrutinize her, while his expression spoke clearly of mocking disbelief, and said, "It doesn't look like nothing."

"Well, you see," she continued, "I had an accident…last night. But I'm alright…there's no need to be concerned."

Rebecca felt as if she was babbling but the officer didn't seem to notice. Instead, he shook his head and continued on his way, muttering under his breath, "I didn't say I was concerned."

Rebecca breathed a sigh of relief after he had passed, for the last thing she wanted was to see Eddy punished for the unfortunate accident. Glancing over her shoulder, she caught sight of Captain Jameson peering at her from the quarterdeck. She hoped the young lieutenant wouldn't speak of his encounter with her lest the captain press her further for details of the incident, and she was quick to turn her head away from him for fear that he too, would catch sight of her wretched appearance. With a quick step she hurried on towards the sick berth, relief washing over her at the sight of Dr. Ammons carefully tidying up the cupboards.

"Oh my," she said with a breathless sigh, "am I glad to find you here!"

He turned towards her at hearing the sound of her melodic voice, a smile splayed across his face, but the smile was quick to dissipate when he saw the bruises that stained her fair complexion. "Rebecca!" he exclaimed. "What's happened to you?"

Rebecca shirked off his concern with a flippant wave of her hand and replied, "Nothing that couldn't have been avoided if I had been a little more careful."

His expression firmed and he asked, "Is there someone who is harassing you?"

She struggled to offer an explanation that would be truthful. "I lost my footing and fell, Dr. Ammons, last night in the galley. It was a dreadful accident, but one I don't intend to repeat."

Rebecca gave him a lopsided grin, determined to convince the man of her story, but he continued to study her with a skeptical countenance, unsure of whether to press the matter further or lay it to rest.

"Can you make me a bit more presentable?" she asked. "It's a little difficult for me to do without a looking glass."

He led her by the arm toward a chair, and then proceeded in a sullen disquiet to the supply cabinet to gather what he needed. He pulled several cotton cloths and a bit of witch hazel from the shelves before returning to where she waited. Wordlessly he began to swab at the wounds on her bruised skin, feeling a fresh stab of guilt with each grimace that sprang to her face. "I want you to be truthful with me," he chastised in a low voice.

"I'm being as truthful as I can be, sir," she murmured.

He continued to work without meeting her gaze and when he had finished he retreated to the cupboard and said, "I've done all I can, Rebecca. You're free to go now."

He braced his hands against the cabinet but kept his back towards her, his stance speaking clearly of the anger that smoldered within. Rebecca, realizing that she had upset him, sat for a moment, torn between confessing everything that had happened and leaving without a saying a word, but upon further deliberation she got up from the chair and moved to where he stood, silent and still.

"Please don't be angry with me, Dr. Ammons," she plead. "I'm just trying to fit into a very difficult situation."

"Difficult for who?" he demanded, spinning on his heal to look at her. "Difficult for you, or for the man who beat you?"

"No one beat me…I assure you. It was truly just an accident. Please, let's leave it at that and forget that it ever happened."

"I think the captain will want to be informed of this," he stated, his gaze leveling on Rebecca's face.

Rebecca felt a wave of unexpected fear welling up within her, and was aware of her thoughts giving way to panic. She closed her eyes tightly to pray that the Lord would sway the mind of Dr. Ammons, pleading with Him to rescue her from the precarious situation she had stumbled into.

Dr. Ammons stared at the girl for several moments thinking she was suffering ill effects from the battering she had received and was about to faint. He took hold of her by the arms and gave her a firm shake, hoping to snap her out of it before she lost consciousness. "Rebecca!" he shouted.

Rebecca eyes flew open with startled apprehension. "What?" she cried.

"What is it? What in Heaven's name is the matter with you?"

"Nothing," she stammered. "I was just praying, sir."

"Praying?" he repeated incredulously. "Why on earth would you be praying at a time like this?"

"Dr. Ammons, if I promise to tell you the next time someone harasses me, will you keep this incident just between the two of us? Please?"

He stared at her with a look of disbelief while she took his hands in her own.

"Please, sir, just this once…I beg you," she whispered.

Dr. Ammons waited a moment before nodding in resignation, certain that he would regret the decision later. Rebecca flung her arms around him in a hasty expression of gratitude and offered a quick thank-you before departing, leaving the man standing in the middle of the sick berth peering after her with a baffled expression on his face.

Rebecca hurried to the galley, concerned that Eddy might be irritated by her delay, but finding the room empty she pulled a large kettle from the shelf beneath the cupboard and began to fill it with fresh water, intent on making a hearty stew for the crew's lunch. When she had finished she set the kettle on top of the wood stove where the fire would bring it to a rolling boil.

"It'll take a long time to heat that water without a fire."

Rebecca twirled around in surprise at the statement, taken aback by the sharp intonation in the cook's voice. She saw him standing in the doorway, obliterating what little light came from the corridor, while his expression remained distant and aloof. His arms were laden with slivers of wood and he did his best to avoid her gaze as he walked to the corner of the room to let them fall with a clatter to the floor, picking out the largest pieces to add to the smoldering ashes in the stove.

"Oh," Rebecca replied, knowing that Eddy had always been the one who took on the task of keeping the stove burning up until now. She stood for a moment, uncertain of what to do next. It was obvious to her that an awkward tension still lingered between them and she was hesitant to do something that might provoke his anger once again.

He brushed his hands against his legs to dispel the dust that remained and walked to the barrel of salt packed meat to remove a large shank of mutton. Wordlessly he began to cut it up, tossing the pieces into the water she had tried to set to boiling.

Rebecca slipped over to the potato bin to pick out several large, yellow potatoes to add to the pot. Taking a good sized bowl from the shelf behind her, she settled herself at the counter where she began to peel the skins away from the starchy, white root with a small paring knife. The two continued to work side by side, never speaking a word to one another, nor making eye contact. It wasn't long until the first of the men began to trickle in, some giving Rebecca a sidelong glance, and others looking past her as if she weren't even there, while Eddy and Rebecca remained oblivious to them all, only consumed by the uncomfortable silence which hovered between them.

Dinner was more subdued than it had been previously, for most of the crew remained wary of the girl's presence. Instead of lingering in conversation after the evening meal as was the custom, the men filtered out, preferring instead to partake in camaraderie in the solitude of their berths below. After most of them had left, Rebecca and Eddy set about cleaning up the mess left behind. Although Rebecca had never offered much in the way of conversation with Eddy before her identity was discovered, she found she missed his endless chatter that had always seemed to distract her mind from boredom. Now however, he remained stoic and silent, and she wondered if the lingering contention would ever resolve itself. A quiet sigh of resignation escaped her as she dipped her hand into the hot, sudsy water to retrieve the rag she had been wiping the countertop with. Having finished with that, she moved onto the floor, crawling on her hands and knees as she scrubbed at the grease and the grime that saturated the wooden boards. She stretched her arm along the length of the cabinet that held the pots and pans to give a quick swipe with the soapy cloth, only to dislodge the shriveled carcass of a rat.

"Ugh!" she grimaced in disgust, taking hold of the creature by the tail to sling it into the trash bin placed next to the where Eddy worked.

Eddy glanced over his shoulder to see what the commotion was about and was struck in the middle of the back by the carcass sailing through the air. A stunned grimace of disgust sprang to his face as he looked first at Rebecca, then at the dehydrated body of the rodent which had dropped at his feet, and then back to Rebecca again.

Rebecca rested on her knees in a startled silence, an impish grin beginning to pull at the corners of her mouth. She lifted her hand to stifle the giggles that she knew would come but her laughter erupted before she could contain it. Her head fell back in her mirth while she dropped the rag into the pail, sending water sloshing over the sides of the bucket and onto the wooden planks of the floor. "Eddy," she gasped at last. "I am so sorry! I was aiming for the garbage barrel, not you!"

Eddy remained frozen in place peering down at her. Then, without a word he stomped out of the galley, leaving Rebecca staring after him with eyes dazed and confused. She collapsed against the side of the cabinet, her laughter dying in her throat, as she gazed about the room in a troubled silence for several moments. Before the roots of resentment and self-pity could take hold, she began to whisper with fierce determination as she willed herself not to cry. *"And He shall sit as a refiner and purifier of silver, purging them as gold and silver, that they may offer unto the Lord an offering in righteousness..."*

She paused in guilty contemplation, thinking if she were the sacrifice to be offered, she certainly didn't feel as righteous as she ought to just now. A heavy sigh prompted her to her knees and she began to pray for Eddy with an impassioned voice that was mostly spurned on by frustration and anger rather than compassion and concern. Before long the sound of someone approaching caught her attention and her voice grew quiet while she waited for the cook to return to dispense his wrath. She peered through the hazy light reflected in the corridor to see the shadowed form of not the cook, but the petty officer looming in the doorway.

"Missy, is that you in there?" he asked, glancing about the galley.

"It's me," she said, a sheepish grin spreading across her features.

"Who's in there with you?" he continued.

"No one."

"Who're you talking to then?"

"God," she answered without hesitation.

"Well it sounds to me like you're awfully upset with him..."

"Not with Him, Mr. Andrews, just with circumstances," she sighed.

"Oh. Might you be needing some company?"

"No, Mr. Andrews," she smiled. "I think I need to keep this between myself and the Lord."

"Well then, I suppose I should leave you to your arguing."

He continued on without another word, his features still hidden from sight in the seclusion of the corridor while she turned back to stifle a much needed chuckle, and set about finishing the task set before her.

Rebecca returned to her quarters after she had finished cleaning up the remainder of the galley. Eddy never did return, but she was grateful to have had the time alone to ponder her circumstances and she knew without a doubt that she must take her leave of the Redemption as soon as she was able to. She persisted in questioning God as to why He had allowed this situation to occur in the first place, while she prayed without ceasing for her life to resume its course from where it had been so unexpectedly interrupted.

Although Rebecca had hoped things with Eddy would improve over time, the air between them continued to be tense and uncomfortable, their silence speaking louder than any mere words could have. She half-heartedly expected him to banish her forever from the galley at some point and almost wished that he would, but he continued to tolerate her presence there, even though it was obvious to Rebecca that it caused him a great deal of distress. On occasion she would cross paths with Lieutenant Burgess but he would not speak to her either. In fact, when he saw her approach he often turned and walked the other way. She was aware that he was avoiding her, however she remained diligent to pray for him, never giving up on what the Lord had in store for his life. The captain on the other hand, seemed to be watching her with relentless distraction, as if he were waiting for her to commit an infraction of some sort. When Rebecca felt his piercing gaze upon her, she would smile up at him with a cherubic radiance and nod her head in a respectful greeting. She was determined not to evoke his anger, nor the anger of his crew during the remainder of her time aboard the Redemption, however long, and difficult, that may be.

Dr. Ammons was a more forgiving soul and welcomed Rebecca into his presence with joyous adoration. He was a never-ending source of encouragement to her and willingly took her under is wing to provide her with some semblance of continuity. With him she was able to speak of most anything... her apprehension at being aboard a ship full of men who resented her presence, her longing to return to her family in Portsmouth, and even her deferred but hopeful plans for the future. It was in the sick berth that Rebecca truly felt accepted, and she spent most of her free time there, away from the wary glances of the men.

The ship was continuing its path toward the rendezvous point, where Captain Jameson would receive Admiral Charles Perry on board, and in preparation for his visit, the crew was busy readying the frigate for the admiral's inspecting eye. Even Eddy seemed caught up in the fervor of tidying up the galley, though he never said so to her, but it was obvious to Rebecca that he wanted to make a good impression on the admiral as well. In fact, it seemed to Rebecca that the nearer the time drew to the man's arrival the shorter the tempers of the men grew. Anticipation was as prevalent among them all as irritation and Rebecca tried her best to remain inconspicuous and quiet lest she evoke someone's wrath.

Dinner had come late one evening when a surprise inspection by the captain led to an additional hour of duty on deck. Eddy grew irritated by the delay, leaving Rebecca tiptoeing around his belligerent form until eventually the hoard of men began to trickle in, their faces taught with fatigue, frustration and hunger. She busied herself at the washbasin, intent on staying out of everyone's way until she could return to the safety of her berth, the warm suds of water soothing the tension she held in her limbs.

From the small window behind her, a young midshipman was trying to catch her attention in the hopes of convincing her to give him a second serving of boiled mutton. "Hey! You there!" he called over the ruckus of men's voices.

Rebecca, caught up in her daydreaming, was oblivious to his presence and continued scrubbing the large kettle wedged in the basin. Eddy on the other hand, was only anxious to get things cleaned up for the night and remained in the common area gathering the plates from the men who had already finished eating.

"I said hey!" he shouted at her again, growing agitated by her apparent indifference.

"Come on now…leave her alone, Pete," Petty Officer Andrews chortled. "It's obvious to me that she doesn't care for the likes of you."

The petty officer had long been aware of the crew's attitude of disdain towards Rebecca, but found himself helpless to do anything about it. Instead he avoided her as best he could along with the rest of the men and was grateful when she didn't intentionally seek out his company.

Pete Jones, disgruntled at being ignored by the insolent girl, grabbed a heavy pewter mug resting on the counter and slung it through the small opening of the kitchen to where Rebecca stood. It struck her at the base of the skull, the sickening thud silencing the room and snapping the cook to attention.

"What the devil are you doing, man?" he shouted over at the midshipman standing in a stunned silence, his face draining of color as he watched Rebecca slip to the floor.

Eddy saw the dread which filled the man's startled gaze and he hurried to the small confines of the galley to see what had happened. His eyes lit upon Rebecca lying dazed and groaning on the ground. He rushed to kneel at her side, lifting her head onto is lap and feeling a stab of guilt at the grimace of pain which furrowed her brow.

"Someone get Dr. Ammons!" he shouted, his voice filled with alarm.

Rebecca was only semi-conscious and kept her eyes shut tight against the brightness of the lantern hanging above her.

She was aware of the eerie silence that fell over the men but was in too much agony to give them much thought.

"Rebecca?" Eddy whispered. "Are you alright?"

She stole a glance through half-closed lids at the mention of her name, but remained silent except for the groans that escaped her lips.

Eddy struggled to remain calm against the panic he felt rising in his gut while all around him were eyes wide with dread, both at the thought of harm befalling the girl, but also with the understanding of a sure punishment to follow for the one who had thrown the mug.

Dr. Ammons flew through the door of the galley, his face pale against the darkness of the night air. "Where is she?" he shouted, seeing Rebecca crumpled on the floor near the cook as soon as he had uttered the words. He dropped to his knees beside her, prying open first one eye with a tentative finger and then the other. He saw that her pupils were large and unchanging, in spite of the light flickering overhead.

Gathering Rebecca up in his arms, he proceeded to carry her to the sick berth with several of the men trailing along behind him.

"Mr. Andrews," he called. "Find Lieutenant Burgess and tell him to summon the captain immediately."

When Dr. Ammons entered the sick berth, only Eddy followed him in. The other men were quick to disperse to the crew's quarters below, not wanting to be near when the captain discovered what had happened. Dr. Ammons laid Rebecca on an examination table in the center of the room where Eddy hovered over his shoulder trying to catch a glimpse of her listless form.

Rebecca began to stir with the movement and made a futile attempt to sit up.

"Rebecca!" Dr. Ammons cautioned. "Lie still."

"I'm alright," she groaned. "Don't call the captain."

"I already have," Dr. Ammons replied, his voice laced with anger.

Rebecca cringed at the thought, knowing she would have a hard time convincing Captain Jameson that this was the result of a mere accident, especially now that she had Eddy to contend with as a witness.

She glanced up into the anxious eyes of the cook to give him a feeble smile, in spite of her pain. "Sorry about this, Eddy," she said. "You can leave the dishes in the washbasin...I'll finish them later on tonight."

Before Eddy could respond, Captain Jameson stormed into the room with an irate Lieutenant Burgess on his heels. "What the devil is going on?" he demanded.

Dr. Ammons took him by the arm and led him away from Rebecca, murmuring to him in low tones as they walked. The two men stood in the corner for several moments discussing the matter in hushed voices, and when they had finished Captain Jameson approached the table where Rebecca lay.

"Who did this to you?" he demanded, a look of grim consternation on his face.

"Captain," Rebecca whispered. "May we please speak about this in private?" Her only concern at the moment was keeping Eddy quiet, lest he reveal the name of the man who had injured her.

"I'll tell you who it was, sir," Eddy piped up.

Rebecca gave an inward groan at the sound of the cook's voice.

"It was Pete, sir. Pete Jones," he continued.

Captain Jameson began to pace about the small room, agitation clearly evident on his face. Directing a piercing gaze at Lieutenant Burgess he ordered, "Assemble the men below. I will attend presently."

The officer made a hasty retreat with the cook following close behind him, while Rebecca again attempted to sit up.

"Lie down!" Captain Jameson and Dr. Ammons shouted in unison.

"Please, sir," Rebecca plead. "I'm sure he meant no harm..."

An incredulous look crossed Dr. Ammons face. "Good heavens, Rebecca!" he exclaimed. "Do you really intend for us to sit back and watch them beat you to death?"

"No," she murmured. "I just don't want to see a man punished on account of me."

"Oh, see him punished, you will," Captain Jameson growled. "I assure you, his punishment shall be swift and severe." The captain stormed from the room leaving Rebecca staring after him through eyes large with dismay, while Dr. Ammons proceeded to palpate Rebecca's head.

"What's going to happen to him, Dr. Ammons?" she groaned.

He glanced down at her for a brief moment, his mind intent on determining the severity of her injury. "A flogging, most likely," he replied.

He continued moving his fingertips through her hair, searching for broken bone or torn flesh and not pausing until he felt the moist warmth of her tears on his hands. He stopped then and leaned heavily on his arms while he stared down at her with eyes full of disbelief. "Why do you weep for him?" he asked, irritated by her contrite nature. "In fact, why is it that you must always seek to protect the very ones who would do you harm?"

"The men already despise me, Dr. Ammons. This is only going to make matters worse."

"Well not if you'd let us protect you, it won't."

She sighed, sounding as if she carried the weight of the world upon her shoulders.

Just then Lieutenant Burgess reappeared in the narrow doorway, his face flushed with irritation. He resented the fact that one of his own crew members was going to suffer a flogging because of the girl. If she hadn't been so deceitful in the first place he determined, and had stayed in Portsmouth where she belonged, none of this would be happening now. His resentment welled at the thought and while he wished her no serious harm, he thought that she had again gotten just what she deserved for intruding into their world.

"The captain is ready, sir," he announced, glancing only at Dr. Ammons in an effort to avoid looking at the girl.

"Very well," the doctor replied. "I'll be there presently."

Dr. Ammons hovered over Rebecca a moment longer, his compassionate gaze settling on her disconsolate face. "Will you be alright if I leave you alone for a bit?" he asked.

Rebecca nodded, bringing a fresh spasm of pain coursing through her head. She watched his retreating form until he had nearly disappeared through the doorway.

"And stay where you are," he warned, glancing back at her over his shoulder. "In fact, if you so much as move one finger off of that table young lady I will see you flogged as well, do I make myself clear?"

Rebecca nodded again through her misery, anxious to be left alone to pray, but she found the words slow in coming due to the distracting sounds emanating from below deck. She first heard the stern tone of the captain as he began to address the men, while all else was eerily quiet. When the sound of his voice finally quieted, Rebecca was horrified to hear the harsh crack of a whip striking a man's flesh, a sound she hadn't heard since her days aboard the Defiance, while a loud voice called out the strokes as they were administered. Anxious to escape the sickening noise, she stood to her feet to take refuge at the rear of the ship, where the echo's of Pete Jones's agony would be muffled by sheer distance alone. Remembering the cautionary words of Dr. Ammons, Rebecca dashed back into the sick berth to scribble a hasty note which read 'back of ship'. That done, she hurried out into the chill of the night air, anxious to hide herself from the guilt that tormented her soul.

The flogging continued with unrelenting severity until Pete Jones, in his great agony, faded into blackness. The punishment was declared sufficient and the men were dismissed. All returned below to the solitude of their quarters where they remained quiet and sullen, grateful that the accused had finally been released from the shackles which had held him. None spoke as they retreated into the darkness, for there would be no revelry below deck tonight as the memory of the harsh beating cast a dark oppression over all. Instead, they crawled wordlessly into their bunks save for the few who tended to the penitent sailor.

Captain Jameson proceeded immediately to his stateroom, just as disturbed by the incident as the rest of the crew, as floggings were seldom necessary onboard the Redemption. Dr. Ammons in turn, was only anxious to return to the sick berth where Rebecca lay injured and distraught, but with a disgruntled sigh, he found the sick berth empty and his anger flared with the realization that she would dare to leave against his admonition to remain. It was only when he tossed his overcoat onto the chair that he took notice of the note she had left for him. Grabbing it up in his hand, he hurried out the door to find her.

Rebecca remained in her sanctuary at the rear of the ship, buffeted by the wind but secure in the silence that enveloped her. Tears of desolation coursed down her cheeks with the realization that she had brought this horrible thing upon Pete Jones and in her mind she was certain that all were certain to abhor her presence now, including Eddy and Dr. Ammons.

Dr. Ammons saw Rebecca when he rounded the corner of the frigate, her small form bundled in the blanket that had covered her in the sick berth, while the wind whipped dark tendrils of hair about her face. He stood for a moment watching her and soon caught sight of the pained expression which masked her features. He was filled with pity at the vision of despondency before him but was at a loss as to how to comfort her. With cautious steps he moved nearer to her. "Rebecca," he said in a compassionate tone, "Why are you so troubled by this? The man might have killed you."

She glanced up at him in surprise, but quickly lowered her head in an attempt to hide the tears that continued to course down her cheeks.

Dr. Ammons knelt down beside her, gathering her into his arms with tender affection. He patted her head and murmured soothing sounds of comfort, allowing her to release the emotions she was trying so hard to contain. "It's alright, my dear," he soothed. "Everything is going to be alright."

Rebecca sat enfolded in his embrace for several minutes, her mind drifting to thoughts of her home where her father had so often comforted her in much the same way. The memory of what had been left a cavernous hole in her heart and the loneliness threatened to engulf her. "I'm sorry I left the sick berth, sir," she began. "I just couldn't bear to listen to the sounds coming from below."

"It's alright, Rebecca," he said, remembering only now why he had gone in search of her in the first place. "Are you feeling yourself again?"

She nodded gingerly, her head still throbbing with any sort of movement that she made.

Just then Eddy appeared before them, a worried look shadowing his eyes. It seemed to him that no matter what he did, he just managed to bring further havoc down upon the girl. Surely, he realized, she was bound to detest him now and would have nothing more to do with him or his galley. "There you are!" he exclaimed. "I've been searching all over for you!"

Rebecca stared up at him in dismay. "Oh, Eddy," she murmured. "I forgot all about the galley. I'll go there right now and finish things up."

He gave her a look of exasperated disbelief when she struggled to stand and shouted, "Blast it, Bec, I'm not here about the bloody galley!"

She stared up at him through startled eyes.

"You've had a whale of a bump on your head and all you think I care about is the galley? We thought you were dead!" He raked his fingers through his hair and kicked at a board jutting up on the deck.

Rebecca, sensing his frustration, hurried to stand to her feet and both Dr. Ammons and Eddy caught a glimpse of the grimace of pain that sprang to her features. She swayed for a moment before she gathered her bearings and then approached Eddy with tentative steps. "Eddy, I'm alright," she assured him, taken aback by the unexpected concern in his eyes.

He stood for a moment staring down at her, his knuckles glowing white in his clenched fists, until in a sudden move that startled even Dr. Ammons he reached out to embrace her, releasing her in a swift motion that almost sent her reeling backwards.

"Alright, then," he muttered, stepping back. "I'll be seeing you in the galley when you're feeling up to it?"

Rebecca gave another slight nod, hoping to spare a fresh spasm of pain, and murmured, "Yes."

Dr. Ammons took Rebecca by the arm and turned her towards her berth. "Come on then, you've had enough excitement for one night, young lady. Now it's time to retire to your berth."

She followed him without hesitation, anxious to seek solace in the comfort of her room so that the ache in her head would dissipate some, but before they had even arrived at the corridor Lieutenant Burgess approached them from where he stood watch on the quarterdeck.

"Sir," he said, speaking to Dr. Ammons. "The girl is to report to Captain Jameson's quarters immediately."

Rebecca cast a weary glance at Dr. Ammons, who silenced her with a shake of his head. "I'll report to the captain myself," he began. "This girl is in no condition to be chastised tonight."

"He won't appreciate her delay in his present mood, sir," the officer warned.

Rebecca rested her hand on Dr. Ammon's arm and said, "I'll go. I don't want to prolong this incident beyond tonight anyway. I'd rather deal with the matter now and be done with it."

Lieutenant Burgess watched their exchange for a moment and then turned on his heel to return to his watch on deck. He hoped the captain would deal harshly with the girl, as she deserved nothing less than the severe beating Pete Jones had taken on account of her.

Dr. Ammons gave Rebecca a stern look of admonition before relenting, knowing that it would indeed be best for her if the matter were laid to rest this night. He reached out to pat her cheek before she left and offered to accompany her to the captain's berth, but she refused, preferring instead to be chastised by the captain alone.

Captain Jameson paced in his stateroom, angered by the events of the evening but even more so upon being informed that a similar incident had occurred prior to this one that he had not been told of. He realized then that he had taken little initiative to assure the girl's safety, assuming that if there were any altercations he would hear about them from his officers. Apparently, he realized with irritation, this was not to be the case. The slight tap announcing the girl's arrival interrupted his thoughts but instead of calling out for her to enter, he strode across the room to fling open the door himself.

Rebecca took an apprehensive step backward at the sudden appearance of Captain Jameson and she watched him give an exaggerated wave of his arm motioning for her to enter. She could sense the tension in the room well before she turned to face the foreboding officer, but still her breath caught in her throat at the sight of his stern expression, leaving her once again speechless and trembling before him.

Captain Jameson towered over the girl, determined to disrupt the calm reserve she had displayed at their last meeting. If breaking her will and bringing her to the point of utter terror was what it would take to instill some sense into her, then by all means that's what he was prepared to do. He glared down at her with livid eyes, intent on compelling her to speak first.

The two contemplated one another for several, uncomfortable moments until Rebecca finally opened her mouth to say something, but then thinking better of it, she snapped it shut again. She was hesitant to say anything at all lest she upset the man even further and she uttered an inward prayer while she waited in silence for some sliver of mercy to be miraculously bestowed in the man's heart lest he kill her right here and now where she stand.

Captain Jameson became even more incensed by the girl's stubborn silence and turned away to pace back toward the window, oblivious to the precautionary step Rebecca took towards the door. "Well," he growled, not bothering to turn around and look at her. "Are you, or are you not going to tell me what happened?"

"I'm afraid I cannot tell you, sir" she whispered, unsure of how she had been injured.

He spun on his heel and marched back to where she cowered, thinking if it was terror he hoped to instill in her it would appear as though he had already succeeded. Rebecca shrank back against the wall in an effort to gain some semblance of self-preservation, watching the ominous form of Captain Jameson advance upon her.

"You will tell me on your own volition," he warned darkly, "or I will force it out of you on mine."

"But, Captain," she confessed in a contrite tone. "I don't know what happened."

He stared at her for a moment, caught off guard by her statement. Surely something must have had led up to the attack. "Apparently this isn't the first time you were assaulted, is that right?" he questioned, his angry gaze never wavering.

"No," she corrected truthfully. "This is most definitely the first time."

"Do *not* lie to me," he warned.

"I'm not lying, sir," she murmured, her features clouded with panic.

He gave her a look of enraged disbelief, having already been told of the bruises found on her face by Dr. Ammons. Glaring at her through livid eyes he retreated angrily to his dining table where he rang for his steward. Within minutes the ruddy face of George Robbins appeared.

"You rang, sir?"

"Get Dr. Ammons," the captain ordered.

Rebecca's stomach clenched in apprehension while she remained rooted in place, her gaze fixed warily on Captain Jameson. Dr. Ammon's rap on the door came within minutes. The captain called for him to enter and he hurried into the room, his eyes heavy with concern. "Oh, thank heavens," he breathed upon seeing Rebecca. "You're alright."

Rebecca's eyes moved from the captain to Dr. Ammons, and then back to the captain again, while Captain Jameson turned his full attention on the doctor.

"Dr. Ammons, would you be so kind as to repeat," he began with a noticeable hint of sarcasm, "what you so kindly told me in the sick berth this evening?"

Dr. Ammons glanced at Rebecca before replying. "I said this was not the first time someone has assaulted her."

"And when was the first time, pray tell?"

"Fourteen days past, sir."

"And why, might I be so bold as to ask, was I not informed of the incident?"

Dr. Ammons sat back heavily in the chair. "She asked me not to say anything, sir."

Captain Jameson glanced sharply at Rebecca through narrowed eyes and growled, "Your prevarication is testing my patience, Miss Halloway."

"It wasn't an assault, Captain," she assured. "It was simply an accident."

His fist slammed against the edge of the table in rage causing Rebecca to pale in alarm. "Then why did you try to hide it from me?" he demanded.

Rebecca remained silent, her eyes large with remorse.

"An assault aboard my ship...on a female no less...and my very own officer neglects to tell me," he muttered. "Do you realize the punishments that have been inflicted upon men who have withheld pertinent information such as this from a commanding officer?" he demanded.

A pained expression crossed Rebecca's face. "Oh, Captain," she breathed. "This is all my fault. The matter didn't concern you so I persuaded Dr. Ammons to keep it to himself."

"Everything that happens aboard this ship concerns me!" he bellowed. "There are two hundred men who serve on this frigate and I will maintain order!"

Captain Jameson's face was flushed with fury and Rebecca was aware that she had pushed him near the limits of his self control. She lowered her gaze in deference and responded in a soft tone, hoping to somehow diffuse the man's anger, "Never-the-less, sir, it is I who am at fault and I beg you to inflict whatever punishment you deem necessary on me, and me alone."

"You escaped a punishment the last time we met...I don't think you will be as fortunate this time," he growled.

"Still, I'm willing to accept any punishment you deem necessary in order to spare the good name of Dr. Ammons."

"Have you ever seen a man flogged, Miss Halloway?" he asked coldly.

Horrifying images of Captain Cromwell's men being beaten beyond recognition sprang with instant clarity to her mind but she remained silent, certain that Captain Jameson was not questioning her past experience with maritime punishment at that particular moment. "Captain, please..." she whispered, desperate to deflect the captain's wrath away from Dr. Ammons.

"No! I will not lay this matter to rest," he shouted. "I must maintain order aboard this ship and if that means seeing someone punished, then I will not delay."

"Then do what you must, sir, but do it to me," she begged.

"And if I choose to string you up by the neck and hang you from the lanyards?" he threatened, his piercing gaze searching her face for some minuscule hint of fear that would induce in her an attitude of submission.

"Then I shall die by your hand, Captain," she whispered, her gaze unwavering.

He paced back and forth before her to contemplate his next action. He knew he was at liberty to punish the girl somehow, and if she were one of his own crew he knew that discipline would be severe. Glancing at Dr. Ammons he growled, "Might you have any suggestions to offer, Dr. Ammons?"

Dr. Ammon's head rested wearily on his hand and he lifted it only to give it a quiet shake, while his gaze settled on Rebecca. "I don't know what we can do to keep you safe, Rebecca, short of locking you up until we moor in Portsmouth," he sighed, his eyes heavy with concern.

A knock at the door interrupted their deliberations and Lieutenant Burgess stepped through the portal at the captain's call to enter. "Sir, I apologize for the interruption, but your presence is needed on deck when you are finished here."

Captain Jameson glanced one final time at Rebecca who stood with an apologetic expression of penitence. "We'll settle this matter on the morrow," he said in a gruff tone, grateful for the interruption. "You have tested my patience enough for one day."

With that he stormed from the room, leaving Dr. Ammons and Rebecca alone in an uncomfortable silence. She glanced at him with woeful eyes and whispered, "I'm so sorry…I never meant for any of this to happen."

"What did happen, Rebecca?"

"I don't know, sir. The men were eating dinner and I was washing the kettles. I only wanted to stay out of Eddy's way... he hasn't been the same since he found out..."

She paused for a moment and glanced away sheepishly.

"Found out what?" he asked.

"Since he found out that I wasn't who he thought I was."

"I see," Dr. Ammons replied, finally gaining some perspective on the complicated predicament of the girl's situation. "Might that have been the night you received those nasty bruises on your face?" he asked with a hint of sarcasm.

Her eyes met his with a polite, but determined gaze. "Yes, it was, and what happened that night was an accident, just as I told you. I did not lie to you Dr. Ammons, not in the past, not now, and I will not in the future."

"I'm afraid I'm not the man you need to convince of that, Rebecca," he mused, knowing Captain Jameson had little reason or inclination to trust the girl, especially after the events of this evening.

Rebecca felt her throat welling with tears of frustration but she willed herself not to let her vulnerability show, while Dr. Ammons felt a brief stab of guilt at her sudden expression of despair. "You're exhausted, Rebecca," he murmured. "Let me walk you to your berth so you can rest. Apparently this matter won't settle itself as quickly as you had hoped, but there's nothing that can be done about it tonight."

She nodded in acquiescence and felt his arm encircle her shoulder. She let herself lean against him, grateful that he harbored no ill will after the captain's stern rebuke, and before long they stood in the corridor which held the small room that beckoned her to its sanctuary. "I truly am sorry, Dr. Ammons," she whispered.

"I know, my dear," he assured, giving her a gentle push through then narrow doorway. "Now get some rest."

Rebecca breathed a sigh of relief at having returned to the safety of her berth and she was quick to fall to her knees in an attitude of reverent submission, whispering with passion the words of scripture nestled deep in her heart. *"Because or your great love, oh Lord, I will not be consumed, your compassions will never fail me...no, they are new every morning. How great is your faithfulness to me o God. Be now my portion and my cup and sustain me while I wait for your deliverance!"*

With a complacent sigh she crawled into her bed and burrowed beneath the warmth of the heavy covers, the dull pain in her skull fading with the approach of slumber, and her eyelids drifting shut under a heavy shroud of fatigue.

The morning came much too soon for Rebecca and the knot of dread that had planted itself in her belly the night before had begun to take root and grow. Sighing in resignation she rose to freshen up a bit, hoping to attend to Eddy in the galley before her final day of freedom came to an end. She wasn't sure of what punishment Captain Jameson had in store for her, but she had no doubt in her mind that it would be unpleasant. Her head still throbbed with pain at each movement that she made but she brushed it off, intent on leaving her small quarters before the captain decided to attend to their unfinished business. She noticed that the men gave her a wide berth as she passed by, but she was grateful that her presence didn't appear to be as blatantly despised as she had expected it would be. Steering herself into the galley she came face to face with the cook, who glanced up in surprise when he saw her.

"Hey!" he exclaimed. "What're you doing here?"

Rebecca's smile darkened upon hearing his words. "I said I'd be here to help you...don't you remember?"

"Well, yeah," he said. "You said you'd be here to help but I didn't want it to be today."

Rebecca sighed in exasperation, weary of the unpredictable nature of the male species. "Fine, Eddy...you let me know when the time is right." She spun on her heel to leave.

"Wait!" he called.

She stopped for a moment but did not turn around to meet his gaze.

"I only meant you shouldn't be here...not yet anyway. You were hurt awfully bad, Bec...we all thought you were dead. Are you sure everything's all right with your head'n all?"

"It's fine," she said, still feeling confused and irritated by his behavior.

"Then go ahead and stay," he murmured, taking refuge near the safety of the stove.

She lowered her head as if in great deliberation before turning to move with a cautious step back into the room, an awkward silence enveloping her. She was aware of Eddy's eyes upon her and only breathed a quiet sigh of relief when his attentions returned to the simmering pot of porridge on the hot burner. The two of them remained quiet, Rebecca watching the solid, broad shoulders of the one whom she had considered her trusted friend since her early days aboard the Redemption, and Eddy keeping his eyes fixed on the task before him.

Eddy maintained his gaze on the steaming gruel, his guilt returning with a gut-wrenching force as he felt the eyes of Rebecca on his back. He was aware that he had hurt her deeply yet he was at a loss as to how he could he mend the shattered trust that they once seemed to share. She had every right to despise him he realized, and it appeared as though she was considering that option at that very moment. He muttered a forceful curse under his breath and leaned heavily against the stove, in spite of the heat emanating up in his face.

Rebecca sensed his anger from across the expanse of the room and lowered her gaze in self reproach, certain that her prayers for reconciliation had gone unheard. In her discomfort she yearned for a quick escape from yet another altercation with the cook. Glancing up one last time she mumbled in a voice heavy laden with remorse, "It's alright, Eddy. I'll leave. Please... just don't be angry anymore."

He spun around and shouted, "No! I don't want you to leave...I want to pretend none of this ever happened...I don't want to wonder every time I see you if you still despise me for what I did to you!"

"I don't despise you," she said, her eyes widening in surprise.

"How could you not?" he scoffed. "I've given you nothing but trouble since that beating you took on deck...and even that was my fault!"

"How was that your fault?" she stammered, confusion etched on her features.

"*I* was the one who drug you out of the galley, and *I* was the one who pushed you into the hands of the men. You begged me not to, don't you remember?"

"But Eddy, you didn't know-"

"How could I not have known, Bec?" he muttered. "I'm not blind."

Rebecca was stunned. She continued to stare at him while uttering a quick plea to God for guidance. "Dearest Lord Jesus," she began, raising her eyes toward heaven in a pious gesture of penitence, "Please help me convince Eddy that there is nothing but your love for him in my heart. Help me to make him understand that I have forgiven him just as you have forgiven me. And help me, Lord, to show him a bit of your kindness and mercy with each day that you give to us."

He stared down at her in surprise as she offered her humble prayer aloud and when she had finished, she met his gaze, her face lighting up with a radiant smile, while her eyes glistened with a sheen of tears. "Eddy, there is nothing you can do that will ever make me despise you...ever."

He contemplated her in an apprehensive silence until he watched a single tear slide down her cheek. "Don't...you...cry..." he warned.

"Oh, Eddy," she whispered. "They're happy tears."

Another tear slid haphazardly down her cheek while an infectious giggle began to rise in her throat. Eddy's grin broke free at last and the two of them erupted into a loud chorus of laughter. He reached out to embrace her firmly before holding her at arm's length.

"Forgiven?" he asked.

"Yes, forgiven completely," she sighed.

They reveled in their joy of reconciliation for several moments before they grew quiet, allowing Rebecca a moment to glance around at the cluttered room and the unwashed dishes of the past day stacked precariously on the counters.

"Oh my," she smiled. "It *is* quite a mess in here, isn't it?"

Eddy gave her a playful slug on the shoulder and said, "Looks like you'd best get busy then."

The two of them began to attack the chaos strewn about with determination, grateful to have dispelled the contention between them at last. They worked in a comfortable silence for a time, needing no words to enhance the air of camaraderie in the tiny galley, and when the men finally began to trickle in for the morning meal Eddy hovered over Rebecca protectively, giving a warning glance at any who might seek to do her harm. His concern was unwarranted though as the severe beating which took place the night before left a stark impression on the rest of the crew, and now none dared go near the girl, much less look at her.

Petty Officer Andrews didn't enter with the rest of the men but stood in the narrow doorway eyeing Rebecca from a distance, concern etched through the myriad of lines on his face, until he finally mustered the courage to approach her. He was stopped short by the cook who gave him a wary look of caution as he placed himself between the old man and the girl.

"What do you want with her?" Eddy growled.

Rebecca, hearing the harsh tone of his voice, turned around in surprise to see who it was that he spoke to. "Mr. Andrews!" she exclaimed. "What are you doing here?"

"I just came by to see if you're alright, Missy," he said. "I felt awfully bad about what happened last night."

Rebecca stepped around the lurking form of Eddy to reassure the petty officer that she was indeed alive and well and thank you very much for asking, convincing him only when she began to inquire as to the whereabouts of Captain Jameson and Dr. Ammons. "I'm afraid this whole thing has left them spitting mad!" she whispered, a mock grimace on her face.

Not bothering to answer her question, he patted her cheek affectionately and stepped out, anxious to put some distance between himself and the irate cook.

Captain Jameson's promise to see her punished had gone forgotten in the arrival of the most recent news announcing that the honorable Admiral Perry would pay his visit to the Redemption seven days earlier than was previously expected. The tension aboard the frigate soon grew intense as the crew made a hasty attempt to prepare the ship for the inspecting eye of the admiral, while the officers struggled to keep the tempers of the exhausted men at bay. Eddy and Rebecca worked just as diligently in the galley, waxing the floor boards and the cabinets until they glistened with a fine sheen. Rebecca's only wish was that the men would take their meals on deck until after the admiral's arrival so as to preserve what little they had worked so hard to accomplish. Instead, the men filed in night after night, leaving Eddy more disgruntled than ever at the mess they left behind.

Rebecca, in her discomfort with the contention that lingered between herself and Captain Jameson, was consumed by the fact that a sure punishment awaited her, and having not heard from him in more than two days posed a distraction greater than any irate crewmember ever could have. She remained quiet and forlorn throughout most of the evening's clean-up duties, and determined in her mind to pay a visit to the captain as soon as she could convince Eddy to let her leave. He too, was quiet, his thoughts lingering only on the impending visit from the high ranking official who would be arriving in just two more days, so when she informed him that she was finished for the night he barely gave her a second glance, but simply lifted his hand in acknowledgement of her statement.

Rebecca left the confines of the galley and meandered across the broad expanse of the deck, in no hurry to confront Captain Jameson. The sun was setting low across the water leaving a rose-tinged hue on the horizon, and it didn't take long for Rebecca to recall how much she enjoyed the peace and solitude that was to be found on deck after the fading light of day had driven the crew to their quarters below. She took a moment to gaze upon the beautiful sunset and uttered a quick prayer, asking the Lord to give her the courage to do what lay before her. When she had finished she continued on her way, stopping in front of Captain Jameson's quarters to calm her nerves before knocking at his door. Finally, with a sigh of resolve, she rapped firmly three times and waited for his call to enter. Much to her surprise, she was greeted by Lieutenant Burgess, who gave her an indifferent glance of curiosity before asking, "May I help you?"

Coming from any other person the words would have been received as gracious and hospitable, however the lieutenant's very air made them sound more like a task that one must persevere through, even though dreaded as it was expected to be. Rebecca hesitated for a moment before proceeding, as she had hoped to have found the captain alone in his stateroom. "Might I speak with Captain Jameson for a moment?"

"Is he expecting you?"

"No, sir, he's not," she answered, half-heartedly wishing the lieutenant would send her away.

"It's alright, Mr. Burgess," she heard the captain say. "I'll see the girl."

Lieutenant Burgess stepped away from the portal and motioned for Rebecca to enter, grateful that his business with his commanding officer was finished. He didn't want to be in the girl's presence any longer than was absolutely necessary and so he bid the captain a quiet goodnight before departing, pulling the door shut with a soft clang behind him.

Captain Jameson was seated behind a large, mahogany desk, scrutinizing Rebecca with a suspicious scowl. He found himself regretting his decision to let her wander about at will on the frigate and deliberated confining her once again to the hold, where he at least had some aspect of control over who came into contact with the girl.

Rebecca did not approach the captain, but remained rooted in place near the safety of the corridor. "Sir," she began. "I wanted to apologize again for what happened the other night."

"An apology doesn't change the fact that a punishment is warranted," he admonished.

"I understand that, sir, and I was hoping we might discuss that now."

"Tell me," he asked, a hint of sarcasm lacing his words, "What might *you* consider an acceptable punishment?"

Rebecca pondered his question for a moment, but having never found herself in such a predicament before, she was at a loss for both words and ideas. "I don't know, Captain," she sighed, a shadow of remorse clouding her features.

He stood to his feet and began to pace while he again found himself contemplating his options for punishing the girl. Were she a child he would turn her over his knee and give her a swift swat on the backside, but dealing with a young woman such as herself was a different matter. He couldn't very well lock her up until they reached Portsmouth, nor could he bring himself to inflict a physical punishment on her either. A sudden idea came to mind and he spun on his heel to face her. "From here on out," he began, "If there is so much one hair on your head out of place, I will see to it that whoever is at fault receives a dozen lashes… delivered by you!"

Rebecca's eyes grew wide with dismay. "I couldn't," she whispered.

"Oh, you will," he assured, "or every man aboard this ship will suffer the consequences for your disobedience. Do I make myself clear?"

Rebecca appeared to be near tears and Captain Jameson felt an unexpected twinge of remorse at having dealt with her so harshly. No matter, he thought, better to keep her safe than complacent until they could be rid of her. Rebecca remained silent, still too distraught to speak.

"I said, do I make myself clear," the captain repeated in a menacing tone.

Rebecca was hesitant to open her mouth for fear of what might come forth, so she gave a quick nod, wanting only to escape to the solitude of her quarters before she erupted into sobs.

"Then you are dismissed," he said, turning his back lest she see the guilt etched in his features.

Rebecca hurried from the captain's cabin without another glance, biting at her lip until she was in the corridor where her breath came in great, ragged gasps. She proceeded to the confines of her berth lest someone catch a glimpse of her in her present state, and when she finally reached the tiny room, she slipped inside and fell back against the door, her tears coursing in silent streams while her shoulders shook beneath the weight of her despair. She would have gladly taken a dozen lashes rather than see any of the crew suffer such a demise on account of her. Sliding to the floor, she buried her head in her hands and uttered despondent prayers for deliverance, her tears of desolation flowing unchecked long into the night.

The new day dawned bright and clear but Rebecca groaned at the sounds of the days activities above her, wishing only for the silence to envelope her once again. Instead of rising she burrowed deeper into the folds of the blankets and pulled them up over her head to drown out the noise. She soon returned to the slumber which she had been awakened from, stirring only when the sound of the ship's bell announced the noon meal. She flipped herself onto her back with a weary sigh, determined to remain in her berth until she was finally delivered in Portsmouth. That was the only way to be certain that another mishap with one of the ship's crew wouldn't occur she realized, thus sparing her from having to deliver any lashes to any man onboard the Redemption.

Rebecca tossed about in her darkened berth late into the evening, when she simply could not stand to spend one more moment in idle dawdling. She crawled from beneath her covers and tried to put some order to her hair before she ventured out among the men. The one good thing about having naturally unruly hair she mused, was that it always appeared to be in a state of disarray, so when it really was no one took much notice. She grinned at her good fortune and slipped into the corridor, anxious to help Eddy make his final preparations before the admiral's arrival in the morning. When she first set eyes upon the ruddy, young cook, she nearly laughed out loud. His arms were buried up to the shoulders in sudsy bubbles, while dirt-streaked rivulets of sweat coursed down his face. She covered her mouth to stifle a chuckle, silencing it only when he twisted around at the sound of her voice.

"And just where have you been?" he demanded, in a tone laced more with exasperation than with anger.

"I was hiding in my berth, Eddy, so I don't get myself into any more trouble, but then my guilt got the better of me when I thought of you all alone down here," she smiled. "I'm sorry for leaving you to take care of matters on your own, but I'm ready to go to work now. What do you need me to do?"

"Well," he began, looking around. "Let's get the rest of these walls cleaned up a bit and then we can work on the cabinets. We'll save the floors until last..."

He glanced down at Rebecca to see her smug grin.

"What's so funny?" he asked.

"So, I should just expect to get no sleep tonight, is that what you're saying?" she teased.

"Well it seems to me that you've been sleeping all day! Why would you think you'd need to sleep tonight?"

A sheepish grin spread across his face when he heard the giggle that bubbled up from within her and he added, "I suppose we will need to stay a bit later than usual, if you're up to it?"

"Then I suppose I'd better get started," she laughed.

Rebecca took to cleaning the walls with gusto, knowing how important it was for Eddy to have an impeccable galley to present to the high ranking admiral, and the two of them chatted long into the evening while they scrubbed down the walls, the cook stove, and finally the floorboards. Eddy brewed them a pot of strong coffee to enjoy while they worked and when they had finished, they sat back and gazed about with exultation at what they had accomplished. The room grew quiet around them as they rested, and it wasn't long until they became aware of a fierce gale which had begun to rock the Redemption from side to side, tossing the massive frigate about like a leaf on the wind.

"It's going to be a howler this night I'm afraid," Eddy sighed, taking extra care to secure the contents of the galley within the spaces provided.

Rebecca nodded, too exhausted to respond to his comment.

"I suppose we should turn in and call it a night," he continued. "I sure appreciate your help, Bec. You know I couldn't have done it without you."

Rebecca stood to her feet, grimacing at the unexpected ache in her stiff muscles.

"I'm more than happy to have helped, Eddy." she said. "It looks just beautiful in here. Now if only we can keep it this way until Admiral Perry arrives."

She bid him a goodnight and made her way to the deck, only to be greeted by a spray of cold, salty water. From where she stood, she could hear the wind screaming and the sound of the sails slapping in the fury of the storm. She saw that there was more activity than usual on the frigate for this time of night, as several of the crew struggled to secure the rigging against the onslaught.

"You there! Reel in those lanyards!" a voice bellowed from out of the darkness.

Rebecca glanced around to see who it was that spoke and found an unfamiliar face barking the order at her from the quarterdeck, his officer's uniform easily distinguishable even beneath the rain slicker that he wore. She stared up at him in confusion, trying to make sense of what he had said and hoping he hadn't been speaking to her.

"I said reel in those lanyards, boy!" he screamed again, his gaze leveling with hers.

Rebecca remained puzzled by the odd command and peered about in frantic haste in the hopes of discovering what he might be referring to. Much to her chagrin, she watched as the young officer stalked down to where she stood with an ominous grimace on his face as he repeated the order yet again. She eyed him with wary hesitation saying, "Please, sir! I don't understand what it is you're telling me to do…can you just show me?"

The officer seized her roughly by the arm, forcing her down toward the pile of jumbled ropes scattered about the deck. "Pick them up!" he ordered.

Just then a massive wave rocked the Redemption with unexpected force, flinging Rebecca from the angry clutches of the lieutenant and slamming her against the wall of the vessel. She was blinded for several moments by the salty spray which stung her eyes and she wiped at them in desperation, trying to clear her vision before the officer approached a second time. She attempted to stand on shaky legs in an effort to regain her balance on the reeling ship and glanced up to see Lieutenant Burgess, who had seemingly appeared out of thin air, shouting something in the officer's ear, while the angry officer reeled back on his heel to tower over her once again.

"I don't care *who* you are," he bellowed, "If you're going to be on this deck you'll learn the commands like everybody else, do you understand?"

"Yes!" Rebecca shouted above the din, praying they could hear her. She watched as the man took an abrupt turn and stormed away, leaving Rebecca standing face to face with the irate Lieutenant Burgess.

"Well, I see you've had the pleasure of meeting Lieutenant Edwards," he grumbled, glowering at her from beneath the brim of his rain drenched hat. "And now," he seethed with an air of irritation, "seeing as how I have already rescued you once this night, I would suggest that you return to your quarters, because if you should get swept overboard in this infernal wind, I do not intend to rescue you a second time."

Rebecca, needing no further prompting, turned and staggered off on unsteady legs towards her room, her eyes still stinging from the spray of the salt laden sea water. Once inside she collapsed on her bed, both from exhaustion as well as from relief at having survived her run in with the disgruntled officers. She struggled out of her wet clothing without bothering to stand up and soon slipped into a restless slumber, oblivious to the storm that raged outside.

The gales continued throughout the night and well into the next day, leaving the air cold and damp and the men somewhat ill tempered. Rebecca was hesitant to leave the safety of her quarters, but felt guilty at leaving Eddy to face the irritable crew alone yet again. She poked her head from behind the door into the passageway before stepping out, hoping to pass unnoticed to the galley. Seeing no sign of Mr. Burgess or Mr. Edwards, she hurried from the narrow hallway towards the deck, but no sooner had she left the safety of the corridor did she find herself in the path of Lieutenant Burgess, who was striding towards her. She stepped back in surprise, stumbling on the trousers she wore, and glanced up in embarrassment at the approaching officer who studied her with indifference, but made no move to help her secure her footing.

"Captain Jameson requests that you report immediately to his quarters," he said, his face void of all expression.

Rebecca stared at him for a moment to study his face. She considered him to be a handsome man, with kind eyes well lined in the areas that bespoke of one who laughed often. His shoulder length, dark hair was secured in a tight band behind his head, and Rebecca found herself wishing she could find favor with this man, for she was uncomfortable with his contention. However, at a loss for words, she simply nodded her head and turned on her heel to proceed to the captain's quarters. Rebecca was unsure of what Captain Jameson might want to see her about, but she had a sinking feeling that it had to do with the altercation she had had with his officer on the previous night. She stood for a moment to collect herself before knocking on the door, and then listened for the captain's command to enter.

"Come!" he called.

She stepped inside the stateroom just far enough to close the door behind her and began to feel the familiar knot of trepidation forming in her belly, while she waited in attentive silence for the captain's swift rebuke.

Captain Jameson gazed at her curiously, again taken aback by this girl of so few words. He hadn't, until now, met a woman who didn't chatter on incessantly about nothing, which was one of the very reasons he chose to avoid them. "Yes, well please, do come in," he said, motioning her to a chair near a small table in the center of the room.

She did as he asked, while wondering why he would invite her to sit. His reprimands in the past had always come swift and sure.

"I trust you are haven't suffered any further assaults by the crew?" he asked, his voice tinged with a hint of sarcasm.

"No, Captain," she replied, instinctively running a hand through her hair to make certain none were out of place.

"Good, good," he continued. "As you know, we will be taking on a guest for a short time."

Rebecca nodded, wondering where this conversation might be headed.

"I regret to say he does not travel alone. He is bringing his wife and her sister aboard with him. As there are no other women onboard the Redemption, I would like you to dine with us in order to provide them with some female companionship."

Rebecca remained pensive for a moment, waiting for the words of the captain's request to register. Expecting a firm rebuke, she had set her mind on explaining why she was on deck at such a late hour, and now she was left to sort through the myriad of confusing thoughts coursing through her mind. She was bewildered as to why the captain deemed her worthy to dine with his guests, especially one of such an honorable rank, and she did not know how to express her reluctance to him.

He in turn, regarded her with an inquisitive expression, wondering why she hadn't been more enthusiastic in accepting the invitation, for surely he thought the girl would appreciate the opportunity to dine with more refined company after having spent so much of her time cooped up with the ill-mannered crew of the Redemption.

Rebecca lowered her head to stare at her hands folded in her lap, feeling suddenly shamed by his request. "Captain," she began in a quiet tone, "I hardly think I'm worthy to dine with your guests, sir. I am of no more importance than a simple deck hand and I fear I would disgrace you with my manner of dress, as I have nothing but the clothes on my back to wear."

Captain Jameson was stunned by her rueful manner, for it was the first time she did not speak to him directly, averting her gaze toward the floor instead. He felt a sudden twinge of regret for having brought this notion of humiliation upon her. "I'm not asking you to attend a fashion show, just a simple dinner," he remarked in a candid voice, hoping to bring a hint of a smile to her face.

Rebecca glanced up briefly, her demeanor doubtful.

"We can get Mr. Andrews to find some other clothing if that's what concerns you, but I see no reason to trouble yourself over what to wear."

"Alright, sir," she agreed meekly. "I will do as you wish."

He couldn't help but notice how the intonation of her words made it sound as though she were a lamb being led to the slaughter and he struggled not to let the grin that hovered near rise to the surface. "Good. It's settled then. They'll be arriving onboard the Redemption on the morrow, and I will inform you as to the hour of dinner when it has been decided upon."

She nodded her understanding and stood to leave.

"I haven't dismissed you yet, Miss Halloway," he rebuked in a low tone.

Rebecca lowered herself back into her chair and offered a contrite apology, unaccustomed to the deferential protocol of those in the service of the queen, while Captain Jameson studied her contrite form for some time, his silence causing her a great deal of discomfort. After several unnerving moments he began to speak.

"Dr. Ammons tells me you enjoy reading literature," he remarked, a hint of intrigue in his voice.

"Yes, I do, very much so, sir."

"I have several books in my cabinet if you'd like to see them."

A brief hint of confusion skimmed over her features and she wondered why the captain thought she might be interested in looking at his library, but not wanting to appear rude she accepted his offer and stood to follow him to the cabinet. Glancing over the shelves of books, of which none were titles she recognized, she realized again how much she missed being able to lose herself in a good story. Books had always offered her a welcome solace from the unexpected trials of life, and she felt now was a time when she especially needed some solace, because the trials had been many these past several months. Weary beyond description, she cast a dutiful glance across the shelves, hoping to soon be excused to return to her quarters.

"Go ahead...choose one that you would enjoy," the captain encouraged.

Rebecca stared at him with an incredulous expression, overwhelmed by his generous offer and wondering what favor had suddenly been bestowed on her to make the captain offer up one of his treasured works of literature. Never, she soon realized, had she seen such a vast selection of books in such a small space, and it became apparent to her that he must enjoy reading nearly as much as she did.

"Well," he continued, "Which one will it be?"

"I'm not sure...I don't recognize any of the titles," she murmured.

"If there are none to your liking, Miss Halloway, then don't feel as though you must take one."

He seemed to take offense at her reluctance to choose a book, yet she remained contemplative about the nature of his unusual offer, for although he had never intentionally treated her harshly, she had been aware of his disdain towards her since her presence had been discovered onboard his frigate. "Which book are you most fond of, sir?" she asked at last.

He was taken aback by her query, as no one had ever expressed an interest in his reading preferences before now. Glancing at the myriad of options he had presented her with, his eyes soon settled on *A Wayfarer's Tale*. "This one has always been my favorite," he remarked, pulling the worn copy from the shelf and handing it to Rebecca.

She took the book from his hand and gazed at it with an expression of genuine interest, its tattered cover a testament of the truth to be found in the captain's statement. "I'd like to start with this one then, if that's alright with you?"

He studied her for several moments, until she began to shift on her feet in apparent discomfort. "Why?" he asked, a glimmer of curiosity radiating from his eyes. "Why would you choose to read that one, rather than any of the others?"

She gazed at him for a quiet moment before answering truthfully, "Because it might help me get to know you, sir."

Captain Jameson felt an odd sensation stirring within him upon hearing her words, and he suddenly found himself rendered speechless. Rebecca held the book in a cautious embrace, her expression of honest trepidation speaking more clearly than any words could have. The two contemplated one another with great curiosity for a time.

"May I be excused now, sir?" she finally asked.

"Yes, of course," he replied, ushering her toward the door. "If you find that book is not to your liking, then you're welcome to choose another."

She smiled, knowing that regardless of what she thought of the book it was one that she would read to the end, if only to gain insight into the man who held her very life in his hands. "I don't know how to thank you, Captain," she said, still puzzled by his kind offer.

"Oh, come now…it's only a book," he said, waving his hand in nonchalance. He was happy to have afforded her this one luxury to bide her time until she could disembark, certain she must be growing weary by now of the Redemption and her crew.

Rebecca nodded, giving the captain one, last timid smile before hurrying to her berth. Once behind closed doors she stared at the book in her hands for several moments, wanting to understand every aspect of the story it told. She remained perplexed by the captain's request that she join his dinner party and tried to think of something that could be fashioned with the makeshift tunics she wore, in order to make herself more presentable to the admiral and his family. Instead of troubling herself further with thoughts of dinner parties though, she opened the book the captain had given her and began to read, her thoughts of admirals and officers slipping without a care from her mind.

Chapter 6

THE TIME LEADING up to the admiral's arrival passed without notice while Rebecca worked with fervor for several hours the next day, piecing together a fashionable skirt and chemise from the discarded clothing and random bits of material she had collected from Mr. Andrews. The outfit was beginning to take shape and she thought it not bad for a novice seamstress such as herself. At least it was better than the graying tunic and trousers that she usually wore, she mused.

Admiral Perry's arrival came in the early afternoon and Rebecca stood on deck enjoying the formality of his welcome while he, his wife and his sister-in-law were bustled on board. She was beginning to grow apprehensive at the thought of dining with the captain, as well as with those he hoped to impress, and she marveled at the absurdity of it all. She had lived in several different countries, shared her faith with countless foreigners, and spoke without ceasing to the almighty God himself, yet she was terrified at the thought of this paltry dinner party. While the thought of being in the presence of the admiral and his family did not trouble her, she realized that her utmost concern in the whole affair was pleasing Captain Jameson, for she was desperate to find favor with the man who had taken her in and provided her with safe refuge during her confinement aboard his vessel.

Rebecca returned to her berth after attending to her duties in the galley to finish stitching together her evening attire. She proceeded to try them on for fit, still having plenty of time to make adjustments if necessary, and she was delighted when the skirt and chemise slipped over her lithe form without any difficulty. How she wished she had a mirror to make certain the outfit looked as wonderfully as it felt. It seemed so unusual she realized, to be wearing a skirt once again, as she hadn't worn one since the night she had been abducted from Portsmouth. She twirled about, enjoying the feel of the flaring drapes of fabric about her legs, until with a happy sigh of satisfaction she donned her old, familiar clothes and set out for the deck in the hopes of finding a bucket to fill with fresh water. She had planned an unhurried bath before the dinner party was scheduled to begin, for she desperately wanted to present herself as a civilized young lady rather than a tattered stowaway. Walking out into the bright, afternoon sunlight, she came upon Mr. Andrews reclined against the rail near the back of the frigate, observing the crew while they worked in the hot sun.

"Hello, Mr. Andrews," she said as she approached.

"Hello, Missy," he replied, giving her a genuine smile of welcome.

"I am in dire need of a thorough bath just now...do you know where I might find a bucket?" she asked, not seeing any where they usually hung.

"Aye, they're scattered about here and there, and it's not likely you'll be getting your hands on one...not until the admiral takes his leave, that is!" he chortled.

She followed the direction he pointed and saw several of the crew scrubbing and polishing the wooden planks of the deck until it glistened with a fine sheen. Upon seeing her look of disappointment, he teased, "Why don't you just jump overboard? Ocean's as good a place as any for a bath."

"Oh, could I?" she breathed.

He glanced over at her in surprise, thinking she was speaking in jest. He had never seen a woman take willingly to the water before this time, and he paused to consider if she even knew how to swim.

"Please, Mr. Andrews?" she asked again, her eyes hopeful.

"Now wait a minute," he began. "Can you manage in the ocean on your own?"

"Yes, I've been managing very nicely since I was a child," she laughed.

"Alright then," he said, glancing around at the others on deck, "but make it quick, I wouldn't want the captain catching wind of this."

Rebecca slipped over the railing, descending the rope ladder with ease. She figured it was just as good a time as any to scrub out her tunic and trousers while she was at it and enjoy a relaxing swim in the meantime. Having spent much of her early childhood on the coast of Africa, her father had seen to it that she would be safe in the water, and taught her how to swim with a natural agility. Rebecca was grateful for his prudence, and considered herself to be an adept swimmer, comfortable in most any body of water.

Mr. Andrews, not really expecting she would take him up on his offer of bathing in the ocean, was careful to keep a watchful eye on her as she lowered herself into the waves, making sure she didn't succumb to her death below the murky depths, but when he caught sight of how much she seemed to enjoy frolicking in the water, he allowed her to swim for as long as she wished, happy to oblige her this one small request, while keeping his eyes trained on her in case she grew overwhelmed by fatigue.

After a time, the chill of the ocean began to grow uncomfortable, and Rebecca took hold of the rope ladder to climb back up towards the deck. She felt more refreshed than she had in months as she threw herself over the side of the frigate, and she was quick to bestow a grateful smile on the petty officer when he reached out to offer her a hand. She allowed him to pull her to her feet, and gave him a contented sigh when he wrapped a thick, cotton blanket around her shivering form. Rebecca grinned her appreciation from beneath the folds of the heavy blanket and watched while he pulled the ladder up behind her, again offering her most gracious thanks for his kindness before dashing off to her berth to prepare herself for the captain's dinner party.

Using the blanket as a towel, she dried off as best she could, taking special care to extract as much moisture from her head as she was able to lest the unruly curls take over. Unsure of how to style her hair without the benefit of a looking glass, she sighed in exasperation at the loose tendrils that curled around her face, but rather than try to tame them into something more presentable, she relented, and bound them into a loose coil that rested at the base of her neck. She had never had the patience for long hair before, even though it was the style in Portsmouth, but preferred instead the short carefree curls that didn't require so much of her time. After the past several months at sea however, her tresses had grown well beyond their customary length, leaving her wondering how best to manage them. One final glance at her reflection in the window convinced her that her curls were about as tamed as they would ever be, and without further thought she stepped into the chemise and skirt she had fashioned, wishing again for a looking glass to study her appearance one last time. She hadn't had one of her own since she had been at sea, nor she did lament over not having one, for she had never been a girl won over by vanity, so rather than fretting over her appearance any longer, she made her way down the narrow corridor to the captain's stateroom, excited at the prospect of conversing with women for a change.

Rebecca stood for a moment before the door, hesitant to knock. She had been anticipating the dinner party up until this moment but now felt an unexpected rush of panic come over her. She took a deep breath to calm her nerves before tapping with a light hand on the door. Within seconds it was flung open and she found herself face to face with the all too familiar Lieutenant Edwards. Rebecca was aware of his confusion as he stared at her, no doubt speculating she realized, why she was calling on the captain in such a manner. For a moment she wondered if he would mention the incident that had occurred on the deck the night before, but he remained silent and aloof. If he recognized her from their haphazard interlude during the storm, he did not make it apparent to her. Instead, without speaking a word he stepped back, opening the door wide to let her pass. The eyes of all those in the room turned to see who had entered and Rebecca suddenly felt ridiculous in the patchwork outfit she wore. She watched through a discomfited gaze as the captain approached her, a hint of amusement splayed across his features.

"You decided to do a fashion show after all, eh?" he remarked, touched by her efforts to impress his guests.

Rebecca gazed down at the hand stitched garments before casting a sheepish grin at Captain Jameson. "I suppose this looks rather silly right now, doesn't it?" she whispered.

"No, I don't think it looks silly at all," he replied with a complimentary smile. "In fact, you did a fine job of sewing those old rags together. Now come, and let me introduce you to Admiral Perry and his guests."

He took her by the elbow and led her toward an older looking gentleman and two women whom, Rebecca was quick to note, were adorned with impeccable perfection. Before she had entered the state room, the women had been involved in an intimate conversation with Lieutenant Burgess, but now, as she approached them at the captain's side, she saw that they all watched her with a mixture of intrigue and disbelief.

"Admiral Perry, ladies," Captain Jameson began, "I'd like to introduce you to Rebecca Halloway, a young lady sailing with us to Portsmouth."

Rebecca offered her hand in a respectful greeting and said "It's a pleasure to meet you all."

Admiral Perry grasped her hand with exuberance and kissed it saying, "The pleasure is mine, milady!"

Rebecca gave him a curious glance, having never been in the presence of maritime royalty before, while the eyes of the women settled on her garments. Rebecca, ever quick to note their look of condescension, turned to them and murmured, "And it's a pleasure to meet you both as well, Mrs. Perry and ...?"

"Gladys," the woman remarked with a long glance down her nose. "Gladys Merriweather. But you may call me Mrs. Merriweather."

Rebecca smiled and nodded, thinking it most likely wouldn't be necessary to call the woman anything at all, as her disapproval was clearly evident to her. Both ladies in turn, continued to regard her with obvious disdain, neither one bothering to take the hand she offered them in greeting. Rebecca blushed as she withdrew her arm, feeling suddenly self-conscious in the outfit she had fashioned. It was incomparable to the finery the two women were dressed in and they made it clear to Rebecca that she did indeed look ridiculous.

Admiral Perry reached out to take hold of her elbow and led her off to a small table which held a variety of fine wines, as well as the customary rum to mark the special occasion. Pouring her a glass of a burgundy colored merlot, he handed it to her. "This came straight from Italy, milady, where it was prepared in the cellars of Rome. I trust you will find it as unique as I find you to be."

Rebecca took the goblet he offered to be polite and allowed herself to be escorted to the dining table, where Admiral Perry pulled out a chair for her to sit on. She lowered herself to the table with a grateful smile, taking care not to spill the wine on the fine linen tablecloth. No sooner had he taken a seat next to her than he began to launch into a colorful monologue about his myriad of travels and adventures at sea, while Rebecca listened with rapt attention. He was a short man, and balding in all of the wrong places. His lips were moist as he spoke and random drops of spittle flew when he became especially excited over one tidbit of information or another. Rebecca enjoyed watching him and hoped it wasn't too apparent that she was more interested in his strange, paunchy mannerisms than in the exaggerated stories of his many adventures at sea.

From the corner of the stateroom, Lieutenant Burgess scrutinized Rebecca with a contemplative look. She appeared to be at ease in the company of the admiral and seemed to be listening intently to what the arrogant man had to say. From his conversation thus far with the admiral's wife and her sister, the two had just as much meaningless dialogue going as Admiral Perry did, only he had lost interest in the women's trivial gossip long ago. He watched as Captain Jameson made his way to the table to join the girl and his guest. Why she stirred up such contention in him he did not understand. He had spoken less than three times to her, yet he always ended up irate and frustrated afterwards. Perhaps it was her initial deceit at having passed herself off as one of the crew that perturbed him the most, but whatever it was, he intended to stay as far away from her as possible tonight, preferring instead to consort with Lieutenant Edwards and the other officers present. If only he could break free from these blasted women, he thought. They had already drunk much more wine than they could tolerate judging by the slur of their words as they rambled on, as well as by the indecency of what they were saying. Until the girl had arrived, their mindless gossip had revolved around dinner parties and men. Now, however, their conversation turned with malicious intent toward the girl, while they spoke in loud tones of the clothing she wore, her unattended hair and her easy manner, even going so far as accusing her of soliciting favors from Admiral Perry.

Lieutenant Burgess excused himself from their circle, having already heard more than he cared to, and moved to join Lieutenant Edwards who was near the entrance of the stateroom observing the dinner party in silent contemplation. The men watched Dr. Ammons enter the room, and after greeting the two officers who had taken refuge near the doorway, he made his way toward the table to sit on the other side of Rebecca, who by this time was looking a bit overwhelmed by the attention of the admiral. There were several other young officers mingling about, and they all moved to sit at the long table when Captain Jameson announced the commencement of dinner.

The captain's steward began to serve the first course and Rebecca, without thought to protocol, stood to offer her assistance, for she was surprised to find that he was serving such a large group by himself. The steward's mouth gaped open in disbelief, having never been offered help before when serving a formal dinner party.

Captain Jameson was irritated by her breach in etiquette and cleared his throat to say, "Dinner guests are not allowed to serve, Miss Halloway. You will remain seated if you please."

The admiral's wife snickered and remarked under her breath, "Most likely what she's used to when she's in her customary surroundings."

The comment brought a peal of laughter from her sister, and Captain Jameson gave a small grin that was prompted more from humiliation than from complacency. Rebecca noticed that he seemed a bit offended by her actions, even though he attempted to make light of the incident, and she prayed she hadn't embarrassed him. She was growing quite weary of the lewd advances of the admiral by now, and in offering to help serve the guests she had only hoped for a chance to escape his incessant talking for a time. This would have been the perfect opportunity she mused, however having been rebuked by Captain Jameson, she remained in her seat with a penitent look settling on her face.

Dr. Ammons broke the awkward silence by saying to her, "Well, I see you stitch up garments as well as you stitch up men, Rebecca!"

Those present glanced at him with curious faces but Rebecca gave him a grateful smile and said, "Thank you, Dr. Ammons. I do hope that's a compliment, sir."

Turning to the confused guests he explained, "This young lady is the daughter of a medical doctor and I'll be darned if she doesn't stitch men up as well as the rest of us!"

The two women gazed down their noses in haughty contempt, unimpressed by the doctor's comment. Admiral Perry's wife could be heard remarking under her breath to her sister, "I'd expect the daughter of a doctor to be dressed a bit more respectably."

The two women again attempted to draw Lieutenant Burgess into a conversation and Rebecca was relieved to have their attention drawn away from her for a time, having already been humiliated on more than one occasion this evening by their snide remarks.

Once everyone had been served the first course the group began to eat. The food was very rich for Rebecca, whose meals up until now had consisted mostly of stringy mutton and boiled potatoes. She took small bites trying to savor every morsel, knowing her stomach would not tolerate much of this extravagant fare. Suddenly, and without warning, she felt the clammy hand of Admiral Perry slithering up her thigh. He had become more and more unrelenting in his advances toward her and her subtle rebuttals didn't seem to be discouraging him. She was at a loss as to how to handle the situation, having never found herself in one quite like it before. The men continued to talk around her, oblivious to her discomfort, while Rebecca remained silent unless she was spoken to, directing her energies instead at deflecting the wandering gropes of the admiral.

It was during the serving of the third course that Rebecca had finally had enough of Admiral Perry's audacious behavior, and she stood with an abrupt sigh and stepped away from the table. All eyes focused on her perplexed features, which were by now flushed with the bright hue of embarrassment. Directing her gaze only at Captain Jameson, she stated with remorse, "If you'll excuse me, sir, I'm afraid I must take my leave from this lovely dinner party now."

Without waiting for a reply she hurried from the room. The confused glances of the guests followed her to the door and remained there for a few moments after she had gone, almost as if expecting her to reappear again. Captain Jameson's eyes met those of Lieutenant Burgess and their silent exchange went unnoticed by the others present, who soon resumed eating when they realized the girl would not be returning. Lieutenant Burgess excused himself to follow after her, while Captain Jameson watched him disappear through the doorway, his expression grim.

Rebecca hurried towards the galley grumbling under her breath in agitation and knowing she would find a sympathetic ear with Eddy. She brushed at her skin while she walked in an attempt to dispel the lingering sensation of the admiral's shameless gropes, but before she was even twenty feet from the captain's stateroom she was brought about by the rough grasp of Lieutenant Burgess.

"You do not walk out on a dinner party with the captain, much less an admiral," he hissed with admonition, towering over her in his anger.

Rebecca was stunned by the sudden appearance of the officer, as well as by her close proximity to the man, and she took a precautionary step backward to allow for more distance between the two of them. "I don't expect you to understand, sir, but I couldn't stay," she replied in a halting voice.

"You will return to the captain's stateroom at once, offer your apologies for the disruption, and continue with your meal," he ordered.

"I'm sorry, but I cannot do that," she mumbled in a meek whisper.

"Do not make me humiliate you further by dragging you back in there like a child!"

"I won't resist you, Mr. Burgess, but if you force me to return I assure you, I will leave again," she said, unrelenting in her effort to steer clear of the admiral's presence.

"Then I will see you flogged for your insolence!" he shouted in her face.

"You may do to me what you wish, sir," she pronounced, becoming infuriated by his harassment, "but I will not subject myself to the lewd advances of the admiral any longer."

"Advances towards you?" he scoffed. "You flatter yourself!"

The cruel comment stung Rebecca and she struggled to maintain her composure, choosing to remain cautious but quiet at that point rather than say something that she would only have to repent of later. Watching Lieutenant Burgess through guarded eyes, she lingered in a passive silence and waited for him to speak.

He continued to glare down at her, his hands clenched in anger, until he finally turned away in frustration at her obstinate manner and stormed off muttering, "You'll regret this when the captain hears that you've refused to return."

Rebecca stared after him until he was out of sight, worried that he might return to dispense the flogging he had threatened. She longed for a quiet place of solitude to rid herself of the resentment rising within her and so she hurried to the rear of the ship where she would be alone. Sliding down onto the wooden planks of the deck she began to pray with a passionate voice, while her anger began to ebb like a receding tide as she cried out to God in her despair. Pouring her heart out to Him had always lifted her spirits in the past but now she found herself feeling confused and betrayed at not having been delivered from the Redemption, and from all of the trials that had come upon her here. She shut her eyes tight against the darkness that lingered in her soul and willed herself to speak reverently before the Lord, in spite of what her heart was feeling at that particular moment. "*Lord,*" she began, a single tear sliding down her cheek, "*all I've ever wanted to do was serve you...to be in the mission field where I could minister to your sheep, and draw the lost into your fold. I don't understand why You've brought me here, where my presence is so blatantly despised, nor why You've kept me here where I do not want to be, but I beseech you to grant me understanding, and patience as well, so that I might persevere through this difficult time until I am delivered at last into the plans that you have in store for me.*

Rebecca turned a weary gaze upward to fix her eyes upon the stars shimmering in the darkened sky. It never ceased to take her breath away when she considered the celestial bodies placed with such divine precision in the galaxy, and Rebecca felt she was looking into the very depths of heaven when she was lost in her universe. She was struck with an unexpected longing for her father, who had taught her many of the constellations that were to be found in the evening sky, and now, missing his nurturing presence desperately, she tried to locate the ones that were visible to her. When at last her heart grew comforted by thoughts of Colin Halloway, she burrowed into a corner of the frigate and contemplated sleeping on deck for the remainder of the night in the event the admiral should decide to go in search of her quarters.

Rebecca had slipped into a restful slumber for a time when she was awakened by a strange noise nearby. Opening her eyes, she lay frozen in fear, thinking perhaps it was the admiral roaming about searching for her. With her heart pounding in her chest, she peered with a cautious glance from behind the barrel she was propped against, only to see the admiral's wife stumbling around in a drunken stupor. She had come to the deck to relieve herself but was having a difficult time figuring out where to do so. Rebecca covered her mouth to stifle a giggle and continued to watch on in amusement, not wanting to reveal her whereabouts to the woman lest she begin her verbal assault once again. Instead, she slid back against the wall and waited for the ill-mannered woman to be done.

Suddenly Rebecca heard a loud scream followed by a horrific splash. She jumped to her feet and ran to the rail to peer into the darkness of the murky water below, where she could see the woman flailing in the waves, the salt water rushing down her throat and preventing her from crying out for help. Rebecca screamed with frantic desperation to the midshipman on watch, "Help! Man...uh, woman overboard!"

Rebecca dashed behind a large water barrel to shed her skirt lest it drag her under the waves with its weight, and hurried back to the railing to dive into the frigid water in search of the admiral's wife. The midshipman on watch began to sound the alarm and soon the deck was brimming with men, curious to see what the cause for the commotion might be. It wasn't long before Rebecca heard the admiral's wife sputtering and flailing about through the spray of salty water crashing over her, and she approached her with a watchful eye, shouting out in an attempt to get the woman's attention.

"I'm over here, Mrs. Perry! I've come to help you, but you must calm down!"

The air was cut off from her lungs when the woman turned towards her in panicked desperation and wrapped her arms in a viselike grip around Rebecca's neck. "Help me!" she screamed.

Rebecca felt the air being cut off from her lungs and she cried out, "Let me go...Mrs. Perry, you have to let me go!"

The woman did not heed the request and continued to claw at Rebecca, her only chance for survival.

Plunging beneath the waves, Rebecca pushed herself out from beneath the woman's grasp and swam away, frantic to reach the surface to fill her lungs with air. She drifted back several feet to put a safe distance between herself, and the hysterical woman.

"Please!" Rebecca called again from where she bobbed on the waves. "Calm yourself and I can pull you to the ship!"

Captain Jameson heard the sound of Rebecca's voice before he caught a glimpse of the struggle taking place in the murky depths below, and as he peered through the darkness to where she struggled with the admiral's wife his breath caught in his throat. Seeing her tiny frame being tossed about on the waves, he wanted to call out to her, to tell her to leave the cursed woman to her deserved demise and save herself, but instead he remained silent, angry that she was putting her own safety in jeopardy to save such a despicable soul.

Before Rebecca could approach the panic-stricken woman a second time, Mr. Andrews had located their shadowy forms in the water and tossed them a rope fashioned with a hang man's noose at the end. Rebecca swam to take hold of it and quickly opened the loop wide while struggling to stay afloat in the turbulent darkness. She saw the admiral's wife slip beneath the surface once again and despite her sense of caution Rebecca dove to retrieve her, but the woman took hold of her anew and clung fast to her in frantic desperation, leaving Rebecca gasping for a choked breath through the viselike grip. She made a conscious effort not to panic as the air was squeezed from her lungs yet again, and fought to break through to the surface of the water.

Rebecca realized she must act quickly, so diving deep behind Mrs. Perry, she slipped the loop in a haphazard manner up over the woman's legs and gave it a quick tug, signaling Mr. Andrews to begin pulling the woman toward the frigate. She separated herself once again from the admiral's wife and breathed a weary sigh of relief when she saw Mr. Andrews hoist the rope toward the Redemption, dragging the terrified woman with it. Rebecca remained where she was, her breath coming in harsh, ragged spasms. She peered through the darkness and waited in an attentive calm until the woman was hauled back onto the deck, her husband clucking over her with pity while the captain watched on in silent irritation.

Mr. Andrews was quick to free the woman from the noose and he tossed it back to Rebecca who swam in slow circles around it, wishing the men would return below and allow her some semblance of privacy, but instead she saw that they remained where they were, their eyes fixed on her. She began to maneuver through the waves toward the rear of the ship in the hopes of escaping their curious glances, for she was not about to go aboard with her legs uncovered. She wished she hadn't been so quick to discard her skirt before jumping in and wondered if she would succumb to death by hypothermia before the men would disperse.

"Missy! You'd best get out of that water before you catch your death of a cold!" Mr. Andrews shouted down at her.

"I need my skirt, Mr. Andrews," she tried to call in a hushed voice.

"Your what?"

By now Mr. Burgess, Mr. Edwards, and Captain Jameson were all staring down at her with impatient faces. She cast a gracious smile up at them and stammered through blue-tinged lips, "F-fine night for a s-swim, don't you th-think?"

Rebecca was so chilled she was certain that she would never again regain any feeling in her limbs. She shivered uncontrollably while the captain looked on in dismay, incensed that she was making no attempt to remove herself from the frigid ocean.

"For heaven's sake!" he shouted at her. "Get out of that water this instant! I do not plan on coming in after you!"

The rope floated nearby, yet she did not take hold of it. Instead, she gazed at him with a forlorn expression while the two officers stared down at her in disbelief.

"S-S-Sir, perhaps y-y-you ought to a-attend to the admiral's w-wife," she suggested, having a difficult time speaking through her rattling teeth. "I'm s-sure she's quite sh-shaken up."

Mr. Andrew's wary grimace darted back and forth between the captain and the girl when he spotted her garment lying in a crumpled heap on the deck. He finally understood what it was

Rebecca was grappling with and he cleared his throat in the hopes of drawing the attention of the officers. To his surprise Lieutenant Burgess glanced up for a moment, and Mr. Andrews was quick to motion him away from the railing, but instead of moving Mr. Burgess stood fast, his exasperation evident as he glared at the petty officer.

"Do something, Mr. Andrews!" he shouted.

Mr. Andrews sighed in resignation and said, "She's not about to get out of that water in her current state, sir."

The men looked on in confusion while Rebecca continued to bob up and down on the waves, by this time looking extremely uncomfortable, her face appearing rather blue. Without warning they caught sight of her skirt on the deck, and in their haste to move away from the railing they stumbled over one another in their embarrassment. They proceeded to where the admiral stood, still trying to calm his hysteric wife, while Petty Officer Andrews again tried to coax Rebecca from the churning waves.

Rebecca, ever so grateful to see the men leave, climbed with stiff but deliberate steps up the rope ladder, relishing the warmth of the soft blanket Mr. Andrews wrapped her in once she cleared the railing. She collapsed against him with gratitude and watched the unraveling situation with the admiral's wife, while an amused smile hovered over her face. The woman was still prattling on about her near death experience and the 'wench' who had refused to help her. Rebecca felt a giggle rising in her throat and she thought to herself that the woman received no less than what she deserved for her calloused behavior at the captain's dinner party. Feeling a minute semblance of guilt, it surprised Rebecca to realize that remorse was not so quick in coming this time, and she attributed it to the fact that she was nearly delirious with fatigue, while she hoped that the Lord shared her sense of humor.

Petty Officer Andrews began to lead her toward her berth, but Rebecca resisted.

"Come on, now..." he urged. "You'll catch your death of a cold if you stay out here much longer."

"I'd just like some time alone, Mr. Andrews," she began. "Just a few minutes...I promise."

He gave her a scowl of admonition before allowing her to linger in the cool evening air. "Don't tarry long, Missy," he warned.

She watched him walk away, grateful for his friendship, and was still peering after his retreating form when he turned back to say, "I'm glad you're alright, Missy. That was a brave thing you did."

She smiled, feeling unexpectedly warmed on the inside by the petty officer's words. She nestled her face down into the inviting folds of the blanket and gave a soft sigh of content, in spite of the chilly air of evening.

Captain Jameson had moved to the quarterdeck, wanting to distance himself from the precarious woman and her husband, preferring instead to observe the situation from afar. He was aware of Rebecca's presence on deck and he wished the petty officer would take her inside where it was warmer. When the commotion began to die down some, he watched the crew return to their boisterous revelry below while the admiral accompanied his wife to their berth. He saw Lieutenants Burgess and Edwards retreating to the comfort of his stateroom, no doubt believing that he had already gone there, but still, he realized, the girl lingered on deck, the blanket wrapped tightly around her. He waited and watched, hoping she would soon make a move to leave, and he found himself growing concerned by her listless manner as she rested her head in the thick folds of the cotton cover she held close about her.

Rebecca was exhausted beneath the warmth of the blanket and wondered if she would be able to muster the energy to carry herself down to her berth. She found herself still shaken from the desperate rescue attempt but relieved that the admiral's wife was safe, even though the woman had been relentlessly cruel and harsh towards her. With a determined groan she set out to force her still chilled limbs down the steps to her quarters, in spite of the fatigue that lingered. There would be no sleeping on deck tonight she reasoned, for she was still soaking wet and shivering. Walking near the quarterdeck, she was startled to hear the captain's voice speaking to her. She had been unaware of his presence until now and was under the impression that he had returned to his stateroom long ago.

"Do you feel compelled to save the *whole* world?" he asked, his voice laced with sarcasm.

It took her a moment to locate him peering down at her from where he stood on the quarterdeck, but when she found him she answered without hesitation, "Yes, sir, I do."

For all of her young life she had envisioned taking the message of salvation to the lost, just as her father had done for so many years. Saving the world she knew, had been her intention all along.

"That woman treated you despicably all evening and still you risked your very life to save her. Why did you do that?" he demanded, still irritated by her reckless determination.

"She fell overboard, Captain," Rebecca replied. "She would have drowned without my assistance. Anybody would have done the same, sir."

"No, anybody would not have done the same!" he shot back, sounding much harsher than he had intended to, but knowing most would have preferred to see the ill-mannered woman lost at sea.

Rebecca gazed up at him with a feigned expression of innocence and murmured, "Do you mean I saved her for naught, sir?"

Captain Jameson regarded her with a look of surprise, taken aback by her quick rebuttal. The befuddled expression on his face brought a peal of laughter from Rebecca, and he was immediately captivated by the delightful resonance of her voice, certain that he had never before heard anything so lovely. He could feel the radiant warmth emanating from her countenance in spite of her blue lips, and he found he could not take his eyes from the sight of her.

Shaking her head in delight, she turned and walked toward the narrow corridor that would return her to her berth. She lifted her hand in a slight wave and called out over her shoulder without looking back, "Goodnight, Captain Jameson."

He stared after her retreating form long after she had disappeared into the corridor, struck anew by her charming innocence, and he found himself wondering again as to the nature of this one thrust so unexpectedly into his world. A heavy sigh of realization escaped him as he began to comprehend the weight of his responsibility in keeping her safe until her return to Portsmouth, but not wanting to linger any longer on deck, he began to make his way toward the admiral's cabin, with the intention of seeing his guests secured for the night before turning in himself.

Chapter 7

Rebecca slept later than usual the next morning and the captain was growing a bit concerned at not having seen her moving about. He resisted the urge to send Lieutenant Burgess to check on her, not wanting to wake her if she was still resting. He expected she would be exhausted after her daring plunge in the ocean the evening before and he feared she would become ill after spending so much time in the chilly water. He determined to wait just a half hour more before going to her quarters to check on her himself.

The admiral and his wife, along with her sister, had been lounging about in their guest quarters waiting to take breakfast with Captain Jameson. Hearing a soft knock at the door announcing his arrival, the admiral called out for him to enter.

"Good morning, Captain!" he exclaimed. "I trust your young lady passenger is faring well after the excitement of last evening?"

"As well as can be expected I hope… I have not yet seen her today," he answered.

While they exchanged pleasantries, the captain's steward entered carrying a large tray filled with pastries and hot coffee. Admiral Perry and the women gathered at the table and began to eat with hearty gusto. Captain Jameson found himself perturbed by their manner and anxious to see them depart, for he had long ago grown weary of the incessant babbling of the women. He didn't know if he could stomach even one more night with them onboard his ship.

"Will she be joining us this morning?" Admiral Perry asked through a mouthful of cherry filled pastry.

"No, no…I believe she is otherwise disposed of for the day," the captain answered, well aware of the relentless torment the women had subjected the girl to at the dinner party. He wanted to spare her even one more moment of heartache at the hands of the vicious wenches, and he had a nagging suspicion that that had been the reason for her hasty departure from the table.

"Pity," the admiral remarked. "I do hope I'll get another opportunity to visit with her before we take our leave. I simply must thank her for her heroic efforts at saving my wife."

"I'll try to arrange for that, Admiral," Captain Jameson assured with a polite nod, having no intention of doing so.

A knock at the door interrupted their conversation and Captain Jameson stood to answer it. Seeing Lieutenant Edwards standing before him, he stepped out into the corridor to speak with his officer, away from the ever attentive ears of his guests.

"Sir, I apologize for the interruption, but your presence is requested on deck."

"Thank you, Mr. Edwards," he replied, grateful for the opportunity to escape the company of the admiral and his family. "Tell me," he added, "have you seen the young lady about this morning?"

"No sir, I haven't."

"Check her quarters to make sure she is up and about this morning," he said, "and report back to me what you find."

"Of course, sir, I'll go there directly."

Captain Jameson made his way up to the deck, while Lieutenant Edwards proceeded toward the berth the girl had been assigned to. Knocking twice on her door, he waited for her call to enter, but after several uncomfortable moments of silence, he paused to contemplate his next move. With a cautious hand he pushed the door open, not expecting to find her inside, and he breathed an appreciative sigh of relief when he found the cabin was indeed empty. He caught sight of the outlandish outfit she had worn the evening before, folded with care and lying at the foot of the bed, and with a disgruntled shake of his head he glanced throughout the room one final time before he turned to go in search of her elsewhere, irate at having been the one called upon to deal with the matter of finding her.

Down in the galley Rebecca hovered over the steaming pot of gruel she was stirring. She had drug herself out of bed, still feeling exhausted after the emotional and physical turmoil of the previous evening, and now she stood with a large yawn interrupting her face while Eddy droned on and on about her courageous activities, and she grew even more tired just listening to him.

"Eddy, it wasn't that spectacular...anyone one of you could have pulled her to safety."

"Anyone of us could have maybe but it was you that did it! That's what makes it so spectacular! You, just a girl, and with all the men scoffing at you because you're a *woman*...and then you go and save the wife of an admiral!" he laughed, slapping his knee.

"Who scoffs at me?" she asked with an indignant look.

"Oh, don't pay them any mind," he answered, tossing his hand in the air as if it didn't matter. "They won't be scoffing at you now!"

With a loud chortle he returned to the task at hand expecting she would put the matter behind her, but Rebecca continued to stir the gruel, pondering his words with a forlorn face. She would have been willing to risk her very life to save any one of the men onboard the Redemption, and it troubled her to know that there were still some who resented her presence on the ship, but instead of sharing her woes with Eddy she remained silent, determining in her heart to stop feeling rejected over such a petty grievance.

Lieutenant Edwards was growing frustrated at having been unable to find Rebecca, and passing Lieutenant Burgess on deck, he asked, "Have you seen the girl about this morning?"

"No," he commented through a cynical scowl, "and I try my best not to."

"As do I," Mr. Edwards mused, "but the captain wishes to know her whereabouts, and I'll be darned if I can find her."

"Have you checked the galley?"

"Not yet, but I'll go there directly if you think that's where she might be," Mr. Edwards answered.

"I am most certain you will find her there as it is the one place she is tolerated aboard this vessel," Mr. Burgess scoffed with disdain.

He stood watching Lieutenant Edwards continue on toward the galley, grateful that it was not he who had to consort with the girl for a change.

Rebecca still had not spoken to Eddy, who seemed completely unaware of the emotional upheaval he had tossed her into, and so instead of trying to make idle conversation she began to utter a silent prayer spurned on by her resentment and frustration. *"Lord, you know I don't expect to receive accolades for my service aboard this ship, but I hadn't expected such hostility either. How long will you have me be delayed here, away from the multitude of the lost, where I thought you wanted me?"*

Rebecca was startled out of her piteous musing by the unexpected appearance of Lieutenant Edwards who had suddenly materialized in the doorway. She had never before seen an officer approach the galley prior to this day and she wondered what business might have brought him here. Rebecca held her breath in nervous apprehension, hoping that it had nothing to do with her. She caught his eye as he glanced at her, and then without uttering a word he turned on his heel and left just as quickly as he had come. Rebecca breathed a heavy sigh of relief as she peered over at Eddy, not expecting to see the shadow of condescension that darkened his face.

"What is it? What's the matter?" she asked.

"Why do you fear them so?" he admonished with a hint of annoyed accusation.

"Because I enjoy living," she said.

"You know they can't lay so much as a finger on you without seeing the captain's wrath," he chided.

"It doesn't matter, Eddy. They still invoke the fear of death into me," she sighed, turning to face him, her tanned skin flushed from toiling over the steaming pot. Rebecca was caught off guard by the angry scowl that continued to linger on Eddy's face, and she suddenly felt uncomfortable beneath his scrutinizing gaze. A tense silence hung in the air and she spun back to stir the gruel to avoid the apparent contention on his features.

Eddy was aware that he had hurt her feelings but he found himself incensed that the officers were able to intimidate her so easily. A wave of guilt caused him to glance away in shame and he paused to consider how protective of her he had become. "I'm sorry, Bec," he began. "I didn't mean it to sound like that."

He saw her nod her head in acknowledgement of his apology.

"You just stay down here with me," he reassured her. "None of them ever come down here."

She gave him a look that spoke her disbelief, having just come face to face with an officer in the galley.

"Alright, not usually anyway," he added with a sheepish grin.

Rebecca couldn't help but offer up a hearty giggle at seeing the impish expression on the face of her friend in spite of the tumultuous feelings coursing through her, and she resolved to mask her emotions better in the future lest she instigate contention between Eddy, and the officers who could see him punished for defending her against their onslaught.

Lieutenant Edwards made his way to the quarterdeck where he found Captain Jameson.

"Ah! There you are, Mr. Edwards. Did you find her?" Captain Jameson asked.

"Yes, sir," the officer replied. "The girl is below in the galley, working alongside the cook."

"Very well," the captain said, dismissing his officer. He was relieved to hear that she was up and about and had an overwhelming desire to go and see for himself that all was well, but he resisted the urge. He had no intentions of resuming his breakfast with the admiral however and chose instead to linger on deck with his crew, contemplating the peculiar happenings of the evening before.

Rebecca remained with Eddy until they had finished the morning's chores. She still felt somewhat exhausted from the activities of the previous evening and excused herself to return to her quarters with the hopes of resting a bit before the noon meal. Walking down the narrow corridor, she saw Admiral Perry headed straight for her, making his way up to the deck she assumed. She stopped in her tracks and tried with desperation to think of some place she could hide herself from the man before he caught sight of her. Taking a quick step backwards, she slipped into the room nearest her, turning to ease the door shut behind her. Rebecca stood listening with her ear pressed to the door for the sound of his passing and was nearly startled out of her skin when she heard a voice say with calculated coldness, "May I help you?"

She whirled around in surprise to find several young officers seated around a table staring at her, Lieutenants Edwards and Burgess among them. She gazed back at them through a perplexed expression, her mouth agape in shock at the situation she had found herself in.

"Well," Mr. Edwards demanded in a loud voice, "what excuse have you for interrupting our meeting?"

"I uh... I have no excuse, sir," Rebecca stammered, not wanting to revisit the issue of Admiral Perry and his lascivious behavior in the presence of Mr. Burgess.

"Oh?" he taunted, his voice mocking and cynical. "Then how long have you made a habit of barging into other people's quarters?"

Rebecca sighed in defeat and admitted, "I'm just trying to avoid a difficult situation, sir. I'm terribly sorry for interrupting your circle."

She retreated into the corridor, hoping to resume her course without attracting the attention of Admiral Perry, while Lieutenant Burgess leapt to his feet, curious as to whom the girl sought refuge from. In his abrupt movement, the chair he had been sitting in tipped over backwards where it crashed to the floor. Rebecca was startled by the noise and spun around in surprise, her face draining of color when he strode towards where she lingered in the doorway. Her eyes were darkened with alarm as he maneuvered between her rigid form and the portal to peer out into the hallway.

Seeing Admiral Perry nearing the top of the narrow stairwell, the lieutenant called out, "Excuse me, sir, perhaps I can help you find what it is you're looking for?"

The admiral offered a hearty smile and returned to speak with the young Lieutenant, chortling in delight when his eyes lit upon Rebecca, who was cringing behind the officer's back in an effort to remain unseen. Her apparent discomfort in the admiral's presence was obvious to Mr. Burgess and he felt a brief stab of guilt at having revealed her whereabouts to the man.

"There you are, milady!" the admiral exclaimed with cheerful exuberance. "I was hoping we could spend a little more time together before I must take my leave."

Lieutenant Edwards stood to his feet and announced through a cordial smile, "You're welcome to use this room, sir… we were just leaving."

His eyes met Lieutenant Burgess' in a mocking silence, knowing that the last thing the girl had anticipated was to be left in the room alone with the admiral. He nodded to the other officers who took his cue and stood to leave, while he watched Admiral Perry lead Rebecca by the arm to a chair setting near the corner of the room.

Lieutenant Burgess caught a glimpse of the panicked expression that shadowed the girl's features as she watched them depart, but with an air of indifference he pulled the door shut behind him. Thinking the girl might try something foolish in her precarious frame of mind, he chose to linger nearby for a time rather than join the other officers on deck.

Rebecca heard the latch drop into place with a resounding clang and she fought to subdue the panic rising in her belly. She made a conscious effort to control her breathing lest the admiral hear the ragged breaths that threatened to overwhelm her, for she did not want him to know that he terrified her with his presence.

"I've been waiting for this moment all morning," he murmured, sidling up next to her. "After all, it's only proper that I show my appreciation for your heroic efforts in rescuing my wife."

Rebecca struggled to maintain a sense of composure when he drew near and attempted to stand to her feet, wanting to put some much needed distance between the two of them. His breath felt hot and sticky on her face and thoughts of escape consumed her as he continued to babble on, but his words fell on deaf ears.

"Admiral Perry," she breathed in admonition, "I think your wife might take offense at this demonstration of appreciation, sir."

He took hold of her arms and pulled her with a firm grip back into the seat, a low chuckle rolling from his throat. "Mrs. Perry isn't here, my dear."

An overwhelming sense of alarm came over her and she began to pray in silent desperation for deliverance from the precarious situation she had found herself in.

The admiral continued with his lascivious prattle, but Rebecca remained oblivious to every word that was uttered. Her only concern centered on keeping his hands at bay until she could somehow work her way around his bulky form and excuse herself from the room. "Admiral," she coaxed, "why don't we go up to the deck to visit…it'd be much more comfortable there."

"No, my dear," he teased. "I prefer to have you all to myself."

Rebecca was horrified to feel his sweaty palm sliding up her leg and she jumped from her seat in repulsion. Without warning he took hold of her and tried to pull her onto his lap, while Rebecca fought against his strength. A low groan of dismay rose deep within her but he was quick to clamp a clammy hand over her mouth as he persisted in subduing her. The admiral seemed to take perverse pleasure in her resistance, in spite of the grimace of disgust that darkened her features. Rebecca, weary and gasping for breath, again made an attempt to call out for help only to find that no sound would come forth. In panic stricken horror, she watched as the officer lowered his face to hers in an attempt to cover her mouth with his. "Oh, God," she plead, "help me!"

Without warning a surge of bile welled up in her throat and it exploded with such vehement force that it struck the admiral squarely in the face, blinding him for several terse moments. She felt him recoil in disgust at the foul liquid that dripped from his hair, and he was quick to release his hold on her. Rebecca fell back against the wall, where she watched in stunned disbelief as he attempted to brush away the putrid vomit staining the starched, white linen jacket he wore.

Rebecca, in her giddy release, began to giggle at the Lord's idea of deliverance, and it occurred to her at that very moment that He did indeed share her sense of humor.

The admiral glared at Rebecca through livid eyes, incensed that she would have the audacity to laugh at him. Muttering a forceful curse under his breath, he landed a fierce blow across the side of her head which sent her reeling to the floor.

Rebecca cringed low to the ground in contrite silence where she expected the beating to continue, but instead the door flew open and Lieutenant Burgess rushed in, his eyes registering shock at the upheaval that greeted him. He was quick to remove the enraged officer from the room in an effort to get him away from the girl, while he made a determined attempt to tame the man's wrath.

Rebecca, in her shame, kept her eyes averted from both men as they left and crawled to her knees to offer a heartfelt prayer of thanks to God for his perfectly timed deliverance from the wiles of the admiral. When she had finished, she stood to her feet, in no mood to tarry lest the admiral return to finish what he had started. Her face smarted where the man had struck her however, glancing down at her tunic she realized not a drop of the vomit had been spilled upon her and she began to laugh once more. It was obvious to her that the Lord knew where to direct his wrath, but her laughter soon succumbed to tears of relief as she began to walk on trembling legs toward the corridor, while trying to breathe through the wrenching sobs that escaped her.

Lieutenant Burgess, having disposed of the irate admiral, reappeared in the doorway and eyed Rebecca with guilty apprehension. Rebecca was startled by his presence and hovered in mid stride for a moment before taking a cautions step around him, being vigilant to keep her eyes averted from his face. He stood silent, letting her pass, and then turned to watch her retreat down the hall.

Admiral Perry gagged in disgust as he scrubbed at the putrid bile drying on his skin. He had been determined to have the girl before taking his leave from the Redemption but now it appeared as though his time was running out. He had a back up plan already set in motion however, and if all went according to schedule, she would be returning with him to his ship on the morrow. He smiled through his revulsion at the thought, enjoying the idea of what he would do with the girl once he had her in his possession, away from the watchful eyes of Captain Jameson and his crew.

Rebecca dropped onto the bed, using her cotton blanket to dry the tears which remained on her cheeks. She felt drained of all emotion and soon fell asleep, her dreams returning her to her home and to the loving arms of her mother and father. She awakened just two hours later to a sharp rap on the door, and she was relieved to see that it was an irate Lieutenant Edwards who called on her, and not Lieutenant Burgess for a change.

"You are to report to the captain's quarters at once," he stated, leaving her standing in his turbulent wake without waiting for a response.

Rebecca lingered until she heard the sound of his footsteps retreating down the narrow corridor before making a hasty attempt to straighten her hair and adjust her clothing. She hurried to Captain Jameson's stateroom where she was greeted by an indifferent Lieutenant Burgess, who pulled the door open and waited for her to enter. Rebecca slipped around his ominous form with a cautious step, allowing him a wide berth as he motioned for her to proceed to the center of the room. Glancing about in confusion, she was surprised to see that Mr. Andrews, the captain's steward, and a few of the other midshipmen were also present and glancing about the room in an uneasy silence. She peered through inquisitive eyes at Captain Jameson, who would not meet her gaze, but instead stared in a solemn manner out the window. The admiral and his wife were both in attendance as well, with haughty looks darkening their features. The tension in the air was thick and filled with uncertainty. Rebecca peered across the room to where Mrs. Perry and the admiral lingered, and she saw the woman whisper something under her breath to her husband while flinging a nasty glance her way. Rebecca remained in passive silence, waiting for someone to explain why she had been summoned, while a hard knot of dread began to weave itself through her belly.

The captain cleared his throat and began to address the group in a terse voice from where he stood. "It has been brought to my attention that a valuable article belonging to the admiral has disappeared without explanation. We have brought those of you who have come into contact with our guests together, to inquire as the whereabouts of the article in question."

Rebecca glanced over at Mr. Andrews and wondered when he had come into contact with the admiral, while the captain waited with an expectant pause for someone to confess to the theft. Apprehensive glances roamed about the room as an uncomfortable hush fell over those present, but the admiral's wife continued to glare at Rebecca with loathing hatred spilling from her eyes. The captain finally turned his piercing gaze towards the crew who were standing in a nervous disquiet before him.

"Well," he barked, having a difficult time concealing the anger which laced his voice, "since none of you are willing to volunteer any information, I will have to demand that you empty your pockets."

Rebecca watched the men reach deep into their tunics, and then their trousers, bringing up minimal items of interest. Reaching into her own tunic, she felt something cold and hard fill her hand. Her face bore an expression of interest as she pulled it out to examine it. In her palm lay a beautiful gold-plated pocket watch, carved with intricate detail and design. Realizing what it was that she held, she lifted her perplexed gaze to meet the captain's and was quick to note the grimace of dismay which sprang to his face, while some in the room gasped in alarm.

The admiral's wife began to hurl obscenities at Rebecca and rushed towards her, striking her with a resounding slap on the face while snatching the pocket watch from Rebecca's open hand. Rebecca winced in pain at the blow but stood her ground in submissive silence, not knowing what else she could do except be grateful that the woman had struck the side of her face that hadn't been struck earlier by her husband.

Captain Jameson stormed toward the two while shouting in a loud voice, "Madame! You will control yourself!" Taking the pocket watch from the reluctant grasp of Mrs. Perry, he waved it in front of Rebecca and demanded, "Explain this!"

Rebecca stood transfixed by the intensity of Captain Jameson's fury, and utter confusion was reflected in her countenance. She had never before seen the captain appear so angry, and never would she have expected that anger directed towards her. She felt the eyes of all in the room resting on her while she stood on trembling legs.

"I don't know how that came to be in my tunic, Captain, nor where it came from..."she murmured.

"You took it from my husband, you lying little wench!" the admiral's wife hissed.

"I would never take anything that didn't belong to me," Rebecca implored, beginning to look frightened.

The others present in the room remained in bewildered confusion while the captain contemplated how to respond to the accusation. Never in all of his seafaring years had anyone stolen something from a guest aboard his ship and now, the one person he least expected it would be turned out to be the thief. "Take her below, Mr. Burgess, and lock her in the hold," he ordered in a sharp tone.

Rebecca, her eyes large with disbelief, stood frozen in place, stunned by what had just come to pass. She cast imploring eyes at Captain Jameson, but he would not meet her gaze. Instead, he moved to the large picture window and turned his back to them, as if to dismiss all who lingered.

"Captain, please," she whispered, "You must believe-"

"I said get her out of here!" he shouted, not bothering to turn around.

Rebecca felt the hand of Lieutenant Burgess take hold of her arm as he began to pull her from the cabin. She did not resist him, nor did she acknowledge the suspicious glances of those present, but instead she lowered her face in shame as she was removed from the room.

Captain Jameson was quick to excuse the assemblage from his stateroom before turning to speak with Admiral Perry. With weary humiliation he said, "I apologize, Admiral. I never would have thought..."

"Oh, come now," Admiral Perry replied. "How could you have known the girl was a vagrant and a thief?"

Captain Jameson paused to consider his words, thinking perhaps he had been too quick to fall for the innocent wiles of his captive stowaway. It was a brutal reminder of his resolution to avoid the female gender as much as was feasible, both in the past, and now even more so in the future. Never again, he determined, would he let his guard down for the likes of a woman. "If you will excuse me, Admiral, I would like to be alone for a time to consider the options for punishment," he murmured.

"Perhaps I can come up with some ideas as well," Admiral Perry suggested.

"Yes, yes..." the captain said. "We'll discuss them at dinner if that is alright with you, sir?"

Captain Jameson was relieved to see the admiral nod his head in agreement, wanting only to be left alone with his tortured thoughts. He stood in respectful silence while Admiral Perry escorted his wife back to their quarters and then lowered himself into a chair, finding himself once again at a loss as to how to punish the girl. No doubt the admiral would insist she hang for her thievery, and with just cause. She deserved no less he realized, but regardless of the consequences, there was little he could do to sway the outcome of the admiral's decision, whatever the penalty may be.

The remainder of the crew immediately returned below deck to discuss what had taken place. Eddy and Mr. Andrews were the most visibly upset, both of them realizing that some form of trickery had occurred but unable to identify who, or why someone might want to bring this havoc down upon Rebecca. Even Lieutenant Burgess himself doubted the allegation and felt somehow responsible after leaving the girl alone with the man earlier in the day. He did not speak as he led her below and he was grateful when she followed him in silence. He had anticipated a tearful outburst, or a voiced plea for mercy, or even a hateful accusation, but instead she remained pensive and detached, almost as if in a state of shock.

Rebecca watched Lieutenant Burgess open the heavy door and then crept inside, still not saying a word. She did not turn around when the lock clanged into place behind her but remained where she was until she was certain he had gone. When at last she heard the faint click of his heels retreating up the steps, she fell to her knees in despair and began to pray that her death would come quickly. A scripture verse that she had memorized as a child sprang with instant clarity to her mind and she began to utter the words with a heavy heart, her voice rasping with desolation. *"One thing I ask of the Lord, this is what I seek: that I may dwell in the house of the Lord all the days of my life, to gaze upon the beauty of the Lord and to seek him in His temple. For in the day of trouble he will keep me safe in his dwelling: He will hide me in the shelter of His tabernacle and set me high upon a rock. Then my head will be exalted above the enemies who surround me: at His tabernacle will I sacrifice with shouts of joy. I will sing and make music to the Lord!"*

A sob broke free, and with desperate fervor she continued, "Keep me safe within your dwelling, Lord…hide me even now in the shelter of your tabernacle…"

Tears flooded her eyes as she became aware of the presence of God there in the midst of the dark, dank hold. She envisioned Daniel facing the angry lions, and Shadrach, Meshach and Abednego confronted by the flaming fire, and all the martyrs of the faith who had gone before her. She began to praise God with a passion she hadn't felt in some time while singing songs of praise and thanksgiving to Him, her despair quickly draining from her like a sponge over-saturated with water.

Mr. Andrews lingered near the bow of the ship discussing the precarious situation with the cook when they heard the commotion emanating from the hold. Afraid for the girl's safety, they hurried down the stairwell thinking Rebecca might be in some sort of trouble, but when they drew near they realized it was only her voice they heard. Both men shifted in nervous apprehension before the door, hesitant to disturb the girl, until Mr. Andrews finally called out, "Missy?"

"Mr. Andrews?" Rebecca replied, wondering why he had ventured below deck.

"What're you doing in there?" he asked, a hint of curiosity in his voice.

"Praying…what are you doing out there?"

"Talking to you," he smiled.

"Is the captain alright, Mr. Andrews? I'm afraid I've upset him terribly."

"He'll manage, Missy. Do you have any idea how you ended up with the admiral's pocket watch?" he asked her.

"Well, I certainly have some suspicions but I doubt I could prove anything," she sighed.

Hearing the sound of approaching footsteps, the two men glanced at one another before retreating into a darkened corridor lest they be caught consorting with the accused. Rebecca heard their hasty departure and wondered what it was that had sent them scurrying away in such a manner.

Captain Jameson made his way down the dark corridor toward the hold. He didn't make a habit of going below deck and he resisted it this time more than ever. He was determined to question the girl though, to see if she had an explanation as to why she would have stolen the pocket watch from the admiral. He didn't really know her character he reasoned, so why did it surprise him so to realize she was a thief? He made a note to check his quarters for any missing valuables, recalling that he had left her unattended there on more than one occasion.

When he approached the hold he slowed his steps and stopped just beyond the entrance. It was silent inside, and he wondered if perhaps the girl was sleeping. No, he reasoned, she would most likely be too upset for sleep to come with ease. He paced back and forth in front of the door, hesitant to enter.

Rebecca's heart began to pound in her chest when she heard the sound of approaching footsteps, certain the admiral had come to finish what he had started. She held her breath and listened at the door for some clue as to who might be lurking there, until her knees began to shake, making it difficult for her to stand. She leaned against the wall and slid to the floor, where she again beseeched the Lord for deliverance.

Beyond the confines of the hold the captain continued to pace, unsure as to why he hesitated to speak with the girl. After what seemed to him like hours, he retreated to the solitude of his stateroom, where it would soon be time to receive the admiral for dinner. He would leave the girl to contemplate her wrongdoings he determined, and deal with her indiscretion when a satisfactory punishment had been decided upon.

The admiral arrived as expected and Captain Jameson was relieved to see neither of the women accompanied him. The two men sat in amicable silence at the table, waiting for the steward to deliver their dinner. The admiral was the first to speak.

"I believe I have come up with a solution to our problem, Captain."

Captain Jameson contemplated the comment he made, wondering what problem it was that he was spoke of, until he remembered the incident involving the girl. Funny, he thought to himself, he had never considered her a problem before tonight.

"The young lady can return with my wife and I, work off the debt of her transgression, and when our mutually decided upon time is complete I will return her to Portsmouth myself."

Captain Jameson remained silent, still deep in thought. He wasn't sure what he had expected to hear, as the options for punishing a woman were few. He was relieved to hear that Admiral Perry hadn't demanded the girl hang, but he never thought for a moment that the man would want the girl to return with him. For reasons he could not understand, he was hesitant to let her leave. "Come now, Admiral…I'm sure there are other options that wouldn't require your having to take the girl with you. After all, I would hate to burden you with the responsibility of having to return her to England."

"It would be no burden at all," Admiral Perry assured him. "My wife could use the help, and I would consider the punishment for the offense adequate…unless of course, you had something better in mind?"

He didn't. He had deliberated his options all afternoon to come up with an appropriate punishment that would appease the admiral, but he had been unable to. Now, when faced with the prospect of the girl's departure, he felt suddenly torn. He realized he had come to enjoy the girl's presence on board his frigate, and the spontaneous energy she brought to the dreariness of war. Her exuberance and humility were like a palliative solace to the men who enjoyed her company…Dr. Ammons, Eddy the cook, and the Petty Officer, Mr. Andrews. Never-the-less, he deliberated, he did not want her to remain onboard if he could not trust her integrity.

"Captain?"

He turned again to the admiral and said in a curt manner, "Very well, she shall go with you and you can do with her as you see fit, sir."

Captain Jameson excused himself for a moment to go in search of Lieutenant Burgess. He wanted to finish this once and for all, before he had time to reconsider their decision, knowing he had little chance of overriding the judgment of the admiral.

"Mr. Burgess," he called to the officer standing watch on deck.

"Sir?"

"Find Petty Officer Andrews and have him bring the girl to my quarters. And I'll expect you to be present as well."

Captain Jameson returned to his berth while Lieutenant Burgess went in search of Mr. Andrews.

Rebecca remained seated in the hold, propped against the wall for support. She again heard the sound of approaching footsteps, and slowed her breathing in order to determine who they belonged to. This time though, she heard a key turn in the lock. She glanced up in apprehension to catch a glimpse of the face that entered and was relieved to see that it was only Mr. Andrews. He had a solemn look on his face as he fixed his eyes on her.

"You'll have to come with me, Missy. Captain Jameson and the admiral are ready to speak to you."

Rebecca stood to her feet, preparing herself to face the captain's wrath once again. She had no regrets about the confrontation that was certain to follow with the admiral, but in her heart she despaired over having so greatly upset Captain Jameson.

"I'll do what I can to help you," Mr. Andrews said in a worried voice.

"Thank you, Mr. Andrews," she replied, a weary exhaustion settling on her face. "But you needn't be concerned for me, sir. I am prepared for whatever may come to pass tonight, for I must remain confident that the Lord has ordained these steps even before I was born."

He gave her a look of irate disbelief upon hearing her pious statement, but was too concerned with the battle which was sure to ensue to chastise her further. With a quick shake of his head he climbed the stairs, Rebecca following him the rest of the way in silence, while both of them contemplated what would come to pass once they arrived at the captain's quarters.

Lieutenant Burgess was seated at the table with Captain Jameson and Admiral Perry, waiting for the girl to be brought before them. He remained attentive but silent while they explained their intention for punishment, and like the captain he was relieved that the girl would not be sentenced to hang. For as much as she infuriated him, he still did not wish to see her dead. A knock at the door interrupted their deliberation and Lieutenant Burgess stood to open it. Seeing Mr. Andrews standing with Rebecca at his side, he waved them into the room before returning to take his seat.

"This won't take long, Mr. Andrews," Captain Jameson said in a terse voice, standing to face the petty officer while keeping his gaze averted from Rebecca. "You might as well just wait here until we've finished with her."

Petty Officer Andrews considered the words Captain Jameson spoke, thinking that one overhearing the conversation might have thought they intended to devour the girl like a pride of hungry lions. He hoped instead that they would be merciful, for surely the captain must realize that Rebecca was no thief.

Captain Jameson spun on his heel and moved to the window, leaving Rebecca and Mr. Andrews staring after him with nervous apprehension. The three officers studied her contrite form without speaking until the captain finally said, "Do you have anything more to say for yourself?"

"No, sir," she whispered, her eyes downcast.

She couldn't bear the thought of the captain thinking she was a thief, yet she was at a loss as to how to convince the man otherwise. Any punishment they chose at this point would pale in comparison to the knowledge that she had so greatly disappointed this man with her supposed crime.

The captain began to speak then, keeping his eyes averted from Rebecca. "You will sail tomorrow with Admiral Perry. A definitive amount of time will be established between the two of you, during which you will work in his employ to make arrears for your transgression. Upon completion of that time you will be returned to Portsmouth, where, I hope, you will change your ways and turn to a life of more admirable living." Turning to the admiral, he said, "Admiral Perry, I hereby bequeath to you this girl and all that goes with her."

Rebecca was stunned by the words he spoke and grew indignant at the notion that the captain thought he could give away to this swine of a man the faith and the innocence she had held so dear for all of her years. Fixing a direct gaze on the captain, she reprimanded him in a low voice. "Captain, what I have is not yours to give away, sir."

Lieutenant Burgess paled in shocked disbelief at the girl's bold rebuttal, while Captain Jameson cursed forcefully under his breath and spun on his heel to glare at her. Storming toward her with an angry grimace he shouted, "Everything you have right down to the shirt on your back belongs to me, and I will not stand idly by and let you tell me otherwise!

Rebecca peered up at the man glowering down at her with such blatant contempt, but instead of seeing the livid eyes that blazed with rage, she saw through to the kind soul of the one who had taken her in to provide her with a safe haven in the midst of great uncertainty, even though she had no way of repaying him. The very one who gave her a comfortable bed to sleep in at night, fed her during the day, and offered her a sanctuary from all she feared most at being alone on his ship, far from the comforts and love of her family and home. Her face took on a look of utter remorse and she lowered her gaze to whisper with humble contrition, "You're right, Captain Jameson. What I have you have provided for me unselfishly and I shall forever be in your debt, sir. Please, forgive me."

He stepped back, caught off guard by her unexpected display of repentance. He had anticipated, and even hoped for a fight, to make doing what he had to do come more easily, but to his great dismay he realized that she was not about to give him one. Turning to the admiral, he said with a weary voice, "This burden is now yours, Admiral Perry."

Captain Jameson kept his head lowered as retreated to the refuge of the window, appearing as though the weight of the world rested upon his shoulders at that very moment, and as he gazed at the vast beauty that beckoned from the confines of the small room Rebecca's heart broke with compassion at the sight of him. Her cry of helplessness caught in a thick lump in her throat, for she was determined not to let the admiral catch a glimpse of her anguish.

"Wait!" called Mr. Andrews, his eyes darting about in nervous anticipation.

Captain Jameson twisted back to face the contrite figures of the petty officer and the girl standing before him.

"T'was I, sir, who took the pocket watch from the admiral."

Rebecca shifted her gaze to peer at Mr. Andrews, stunned by his statement.

"Nonsense," the admiral said with a flippant wave of his hand. "She's the thief."

Captain Jameson, Lieutenant Burgess and Rebecca all remained motionless and silent, their glances moving between Admiral Perry and the apprehensive petty officer, while the two continued their verbal exchange with one another.

"I took it myself, sir… didn't think anyone would notice."

"You lie," the admiral growled.

"No, t'was I, sir, and my conscience just won't let me watch the girl go off and serve the punishment for my crime. Looks like you'll have to take me back with you, admiral."

"No!" shouted the admiral. "She took the watch, not you! Imbecile!"

"T'was I sir…"

"It was in the girl's pocket, you fool!"

Petty Officer Andrews shook his head, his confidence growing as that of the admiral waned, and a smug grin spread over his face. "I only put it there to save my own skin until you left, Admiral."

"Captain Jameson, I demand you dismiss this man at once."

Admiral Perry began to pace fretfully about the room, his face flushing a bright crimson hue while he glared at Petty Officer Andrews in agitation. Captain Jameson stood speechless, contemplating the curious argument between the two men.

"Captain," Mr. Andrews began, "I, myself, am the thief you must punish. I took the watch from the admiral's stateroom while he attended your dinner party, sir." And then turning to face Admiral Perry, he added, "Looks like I'll be the one sailing with you tomorrow, admiral."

"Liar!" the admiral roared, shaking his fist in the air. "I put it in *her* pocket, not *yours*!"

All those present in the room turned to stare at Admiral Perry with incredulous expressions, all except for Mr. Andrews that is, who was simply relieved that his plan had worked. A sudden burst of commotion erupted when the captain, Mr. Burgess and the admiral all began to argue at the same time, while Rebecca stood transfixed by the chaos unfolding before her. Mr. Andrews watched from where he stood with a wary expression on his face, hoping the captain had heard the admiral's confession lest he be punished for his feigned thievery after all. Neither he, nor the other men, took notice of Rebecca slipping without a word from the room.

Rebecca felt as if a knife had pierced her heart while the words the captain had uttered replayed themselves over and over again in her mind.

"This burden is now yours…"

Never had she known such personal anguish, even upon having been taken from her home. It grieved Rebecca to know that the captain still considered her presence a burden when she had tried with such diligence to stay out of his way, to make herself scarce, and to work with meticulous dedication in the hopes of repaying him for his kindness. She would depart with the admiral after all she determined, in spite of the threat he posed to her, if only to give Captain Jameson the freedom from her that he sought. Perhaps, she thought, it would be easier to just throw herself overboard once they were out of sight of the Redemption. Yes, she resolved, she would rather swim home to England, or die trying, rather than let the horrid Admiral Perry steal from her the innocence that she had guarded for all of her eighteen years.

Rebecca made her way to the stern of the ship, the one place she could formulate her plan undisturbed. She desperately wanted to bid farewell to Mr. Andrews and Eddy before she left, for she was certain she would never see them again. The two men had been her dearest friends during the past several months and she was overcome with despair at having to leave them in this manner. She reached the rear of the frigate, her heart heavy with grief, and she slid down onto the wooden planks where she sought refuge in the presence of her Lord.

It took a few moments before the uproar in the captain's stateroom had calmed enough for the men to take note of Rebecca's absence. Glancing around in alarm, Mr. Andrews exclaimed to Lieutenant Burgess, "Where'd she go, sir?"

"I don't know, Mr. Andrews," Lieutenant Burgess replied, "but we'll find her soon enough no doubt."

Captain Jameson remained in his quarters to settle matters with the admiral, while Lieutenant Burgess and Mr. Andrews set out to find Rebecca. They split up, each heading in opposite directions on the deck.

Rebecca lingered in a despondent silence considering the things that had come to pass that evening, and while she thanked the Lord that the truth had been revealed, her heart was heavy with the realization that the captain had believed her to be the thief. At least now the captain would know that she was innocent, she mused. As she gazed up at the stars shining in the sky she became aware of how much she would miss these nights aboard the Redemption, where the sky seemed ablaze with the glory of God and she could daydream about the places she would go, and the people she would minister to. She also thought of the crew whom she had grown so fond of and regretted having to leave them so much sooner than she had anticipated, and even more so before she had taken the opportunity to speak to them of Lord's redeeming love. A weary sigh escaped her as she felt the heaviness of heart descend into her soul.

Lieutenant Burgess rounded the corner of the sick berth and headed to the back of the frigate, where he saw Rebecca's foot extended in a relaxed manner across the deck. She was hidden from sight behind a large barrel and he came to an abrupt halt lest she catch a glimpse of him. He had not intended to find her and did not know what he would say to her when she became aware of his presence, so instead of approaching her where she sat, he retreated into the shadows and proceeded to report to the captain's stateroom. Upon entering, he saw that the captain was alone, and pacing about in nervous anticipation.

"Did you find her?" Captain Jameson asked, casting an anxious glance at Mr. Burgess.

"Yes, sir. She is at the rear of the ship resting quietly."

"Thank you, Mr. Burgess. We'll leave her undisturbed for now. I'm sure she must be overcome with emotion."

"As you wish, sir," the lieutenant replied.

The captain studied his young officer for a moment before saying, "Tell me, Mr. Burgess, did you believe her to be the thief?"

Mr. Burgess considered his question with great care and answered, "No, sir, I did not."

"Then you have extended her more grace than I," he sighed.

Lieutenant Burgess hesitated in the uncomfortable silence for a time and then asked, "Is there anything you need me to do in the matter of the admiral, sir?"

"No, I've handled that matter myself, and I must say, I will be glad to see them depart on the morrow."

"Then perhaps I should inform the petty officer of her whereabouts?" Mr. Burgess asked.

"Yes, by all means, Mr. Burgess. He will no doubt be relieved to hear of her safety, but tell him not to disturb her for the time being." Captain Jameson paused for a moment before remarking in a thoughtful voice, "A wise move he made, don't you think?"

"Yes, captain, very wise," Lieutenant Burgess answered, nodding through a wry smile.

The captain studied the officer's retreating form while he considered the distressing upheaval the girl must be experiencing. He despised himself at that moment for believing the lies of the admiral, and for not being more willing to defend Rebecca against the man's accusation. He was desperate to speak with her, to apologize, to beg for her forgiveness…whatever it would take to heal the wound he had inflicted upon her, but unsure of the emotional state of his young stowaway, he continued to pace about feeling helpless and at a loss as to how to approach her.

Rebecca remained where she was, not wanting to lose even one precious second of solitude on her last night aboard the Redemption. She gazed through tear filled eyes into the vast heavens beyond and was startled by the abundance of stars which glistened in the cloudless sky above her. It brought to mind the night she had escaped her captivity from the Defiance, seeking refuge in Cadiz, and she recalled the moment she had first set eyes on the Redemption and of how brightly the name of the frigate had been illuminated by the light of the moon. She had been convinced then that the name *'Redemption'* had been a sign to her from God that this ship would be her means of returning home, but as she sat contemplating the situation she now found herself in, she wondered if she had ever really heard the voice of God speaking to her at all. She laid her head back with a weary sigh and closed her eyes, taking deep breaths of the pungent, salt laden air that had consumed her lungs these past several months. In a voice heavy laden with dejection, she began to call out to God in her anguish with the scripture verses she held so dear to her heart. *"Hear my prayer, O Lord, and give ear unto my cry; hold not thy peace at my tears, for I am a stranger with thee, and a sojourner, as all my fathers were. O spare me, that I may recover strength before I go hence, and be no more!"*

Rebecca was startled out of her meditations by the sound of someone approaching. She remained motionless and still, trying to keep her presence concealed from the passerby, for she did not wanting her peaceful interlude to come to an end so soon. Shutting her eyes against the darkness, as if that would help to keep her hidden from sight, she held her breath to avoid letting even the tiniest bit of sound escape her. The footsteps continued to advance with purposeful yet discreet strides, and when they finally came to a halt she peered up through a hesitant glance, hoping that whoever had been passing by had gone on without taking notice of her, but the first thing her eyes beheld from where she sat was a pair of legs positioned before her. She followed the legs upward and was astounded to see that it was the captain who had approached, and was staring down at her with a somber look upon his face. Rebecca, in her discomfort, made a hurried attempt to stand to her feet.

"No, no," he exclaimed, holding up his hand. "Please, stay where you are."

Without speaking, she lowered herself back onto the floorboards, keeping her apprehensive gaze on Captain Jameson.

"Do you mind if I join you?" he asked, certain the girl must despise him after all that had happened.

"Of course not, sir," she answered, "but wouldn't you be more comfortable in your stateroom?"

"No one will disturb us here," he replied.

He moved down to where she sat with an awkward grace, having never positioned himself in such a fashion before, but in this instance he wanted to be where the girl felt most comfortable and where they would have the least amount of distractions.

Rebecca grew a bit flustered by the awkward situation and found herself at a loss for words. It seemed strange to be sitting on the wooden planks of the deck with the captain seated next to her, and she wondered what sort of conclusion a passerby would construe upon seeing them together in this manner. She glanced at him in her discomfort, waiting for him to say something. She was unsure as to whether or not he was still upset with her and she was hesitant to exacerbate the matter further with meaningless dialogue. After what seemed to her like hours, the captain began to speak in a quiet voice while he gazed out over the vast waters of the Atlantic Ocean.

"Tell me the story of how you came to be here."

Rebecca could hear the weariness and exhaustion in his voice and she wanted to wrap her arms around him and tell him that everything would be alright, that she wasn't angry with him and that he had treated her better than she had ever hoped he would, but instead she said, "*Right* here, sir?", thinking perhaps he meant at the rear of the frigate.

"On the Redemption," he answered, turning to glance at her.

Rebecca paused for a moment while they sat side by side, staring out over the rolling waves. It had seemed like a lifetime since she had last set eyes upon her beloved England, and now she wondered if she could even remember the strange series of events that had brought her here. With a thoughtful expression on her face she began to speak, her voice tentative as she tried to retell the incidents in the order in which they had occurred.

"I'm from Portsmouth, sir," she said in a soft voice.

"Yes, I recall you telling me that once before," he said, a pained grin tugging at the corners of his mouth.

She paused for a moment, and then glanced at him to say, "This might take some time, Captain."

He motioned with his hand and said, "Go ahead then, I have all night."

Rebecca leaned back against the wall with a contemplative sigh and began to recount her story. "There was a revival service…it was the last night. Everyone brought desserts to share afterwards, but I decided not to stay. I wanted to take a walk along the shore instead. Moira wasn't happy about my decision and tried to convince me not to go, but I chose to leave anyway."

"Moira?" he questioned.

"A dear friend...no, more like family I suppose. She had taken it upon herself to mother me when she felt it was necessary, which was pretty much all of the time." Rebecca grinned at Captain Jameson, but her face held a shadow of regret. "I should have listened to her..."

She paused for a moment, trying to remember what had happened next. "It was a beautiful, clear night, much like this one. In my mind I can still see how brightly the stars were shining and smell the scent of the ocean air, hear the sounds of the activities in the city..."

A troubled look darkened her features and she grew silent. Captain Jameson peered over at her to find her staring off into the darkness, deep in thought. After several moments she began to speak again. "The only thing I remember beyond that is seeing a man standing on the path in front of me. He was talking to me, but I can't recall his words, only that he smelled strongly of rum." She looked at Captain Jameson and gave a fitful toss of her head. "Next thing I know I wake up with a splitting headache in the belly of a ship called Defiance."

Captain Jameson gasped in astonishment. "The Defiance?" he repeated. "That's Captain Cromwell's ship!"

Rebecca gave a quick nod of her head.

"How long were you on Cromwell's frigate?" he asked.

"I'm not sure, sir, but I'd guess about three months."

"Captain Cromwell, indeed..." he said, shaking his head. "Then you have seen a man flogged, no doubt," he muttered, realizing the girl would have witnessed much harsher cruelties than a mere flogging at the hand of Cromwell's men.

Rebecca cringed even still at the horrible memories and whispered, "More floggings than I care to remember." She kept her eyes averted and continued, "Is Captain Cromwell a friend of yours, sir?" She waited with baited breath for his reply, fearful of what he might say.

"No, he most certainly is not. I'm not fond of officers who maintain control of their command by brute force."

"Neither am I, sir," she sighed, relieved to hear that he found Captain Cromwell just as despicable as she had.

He cast a sidelong glance at her and said, "Were you ever... did they know..."

"My identity was never discovered, Captain," she assured, rescuing him from his troubled thoughts. "I realize now that I was very fortunate to have escaped many horrible experiences while aboard the Defiance."

She continued to speak in a soft voice of her memories of the recurrent floggings, the brutal fights that often broke out, and the horrendous effects of the rum which flowed much too freely, while the captain listened with a pensive expression on his face. A guarded expression shadowed her features, and her voice grew quiet at the disturbing images that would forever be burned into her mind.

"You say you were on the Defiance for three months?" the captain asked.

Rebecca nodded, her gaze distant.

"What happened then?" he asked.

"I found you, sir," she murmured through a soft smile.

His eyes widened in surprise.

"When the Defiance sailed into the port of Cadiz I was able to escape onto a dinghy taking men ashore. Once we arrived on dry land, I hid myself away in a thicket of shrubs and waited until I heard a group of men speaking of Portsmouth. They were your men, captain."

He shook his head in bewildered disbelief. "How then did you happen onto the Redemption?"

"Well," she began, "I waited until your men made a move toward the shoreline. It was easy enough to slip in behind them then, as there minds were already lost to drink. No one took notice of me as far as I could tell." She smiled as her recollection of the evening stirred an unexpected wave of emotion. "When I heard them say the name of your ship, *Redemption*, I thought surely this was the deliverance I had prayed for. My redemption had come at last..."

Her voice quieted to a mere whisper, and she felt tears brimming at her eyes. In her embarrassment she averted her face, hoping that the captain would not take notice of them. "And so here I am," she murmured in a soft tone.

The captain remained silent, listening with rapt attention and finding himself amazed at her resilience after hearing of all that she had been through, while a knot of guilt suddenly clenched at his gut. "I'm certain this is not the deliverance you had prayed for," he muttered.

Rebecca leaned briefly against Captain Jameson's shoulder, more so to reassure him than for support, and said, "You are exactly what I prayed for, sir. You have shown me a patient and kind spirit and have given me a safe haven in the midst of a very lonely and vulnerable time. I thank God every day for the accommodation and protection you've provided for me."

She grew silent then as her tale came to an end, and she turned to catch a glimpse of the captain's expression, certain she must have bored him senseless by now. Instead, she was startled to see his face etched with a sorrow so deep that it threatened to engulf her and she was quick to look away, uncomfortable with his visible display of emotion. The two of them remained silent for several moments until Captain Jameson spoke, his voice heavy with remorse.

"I'm aware that I have wronged you severely and I fear you shall carry the resentment of this night long into your future."

Rebecca laid her hand softly on his arm to draw his gaze towards her. "Captain," she whispered in passionate determination, "what happened with the admiral was no fault of your own. I harbor no resentment towards you, sir, and I will put this incident behind me this very night."

He saw that her face held the appearance of truthfulness with which she spoke, and he wondered how he could have ever doubted her integrity in the first place. "I am so very sorry for believing his lie," he said, resting his head with a weary heaviness in his hand.

Rebecca turned back again and reclined against the wall of the Redemption, her eyes lowered to the deck. She did not know how to convince the man that she had never even once considered him to be at fault for what had happened, and for a moment she debated on telling him that she would be leaving with the admiral after all to ease the burden he felt with her presence onboard his frigate. After some time though, she determined it would be best to withhold the information from him. Morning, she knew, would come soon enough.

The two remained seated on the deck of the frigate for a few moments more, neither of them wanting to break the quiet solitude that had encompassed them, until the captain finally spoke.

"I suppose you are quite exhausted?"

"Just relieved right now, sir," she whispered.

Captain Jameson sighed through a solemn nod. "Then I'd best return to settle matters with the admiral. Will you be returning to your quarters?"

Rebecca, knowing this would be her last night aboard the Redemption, wanted to savor every single moment she had left. "Soon, Captain," she answered. "I'd like to stay out here under the stars for just a little while longer. It's not often we're able to see so many of the constellations this clearly."

His face took on a look of intrigue as he pondered her words. "You're familiar with the constellations?" he asked.

She nodded through a sleepy yawn. "My father thought it his duty to enlighten me to the wonders of our universe."

"Tell me then, what do you see up there now?" he asked with a hint of curiosity.

He watched as she directed her gaze upward to look at the bright specks flickering overhead and he was amazed by the utter peace that glistened in her countenance, with a serenity that shone brighter than any star he had ever set eyes upon. She remained silent for some time, her eyes searching the darkness of the night sky as if seeking out some great revelation.

"I see the Andromeda constellation," she said at last, lifting her hand to direct the captain's gaze into the broad expanse of darkness. "It's there, about ten degrees north of the Alrisha star, which is actually located in the Pisces constellation off to the left…there."

His gaze followed her arm moving in a graceful arc across the firmament before looking back at her in surprise.

"Because of its easy visibility," she continued, glancing at him with an impish grin, "I'd guess the month is November?"

His incredulous laughter broke the silence which surrounded them and he found himself utterly captivated by her knowledge of the galaxy. "You are correct," he said.

"You seem surprised, Captain," she smiled.

Through a wry grin he said, "I can't help but wonder why you bother to retain such information."

Rebecca remained in silent contemplation for a moment before answering, her face reflecting a radiant glow, and then she began to speak in a soft, melodious tone the words of scripture written on her heart. *"When I consider Your heavens, the work of Your hands; the moon and the stars which You have ordained, what is man that You are mindful of him, and the son of man that You visit him…"*

She cast a shy glance his way, wondering if he could possibly comprehend the depth of her conviction, but seeing his face staring with a blank expression back at her, she went on to explain further. "It helps me to remember, Captain, that if God, in His infinite mercy, took such great care to place the stars in the sky, how much more mindful is He of me, His humble servant here on earth?"

Captain Jameson contemplated her contrite response, and found that the unwavering expression of faith in her countenance bore evidence to the truthfulness with which she spoke. He suddenly felt unworthy to be in her presence, and in his great discomfort, he stood to his feet and peered down at her one last time, regretting having ever brought Admiral Perry on board.

Rebecca gazed up at him with humble sincerity and murmured, "Good night, Captain Jameson."

He found it difficult to speak, but instead nodded his head in a curt manner and turned to leave.

Rebecca remained where she was for a long while, pondering the peculiar events of the evening and wondering whether or not she would sleep on deck. She could hear the boisterous activity below and suddenly realized how much she would miss being among the men whom she had come to consider her friends. Instead of tarrying any longer, she decided to go in search of Eddy and Mr. Andrews to bid them a final farewell. A heavy sigh escaped her as she plucked herself from the solitude of the moment, stood to her feet, and headed back towards the quarterdeck. She caught a glimpse of Mr. Andrews leaning over the rail of the ship and gazing out over the water. She was thankful he was not below with the rest of the crew, for she wanted to speak with him in private, where other ears couldn't hear what she wanted to say. She advanced upon him with a quiet step, not wanting to startle him or interrupt the pensive moment he seemed to be enjoying.

Mr. Andrews became aware of her presence when she drew near and peered over his shoulder to look at her, a hint of amusement in his eyes at what had come to pass between them that night. He was surprised when Rebecca sidled up to where he stood and wrapped her arms around him in an endearing embrace, while he remained in an awkward silence, his arms hanging like limp lanyards at his sides.

She stepped back to regard him with an expression of heartfelt gratitude and said, "I will never forget what you have done for me, Mr. Andrews, and I shall forever be indebted to you for saving my life. Wherever I am, and wherever I go, I will remember you to God in Heaven for the kindness and mercy you have shown towards me."

Rebecca turned and left just as quickly as she had appeared, not wanting him to see the tears that threatened to spill from her eyes, while he continued to stare after her in a discomfited silence, watching her retreat towards the darkness of the corridor. He did not question the words she had uttered, but instead contemplated her unusual behavior.

After leaving Mr. Andrews, Rebecca wandered down the narrow steps to the galley where she found Eddy, still cleaning up the mess that remained after the evening meal. "Eddy," she sighed with a tired smile, her eyes still glistening with emotion.

"Bec! You're alright! I heard how things turned out for you...big relief for us all, you know. Bet you wish you'd been down here with me, eh?"

She giggled at his rambling words and nodded her head. He always had a keen way of making a situation seem less tragic than she thought it to be. How she would miss these men whom she had come to love, with their easy manner and non-solicitous charm. Until now she had chosen not to encourage those who had displayed romantic intentions for her in the past, thinking marriage and a family were not for those who had decided to devote their lives to the service of the Lord. She had always known in her heart that she was called to be a servant in God's kingdom, and so she maintained her solitary lifestyle in a humble offering to Him, however, Rebecca was surprised to find that the company of men could be very pleasant and comfortable when friendship was the priority and not courtship and marriage.

"Eddy, I just wanted to thank you for being my friend."

"Thank me? What would you do a silly thing like that for?" he asked, a sheepish grin tugging at the corner of his lip.

"I realized tonight that my time on the Redemption is not guaranteed and I wouldn't want to leave this ship without having told you how much your kindness and friendship have meant to me."

"Well just where do you think you're going?" he teased.

Rebecca hesitated before answering but decided to withhold her plans from him for the time being, certain he would try to convince her to remain on board the frigate, and so instead of responding to his question, she smiled and changed the subject to avoid being deceitful. The two visited for a just a few minutes more, until Rebecca gave a sleepy yawn and said, "I'd best get off to bed. It's been a long night."

"Good night, Bec," Eddy called after her when she turned to leave, a puzzled expression lingering on his face.

"Good night, Eddy," she replied, her voice carrying an air of sadness when she realized she would never see the cook again. She retreated with a heavy heart to her quarters hoping sleep would come with ease, but she tossed with restless distraction until the graying light of morning, when at last she dozed off into a dreamless slumber.

The morning of the admiral's departure dawned bright and clear...another perfect day aboard the Redemption, Rebecca mused, until she remembered that this day would be her last day. She lingered beneath the warm folds of the blanket before rising, wanting to prolong her last moments in the tiny berth she had for the past several months called home. When her imminent departure became clear in her mind, she rose in silence to don the faded tunic and trousers that had been placed at the foot of the bed. She took great care to straighten up the small berth, making an attempt to arrange the room so that it would appear as if no one had ever been there. Picking up the book which the captain had lent her, she glanced about at her humble quarters one last time before she departed, pulling the latch into place with a resounding clang behind her. She passed by the captain's quarters on her way to the deck, where she tapped with a light hand on the door. Hearing no one's call to enter, she opened the portal to peer into the room, and finding it empty, she entered just enough to slide the book onto a cabinet. Retreating once again into the corridor, she climbed up the narrow stairwell to the deck, where she would watch and wait for the admiral and his wife to take their leave.

Captain Jameson spent a fitful night fretting over the emotional well-being of the girl, as well as over the events of the evening, but regardless of the lack of sleep he was eager for sunup to arrive so he could bid a final farewell to his cumbersome guests. He had listened with an attentive ear for the girl to return to her quarters after he had left her, concerned that the admiral might make an attempt to pursue her in her berth, and he would not retire to bed until he heard the latch on the door of her berth click softly into place. Now, as daylight approached, he dressed in his uniform and set out to locate Admiral Perry in order to send him, along with the vicious women who accompanied him, on their way.

Rebecca arrived on deck before either the captain or Admiral Perry and she made her way toward the quarterdeck, where she waited in respectful silence to observe the send off. Seeing Lieutenant Burgess approaching from the bow, she turned to face him, well aware that the irate scowl on his face was a sure indication of his ill mood on this day.

"What are you doing up here?" he growled, thinking the girl would have preferred to remain below so as to avoid another run-in with the admiral.

"My intentions are to depart with Admiral Perry, sir," she answered.

"No," he began in a low voice, "I understand that matter was settled last night, and you are to remain aboard the Redemption."

"The matter *you* speak of was settled," she said, "but I'm afraid I have my own matter I must attend to."

She stood before him, a resolute expression settling on her face, while she hoped that the captain and the admiral would soon appear. It was obvious that the young officer was growing irritated, and while she was certain that he would be glad to see her depart she had hoped to avoid yet another altercation with him.

Lieutenant Burgess felt his face flush with resentment once again at the simple words the girl spoke. As if she had a choice to stay or to go he scoffed, knowing full well that many aboard the frigate would have been grateful to be rid of her intruding presence, however, the captain had made it clear that she was to remain aboard the Redemption. "Is Captain Jameson aware of your intention to leave?" he asked, his dark eyes smoldering from beneath the brim of his hat.

"Not yet, sir," she answered.

"Then perhaps you could find the courtesy to make him aware of them," he snapped, certain that the captain would be upset when he discovered what the girl intended to do. He stormed away, agitation clearly evident on his features, and he reclaimed his position at the bow of the frigate, away from the guarded glances of the girl.

Rebecca caught a glimpse of Captain Jameson emerging from the stairwell, followed closely by Admiral Perry and the two women. She saw that he too seemed surprised when he saw her standing on deck and Rebecca's heart began to pound in her chest, dreading the thought of creating another volatile situation like the one she experienced the previous night. She watched as the captain continued on toward her unattended, leaving Admiral Perry and his wife looking on with wary hesitance.

"Good morning, Captain Jameson," she murmured.

"Good morning," he replied with an inquisitive voice. Captain Jameson had thought the girl would have kept herself far away from this place until the admiral was well on his way, but instead he saw that she waited for them, almost expectantly.

"I must say, I'm surprised to see you here," he remarked, watching her expression. "Is there something you are in need of?"

"No, sir," she stammered. "It's just that, well...I've decided to return with the admiral after all. I apologize for not speaking to you of my intentions earlier, but I didn't want to upset you any further."

She shifted on her feet in nervous anticipation, hoping she wasn't about to create a scene right there on the deck of the frigate with all of the men present.

His eyes widened in surprise as he found himself taken aback by her statement. He did not want to force the girl to stay, but he was not about to see her go off with the admiral either. "I'm afraid I cannot let you leave with the man," he replied in a curt tone, "now that I am aware of his intentions."

"Captain," she plead, "I've overstayed my welcome here. "I realize that you bear no responsibility in seeing me home, and as much as I appreciate your kindness at allowing me to remain onboard the Redemption, I cannot bear the thought of burdening you further with my presence."

He stepped back, stunned by her statement and wondering where she had ever gotten the notion that she had been a burden to him. The words he had spoken the night before sprang with instant clarity to his mind and he looked at her in regret, angry at himself for having spoken them with such carelessness. He began to address her then in a calm but direct manner saying, "I'm afraid I cannot let you leave, Miss Halloway. You will return to my quarters and wait for me there until Admiral Perry has departed. We will then discuss this matter further. If you refuse to obey my order, then I will use whatever means necessary to ensure that you are detained. Do I make myself clear?"

Her bright gaze bored into his as she persisted with a hushed voice. "Captain, this is your chance to be free of me for good! Think about it...no more women aboard your ship, peace restored among your men, and you'd no longer be accountable in seeing me back to Portsmouth!"

"You would walk away so easily from the means your God has provided you of returning home?" he scoffed, recalling the words she had spoken earlier.

"Yes," she persisted. "If it eases your burden of responsibility, then I am prepared to do whatever it takes."

"My responsibilities are my own, Miss Halloway," he retorted. "Do not feel as if you have to relieve me of them."

"Captain, please...just let me go," she implored.

Calling to his lieutenant at the bow of the frigate, he instructed in a brusque tone, "Mr. Burgess, kindly escort this young lady to my stateroom."

Lieutenant Burgess was quick to move forward in acknowledgement of the order, in spite of the irritated scowl that lingered on his face.

"No," Rebecca relented, stepping back. "I'll go there on my own accord, sir." With a hint of befallen resignation, she turned to proceed towards the captain's quarters, wanting to ensure a safe distance between herself and Lieutenant Burgess lest he decide to follow after her.

Lieutenant Burgess observed the exchange between Captain Jameson and Rebecca from where he stood near the quarterdeck. He found himself intrigued by the girl's tenacity at withstanding the captain's wrath and he knew few men would have been as brave. Still, he was disappointed to see her return below, hoping instead she would depart as she had planned. Her presence aboard the Redemption continued to cause him great unease, and the mere thought of crossing paths with her by chance on the frigate kept him on edge for most hours of his day. He continued to carry the guilt of the severe beating she had taken on account of him, but, he reasoned, if she hadn't been deceitful about her true identity in the first place, it never would have happened. He became aware of Lieutenant Edwards approaching him from the rear.

"What was that all about?" he asked under his breath.

"Just a foiled plan I suppose," Lieutenant Burgess answered.

"I had heard rumor that she would be departing. I take it we aren't to be so lucky?"

"Not this time, James," the young officer replied with resignation, turning to salute the admiral while he descended over the side of the ship.

Captain Jameson, finally relieved of his guests at last, hurried toward his stateroom where he anticipated a heated argument from the girl at having been detained against her will. He made a vain attempt to formulate a good defense for himself as he neared the end of the narrow corridor, while he realized that he had no right to confine her aboard his vessel, but he was adamant that he would never let the admiral get his conniving hands on her. Standing just beyond the walls of his berth, he paused for a moment to calm his nerves. He had been in charge of several hundred men for well over 15 years, yet he had never before been so keenly aware of the effect his actions and words might have on another person. His enlightenment, he realized, had come the day the girl had made her presence known in his world. For as much conflict the situation had wrought, he rather enjoyed the new aspect of understanding it allowed him, for he had yet to meet such a selfless soul, and he found himself wholly captivated by the young lady's charming nature and depth of character.

In his distress he lifted his hand to rap on the door, and then chuckled to himself at the thought of seeking permission to enter his own private quarters. He took a deep breath and stepped into the room, half expecting the girl to be poised to flee and half expecting her not to be there at all. With a quiet sigh of relief he found she stood by the window, eyeing the portal with an uneasy glance as it slid open. She gave him a timid smile as if anticipating a firm rebuke, but said nothing, and in his discomfort he cleared his throat and glanced about the room, unsure of how to bridge the rift he had created. Spotting the book he had given her lying on the table, he picked up and asked in surprise, "You've finished it already?"

"No, sir," she answered in a quiet manner. "I wanted to return it to you before I left."

"Ah, yes...well I'm glad I convinced you to stay," he teased, a wry grin crossing his face.

Rebecca glanced away for a moment, feeling suddenly uncomfortable in his presence, but remained silent and attentive when he began to speak once again.

"The situation that occurred while the admiral was onboard was unexpected, and I regret not handling it as well as I might have. What I said that evening was spoken in anger and I wish I had remained silent in the matter. You may doubt the sincerity of my words now, but I can only hope that one day you will pardon my transgression. Let me assure you, Miss Halloway, you are no burden."

He faced her with a stoic expression, expecting a tearful outburst and knowing it would be well warranted. He had a sudden realization that he had never really gone out of his way to ensure the girl felt welcomed aboard the Redemption, nor had he protected her from the travails of the admiral. In fact, he had watched his officers treat her with malicious intent at times and had said nothing, while she valiantly defended herself against their onslaught. On occasion, he had even resented her for her intrusion into his world, but now, as she stood facing him with her humble countenance, he realized he would have been willing to give his very life to protect her from further harm. The vulnerability of her predicament overwhelmed him with unexpected suddenness and he strode toward the window, turning his eyes away from her as if it would perhaps alleviate some of the guilt he was experiencing at that precise moment.

Rebecca's heart was still troubled by the recent emotional upheaval she had suffered, but she remained at a loss as to how to convince the man that she bore him no blame. She stood fast, gazing at his back from across the stateroom. "Captain Jameson," she murmured. "I'm not angry with you, sir. How could I be?" She stepped closer to where he stood while she continued speaking. "You've been a safe haven in the midst of this storm I happened into, and I owe you a debt of gratitude that I know I can never repay. My only fear is that your act of kindness will be one day be overshadowed by a burden of responsibility that you no longer wish to bear, and the last thing I want to do is burden you with that responsibility, sir," she whispered.

He cast a quick glance over his shoulder and she was quick to note the pained expression that darkened his features as he turned back to stare out the window.

"As I've said before," he rebuked, "you are no burden to me."

The atmosphere in the small room was charged with guilt and remorse, both from the captain as well as from the girl. Rebecca was aware that she had offended the captain with her decision to leave, and she only hoped she could somehow help him to better understand her intentions. "Captain Jameson, may I share one of my favorite scripture verses with you?" she asked in a soft voice.

He glanced again over his shoulder to see her studying him with an expression of humility instead of one of resentment, and he gave a quick nod of acquiescence.

Rebecca recited the simple verse in a reverent tone. *"My frame was not hidden from You when I was made in the secret place. When I was woven together in the depths of the earth, your eyes saw my unformed body, and all of the days ordained for me were written in your book before even one of them came to be..."*

A quiet assurance rested on her features while she began to explain her thoughts to him. "I had my own plans established long ago, Captain, but the Lord determined He had more important things for me to accomplish first, and so I believe he brought me here, to the Redemption. I don't know why just yet, or for what purpose I'm here for, but I do know that even these days were ordained for me by my heavenly father, and one day

His perfect will shall be revealed to me. Until then, I will trust that nothing can happen to me that is outside of that will, and so you needn't feel responsible for what has come to pass, just as I don't hold you accountable for it."

"Are you telling me that you believe your god brought this entire situation about on purpose?" he scoffed, an incredulous look upon his face.

"Not so much brought it about, Captain, but rather, allowed it to happen," she replied. "God has His plan for my life set in place, and even though I may not be aware of it just yet, I know that He is in control and I remain willing to go where that plan leads me. His ways are so much higher than mine, and although His plan for my life may not always lead me down the comfortable path, I trust Him enough to know that it is the right path."

He continued to study her and saw that she exuded a peace he had not thought possible for one in her predicament, yet she stood resolute, confident in both mind and spirit. In the past, he had considered her very fortunate at having been able to conceal her true identity for so long and had even attributed her success to pure luck, nothing more. However, after hearing of the myriad of harrowing experiences that she had been spared from since she had been abducted, he wondered if there wasn't some greater power at work in her life. He observed her for a moment longer, wondering as to the curious nature of this god she served, and then shook his head in contrite repentance. "I am truly sorry," he offered once more.

"I know, sir," Rebecca whispered. "And I forgive you."

He knew without a doubt that the words she spoke were uttered with all truthfulness and he again wondered why he had ever questioned her integrity in the first place. With a sigh of remorse he averted his gaze, bringing the book he held into view. Glancing back to where she stood he contemplated her for a time, and then said with curious intrigue, "Tell me…what is it you've learned about me thus far from the book?"

Rebecca pondered his words carefully, trying to formulate an adequate response in such a short amount of time. After several moments of deliberation she began to speak in a quiet voice. "I've learned that you are a man of integrity and that you favor harmony over discord. You prefer a life of solitude rather than one of renown, even though the reputation you've established is of critical importance to you. You seek to pursue justice, and you have been faithful to uphold that justice for those who are privileged to call you their captain. You demonstrate a great capacity for mercy but do not hesitate to enforce discipline when the situation warrants it, which is why you have gained both the confidence and the respect of your men, and of me, sir." She paused to consider her reflective summation, and then affirmed in a sincere tone, "I've learned that you are a good man, Captain Jameson, and I trust you with my life."

He found himself rendered speechless by her generous and expressive depiction of his character. "You've learned all of that from the book?" he teased through a wry grin, somewhat humbled by her lavish praise.

"No, Captain," she corrected with a confident air, "I've learned all of that from watching *you*. The book, sir, does not do you justice."

He was again silenced by her gracious response and realized that he had never before felt so undeserving of praise. He hesitated for a time, studying her with humble intrigue, and then remarked in a low tone, "I don't know what to say..."

"You don't have to say anything, sir," she murmured. "I spoke the truth. But may I have the book? I'd like to finish it."

"The book?"

She reached out to take the book from his hand. "The book," she smiled, holding it up before him. As she prepared to leave the confines of his stateroom she whispered with a grateful heart, "Thank you...for making me stay, Captain Jameson."

His look of surprise caught her off guard, causing an infectious giggle to bubble up within her. He studied her retreating form disappearing into the corridor, the sound of her laughter trailing behind her as she went on her way, and he couldn't help but wonder why her god had deemed him worthy of seeing her home.

Chapter 8

THE SEAS HAD been calm for the past two days and the ship listed about in the hot sun. Rebecca had been working on deck with Mr. Andrews, and listened with an attentive ear as he tried to teach her the complicated language of seamanship.

"Man the braces!" he called to her.

Rebecca thought frantically, trying to recall what the command meant. Shaking her head in confusion, he called out another.

"Hoist the rigging!"

Rebecca continued to appear perplexed and again shook her head.

"Ship to larboard!"

Rebecca's eyes lit up as she pointed a confident finger toward the port side of the frigate and shouted, "That way!"

He laughed at her exuberance with having finally gotten something right.

"You'd best not laugh at me, matey, or I'll string ye up with these ropes!" she called out in mock imitation of him.

"Lanyards," he corrected. "And it'd take a lot more than those tiny things to string up an old neck like mine, Missy."

She slid down next to him on the deck to help him coil the lengths of rope lying about, chatting with him in a serene manner while they worked side by side. In her excitement at seeing dry land again with their impending stop at the first port call since she had come aboard, she began to speak of her anticipation of going ashore and the wonderful places she intended to visit when the Redemption would finally put in at Gibraltar. Glancing into the wizened, old face of the petty officer she asked, "What about you, Mr. Andrews? What will you do when we get there?"

"To tell you the truth, Missy, I don't care much for going ashore," he remarked. "Just leads to trouble of some sort... getting robbed blind or just plum drunk. But you know, don't you, that the captain wouldn't think of letting you go ashore by yourself, what with all the men lurking about 'n all."

"But he already told me I could go into the city," she assured in a defensive tone.

The petty officer gave her a skeptical look, knowing full well that the girl would never set foot on dry land unattended.

"Well, Captain Jameson did request that I be accompanied by Lieutenant Burgess," she added.

"Oh he did, did he?" he teased. "No doubt he'll keep a close enough eye on you, I'll guarantee you that."

Rebecca peered at the man with an indignant scowl and tossed a piece of rigging at him saying, "I've never relied on a man for protection before, Mr. Andrews, and I certainly don't need one now, especially one who abhors my presence."

"Well you sure don't want to end up on another frigate do you? Now that we've finally gotten used to your finicky ways and such!" he teased.

She laughed then, and paused to reflect on the situation. She very much wanted to see the sights of Gibraltar, but the thought of going ashore with Mr. Burgess terrified her. She had hoped she could convince Mr. Andrews to go ashore with her, even though the captain had been adamant that she be accompanied by the young lieutenant. She slipped into a pensive silence while they continued to work. "I suppose I'll just have to figure out a way to get off by myself for a bit then," she mused.

"Don't you even consider doing such a thing!" he admonished, his mind conjuring up disturbing images of her surrounded by and at the mercy of hordes of drunken sailors. No doubt, he determined with a grim countenance, he'd best formulate a backup plan to look after her in the event that she was intent on pursuing such a foolish notion, while he contemplated for the remainder of the afternoon how best to keep her safe. He was unwavering in his resolve to see that she was protected from harm lest she fall into the hands of a less genteel crew.

Rebecca spent most of the next day in the sick berth with Dr. Ammons, taking an inventory of the herbs and tinctures that remained in the supply cupboard. She had formulated a grandiose scheme of visiting an apothecary shop while in Gibraltar and she was anxious to introduce the good doctor to some of the more useful and effective medicinal remedies that her father had always stocked his shelves with. She continued on in an animated prattle, thrilled at being able to share some fascinating, new tidbit of information with him. Without pausing for breath she proceeded to ramble several names of tonics and potions she could recall from the recollections of her younger years.

"There's milk thistle...wonderful for infections, bladderwort, hawthorne berry...oh! And fenugreek. Surely you've heard of fenugreek?"

Without waiting for an answer she pressed on, while Dr. Ammons listened with an attentive ear. Her excitement was exhausting, yet he did not want to dissuade her from her good intentions, especially when they were bringing her so much joy. He found himself impressed by her knowledge of curative matters and he had even picked up some intriguing ideas from her unending chatter, during which she spoke of the experiences she had shared while working alongside her father. He would not encourage her to seek out an apothecary shop he decided, simply out of sheer concern for her safety, but neither would he discourage her lest he thwart her enthusiasm.

The Redemption sailed into port in the early afternoon of the following day. Rebecca made sure that she was ready to disembark well before it was necessary, and she spent the rest of the time pacing around her small berth fretting about having to go ashore with Lieutenant Burgess. A knock at the door distracted her from her anxious deliberation, and she opened it to find Captain Jameson standing before her.

"I trust you are ready for your venture into town?" he asked.

"Oh yes," she breathed. "I can hardly wait to set foot on dry land again. But please, sir, may I go ashore by myself? I really would manage just fine, and I do hate to impose on Mr. Burgess on his only day of shore leave...."

She implored him with eyes full of hopeful persuasion, willing him to consent to her one, small request, but instead he answered, "No, I'm afraid it wouldn't be safe to have you wandering about town on your own. Never-the-less, I will instruct Mr. Burgess to see that you are able to call on the places you wish to visit, however I must insist that you be accompanied by an officer."

"Please, Captain," she continued, "I won't stay long...just there and back again."

Captain Jameson, unaccustomed to arguments from his men, gave her an unsympathetic scowl of reproach and said, "If you insist on pursuing the matter, Miss Halloway, I will see that you remain onboard."

"Alright, sir," she conceded with resignation, "I'll do as you say." She was grateful that he was allowing her to go ashore at all and was hesitant to voice anything more that would cause him to reconsider his decision.

"Very well," he replied. "I would like to give you some money in compensation for your many hours of service aboard my ship," he said, taking an envelope from his breast pocket.

"Thank you, Captain, but it's really not necessary," she assured him. "You see, I was fortunate to win several hands of Whist these past few weeks so I can assure you, my pockets are not empty."

He studied her with mixture of feigned shock and consternation. "You deign to play cards?" he teased. "I'm surprised at you…having lowered yourself to partake in the activities of the heathen."

Rebecca's countenance took on a playful and innocent charm as she replied, "One cannot produce a fine wine without first going into the vineyards and toiling in the dirt, Captain."

A boisterous chuckle of delight escaped him at hearing her words and she giggled along with him. He wondered what had ever given his life meaning before she came aboard, while he contemplated how he would ever go on in her absence. Having her onboard the frigate had given him a purpose that forced him to look beyond himself, and created a lively joviality on the ship as well. For the first time in his many years as a sea captain he found himself regretting his decision to relinquish a family for the sake of commanding men at sea. Still grinning, he took her by the elbow to lead her towards the deck, certain that his officer was anticipating an early departure.

Rebecca and Lieutenant Burgess were among the first group taken ashore. They were joined by Lieutenant Edwards and several midshipmen that Rebecca recognized, but did not know by name. She remained pensive during the short trip, and disembarked with restless agitation, her stomach a bundle of nerves as she awaited the orders of the officer who accompanied her.

Without acknowledging her presence, Lieutenants Burgess and Edwards stepped from the dinghy and ambled up the craggy path towards the town, speaking in quiet voices amongst themselves and casting indifferent glances back on occasion to see if the girl followed them. Rebecca trailed several feet behind the two officers for a time, until they finally came to a halt in front of a tavern. The noise inside was deafening, even at this early hour, and Rebecca was suddenly jolted by the dreadful memory of the assault on the shoreline of Portsmouth and the subsequent abduction from her home. Overcome with panic, her heart began to pound in her chest and she cast an uneasy glance through the faces in the crowds, expecting to see the men who had accosted her appear without warning before her. Her eyes continued to dart over her shoulders, her breath coming in short, ragged gasps, until the voice of Lieutenant Burgess stirred her to attention.

"Well, come on then. You're under captain's orders to remain with me until we return to the Redemption."

"Please," she whispered, "can I just wait out here for you?"

"No." he scowled.

Rebecca stood firm, her gaze fixed on the tavern, while she tried with desperation to summon the courage to enter with the officers.

"What's the matter?" Lieutenant Edwards sneered. "Think you're too good for the likes of them, do you? From what I've heard you seem to consider yourself more appealing to men of a higher rank."

Rebecca was stunned by the malicious comment, fully aware that Mr. Edwards was referring to the incident that had occurred with the admiral at Captain Jameson's dinner party. She remained silent, her legs still trembling at the thought of entering the dark tavern.

"If you aren't going to come with us," Lieutenant Burgess warned, "I can certainly find some other officer who would make better use of your company tonight."

Rebecca stumbled forward in quiet submission, realizing with alarm that her safety had been entrusted to the one who most loathed her presence. Moving into the protection of their circle, the three entered the building. There were sailors everywhere, some staggering about, and others appearing as if they had passed out hours ago. Scantily clad women roamed about the room advertising things that shamed Rebecca and brought a warm flush of humiliation to her face. She kept her gaze averted from all who looked upon her lest she attract the attention of someone seeking female companionship, while she followed the two officers to a table near the center of the room.

Back on the deck of the Redemption, Petty Officer Andrews was climbing into the dinghy that would carry him across the waves to Gibraltar. The girl seemed to have planned an agenda of her own he realized, and he doubted she would remain with the lieutenant for the duration of the evening. As much as he disliked being ashore when the frigate was in port, he couldn't bear the thought of harm befalling the girl. The trip on the dinghy lasted less than ten minutes, and when he felt the skiff scrape the sands of the shoreline he hurried over the side, unsure of where to go. Before long, he chose to place himself in a large, central district that was surrounded by various taverns and pubs. It was a place where the girl would be easy to spot should she make an attempt to venture off on her own as she had contemplated doing. Taking a seat in the center of the circle, he watched and waited, examining every face that came and went, while he realized with a heavy sigh that it was going to be a long night.

Inside the tavern, the lieutenants ordered a round of ale, placing a large mug of the pungent liquid in front of Rebecca in a subtle taunt. With barely a glance she left it where it sat, training her focus instead on the raucous crowd which surrounded her. The officers continued to talk to one another, oblivious to her presence, and Rebecca was relieved at not having to make conversation with them. Instead, she scrutinized the activities of the pub with a wary eye. She had never set foot in an establishment such as this before tonight and she felt violated somehow at having been forced in here against her will. She cringed when men moving past her brazenly brushed against her body, some even blatantly reaching out to grab her in their drunken state, while the officers remained indifferent to her discomfort. It wasn't long before a buxom woman cast herself without shame between Rebecca and Lieutenant Burgess, bringing a loud chortle of laughter from Lieutenant Edwards, who encouraged the woman in the lewd activities that were to his delight, humiliating Rebecca and bringing a bright stain of crimson to her cheeks. She began to feel nauseated by the wanton carnality displayed before her and tried with desperation to think of a way in which to remove herself from the tavern without bringing the wrath of the officers down upon her. Rebecca needn't have worried about the wrath of the officer's however, as without warning a glass bottle shattered with vehemence against a wall, sending fine shards of glass flying in all directions. She spun about in alarm to observe the commotion erupting behind her and was stunned to see two men staggering to their feet to pace menacingly around one another. In their drunken state they staggered, fists clenched in fury near their sides. Rebecca remained glued to her seat and continued to watch, even though all common sense told her to flee. The tavern erupted in chaos when the first blow landed and the vicious confrontation soon spiraled out of control, with various patrons beginning to join in on the brawl. Rebecca was unaware of the people scrambling to move out of the path of the onslaught and instead kept her eyes fixed on the horrifying scene playing out before her, her mouth gaping open in stunned disbelief.

Lieutenants Burgess and Edwards were enjoying the melee, having had little to distract them from the monotony of being at sea for the past several months, and moving toward the safety of the tavern's perimeter, they cheered the men on in their fury, while hoping the girl had had the sense to remove herself from harms way.

Rebecca lingered in her confusion and stifled a scream when she caught a fleeting glimpse a large, burly man hurtling towards her. He lost his footing when he neared where she sat, sending him toppling over her chair and trapping her beneath him, crushed by the weight of his massive frame. She cried out in pain and fought the urge to panic as the air was pushed from her lungs. Desperate for a breath of air, she struggled to crawl to safety, her heart catching in her throat at the steel clad boots stomping precariously close to her head. When she felt the man roll a bit to the left, she scrambled out with frantic haste from where she lay pinned beneath him, desperate to escape the angry brawl which continued to rage around her.

The chaos was escalating but the two officers remained in the safety of the tavern's perimeter, enjoying the excitement of the moment. It would have been difficult to locate the girl's whereabouts in the midst of the tumultuous brawl Lieutenant Burgess determined, so neither he nor Lieutenant Edwards made an attempt to search for her. Instead, they ordered a round of rum to sip on until the boisterous activity quieted a bit.

Mr. Andrews heard the commotion from where he lingered and he began to grow restless while he waited for the girl to appear. The activities of the evening were growing more unruly, as they usually did when the town was overcome by sailors who had been at sea for too long. When he heard the fight break out, his first thoughts were of his shipmates, and he hoped that none of them were involved in the scuffle, having been in one too many himself on occasion. He studied a group of people who were stumbling from a tavern off to his left, no doubt hoping to remove themselves from the path of flying fists. Without warning he saw the girl appear, and he would have missed her had he turned his head, for she was fleeing in a panic stricken manner, almost as if being pursued by the devil himself. He jumped to his feet to follow after her lest he lose her in the midst of the unruly crowd.

Rebecca darted through the throngs of people, desperate to escape from this nightmare, yet unsure of where to go. She twisted her head from side to side, glancing about in the hopes of finding someone she might recognize from the Redemption. In the distance she could see the lights of the frigate glimmering in the harbor and she turned to dart in that direction. Without warning, she felt herself being caught up in a sinewy grasp which seized her from behind. Rebecca struggled to free herself and cried out, "Let me go!"

"Missy! It's just me...hold up there!"

She spun around to peer into the familiar face of Petty Officer Andrews before allowing herself to crumple with relief into his beckoning arms, and he could feel her body trembling while he kept her in a firm embrace. Her breath was coming in quick, short bursts, and he realized he must be quick to calm her lest she faint from lack of air. Taking hold of her arm, he led her away from the boisterous activities of the crowd to a place where she could sit and calm herself. He studied her with an anxious expression and saw that she kept her head pressed to his chest, trying to slow her ragged gasps for air.

Rebecca felt as though her lungs were on fire. She could not recall feeling such severe pain since the attack on the Redemption, but now, even though she could not seem to draw any air into her lungs, she was grateful to be in the presence of Mr. Andrews. She was rigid with fear and wanted nothing more than to burst into tears but didn't, knowing it would only complicate her breathing difficulties. Rebecca was furious with Lieutenant Burgess for having taken her into the tavern and even more incensed that he did not think to get her out when the fight erupted. She was prepared for a battle of wills if he should happen to find her, for she was determined not to return to the despicable place, but realizing with alarm that he would force her to return if he found her, she jumped to her feet to flee once again.

"Wait!" the Petty Officer called. "Where do you think you're going?"

"I have to get away from here," she called over her shoulder.

He reached out to take hold of her once more. "I'll have to find Lieutenant Burgess first...you're supposed to stay with him."

Rebecca shook herself free of his hold. "I won't go back in there, Mr. Andrews," she declared.

"I'm not taking you back in there, but I still have to find Lieutenant Burgess so he knows where you are."

"If he knows where I am he'll force me to return. Please, I just want to go back to the Redemption."

She appeared to be near tears, but Petty Officer Andrews was reluctant to let her leave without first informing the Lieutenant of her whereabouts. "I have to let him know you're safe, Missy. There'll be trouble if I don't."

"I won't go back in there, Mr. Andrews," she replied in a determined voice.

"You don't have to...I'll see you back to the Redemption myself if he'll allow it."

"He won't," she replied, again making another attempt to leave.

Mr. Andrews sighed, in no mood to argue with the girl. "I'll just go in and tell him you're safe then...it'll only take a moment."

"I won't stay here if you go in there, Mr. Andrews... he'll come after me. You can try to drag me in there with you, but I'll fight you all the way. Please, just let me go back to the ship."

Tears began to well up in her eyes as she plead with him, and he suddenly felt torn between his duty to report the incident to his superior officer and his desire to protect the girl from further harm. Seeing as how he could not dissuade her from fleeing, he sighed again, this time in resignation. "Alright," he muttered. "I'll see you back to the Redemption before I go to find him then."

He was relieved when at last she nodded her consent, and he wondered what harrowing incident had occurred in the tavern that had upset her so. The two began to walk with hurried steps through the crowds who lingered on the boardwalk in the hopes of evading the two lieutenants. The darkened streets beckoned them with a peaceful silence as they moved further and further away from the boisterous activities of the city. Neither of them spoke, while Rebecca concentrated only on breathing through the pain which stabbed at her ribcage, and Mr. Andrews contemplated the fury he would endure when he eventually returned to speak with the young officer.

The tavern quieted after several minutes and Lieutenant Burgess peered through the faces of the men to discover where Rebecca waited. Finding no sign of her, he approached Lieutenant Edwards to solicit his help. "James, I can't seem to find the girl... do you see her sulking about anywhere?"

Lieutenant Edwards glanced about the room, his face contorted by a wry grin, and he remarked in a low voice, "To tell you the truth, I'd rather we not find her."

Lieutenant Burgess gave a curt nod and muttered, "And I as well, but it we leave Gibraltar without her we're likely to see a flogging for sure."

A loud chortle escaped them both as they began to search every corner and cupboard inside the building before venturing outside, where they grew even more infuriated by her unexpected disappearance. After several minutes of grim contemplation, the two officers decided to return to the Redemption to inform Captain Jameson that the girl was missing. He had chosen to remain onboard for their brief mooring in Gibraltar, but no doubt, they realized, he would want to venture into the city to search for the insolent girl.

Rebecca was vaguely aware of Mr. Andrew's presence as they walked along a quiet path which paralleled the main street, but she was too distraught to make conversation with him. She felt soiled by the filth of the groping hands which had touched her, and forsaken by the men who had taken her to such a vile place, but more than anything, she felt as though she had failed God by her lack of fortitude when in the midst of lost and unsaved souls. Weeping silently in her despair, she began to pray with utter abandon. *"Lord, I have failed you. For so long I thought I was prepared to seek out and serve the lost, yet I can't even face one night in a town of heathens without fleeing in timidity and fear. How long will you have me tarry in this forsaken land, away from the company of your faithful? O Lord, I pray that you would hear my cry and deliver me from my enemies!"*

When she neared a fork in the road, Rebecca paused to wait for Mr. Andrews so he could point out the way that she should go. Turning to find him, she stumbled over a rock firmly embedded on the path, and Mr. Andrews was quick to reach out to steady her. She glanced up to offer a grateful smile when her eyes caught a glimpse of a bright glow in the distance. Squinting for a better look, she gasped in awe, causing the petty officer to peer into the darkness to see what it was that she had caught sight of. Through the trees he saw a mission, stark and plain except for a rugged, wooden cross suspended from the stucco roof. The building was illuminated by the light of the moon and stood out in majestic splendor, in spite of the barren landscape that surrounded it. Rebecca stood mesmerized, while Mr. Andrews waited in a respectful silence until she had a moment to regain her composure. Captivated by its splendor, she was drawn toward the simple structure, her eyes fixed on their course. Mr. Andrews, determined not to leave her side, followed close behind muttering, "I'll see a flogging for this, I'm sure!"

When they finally arrived at the mission, Rebecca paused for a moment before climbing three narrow steps which led her to a broad expanse of stone. Mr. Andrews watched on curiously as she slid down onto the hard, cold surface, her face still flushed with color from the emotional upheaval of the past hour. Resting her face against the cool edge of the granite wall, she allowed her emotions to spill over, lowering her head and weeping without restraint. Mr. Andrews continued to observe her, his heart heavy with pity for the vision of despondency which huddled before him.

The unexpected creaking of a heavy wooden door broke the silence of the night, and both Rebecca and Petty Officer Andrews turned their eyes to see an inquisitive woman peering out at them from beneath a dark, flowing habit. The benevolent face gazed upon Rebecca, who was by this time looking quite miserable. Seeing Mr. Andrews standing nearby and appearing just as miserable, the woman stepped out onto the porch and beckoned to them both saying, "How may I help you?"

Rebecca's heart quickened when she heard the woman speak and she peered into the kindly, old face as if she were beholding an angel. "Please," she whispered through her tears, "may I come in?"

"Of course, my dear," the woman replied, opening both her arms and the door wide to receive them.

Rebecca crept to her feet with a grimace of pain and followed the flowing figure into the central foyer of the building. It appeared to Petty Officer Andrews as though she was being swallowed up by the enormous structure, and he watched on feeling helpless and unsure of whether he should follow her in, or return to inform Lieutenant Burgess of her whereabouts.

"Missy?" he called out.

She turned to glance at him.

"I'm going to find Mr. Burgess to let him know you're safe. Will you wait here until I come back to fetch you?"

"I'll wait here, Mr. Andrews," she answered, retreating into the safe haven which beckoned.

The nun led Rebecca into a large sanctuary filled with simple, rough hewn timbers that served as pews, which encircled a small altar so plain and simple that the sight of it nearly overwhelmed the girl. She sensed a peace here that she had not known since she had last been in Portsmouth, and it seemed as if the Lord himself was present in the room, holding her in His arms and comforting her after her horrendous evening in Gibraltar. Rebecca followed after the woman moving with effortless grace down the aisle, until she saw her stop at a pew near the front and motion for Rebecca to sit. The nun slipped in to claim a seat next to her, taking her hand in a gentle grip and holding it for a moment before speaking.

"My dear girl, why do you weep?" she asked in a compassionate tone.

Rebecca's tears continued to flow unchecked, and in her shame she buried her head in her hands. The force of her sobs caused her frail form to shudder in despair, and she felt the woman's arm encircle her shoulder while she murmured soothing words of comfort in Rebecca's ear. The two sat side by side for several minutes in a hushed silence, until the nun began to speak.

"Rebecca, the Lord has brought you here tonight," she said, her voice confident and sure.

Rebecca peered up at the darkly clad woman in surprise, wondering how she could have known her name. She was keenly aware of the peace which radiated from the woman's countenance and she felt as though she were wrapped in the arms of a heavenly being. The nun continued to speak in a reassuring manner, while Rebecca hung on every word the woman uttered, as if they were a lifeline tossed out to save her drowning soul. Her eyes were bright with a reverent wonder and her mouth slightly parted in awe.

"You have grown discouraged in your heart, Rebecca, but I am here to tell you that God loves you, and you are right where He wants you to be. You have been a faithful servant but your task is not yet complete. You must remember His words, now more than ever...fight the good fight, finish the race, keep the faith, and the crown of righteousness will be awarded to you on that day. You are going to be a powerful servant in God's army one day, but for now you must persevere during this unknown time you believe yourself to be in, and trust God to lead you through."

Rebecca tried to stifle a sob that escaped her throat and said, "But I've failed! I ran away from the heathens because I was... *afraid* of them!"

"Where were you tonight, Rebecca?" the woman prodded.

"A tavern..." she murmured, shuddering at the memory.

"And do you think that was the place the Lord chose for you to minister to his sheep?"

Rebecca studied her face, unsure of how to respond.

"Remember, my dear girl...the Lord wants you to minister to those who are hungry for Him. Not everyone is ready just yet...especially not men who are already lost to drink."

"But how will I know who's ready?"

"Wait on the Lord, Rebecca. He'll show you where to go and who to share His message with. And until He does, let your godly character minister for you. You must always remember... your job isn't to win the lost to Christ, simply to introduce them to Him."

Rebecca leaned against the woman and sighed with weary resignation while the nun continued to console her, rocking her side to side as a mother would comfort a child. Rebecca allowed herself to rest in the soothing embrace, making no effort to dry the tears that continued to course down her cheeks, and the two of them remained entwined for several moments, until Rebecca finally sat up to compose herself. Her eyes lit upon a piano resting in a darkened corner of the room, and the intuitive woman, noting the glint of joy which flitted across Rebecca's features asked, "Do you know how to play, dear?"

Rebecca gave a quiet nod of her head.

"Would you like to play something for us now?"

"May I?" Rebecca breathed.

The nun smiled her encouragement and pulled Rebecca to the mahogany piano, watching the girl lower herself in a graceful move over the bench, where she took a moment to peer down at the simple black and white keys.

Rebecca stared at the ivory keys, wondering how much time had passed since she'd last been afforded the luxury of playing a piano. No matter, she realized…she had not forgotten the tranquility that encompassed her when she poured herself into her music. It had always been the one comfort she found solace in when the trials of life overwhelmed her. Plucking a key in tentative hesitation, she oriented herself to the familiar sound, and then with a soft beam of delight she poised both arms over the grandiose instrument and moved her fingers in a delicate rhythm, as if practicing an exercise.

"Do you need music, dear?" the woman asked.

"No, ma'am," Rebecca smiled. "The notes are written on my heart."

The nun studied the girl with humble regard and waited for the melody to come forth.

She began with a simple rendition of 'The Old Rugged Cross', and then transitioned midway to 'Amazing Grace'. The music seemed to flow from her, and pulsated with elegant energy. Rebecca closed her eyes to savor the precious sound, and the sweet music filled the air, bringing several nuns from their rooms in query. As they gathered around the unfamiliar young visitor, they began to sing along with the hymns she played with such fervent passion. Rebecca soon joined them in their singing, giving thanks to God for being so merciful in His gentle correction of her doubting heart.

Mr. Andrews hurried back down the path they had walked on, half expecting to meet up with Mr. Burgess well before he reached the tavern. He had a nagging suspicion that the officer would have taken notice of the girl's absence by now, and he fretted at the thought of Rebecca having to suffer the officer's firm rebuke yet again. Scanning the faces of the people milling about, he rounded the corner and was halted in his tracks when he saw Captain Jameson himself striding with bold steps toward him, Lieutenants Edwards and Burgess trailing close behind. He was stunned by the pallor in Captain Jameson's face, and the lines of concern etched deep into his forehead. A tense silence ensued as the petty officer watched the men approach, and he stood ready to face the wrath he was certain would follow.

"Mr. Andrews!" Lieutenant Burgess exclaimed in surprise. "I didn't think you were coming ashore."

Mr. Andrews nodded his head and replied, "Change of plans, sir."

Captain Jameson's eyes bored into those of the terse petty officer standing before him, and he demanded through a jaw clenched in anger, "Have you seen the girl pass by here?"

"I know where she is, sir," he answered in a cautious manner, unaccustomed to being addressed by the captain directly.

"Take me there," he growled.

The men followed the petty officer back down the path on which he had just come. Mr. Andrews regretted having to reveal the girl's sanctuary so soon, but he knew this moment was bound to come before too long. He led them up the winding trail toward the mission, and when they rounded the bend in the road he saw the confusion that drifted across Captain Jameson's face.

"Where is she?" he demanded, thinking the petty officer had led him on a wild goose chase in his efforts to protect the girl.

"She's in there, sir," he answered, tilting his head toward the simple, stucco structure in the distance.

Captain Jameson peered into the surrounding darkness, in no mood for games. "In where?" he snapped in agitation.

"In the church, sir...over there," he mumbled, lifting a hand to point out the place of worship. Captain Jameson stared at the building, still illuminated by the yellow glow of the moon, and after several, terse moments he wondered how he could have presumed the girl would have been anyplace else. He stood gazing at the humble structure and contemplated to himself how best to handle the situation. From where he stood he was able to hear the vibrant music which permeated the mud walls, and the voices of those who sang in harmonious unison within them. Turning to the three men who accompanied him, he said, "I will return her to the Redemption myself. You gentlemen are free to go."

The two lieutenants and the petty officer nodded their acknowledgement of his order and turned to leave, all three choosing to return immediately to the Redemption, weary after their stress laden night and in no mood to bear witness to the wrath of the captain when he laid hold of the girl.

Captain Jameson waited for his crew to retreat down the path toward the shoreline before he made a tentative approach to the entrance of the mission, rapping on the door with a heavy hand in the hopes of being heard over the chorus of voices. He lingered on the stone porch for several moments before finally entering uninvited. Once inside, he peered into the dim light of the foyer and glanced about for someone who might know of the girl's whereabouts. Finding no one, he began to walk the length of the corridor that would lead him to where the music was coming from, and in no time at all he came upon the chapel where a group of women were gathered. Their voices filled the room with vibrant emotion, as talented hands gave meaning to the once familiar hymns he could recall hearing as a child. Standing in the doorway, he watched the benevolent nuns for a time not wanting to interrupt their chorus, and when the group finally parted he caught a glimpse of Rebecca seated at the piano, her fingers caressing the keys as they brought forth the beautiful melodies. Even from where he stood he could see the radiant smile that lit up her face as she sang along with the cloaked figures gathered in a protective circle around her. He was quick to slip back into the shadows, not wanting to interrupt her beautiful performance, but wanting instead to observe the girl from afar without being seen. After a time, when the voices began to quiet, he retreated down the corridor from which he had come to take a seat in the foyer, where he pondered once again the peculiar nature of the one who had made such an unexpected appearance into his world. A smug grin spread across his face, and he found himself captivated by the revelation of yet another facet of the girl's character.

A small, heavily robed figure interrupted his pensive musing when she approached from the dimly lit hallway, her face obscured by the dark habit she wore. "Why hello," the woman exclaimed. "I apologize…I didn't realize someone was waiting out here. How may I help you?"

"Yes, good evening," he said. "I am Captain Jameson, of Her Majesty's Frigate *Redemption,* and I'm looking for a young lady I believe you have already had the pleasure of meeting."

"Rebecca? Yes! We have very much enjoyed having her with us. She is a lovely girl. Would you like me to bring her to you?"

"No, no…there's no need to disturb her. I'm more than willing to wait until she is ready to leave."

"Won't you join us in our singing then?" she encouraged.

"I regret to say that I do not possess the spirited talent of you ladies," he smiled. "I truly am more comfortable waiting here, if that is alright?"

"Of course," the nun replied with a sweet face, turning back toward the chapel.

The music continued for a time, and when it stopped he felt the grip of nerves clench his belly, knowing Rebecca would soon be brought before him. He stood to pace about the small foyer, and his breath caught in his throat when he caught a glimpse of the girl walking down the hallway, nestled in a secure embrace beneath the protective arm of the nun who had greeted him. A sudden wave of dread wash over him as he wondered what course of action he would take if the girl refused to return with him to the Redemption, and chose instead to remain here at the mission. Certainly she had the right to stay, he realized, but still, he despaired at the thought of losing her.

Rebecca was unsure of what to expect when she saw the captain, for the nun had told her he waited for her in the foyer. Her heart at peace, she was prepared for whatever was to come, for she knew her life was in God's hands and she remained willing to go wherever He chose to send her, even if that meant relinquishing her passage onboard the Redemption. Peering through the dim corridor, she met the captain's gaze with as much courage as she could muster, but her apprehension soon dissipated when she caught sight of the distressed expression that shadowed his features. "Captain," she murmured, certain something terrible had happened. "What is it?"

"Rebecca," he said in a low tone. "You startled us with your disappearance. I trust everything is alright?"

"Yes, sir," she answered, surprised to hear him call her by her given name, for he had never done so before tonight. A hint of remorse darkened her eyes and she whispered, "I apologize for troubling you, sir."

"Yes, well, I'm just relieved to see that you're safe."

He glanced away for a moment to offer a respectful greeting to the old woman, who was still standing with her arm securely wrapped around Rebecca's shoulders, and he wondered for a moment if he would have to wrestle her for the girl's release.

"Are you ready to return to the Redemption?" he asked.

"Yes, Captain."

Captain Jameson breathed an inward sigh of relief when he heard her response, grateful to have avoided a confrontation. He watched as she turned toward the nun, separating herself at last from the cocoon of safety to embrace the woman, while thanking her with a radiant smile for her kindness. The captain continued to regard the exchange between the two, while he wondered how Rebecca had come upon the mission in the first place, for it was far off the path she would have taken to go into Gibraltar or to return to the Redemption.

When at last the nun released her hold on Rebecca, she walked toward the captain with a tranquil look upon her face and murmured in a soft voice, "Shall we go now, sir?"

Captain Jameson gave a quick nod and thanked the woman again for her kindness before he gestured Rebecca ahead of him through the door, where they descended the steps to walk out into the darkness of the night sky. The two continued on side by side down the path to the shoreline, where an awaiting dinghy would return them to the Redemption. He wondered what thoughts filled the girl's mind as they meandered along in silence, but he resisted asking her to recall what had transpired that evening. He only hoped that she had not disobeyed his orders intentionally when she chose to leave his two officers behind, for he was well aware that she had wanted to go ashore unaccompanied. After refusing her request, it appeared as though she had managed to get off by herself in spite of his command to remain with Mr. Burgess, he realized. He was hesitant to accuse her of wrongdoing though, for he was certain he would hear the story before too much time had passed, and he felt she had experienced more than enough commotion on her first day of shore leave. It was with that in mind that his questions remained unspoken and he chose instead to study her impenetrable expression as the dinghy slid through the murky waters towards the awaiting frigate.

Rebecca remained pensive and still for the duration of the trip back to the Redemption. She knew Captain Jameson was upset with her, yet she was hesitant to tell him of the incident that had occurred in Gibraltar. The relationship between her and his officers was already significantly strained, and she wanted to avoid all pretense of being the innocent victim lest the two men see a flogging because of her. She contemplated how to best answer any questions he might present her with, so as to be able to give a response that wouldn't be deceitful.

When the dinghy had at last returned them to the Redemption, Rebecca was quick to request that she be excused to her quarters. Captain Jameson had hoped that she would have volunteered some information about her eventful evening by now, but to no avail. Instead, she had remained passive and quiet, staring off into the distance in a trancelike state. He considered summoning his officers to hear their version of the incident, but he decided it was only fair for the girl to be present so as to be able to defend herself against their accusations. Still irritated by her seemingly insubordinate behavior, he said, "I'd like to have a chat with you before you retire."

Rebecca paled at the request and murmured, "Please, Captain…can it wait until tomorrow?"

He peered down at her through a suspicious scowl before giving a curt nod.

Rebecca, needing no further prompting, hurried down the length of the corridor to seek solace in the safe confines of her berth. She was aware that Captain Jameson lingered behind to observe her retreat, and breathed a quiet sigh of relief only when she was safely hidden behind the door. In her exhaustion, she slipped into a clean tunic and fell with a thud onto the bed where her eyes closed before she had uttered even one word in prayer. Succumbing to the fatigue, she welcomed the promise of rest which beckoned, while the ache in her ribs faded with the onset of sleep.

Captain Jameson was jolted from a deep slumber by a piercing scream. He bolted from his bed and ran the length of the corridor to where the girl slept. Throwing open the door in alarm, he raced in to find her sitting upright in bed, confusion and blatant fear etched on her features. "What is it?" he shouted. "What's going on?"

Rebecca stared at him through a perplexed scowl for a moment before she realized who it was that stood before her. She had never before seen the captain in anything other than his uniform, and now he stood before her in his nightclothes, looking quite disheveled and distressed.

"Nothing, sir," she stammered. "I just had a disturbing dream...I'm so sorry I woke you."

"Then you're alright?" he asked, relief washing over his face.

"Yes," she mumbled.

He continued to peer at her from across the room, the dim lantern in the corridor casting an eerie glow in the small cabin. After several moments of awkward silence he simply nodded his head and left, shutting the door with a soft thud behind him.

The room was again cast into darkness and Rebecca realized she was drenched in a cold sweat. Her heart continued to pound within her chest as she recalled with vivid clarity the nightmare that had pulled her from her sleep. She was in the tavern, the fight raging around her, only this time she saw a large man bearing down on her with a gleaming blade in his hand. An evil grimace covered his face, and his teeth were yellowed and decayed. She made a desperate attempt to flee, only to feel firm hands grasping her from behind, hands she knew belonged to Lieutenant Burgess even though she could not see his face. She was held captive in his grip while the malicious man stalked toward her, raising the knife high in the air before plunging it deep into her belly while she screamed out in terror, the blade piercing her flesh again and again.

Rebecca crawled from beneath the dampened covers to move to the window, peering into the night sky for a glimpse of a star that might shine a sliver of light into her berth. The sky was overcast with clouds and with a weary sigh she slipped to her knees, knowing that the only source of light which could offer her comfort on this night was just a prayer away, and after receiving the solace she sought she returned to her bed, where she slept without stirring for the remainder of the night.

The sound of the morning's activities pulled Rebecca from her slumber, the nightmare of the evening before just a distant memory. She crawled from beneath the heavy cotton blanket that had covered her and pulled her fingers through her tousled curls to straighten her hair before making her way to the rear of the ship. She was hoping Mr. Andrews would allow her to soak for a time in the cool, ocean water so as to ease the pain that continued to throb in her ribcage, but when she rounded the corner near the stern side of the frigate, she caught sight of Lieutenant Burgess walking with a deliberate gait towards her. A tense grimace sprung to her features and she spun back to retreat into the safety of the galley.

Eddy was seated on a stool at the counter and he glanced up in surprise when Rebecca entered. "You're a little early for lunch, Bec," he teased.

"I know, Eddy," she whispered, peering out from behind the door to watch Lieutenant Burgess pass by, relieved to see he hadn't noticed her. "I'm trying to avoid my least favorite officer."

"I told you, Bec, just stay down here with me and you'll never see any of them again."

Rebecca cast a sweet smile over her shoulder before ducking out of the doorway to continue on her way to find Mr. Andrews. She heard his jovial laughter well before she saw him and offered a warm smile when he lifted his hand in greeting.

"Well! You decided to come back! I thought you might stay and join the order," he teased, hoping her despair from the evening before had eased some.

Rebecca giggled, grateful for his uncanny ability to bring a smile to her face. "Not this time, Mr. Andrews," she said. "But I was wondering…do you think I might have a quick swim?"

He glanced around to see if any officers lingered nearby, thinking some might take offense at him allowing the girl the liberty of a frolic in the ocean. "Do you know of anyone about that might give you a hard time?" he asked.

Rebecca searched the deck with a cautious eye before answering, "No…none that I can see anyway."

"Alright, Missy, go ahead. Holler at me when you're wanting to get out."

Rebecca slipped with ease over the side of the frigate, guarding her side as she lowered herself on the rope ladder to the ripples below. The water was calm and the ship was cruising along at a lazy pace. The coolness of the ocean sent a chill up her spine but it was more refreshing than uncomfortable, and she splashed about with delight, enjoying the feel of the fresh salt water on her skin. Her ribs continued to throb with a dull pain but she had no intentions of seeing Dr. Ammons about it, certain that he would bring the matter to Captain Jameson's attention, and she didn't want to appear as if she were conspiring with him against his Lieutenants.

She floated about for nearly an hour while Petty Officer Andrews continued to peer over the side in an attempt to coax her from the cold water, convinced that she would be so blue by the time she finally did get out that her swimming would no longer remain a secret. After several minutes she began to crawl up the rope ladder that had long ago been lowered down for her, and she flopped over the railing with a grateful smile on her face, feeling renewed both in body and in spirit. Rebecca hurried to dry her dripping hair before returning to her cabin lest she draw the attention of one of the many officers lingering on deck. She shivered beneath the cotton blanket that had been offered to her by Petty Officer Andrews, and she was quick to note the scowl of reproach he gave her.

"You should've come out a long time ago, Missy…you're going to catch your death of a cold floating around in there for so long."

She smiled at his thoughtful concern and tossed him the blanket. One good thing about being chilled to the bone she considered, quivering beneath her wet clothing, was that it helped to dull the ache in her ribcage. Ambling back to her cabin, she again had to divert her path to avoid crossing paths with Lieutenant Burgess, and she determined at that moment that she was going to avoid him at all costs from here on out. She did not care for his haughty manner, nor did she trust him any longer.

Both Mr. Edwards and Mr. Burgess had approached the captain in the early morning hours with a request of speaking to him about the events that had transpired the previous evening. Captain Jameson declined their request at the time and suggested they meet after dinner, with the girl present. The officers agreed to allow Rebecca in on their discussion as the captain suggested, and Lieutenant Burgess set out to find Petty Officer Andrews. He did not want to speak with the girl directly, for he was still enraged by her willful disobedience of the captain's order to remain with him. He mumbled under his breath while he walked, grumbling about the ill mannered audacity of the female gender. Seeing Mr. Andrews mingling with the crew near the quarterdeck, he approached him. "Mr. Andrews!" he called.

"Sir?"

"I need you to find the girl. Inform her that her presence is requested in the captain's quarters after the evening bell."

"Aye-aye, sir," he replied, wondering what sort of trouble she had gotten herself into this time.

Mr. Andrews waited until Lieutenant Burgess dismissed him, and then proceeded to the galley where he expected he would find Rebecca. He heard her infectious laughter well before he saw her and regretted having to dampen her cheerful disposition with the message he was about to deliver.

"Mr. Andrews," she smiled, surprised by his appearance in the galley at such an early hour.

"Captain wants to see you in his stateroom after the evening bell, Missy."

"Why?" she inquired, her smile fading.

"I'm not sure. Lieutenant Burgess just informed me."

"Frankly, Mr. Andrews," Rebecca retorted upon hearing the news he had come to deliver, "I don't care to report to the captain's quarters tonight. I've decided to avoid all officers from this point forward because they are rude, calloused, and not to be trusted... except Captain Jameson, of course, but then no doubt his dreadful officers will be present as well. No, I'm afraid I won't be attending."

"Oh, you'll go alright, if I have to drag you there myself!" he assured her. "The captain doesn't take kindly to one who refuses an order, and you've been testing his patience long enough."

He was quick to note the shadow of apprehension that settled on her face when she sighed over the kettle of stew she was stirring. "What happened last night anyway?" he dared to ask.

"Nothing I shall ever speak of again," she stated in a quiet voice, her expression distant.

He breathed a heavy sigh of frustration before he left, irritated by the girl's obstinate manner.

Dinner came and went, but Rebecca found her appetite lacking. She was still debating on whether or not to make an appearance at the meeting in Captain Jameson's stateroom. She knew he had been curious as to what had happened in Gibraltar, but she only hoped to forget about the incident and move on lest she invoke further wrath from Lieutenant Burgess. She was deep in pensive contemplation when the face of Petty Officer Andrews appeared once again in the doorway.

"Now listen here, Missy," he threatened upon seeing she tarried in the galley, "if you don't go down there on your own two feet, I'm going to haul you there over my shoulder."

"Alright, I'll go," she sighed, not wanting to upset Mr. Andrews any further. "I'll go, but it's not going to do any good I'm afraid."

She left the safety of the galley and made her way across the deck to the narrow corridor that led her to the captain's quarters. Knocking twice, she waited for his command to enter, stepping into his cabin with great trepidation when he called for her to do so.

"Well," the captain said, watching the girl step into the room with a wary glance, "I'm glad you've decided to join us."

A hint of sarcasm laced his words and Rebecca offered a penitent smile, wishing she had arrived sooner. She saw Lieutenants Burgess and Edwards seated at the captain's table, both of them eyeing her with arrogant disdain.

"Please, sit down," Captain Jameson said, motioning her toward a chair placed across from Lieutenant Burgess.

She had never been forced to be in such close proximity to the young officer before and she hesitated for a moment before taking her seat, finding herself much too nervous to breathe easily on this night. The two officers stared at her in silence while she waited for the captain to speak.

"Well then, who'd like to start?" Captain Jameson asked, addressing the two men with a direct gaze.

Mr. Burgess cleared his throat and sat upright, leaning slightly forward with his elbows on the table. He looked at Captain Jameson as he spoke. "I'm not sure what she's told you yet, Captain," he began, glancing at Rebecca, "but I wanted to make sure you heard the truth of the matter."

"She's told me nothing, Mr. Burgess," Captain Jameson remarked with an edge of irritation, "so I'll appreciate your filling me in on the details."

Lieutenant Burgess was surprised to hear that the girl had said nothing, expecting she would have fed the captain an entire account of her maltreatment by now. Glancing at Rebecca one last time, he began to give his recollection of the eventful night, while Lieutenant Edwards continued to stare at Rebecca with hostile resentment. "We went straight to the tavern, sir, where we ordered a portion of ale to drink. While we were there a brawl broke out among some of the men, and it was then that the girl must have left. By the time we realized she had gone, it was too late to locate her whereabouts. That's when we returned to the Redemption, in order to inform you of her absence."

"Might I remind you, Mr. Burgess, that the girl has a name?"

"Yes, sir," he replied. "I'm sorry, sir."

Captain Jameson directed his gaze towards Rebecca and asked, "Did you leave the tavern as they say?"

"Yes, sir," she replied, her voice quiet.

He was dismayed by her answer, knowing that if she had deliberately disobeyed his order to remain with Lieutenant Burgess, a certain punishment would be warranted.

"Why did you choose to leave, after I specifically instructed you to remain with Lieutenant Burgess?" the captain asked, eyeing her with apprehension.

She met his gaze and answered with all truthfulness, "I didn't feel safe in the tavern, Captain."

"You were with two officers," he said, "yet you say you did not feel safe?"

"Yes, sir," she replied, knowing full well that she could never divulge to the captain that his officers would've rather have seen her dead and buried than returned to the Redemption.

"Why didn't you wait for them outside after you chose to leave, where they could find you more easily?"

"I was certain they would have made me return, sir."

"You knew I didn't want you wandering about the town without an officer, did you not?" he asked, trying not to sound angry, but growing annoyed by her apparent indifference to his orders.

"Yes, Captain, and when I left the tavern I came across Mr. Andrews. It was he who offered to accompany me back to the Redemption."

"Well why didn't he go inside to tell Mr. Burgess that he would be returning you to the ship?"

"I asked him not to, and when he insisted on doing so I threatened to go on without him. The fault lies with me, sir."

"I know where the fault lies, Miss Halloway," he growled.

"As I said before, Captain," she murmured, "I expected them to force me to return to the tavern and I didn't want to make matters worse by refusing to obey their orders."

"Well, it's obvious that you still disobeyed my order," he said, his face grim.

"No, Captain, I didn't," Rebecca assured. "You instructed me to remain in the presence of an officer while ashore, and when I left the tavern I was escorted by Petty Officer Andrews. I waited for him at the mission while he went to find Mr. Burgess to inform him of my whereabouts."

Mr. Edwards scoffed, "He's no officer."

Captain Jameson realized that Rebecca most likely would have considered any of the midshipmen onboard the Redemption an officer, as she had little knowledge of seamanship or titles. He certainly couldn't hold that against her, but he remained puzzled as to why she was so obstinate in her decision to leave the tavern in the first place.

"Why did you feel threatened by being in the tavern, even in the presence of my lieutenants?" he asked, still troubled and searching for a clue that would somehow explain her insolent behavior.

"There were men all around, Captain," she began in a tired voice.

"You're surrounded by men here, Miss Halloway," he reminded her, his expression firm.

"A fight broke out..." she murmured.

"I know there was a fight!" he snapped, losing his patience with the girl's evasive manner.

Rebecca breathed a weary sigh, no longer concerned with the malevolent glances of the men sitting nearby. "Captain," she began in a soft voice, "I realize this may be difficult for you to understand, but as a woman I'm more vulnerable to things of this world than you might be aware of. As you are a man, I don't expect you to recognize those threats, but I do hope you will realize that they are real to me. I will obey your orders to the best of my abilities, sir, but I would hope for your understanding when I feel that my immediate safety supercedes your best intentions to protect me."

He looked at her sitting there, unwavering in the defense of her actions, and he paused to consider her words. He realized that she did indeed have reason to be concerned for her well-being, especially after having been surrounded by the burly crew of the Redemption for the past several months. He had not considered the threat she might feel when thrust into the midst of loud, boisterous and intoxicated men, even if in the presence of his two officers. He remained silent for a few moments, while he paced with deliberate steps about the room to contemplate his next actions. Clearing his throat, he turned to glance at the table where the three of them sat. "Well," he began, "I believe we have proceeded as far as we are able to in this matter. I apologize for not giving more thought to your concerns about going ashore, Miss Halloway," he remarked. "I assure you, I will have more foresight about the matter in the future."

Lieutenant Burgess felt himself flushing with resentment. The captain not only declined to punish the girl, he was actually apologizing to her for her insubordination! He felt indignant with his commander's decision but could do nothing about it except resolve to protest any further requests the captain made about accompanying the girl ashore.

The captain dismissed his two officers, asking if they had anything more to add. Shaking their heads in resignation they stood to leave. Once the door was securely shut behind them, Captain Jameson turned to speak to Rebecca.

"I hope whatever it was that happened to you in Gibraltar was not the cause of your disturbing dream last night."

"It was, sir," she sighed, "but I've put it behind me."

"You're certain you do not wish to speak of the matter with anyone?"

"I already have, Captain," she replied with a slight smile.

"Oh? To whom?"

"To God, sir," she answered, her eyes bright and sincere.

He gazed at her with a thoughtful look upon his face, struck anew by her humble nature. He determined the next time the frigate sailed into port he would escort her ashore himself to see the sights that she wished to see, and he wondered why he hadn't considered the notion earlier.

"Captain?" she said, stirring him from his thoughts. "I brought something back for you."

His eyes widened in surprise. "You did?"

She took a small, leather bound bible from the pocket of her tunic. Its cover was worn thin, and the pages were tattered and curled inward from much use. Handing it to him she said, "I know it's not very extravagant in appearance, sir, but I hope you enjoy it…it's *my* favorite book to read."

He stared at the tattered book in her hand for a moment, for in all of his seafaring years he had never received anything from a crew member before, and he knew that even if he had, this one would be by far the most treasured. He lifted the book, with the simple words *Holy Bible* inscribed on the front, from her hand.

Rebecca studied his face with an inquisitive eye in order to catch a glimpse of his expression, hoping that he was not disappointed by the simple gift she offered. For one who had provided her with so much, she had hoped to somehow show her gratitude. When she spotted the bible resting on the piano at the mission, she had asked the nun if she could purchase it from them. Instead, the woman offered it to her as a gift and she had been quick to accept, tucking it into the pocket of her tunic for safekeeping until she could give it to Captain Jameson. Now his face showed little emotion and Rebecca regretted that she wasn't able to offer him something he might have considered more elaborate.

The captain was at a loss for words, so touched was he by her kind gesture, and he cleared his throat in a gruff manner to dispel the tightness that he felt forming there. "You didn't steal this from the nuns, did you?"

An infectious giggle bubbled from deep within her chest and she shook her head saying, "No." Rebecca was grateful that the tension of the evening had been broken and she began to laugh freely, in spite of the bright pink color that spread over her face. She waited for the captain to say something more, but instead he simply stared at her with an impenetrable expression upon his face.

Captain Jameson was again captivated by the young woman's innocent and unpretentious charm, and he was searching for the simple words that would express his appreciation for her thoughtful gesture, as well as his relief and gratitude for her safe return from Gibraltar. He continued to gaze at her, unaware that his silence was causing her to doubt her good intentions.

A shadow of uncertainty sprang to Rebecca's features, and in a hesitant tone she said, "I'm sorry if it's not more to your liking, sir."

"This is a wonderful gift, Rebecca," he assured. "You say it's your favorite?"

Rebecca nodded, still unaccustomed to hearing him call her by her given name.

"Then perhaps it will help me get to know *you*," he smiled. "Do you think you might read me a passage?"

She glanced at the treasured book that lay in his hand for a moment before taking it with great reverence to thumb through the pages with contemplation, hoping to find an appropriate place to begin. A sudden sense of timidity came over her, but she flipped the page open to her favorite Psalm and began to read in a soft voice, "O Lord, you have searched me. You know when I sit and when I rise; You perceive my thoughts from afar. You discern my going out and my lying down; you are familiar with all my ways. Before a word is on my tongue you know it completely, O Lord…"

She glanced over at Captain Jameson to see that he had settled into his chair, his eyes encouraging her to continue. Her shyness began to dissipate some, and her voice grew more confident as she continued, "You hem me in behind and before; You have laid your hand upon me. Such knowledge is too wonderful for me, to lofty for me to attain..."

She wandered around the room while she read, unaware of his eyes upon her as they followed her graceful steps. Her melodic voice carried him off to a far away place and she continued for what seemed like hours. He was startled out of his meditations when her voice fell silent, and he looked up in time to see her stifle a large yawn. He realized then how late into the evening he had kept her there, and he stood to his feet in an abrupt move and said, "I apologize...it's very late and you must be exhausted."

"Yes, I am a bit sleepy," she smiled, tucking the bible close to her bosom.

They stood for a moment in an awkward silence before she retreated toward the darkened corridor. Captain Jameson followed close behind her, anxious to see her returned safely to her quarters for the night. Rebecca turned back before leaving to bid him a final goodnight.

"My gift?" he said, holding out a tentative hand.

"Oh yes...your gift," she giggled, having forgotten that she still held the bible.

She retuned the treasured book to its rightful owner and whispered, "I enjoyed reading it to you, sir."

With a radiant smile lingering on her face she meandered through the portal, while the captain stared after her retreating form without speaking, only now more keenly aware of the stark emptiness that engulfed the room in the absence of the girl's presence.

Chapter 9

THE WEATHER HAD grown cooler as the Redemption sailed north in search of enemy frigates. Life on the seas had been uneventful for the past several weeks and the crew was grateful for the respite from combat. Rebecca continued to avoid Lieutenant Burgess as much as she was able to, a task made much easier by his determination to avoid her as well. She enjoyed spending her free time with Dr. Ammons, immersing herself in his vast wealth of knowledge and gleaning as much information as her mind could absorb during their time together. She had an eager desire to share with him the experiences she had shared with her father, and realized that it offered her great comfort to have found someone who could relate to what had been such an integral part of her life before her abduction and subsequent confinement on the Redemption. Rebecca had forged a close bond with the doctor, as well as with the captain, the petty officer and the galley cook, and it surprised her to realize that she was beginning to consider the men on the Redemption her family, and the thought of leaving them left an unexpected heaviness in her heart. She found herself praying often for the Lord to unveil to them all His redeeming love, knowing that it was the only way she would be certain to be reunited with them once again, after they had parted ways from this earthly realm. It was during one of these pensive moments that Rebecca realized just how quickly their lives could change.

The morning had dawned cold and dreary and Rebecca and Eddy hovered near the stove in the galley, trying to stay warm while they cleaned up after the noon meal. From up above a shrill whistle sounded, announcing the arrival of another frigate. They eyed one another with skeptical glances and wondered which frigate it might be, as none had been expected, nor sighted for some time.

"Ship to larboard!" the watchman on deck shouted, his voice shrill with urgent panic.

The men lingering above could be heard scrambling into action, and Rebecca watched as Eddy ran to join them. She remained in the confines of the galley for a time where she knew she would not be in the way, while she listened carefully for clues as to whether it was an enemy vessel or an ally. Without warning a cannon blast rocked the Redemption, splaying the frigate on her starboard side and sending Rebecca stumbling across the wooden floorboards. She regained her footing and was quick to drop to her knees in urgent prayer, pleading for the lives and safety of the crew. She was startled in the midst of her plea by the sound of a second blast piercing the air, and before the third shot had been fired Rebecca was on her feet, still praying, as she made her way running towards the sick berth to find Dr. Ammons.

Dr. Ammons was pulling supplies from the closet in anticipation of the injuries which were sure to follow. When Rebecca entered, he glanced at her for just a moment, thankful to see she had arrived so quickly. He knew she was adept at handling herself in these situations, and felt no need to give her additional instruction.

Rebecca moved to the closet where Dr. Ammons stood, and began filling her pockets with everything she could think of…suture string, thread, clean cloths for wound dressings, and strips of burlap to use as tourniquets. She continued to gather the necessary provisions until she heard the voice of Dr. Ammons speaking to her.

"No, Rebecca," he commanded. "You stay here in the sick berth where it's safe."

He hurried to pack his own apron with supplies while she looked on. "I'll send those who are still able to walk down to you, and I'll see to the rest of the injured on deck."

He hurried to the door, but glanced back before leaving. "Prepare the sick berth for surgery while there's still time, and I'll return to help you as soon as I'm able to."

With that, he dashed out of the room, leaving Rebecca to arrange the tables and instruments for amputations. In just a matter of moments her first patient arrived and she motioned for him to take a seat. Glancing over his body she assessed the nature of his injuries and found a large gash on his thigh to be the worst of the damage. She was certain more men would soon be following him, so she wrapped and secured the wound with cloth strips, knowing his injury was not life threatening and could be safely sutured after the battle had ended. Before she was able to send him back out to fight, two men carried a second patient into the room. He was twitching sporadically and appeared to be unconscious. Rebecca helped the men place him on a table, where she began to look for visible signs of injury. She attempted to stir the man to consciousness as she gazed into his lifeless eyes, his pupils large black holes in a face void of emotion. Before long the small room was filled with men, and she forced herself to turn her attention to those who still lived.

Up on deck, the Redemption reeled under the relentless blows of the French frigate while rounds of mortar continued to fly. Bodies were strewn about the deck and men jumped over them in their determination to hold their ground against the attack. Dr. Ammons worked with fervent diligence, hoping Rebecca was not overwhelmed in the sick berth, while the captain attempted to call out orders over the noise of the commotion.

Lieutenant Burgess had been screaming directions to the men below on the firing deck, as they shot a round, reloaded, and shot again. The air was thick with the scent of gunpowder and sweat dripped off of the terse face of the young officer, adrenaline coursing through his veins.

"FIRE!" he bellowed, bringing a fury of explosions that rocked the frigate.

The men moved to retract the cannons and reload in order to fire yet again. Lieutenant Burgess turned around to offer his encouragement and was struck by a large shard of metal that was blown from the wall, piercing his arm just below the shoulder. He gasped with the onslaught of pain and ducked down low in case there were more explosions to follow. Grasping his arm in a protective embrace, he realized that the shard was still deeply embedded in his muscle.

"Sir! Are you alright?" a midshipman called out, a concerned look on his face.

"Yes, yes, I'm fine," he replied, urging his men to hasten in their reloading of the guns. He grasped the shrapnel and yanked it out, bringing a fresh wave of pain and a thick stream of blood from the wound.

"FIRE!" he shouted again when the cannons were reloaded.

Another wave of recoil rocked the frigate, and the powder filled shells burst from the cannons. They were reloaded time and time again, and the men grew weary with fatigue from the weight of the ammunition. It seemed to them that the battle continued on for an eternity, and they collapsed with relief when they finally heard Captain Jameson shout in a loud voice, "Cease fire!"

The frigate was strangely silent in the immediate moments following the captain's command, while the men waited for news to determine if the battle had ended. Lieutenant Burgess remained below deck, prepared to issue orders to begin firing again if the situation warranted it. The sleeve of his uniform was sticky and stained with a crimson hue, while the pain in his arm had dulled to a throbbing ache. After a few moments he ventured up on deck, where he found a flurry of activity as the men scrambled about in an attempt to restore order. He saw Dr. Ammons working over the body of one of the crew and approached him to inquire about his arm. The blood continued to flow profusely, in spite of his efforts to stop it.

Dr. Ammons peered up through the smoke filled haze when the lieutenant approached, and he was stunned by the lack of color in the young man's face. Casting a quick glance over the lad, he soon saw the bloodied sleeve of the officer's uniform, giving evidence to the severity of the injury. "Report immediately to the sick berth, Lieutenant Burgess," he ordered, knowing Rebecca could suture the wound.

Lieutenant Burgess turned about and proceeded to the sick berth. He felt nauseous and dizzy and a bit weak on his legs but attributed it to post battle fatigue rather than loss of blood. His men stared after him, fear and apprehension shadowing their features as he passed, and several called out to him offering their assistance. Shaking his head in firm rebuttal, he continued on his way. He rounded the corner that led him to the doorway of the sick berth, where his eyes lit upon Rebecca hunched over one of his crewmembers whose face he could not see. He stopped short when she turned to glance at him, a hint of alarm crossing her face. He saw that she wore an apron over her tunic, and it was soiled with a copious amount of fresh blood. Realizing that she was the only one present in the small berth, he turned to leave, adamant that she would not be the one to tend to his injury.

"Wait!" she called. "You're bleeding!"

"I realize that," he snapped, the throbbing ache growing more severe.

Rebecca approached him with tentative steps. "Please, let me help you."

"I will seek help from the doctor," he stated in an irate tone.

Rebecca reached out to take hold of his arm saying, "You've lost quite a bit of blood, Mr. Burgess. If it's Dr. Ammons you want, then at least wait for him here." She worried at the pallor of his skin, and knew that it wouldn't be long before he lost consciousness, but he shook free of her grasp with an irritated air of resentment and continued on his way.

When Lieutenant Burgess stumbled back onto the deck, Captain Jameson caught a glimpse of his wounded officer from the quarterdeck. He called out to Dr. Ammons who was below, still fervently working over the bodies of the injured men strewn about.

"Dr. Ammons! My lieutenant is wounded and needs immediate attention!"

"Take him to the sick berth, Captain," he shouted, casting a brief glance over his shoulder. "Rebecca's there…she'll tend to his injury."

Captain Jameson took hold of the officer's uninjured arm and escorted him back to the sick berth. When Rebecca saw the two men enter she breathed a sigh of relief. She was grateful that Mr. Burgess had returned, even if forced to do so under the watchful eye of Captain Jameson. Nodding her head towards a chair near the wall, she said, "Please Captain, have him sit there."

Captain Jameson led the young man to where Rebecca instructed, while she hurried to wash her hands in a basin of water that had been placed on the counter. She remained calm and unruffled, in spite of the multitude of moaning and bloodied men scattered about the small room.

"Can you help him remove his jacket, sir?" she asked, glancing over her shoulder.

The captain was quick to discard Mr. Burgess' uniform, pulling it from his body as the young man grimaced in pain. The tunic beneath was pasted to his skin with sticky, crusted blood, and he peeled that away as well, knowing the girl would need to suture the torn flesh. Captain Jameson paled when he saw the deep gash and turned his face away for a moment to regain his composure, while Lieutenant Burgess kept his eyes shut tight in agony.

Rebecca dried her hands on a clean towel and turned to face the men, ready to tend to the wound. She gave a sharp intake of breath when she saw that Lieutenant Burgess was stripped of his shirt, and her face flushed a bright pink at seeing him in his nakedness. The two men glanced at her upon hearing her gasp, and they both regarded her with confusion while she attempted to conceal the color in her cheeks. Although she was accustomed to seeing the scantily clad crew of the Redemption on a daily basis, it embarrassed her to gaze upon the uncovered body of Mr. Burgess, having never seen him out of uniform since that fateful day on the deck of the Redemption. Taking a deep breath she resolved to focus her attention on the injury, examining the wound with a critical eye. Ignoring the discomfort that lingered, she moved in close to the officer with a clean tin of water to begin removing the crusted scab that had already formed over the wound. She began to wipe at his arm with gentle strokes and he cringed at the pain that it wrought. Rebecca stopped for a moment to allow his discomfort to subside some before she continued washing the blood away, never looking at the lieutenant's face but instead keeping her eyes focused on the task at hand. As long as she avoided gazing at him directly she could convince herself that he was just another midshipman, but she felt a fresh stab of guilt each time he winced in pain, for she did not want to hurt him, despite her feelings of ambivalence towards him.

Captain Jameson saw that the girl was managing the undertaking with competence and returned to the quarterdeck to assess the damage wrought upon his ship and his crew, while Rebecca continued to attend to Mr. Burgess' wound for several more minutes. When she finally felt the gash was clean enough to suture, she hurried to the counter to prepare a needle and thread. Casting a cautious glance over her shoulder she said, "This is going to be somewhat uncomfortable I'm afraid, but it needs to be sutured. Would you like anything to ease the pain while I sew it up?"

"No," he muttered. "Just get it over with if you please."

Rebecca returned to take her seat next to the Lieutenant. "Let me know if you need me to stop for a moment," she urged, as she raised the needle to his arm. She faltered at his gasp when the needle first pierced his flesh, and stopped in the midst of the suture. She peered up at him once more, and seeing his eyes closed tightly against the pain asked, "Are you certain you don't want anything to help ease the pain?"

"Yes," he hissed through clenched teeth.

She continued with her suturing, stopping on occasion to give him respite from the agony of the needle. After several minutes had passed, Rebecca felt the gash was closed sufficiently and she wiped away the excess blood, covering the area with a clean cloth. She then bound his arm with strips of muslin that would secure everything in place while she examined the dressing with a critical eye, wanting to be sure it would hold up under the rigorous activity common in the duties of an officer. When she had finished she sat back to gaze at him, still concerned by the pallor of his skin.

He gave the wound a fleeting glance when he realized that she was staring at him. "Are you finished?" he inquired.

"Yes," she answered with a kind voice, "but you'll need to have that dressing changed at least once a day...."

He stood to his feet, swaying in unexpected dizziness. Rebecca stepped closer, not daring to touch him and continued, "Dr. Ammons can do it for you. Try not to use your arm for then next three or four days."

He began to walk toward the doorway, oblivious to what she was telling him and intent only on escaping the stifling confines of the sick berth. He stumbled against a table in his weakened state, and recoiled at the hand the girl extended to help steady him.

"Mr. Burgess," she urged, "you should lie down for a few moments...you've lost quite a bit of blood."

If he heard her he gave no indication, but instead continued on his way. After he had departed Rebecca breathed a sigh of relief, thankful that the awkward situation had passed. She then returned to check on the other men recovering in the room, while she prayed that the officer would make it without further injury to wherever he was going. She considered alerting the captain to his precarious condition, but chose instead to remain where Dr. Ammons was expecting to find her when all was under control on deck. She placed a roll of muslin strips on the counter to remind herself to speak with Dr. Ammons about the lieutenant's wound, wanting to be sure that the dressings were tended to lest an infection set in. With that done, she began to clean the blood from the floor, waiting for the sure return of the doctor.

Chapter 10

THE MEN WERE slow to recover from their battle wounds, while they buried at sea those who had perished. Rebecca never did see Lieutenant Burgess return to have his dressing changed, but Dr. Ammons assured her that the officer had been diligent in seeing to the care of his wound. The entire crew, as well as Rebecca, was glad when the action on the seas had settled a bit, allowing them ample time to repair the damages wrought in the skirmish with the French frigate.

The captain had made plans to sail the Redemption to Norway to replenish their supplies, but the ship's crew speculated that it would take at least two weeks time to get there, assuming the winds remained consistent and strong. Rebecca had no desire to go ashore during their next mooring, not wanting to find herself in another precarious situation like the previous one. Instead, she decided she would be content to remain onboard the ship with Mr. Andrews, secure in the sheltered confines of the Redemption. She continued in her determination to avoid

Mr. Burgess and Mr. Edwards at every opportunity, finding this was most easily accomplished by spending the better part of her days working with Eddy in the galley or along side Dr. Ammons in the sick berth. On many evenings, she enjoyed spending time with Captain Jameson, or Mr. Andrews and his crew, who took it upon themselves to teach her the finer art of playing Whist in competitive teams. They often played for coins, and Rebecca, having not spent what she had won on her last shore leave, was able to increase her purse by quite a sum. The money was useless to her onboard the frigate, but she took pleasure in the time spent with the men in cheerful camaraderie, having all intention of passing the money on to Dr. Ammons. She had been anxious to increase their collection of medicinal tinctures and herbal remedies, but couldn't justify asking the captain to divert the funds from the ship's budget, as it wouldn't be considered a necessary expenditure. She had already won more than enough to buy a plentiful assortment of items to experiment with in the sick berth however, and she was eager to turn those winnings over to Dr. Ammons for his trip to shore once they reached Bergen.

Rebecca had been in the galley helping Eddy for most of the morning and had spent the last thirty minutes mentally calculating the cost of her wish list while the crew finished their breakfast. There had been little conversation between the two of them while they worked, until Eddy, who had up until now been oblivious to her musings, noticed that her mind was not on the task before her.

"Bec!" he called. "Pay attention to what you're doing..."

Rebecca glanced his way, the broom in her hand stilled by the sound of his voice. She realized with a grin that she had swept the same section of floor now for much too long. "Why can't they just eat on deck?" she scowled. "That way they could hold their heads over the railing and spill their crumbs directly into the sea!"

She giggled at Eddy's swift look of reproach and took another swipe with the broom at the rough, wooden floorboards, but the scraps just seemed to scatter with each passing stroke. How she wished she could take a long, languid swim in the ocean and deal with the mess after the dinner meal, knowing fresh crumbs were certain to fall aplenty from the hungry mouths of the men once again. From up above the shrill sound of a whistle pierced the air, announcing a British frigate approaching in the distance. Rebecca and Eddy looked at one another with curious glances, but they resisted the urge to go up on deck before their duties were finished and instead hurried to complete the few tasks which remained. It was not uncommon to sight passing ships in the distance now that they were nearing the port of Bergen, and both were aware that it would be easier to finish their chores now rather than have to return to finish them later.

Captain Jameson appeared from his stateroom when he heard the watchman's whistle, and he glanced out over the water to gaze with interest at the frigate coming into sight on the horizon. From his quarterdeck he peered through his scope, hoping to identify the vessel as it drew nearer. Lieutenant Burgess stood to his right, awaiting any command the captain might issue.

"What do you make of them, Mr. Burgess?" he asked, handing the scope to the officer.

"It looks like the Brisbin to me, sir, but I can't be sure," he answered.

"The Brisbin, you say? That would be Captain Stewart's command. Perhaps they are coming with fresh supplies from Bergen," he mused. "Inform the men that we will invite Captain Stewart to dine with us this evening if they should approach," he added, glancing again at the oncoming vessel.

Rebecca and Eddy finished cleaning the galley in a hurried rush, hoping to get up on deck to catch a glimpse of the passing frigate. The deck was bathed in sunlight as they made their way into the corridor, and they squinted against the glare when they climbed the narrow steps. Seeing the men milling about, they moved to the railing to join the others peering over the waves. A majestic ship with full sails billowing from the sea air greeted Rebecca's eyes, and she was amazed at the beauty of it. Although she had been on the Redemption now for well over six months by her calculations, she had never seen another British vessel sailing from afar like this one, only those moored in port with their sails bound tightly to the masts. She observed the frigate in quiet contemplation alongside Eddy and the other men, until the officers began to call out orders to summon their crew back to their tasks.

"Step lively there, mates! We've got a good while to get the decks scrubbed before the frigate approaches!"

The men set about to return to their duties while Rebecca and Eddy remained for a moment longer to observe the passing frigate. After a time Eddy left to attend to the lanyards scattered about on the planks of the deck, but Rebecca remained at the railing, her eyes glued on the distant horizon.

"Rebecca," a voice called out.

Startled, she glanced over her shoulder to find the captain motioning for her to join him on the quarterdeck. She hesitated for a moment when she saw that Lieutenant Burgess stood near him, but upon seeing that his attention was turned elsewhere, she negotiated a path through the clusters of men to join him.

"Would you like to have a look through this?" he asked, offering her the gold-plated telescope.

"Yes, thank you, sir," she smiled, taking it gingerly from his hand.

Holding the scope to her eye, she attempted to locate the British vessel in the distance, and she soon felt the guiding hand of Captain Jameson bringing it into view for her.

"Oh..." she gasped when she caught sight of it. "It's so beautiful!"

He grinned while he watched her gaze at the ship. Everything that had become so mundane in his life was so exciting in hers he realized, and her captivating zeal for the commonalities at sea charmed him. He determined then to keep her hidden away from Captain Stewart, lest he create another situation like that which had occurred with the admiral.

Rebecca stared through the scope for several moments, enjoying the splendor of the majestic ship.

"It's the Brisbin," Captain Jameson told her. "A British vessel much like this one."

"Where are they coming from, sir?" she asked, lowering the scope from her eye.

"I would expect the same place we are heading towards," he explained. "Bergen is a common port to replenish supplies for the naval fleet."

"Will they pass close by?"

"Yes, I believe so. They may even pull sail, in which case we'll invite their captain to dine with us."

He caught a glimmer of alarm spring to her eyes and quickly assured her, "You will not be required to join us, Rebecca."

She nodded with grateful relief, her memory of the harrowing incident that had occurred with the admiral still too fresh in her mind. She was quick to return the scope to Captain Jameson, knowing he would want to keep abreast of the approaching vessel, and murmured, "Then I think I'll take refuge below if he comes aboard, sir."

The commander gave her a reassuring nod before peering out at the Brisbin once more, adamant to ensure no harm came to her at the hands of Captain Stewart and his men.

Captain Jameson and Rebecca remained on the quarterdeck staring out over the horizon in a contemplative silence, both comfortable in one another's presence. Lieutenant Burgess lingered among them and continued to scrutinize the deckhands working below, until he excused himself to speak with another officer. The ship was making slow progress, and Rebecca, seeing Lieutenant Edwards approaching to speak with the captain, asked if she might be excused as well. Captain Jameson nodded his acquiescence, well aware of her discomfort where his officers were concerned, and she wasted no time in making her way down the steps to the deck.

Rebecca was relieved to have escaped another altercation with the lieutenant, and she hurried to duck into the hallway that would lead her to her quarters. She crawled between the blankets strewn across her bed, hoping to read a few more pages of the most recent book she had received from the captain before having to return to the galley for the noon meal, but before she had read even two pages, her eyelids fluttered shut and she slipped into a lazy slumber.

Captain Jameson had chosen to retire to his stateroom for a time, but was summoned by his officer to return just an hour later when the Brisbin made her final approach. He watched the frigate's crew as they began to lower their sails, signaling their intent to drop anchor. Captain Stewart stood near the deck, giving a smart salute to Captain Jameson, while his midshipmen prepared the dinghy that would transport him over to the Redemption for a casual visit. Captain Jameson anticipated hearing the latest news of the war, but the thought of entertaining the young captain for an entire evening was less than appealing. Never-the-less, he gave a gracious smile as Captain Stewart was lowered into the dinghy to begin the short trip to the Redemption, and as he neared the vessel the midshipman on watch sounded the shrill whistle to announce the arrival of the officer. The crew scurried into formation for his boarding, while Captain Jameson glanced about for a glimpse of Rebecca. He was relieved to see that she remained hidden below, and he returned his gaze to the dinghy moving along side his frigate.

The sound of the shrill whistle stirred Rebecca from her slumber, and a large yawn escaped her as she pulled herself from beneath the warmth of the covers. Running her fingers through her hair, she hurried out to see if the Brisbin was still within sight. The bright sunlight blinded her for a moment and she squinted against the discomfort. Her ears perked though at the unfamiliar call of a large sea bird, a sound she had not heard since her last trip ashore. Clearing the stairwell, she dashed to the bow of the frigate in the hopes of catching a glimpse of the strange animal, but before she could determine its location, her attention was drawn to the men who were gathered alongside the railing, oblivious to the bird circling above them and screeching with relentless distraction for attention.

"An albatross," she breathed, staring up at the magnificent winged creature of the sea. Spying the cook among the group, she called out, "Eddy, look! It's an albatross!"

Eddy either could not hear her she determined, or else he didn't care about this unexpected visit from the beautiful animal. She made her way across the expanse of deck to where he stood, continuing to peer up into the sky to where the bird circled overhead. She took hold of his arm and shook it in her excitement, saying again while pointing into the air, "Eddy! An albatross! Look up there."

Still ignoring her, Rebecca turned to see what it was that held his attention with such dogged determination. She cast a hasty glance over the side of the ship she was startled to see an unfamiliar face peering up at her through cobalt blue eyes. His gaze mingled with hers while she stood transfixed by the sight of the man. Rebecca was taken aback by his rugged good looks, and continued to stare down at him unashamed. He gave her a bright smile and nodded a respectful greeting, while a slow grin spread across Rebecca's features in return. The piercing cry of the albatross broke the spell the stranger seemed to have cast over her, and she moved back toward the center of the frigate to look again at the wondrous creature hovering overhead, forgetting all about the handsome visitor for the time being.

Captain Jameson realized a moment too late that Rebecca was on deck and mingling with the crew, unaware of the young officer's arrival. Hoping to distract his guest's attention away from the girl, Captain Jameson stepped forward to offer his hand in a formal greeting. "Captain Stewart, welcome aboard the Redemption!"

"Thank you, sir! It's wonderful to see you again," the man said in a jovial voice, his blue eyes dancing through the brightness of the noonday sun.

"I hope your plan is to join us for dinner?"

"Yes, yes," he answered. "I'd enjoy that very much, sir."

Captain Stewart stepped through the throngs of men toward the center of the frigate, glancing about as he walked for another glimpse of the young lady. His searching gaze was broken only when the lofty form of Captain Jameson moved to stand before of him.

"Shall we proceed below then?"

Captain Jameson led the young officer to his stateroom for a round of rum while they engaged in casual pleasantries for a time. Anthony Stewart was an acquaintance of Captain Jameson's, but one he seldom saw or chose to consort with, as the age difference between the two men was great. Still, he welcomed the chance to hear the most recent information on strategic strongholds, as well as news of Napoleon's advances, for he had not had word in some time.

"You have a young lady aboard, Captain. I'm surprised at you!" the man teased in a light voice, well aware of the captain's disdain for women.

Captain Jameson was puzzled by Captain Stewart's comment and wondered how the young officer had come to know of Rebecca's presence. He was unaware of when the officer might have seen the girl, for he had been diligent to offer a ready distraction when he realized she had come to the deck.

His expression of perplexed confusion must have been apparent, for Captain Stewart commented, "Oh come now, Captain…it's difficult to hide a woman among a ship full of men. How long as she been with you?"

"Well," he explained, "She fell into our hands quite unexpectedly several months ago. We will return her to her home in Portsmouth when the opportunity arises, but as she poses no inconvenience to me or my men, we will not divert from our orders to take her there at this time. Tell me of the news of the war…" he trailed, hoping to change the subject.

"Might she join us for dinner?" Captain Stewart interjected. "She intrigues me with her charming nature…and with her lovely appearance, I must admit."

The captain paused, desperate to think of an excuse that would keep the girl away from this winsome man.

"Come now, captain…I promise I won't steal her away from you," he laughed, seeing Captain Jameson's apprehensive expression.

"Yes, very well," the captain answered, feeling a bit reluctant to oblige the visitor his request. "Excuse me for a moment while I send someone to inform the girl of our plans."

An irritated grimace darkened his features as he retreated into the corridor to find Lieutenant Burgess, grumbling at the request of his guest. It seemed there would be no hiding the girl away as he had hoped after all, he realized. The irate commander stepped out into the sunlight and found Lieutenant Burgess speaking with Lieutenant Edwards, and he approached the men in his agitated state. "Mr. Burgess," he growled, "Find Miss Halloway and tell her that her presence has been requested at dinner this evening."

"At dinner? But sir…" the young officer began, a look of startled confusion evident on his face.

"Just do it!" the captain barked.

"Aye-aye, sir," he replied, turning on his heel with a quick salute to go in search of the girl.

His first stop was at Dr. Ammons sick berth, for he knew she spent much of her free time there. Dr. Ammons informed him that she had indeed been there for a short while, and had only recently left to go in search of Petty Officer Andrews. Thanking the doctor, Lieutenant Burgess continued on to find Mr. Andrews.

Rebecca, having long forgotten about the handsome visitor who had come aboard, was finally able to convince Mr. Andrews to let her go for a swim. The Redemption had weighed anchor, so she didn't have to concern herself with a drifting vessel, but instead was able to frolic about in leisure. She assured Mr. Andrews that she wouldn't stray far from the frigate, so he left her unattended and splashing with lazy delight in the waves, while he set about coiling the ropes lying nearby. His complacent lounging was brought to an abrupt halt when Lieutenant Burgess appeared before him.

"Good afternoon, sir," Mr. Andrews stammered in a loud voice, hoping Rebecca was able to hear their conversation from where she swam and make an effort to conceal her location from the officer.

"Mr. Andrews," he said, in no mood for pleasantries, "I'm looking for the girl, and Dr. Ammons said she had gone after you...have you seen her?"

The petty officer thought in desperation for a truthful answer, knowing if he was caught lying he would be severely reprimanded, yet he was hesitant to bring further wrath upon Rebecca. Several terse moments passed before the lieutenant's voice cut through the silence.

"Well speak, man!" Mr. Burgess snapped. "Have you or have you not seen her?"

"Yes, sir, she's over there, sir," he said, tossing his head over the side of the frigate.

"Over where?" the Lieutenant demanded.

"There sir, in the ocean."

Lieutenant Burgess stared at Mr. Andrews for a moment, his face livid with disbelief. He stormed over to the edge of the vessel to peer down into the waves lapping at the sides of the Redemption.

Rebecca had been swimming deep below the surface of the water, enjoying the silence beneath the waves. She was oblivious to the exchange taking place between the two men on deck, nor did she realize they were both searching for her at that very instant, trying to determine her whereabouts. When she surfaced for air, she released a long stream of water from her mouth in a carefree moment of frolicking.

Lieutenant Burgess caught sight of the girl when she surfaced, and with his eyes blazing he flung the rope ladder over the side of the ship, narrowly missing Rebecca's head and causing her to glance up in surprise.

"Hey!" she shouted, trying to get a glimpse of the faces that peered down at her through the glare of the afternoon sun.

"Get out of that water immediately!" Mr. Burgess roared.

Rebecca felt her stomach recoil in knots when she heard the officer's voice, and she thought for a brief moment that now might be a good time to start swimming for home. Instead, she grasped the ladder in her hands and began the long climb up, hoping he would be gone before she reached the deck.

Lieutenant Burgess was so infuriated with the girl that he began to pace. She was taking her time getting out of the water he noticed, and he was grateful, for he was unsure of what he planned to say to her when she finally did appear. Glaring at the side of the frigate, he caught a glimpse of her peeking with trepidation over the railing, and he stood scrutinizing her dripping hair, for once at a loss for words.

"You will explain this to the captain, is that clear?" he hissed in an ominous voice.

She observed the irate officer with a guarded silence and nodded, hoping not to anger him further.

Turning to the petty officer, he growled, "Mr. Andrews, please inform her when she is presentable, that she is to report to Captain Jameson's stateroom for dinner at the seventh bell."

With that said Rebecca watched him turn and march off, certain, she thought, to report to the captain her activities of late. With a start, she realized what he had said...report to the captain's stateroom for dinner! A knot of fear began to form in her belly, as visions of the nightmare at the hands of the admiral resurfaced.

"Oh no..." she sighed, flinging her body over the side of the Redemption and onto the rough, wooden planks of the deck.

Mr. Andrews peered down at her, wanting to laugh at her and weep for her at the same time. "I'm sorry, Missy," he apologized, thinking she was troubled by the officer's unexpected visit. "I wish I could have warned you of his approach."

"It's alright, Mr. Andrews," she murmured. "It's not Lieutenant Burgess I fear at the moment...just Captain Stewart. I was supposed to have been excused from dining with him if he came aboard."

She lay there for several minutes trying to formulate a plan to evade the captain's dinner party, while Mr. Andrews called out ideas to her in an effort to ease her fears. With a sudden thought, Rebecca sat upright. "I've got it!" she exclaimed, jumping to her feet.

"Got what?" the petty officer queried.

"The perfect plan," she answered. "I'll go to that dinner party, but I will make myself repulsive to each and every man there."

Mr. Andrews narrowed his eyes and asked, "Just what are you planning to do?"

"Nothing too drastic," she assured. "And if it works, I'll tell you all about it this evening."

Rebecca returned to her quarters, a twinge of nerves fluttering in her belly. She tried to rest for a time but found sleep difficult in coming, so instead she lounged beneath the warm blankets until it was time to prepare for the captain's dinner affair. When at last the hour had arrived, she donned a faded and worn set of clothing, pulled her fingers through her tousled hair, and made her way toward the galley to begin preparing the evening meal. She had a mere forty-five minutes to make herself presentable, and with a determined resolve she began to set her plan in motion.

Eddy arrived in the galley a bit earlier than usual and was surprised to find a whirlwind of activity in the small room, with Rebecca caught up in the middle of it all. "What's going on?" he asked with a curious grin.

She turned to face him then, giving him a full view of her disheveled appearance, and he began to howl with laughter. Her hair was tousled, and stuck in damp ringlets to her face and neck. Her skin, tanned from her unauthorized dips in the ocean, was covered with a sticky layer of flour. Since she hadn't bothered to don her apron, her tunic was splattered with thick clumps of gravy and grease. She gazed at him with a triumphant look in her eyes and waited for his response.

"Just what do you think you're doing, Bec?" he chortled.

"Foiling another dinner party of the captain's," she replied through a smug grin.

"You're not going to go like that, are you?"

"This is it, Eddy. What do you think?" she asked, twirling around in satisfied delight.

"I think if you have the nerve to show up at the captain's stateroom looking like that, you're likely to see that flogging you've been dodging for so long," he admonished.

She paused for a moment to think that maybe she had overdone it just a bit, but decided to report directly to the captain's quarters before she had a change of heart.

Eddy stared after her through a bemused glance, as she marched from the room with a determined grin tugging at the corners of her mouth. He hoped that the poor girl didn't provoke the wrath of Captain Jameson yet again with her mischievous behavior.

Rebecca meandered along to the captain's stateroom, her stomach beginning to churn with anxious flutters. Upon arriving, she stood just beyond the portal for a brief moment trying to slow her pounding heart. Her nerves were in a jumble and she again considered cleaning up a bit before entering, but before she could make up her mind, the door was opened in an abrupt manner by Lieutenant Edwards.

Lieutenant Edwards stared in shocked dismay when he caught a glimpse of Rebecca's unkempt appearance. He knew without a doubt that Captain Jameson would be horrified to see she had arrived in such disarray, but rather than say anything to the insolent girl he stepped back and gestured for her enter.

Rebecca stepped into the room with a faint-hearted grimace, well aware of all eyes turning to see who had entered. She stood glancing around in an uneasy silence until she spotted Captain Jameson striding towards her. Lieutenant Edwards made a hasty retreat from the girl lest he be caught in the angry confrontation he expected would occur, and while the captain stood peering down at Rebecca, she made a timid plea for mercy, saying, "I decided not to dress up tonight, sir."

"Yes," he replied through a bemused grin, "I can see that."

Captain Jameson had a difficult time constraining his laughter. He knew precisely what the girl had set out to do and he thought she had done a marvelous job of it. Taking her by the arm, he led her over to where Captain Stewart stood eyeing her with intrigue.

"Captain Stewart, I'd like to introduce you to Miss Rebecca Halloway," he said.

Rebecca was again struck by the man's rugged good looks, and thought he appeared familiar somehow. She gazed at him with a contrite smile and offered him a flour coated hand, saying, "How wonderful to meet you, sir."

Captain Stewart continued to stare at the girl, wondering what had provoked her mischievous behavior that night. Whatever it was, he thought, the disheveled appearance did little to detract from the girl's beauty which he had observed earlier in the day. He took the hand she offered with gentle ardor and said, "The pleasure is mine, Miss Halloway."

As the two exchanged pleasantries, a haphazard potato peel dropped to the floor, sending Rebecca into a fit of nervous giggles. Captain Stewart couldn't help but be caught up in her infectious laughter and he slapped Captain Jameson on the shoulder saying, "Where ever did you find her, Captain?"

Lieutenants Burgess and Edwards stared on in confusion. They were certain the girl must be bewitched to be able to manipulate the captain the way she did. Had it been anyone else behaving with such impertinence as this, they surely would have received a dozen lashes by now. Their grimaces of disbelief passed unnoticed by the others in attendance as they took their place at the dining table.

Captain Stewart grasped Rebecca's arm and escorted her to a chair nestled between Lieutenant Edwards and Captain Jameson, before proceeding to take a seat across from her. Wine glasses were placed at each setting and the table was adorned with cheeses, nuts and dried fruits such as Rebecca had never seen before.

"I see your larders are full, Captain Stewart," Rebecca smiled, knowing the delicacies had to have come from his ship's stores.

The man laughed with delight at her comment and nodded his head in agreement, commenting on the abundance of goods that were to be found in Bergen.

Rebecca was struck by the familiar ring to his voice, especially in the sound of his laughter. She turned to watch him with a contemplative look on her face, trying to recall why she felt as if she had crossed paths with the man at some point in time. Watching him rise from the table to collect a bottle of wine, she was aware that even his manner of gait was familiar to her, and when he returned to the table, she turned her eyes away from him lest he think she was being flirtatious. After the rest of the men had been seated, the steward hurried to fill the wine glasses with a light, rose-colored port.

Captain Stewart began to engage in casual conversation with Captain Jameson, and the other men soon joined in. Rebecca's inquisitive glance found its way back to the handsome dinner guest, and she stared unashamedly while the men conversed.

"How long will you stay in Bergen, Captain Jameson?"

"Only long enough to replenish our supplies, I'm afraid. Our orders do not give us liberty to tarry any longer than that."

"Well surely you'll allow your men to take their holiday there?" he exclaimed.

"This is a time of war, sir," Captain Jameson reminded him. "My men are not afforded the luxury of time away from the Redemption."

Rebecca found herself lulled into complacency by the soothing sound of the men's voices and her mind drifted as she searched for some distant, hidden memory that would reveal when and where she had last been in the presence of this handsome guest. She was startled out of her distraction by the unexpected mention of her name, and she turned to gaze at the tanned face of Captain Stewart.

"Excuse me, sir?" she said, her face taking on a crimson hue.

"I was just wondering how you came to grace the Redemption with your lovely presence," he smiled, lifting his glass of wine as if to encourage conversation.

Rebecca glanced at Captain Jameson, unsure of how to best answer the man's question, but before another word could be said the steward dispelled the awkward tension by entering with the first course of the meal. Captain Jameson spoke up in an attempt to distract the curious officer, and Rebecca breathed a sigh of relief. How she wished she hadn't been invited to attend this dinner party, and she was at that precise moment trying to think of an appropriate reason to excuse herself. Again the man spoke with the voice of one who had most definitely been in her past, and once more Rebecca began to wonder if perhaps she had seen him in her church congregation at some point in time, or maybe he simply bore an uncanny resemblance to one of her father's patients. She continued to explore her memories with relentless determination, certain that she had known this man at some time during her short lived history. She closed her eyes to better focus her thoughts, hoping for some sort of revelation, until she felt a light touch on her shoulder.

Captain Jameson had leaned in close to where she sat and was peering at her with a concerned expression on his face. The girl was acting in a peculiar manner this evening and he wondered what had brought about this odd change in her behavior. "Are you feeling alright, Rebecca?" he asked.

"Yes, sir, I'm sorry…I'm just a bit distracted," she replied in a hushed tone.

"Distracted by Captain Stewart, no doubt," Lieutenant Edwards remarked under his breath.

The men snickered at his comment while Rebecca lowered her head in shame.

Captain Stewart peered at her from across the table, enjoying the crimson color spreading over her downcast face, and said, "I am flattered if it is I who distracts you, Miss Halloway."

"Forgive me, sir," she murmured, "but I feel as if I've met you before…"

"I'm certain I would have remembered that," he smiled, knowing he would not have forgotten someone so captivating.

The steward began to serve the first course and the men lifted their glasses of wine in a toast. Captain Jameson handed her the goblet which sat in front of her and in her distracted musing, she sipped together with rest of the dinner party, her mind intent on other more important matters. Rebecca was so overcome by her desire to remember where she had crossed paths with Captain Stewart that she didn't realize what it was she was drinking.

Captain Stewart began to recant some of the more exhilarating moments of his adventures at sea, and Rebecca listened, mesmerized once again by the sound of his voice. He told them of his travels to India, China, and Spain, and of trading with the natives in the Americas, while he laughed when he recalled the sword fights, the floggings, and the thievery among pirates. So enamored was Rebecca with his tales, she thought she could have listened all evening, and her eyes took on a glazed look of enchantment as she hung on every word that proceeded from the officer's mouth.

"If you're that smitten with the man, why don't you offer to share your berth with him? I'm certain he'd take you up on the offer," a voice sneered in a hushed tone.

She turned to see who it was that spoke, and found Lieutenant Edwards glowering at her. Just then, Rebecca heard the word that pieced together the mystery of her confusion. "What did you say, sir?" she asked, gazing into the blue eyes of Captain Stewart.

"I said my first ship was the Falcon."

"The Falcon," she whispered to herself, "and you are Captain Stewart."

He nodded his head and flashed a brilliant grin.

"Anthony Stewart?" she prodded, keeping her eyes fixed on his while the men looked on in confusion, wondering where her trivial conversation could be leading.

"That would be me," he assured.

"Did you ever sail to Guinea, Africa, sir?"

"Yes, but only once," he replied. "I was commissioned by a missionary family to take them to the coast."

He studied her curiously, surprised to see grateful recognition light up the girl's eyes.

"Captain Stewart," she said in a soft voice, "that was *my* family you carried."

He was bewildered by her comment and shook his head in disagreement. "It couldn't have been…it was only a husband, his wife and their young child who sailed with me."

"I was five years old, sir."

He stared at her with an intensity that bespoke his disbelief while he did a mental calculation of time in his head. The realization of the truthfulness of her statement shook him to the core. "Becca?" he whispered, a look of recollection springing to his face. "Little Becca?"

She nodded, her eyes bright.

He jumped to his feet with a shout and moved to take her in a firm embrace, and she began to laugh in her delight at recognizing God's unexpected hand of providence. While they embraced, he held her back to look at her time and time again. Her face had become a pasty mess as her tears of joy coursed over the layers of flour which dusted her cheeks, and he wet a napkin to wipe away at them with tender care. When she realized what it was he was trying to do, she began to giggle anew, remembering her plan to foil the dinner arrangement. Captain Jameson and the officers seated at the table gazed around in deference, not wanting to interrupt the affectionate reunion, but listened with great curiosity to the words they spoke in quiet tones to one another.

"It's been so long, Rebecca. You must be sixteen years old by now!"

"Eighteen," she laughed.

"And how have you been?"

"Fine...well, yes, fine..." She made a hasty decision not to elaborate on her past several months at sea.

"And your parents...where are they now?"

"Portsmouth," she said.

"They're both well?"

Rebecca paused for a moment before she realized she couldn't answer the man's question, and she breathed a weary sigh of dismay, suddenly feeling on the verge of tears. "I hope so," she murmured at last. She didn't know how her parents were faring after suffering the trauma of her disappearance. In actuality, she didn't even know if they were still in Portsmouth.

He gazed at her in wonder, still unable to believe this chance meeting.

"Well here," he said, holding her chair for her. "I won't keep you standing any longer...let's have some dinner, shall we?"

Rebecca took her seat, offering the man a gracious smile in spite of the heaviness which lingered in her heart.

Captain Stewart couldn't take his eyes from the girl. He contemplated her in silence for a time, and then said through a wry grin, "Tell me, Rebecca, was it you who set Humphrey free?"

Rebecca appeared puzzled for a moment before a timid hint of remorse clouded her features, but her guilty expression soon broke into smile. "That would be me," she admitted.

"Humphrey was my pet macaw from the Amazon," he explained to the others. "Rebecca was fascinated by the creature, and I should have known better than to leave her alone with him...he disappeared without a trace two days after she came aboard."

The officers present stared at the two in bewildered silence, stunned by the history they shared, while Captain Stewart launched into a myriad of stories involving Rebecca, her mother and her father, before asking her to speak of her recollections of Africa, for he had always been curious as to the wellbeing of the peculiar family he had deposited in Guinea so many years before. Rebecca spoke in a soft, but passionate tone of her family's many encounters, grateful for the pleasant memories it invoked. The young officers gathered around the table listened with intrigue, having never heard the girl speak so many words, and with such eloquence, before this night.

When Rebecca finally grew silent, she contented herself by sitting back and listening to Captain Jameson, Captain Stewart, and the other officers converse. She continued to sip at the fruity wine Captain Jameson had placed in front of her, and soon began to feel a warm flush seeping up through her face and neck. Not recognizing the unfamiliar sensation that comes with intoxication, she leaned forward in her chair to take a deep breath of air, and without warning the room began to spin around her. Rebecca attempted to focus her eyes on the table in the hopes of alleviating the sudden nausea descending upon her, and with an inward groan she realized that she had been drinking the wine brought aboard by Captain Stewart.

The men were distracted by Rebecca's restless fidgeting and studied her with curious expressions, thinking perhaps she was plotting another quick escape, but all present continued to observe the girl with confusion when she remained where she was, her eyes focused with an intent scowl on the place setting before her.

"What is it, Rebecca?" Captain Jameson asked under his breath.

"I'm afraid I don't feel well, sir," she whispered, not wanting the rest of the table to hear.

"Would you like to return to your quarters?"

"Yes, I think I'd better, thank you."

Captain Jameson assisted the girl to her feet and instructed Lieutenant Burgess to escort Rebecca to her berth. Captain Stewart stood as well, offering to accompany her there himself, but instead bid her a sympathetic goodnight when Captain Jameson assured him that his officer would see her there safely.

Rebecca quenched the sudden urge to vomit as the dizziness again overcame her with the movement. Grasping the edge of the chair to steady herself, she waited for a moment before stepping away from the table. The last thing she wanted to do was humiliate Captain Jameson by falling flat on her face before his guest. She made it to the door of the stateroom without stumbling, Lieutenant Burgess following close behind her. He was agitated at having to return the girl to her room, and he wished the captain would call on one of the other able bodied officers to look after her on occasion, instead of expecting him to do so.

She meandered with a cautious step the length of the corridor, leaning against the wall for support. Gazing over her shoulder, she said in a quiet voice, "I can manage, Mr. Burgess. You needn't go with me any further."

Lieutenant Burgess continued to follow her as the captain had requested. "You may choose to disobey the captain's orders as you wish," he snapped, "but I choose not to make a habit of it."

Rebecca attempted to open the door to her berth, but had some difficulty getting the latch to release. She felt the arm of Lieutenant Burgess reach around her to lift it himself, no doubt exasperated by her clumsy efforts. When the latch finally lifted, Rebecca was quick to push her way into the darkness, anxious to escape the suffocating presence of the irate officer.

Lieutenant Burgess stepped into the cabin behind the girl, intent on lighting her lantern himself lest she set the frigate to flames with her intoxicated attempts. Without warning, an unexpected wave rocked the Redemption, sending Rebecca tumbling into the young officer. A grimace of startled apprehension shadowed his features and he pushed the girl to her feet with an abrupt force, watching in dismay as she lost her footing and tumbled into a small table placed near her bed. He felt the momentary sting of remorse as she crumpled to the ground, where she lay unmoving except for an arm reaching out to tug a blanket to the floor, as if to hide herself from his sight. He began to walk towards her to offer his help in assisting her to her feet, when he heard her muffled voice pleading from beneath the heavy, cotton covering.

"I don't need help, sir..."

He peered down at her, his eyes finally adjusting to the dim light in the room. "You can't stay there on the floor all night," he admonished, reaching down to take hold of her arm.

"Please," she murmured, burrowing deeper beneath the blanket, "just go. I can manage on my own." Rebecca didn't want to disgrace herself further by losing the contents of her dinner in the lieutenant's presence.

He stood for a moment in his confusion before leaving her lying on the floor in the darkness, unsure of what else could be done, and his footsteps echoed his retreat down the narrow corridor.

Rebecca remained on the unyielding planks of the floor, where agonizing sobs tore from deep within her, both from the shame at the realization that she was intoxicated with wine, as well as from the pain coursing through her head. Too weary to move, she remained where she was to offer her humble repentance for having imbibed in the drink placed before her. She soon felt a trickle of blood coursing down the side of her cheek, and lifting a tentative hand, she moved her fingers in a gentle fashion over her forehead, trying to determine where it was coming from. She found a small gash just above her eyebrow, and kept her hand pressed firmly in place in the hopes of suppressing the flow. She continued to pray in silence until she drifted off into a deep sleep, bringing welcome relief from the dizziness and pain.

Lieutenant Burgess remained in the corridor just beyond the confines of the girl's cabin, torn between going back in to check on her and returning to the captain's stateroom. He felt shameful remorse at what had happened, having had no intention of harming the girl, and only hoped that she was alright. He listened with his ear to the door for the sound of movement but heard nothing. Lingering before her berth for a moment longer, he decided to rejoin the men in the captain's stateroom, and then return to check on the girl before he retired to his quarters for the remainder of the night.

Captain Jameson glanced up at his returning lieutenant. "All is well with Rebecca I take it?"

"Yes, Captain, she is resting in her berth," he answered, in no mood to elaborate on the girl's present condition.

"Good, good. Thank you, Mr. Burgess," he finished, turning again to speak with Captain Stewart.

Lieutenant Burgess took his seat at the table, where he remained sullen and quiet for the duration of the meal. Lieutenant Edwards was aware of the melancholy mood of his friend and attempted to draw him into conversation, but the young officer was too concerned with the wellbeing of the girl to give much attention to idle chatter.

"What is it, man?" he asked under his breath. "You've hardly spoken a word since you returned."

Lieutenant Burgess was beside himself with worry, certain that Rebecca Halloway lay dead on the floor of her cabin. He cast a nervous glance at his fellow officer and said in a low voice, "May I speak with you in private?"

The two men stood to their feet and excused themselves before slipping into the corridor just beyond the captain's stateroom. "There was an unfortunate accident," Mr. Burgess growled under his breath.

"An accident? Are we rid of her at last?" Lieutenant Edwards teased.

"No…don't even make light of such a thing, James!" he hissed. "She stumbled into me when a wave rocked the frigate and I pushed her away, forgetting she was drunk! She fell into a table and was lying on the floor when I left her. I'm afraid she may be seriously injured."

"Well let's go back and finish the job," he grinned.

"Please, this is no time for humor! I'm concerned for her safety. If anything happens to her, the captain will see me hanged."

Lieutenant Edwards could sense the fear in his friend… something he had never before observed in this confident man.

"Alright, let's go and check on her then," he stated in a calm manner. "I'm sure everything is fine."

They turned and proceeded towards Rebecca's quarters, stopping just beyond the entrance to her cabin. They rapped several times with a heavy hand and waited for an answer, but hearing nothing they entered the darkened berth and waited for a moment for their eyes to adjust to the dim light. Stepping into the center of the room, they saw her still form lying on the hard, wooden floorboards, her head resting on her arm. The men approached her with wary glances until they were close enough to see that she was still breathing. Lieutenant Burgess reached to take hold of the blanket that she had tossed aside, and being careful not to wake her, placed the covering over her still form. She did not stir as they backed out of the room to retreat to the safety of the corridor.

"She looked alright to me," Lieutenant Edwards whispered, hoping to put the man's fears to rest.

"I hope so. Once Captain Jameson hears of this, I'll be the one you'll have to worry about I'm afraid," he replied in a grave tone.

Lieutenant Burgess did not return to the captain's dinner party. Instead, he retired to his quarters, where he spent a fitful night tossing and turning, while his mind conjured up horrifying images of the certain punishment that awaited him.

Rebecca opened her eyes with a groan and saw that it was morning. She wondered for a moment where she was, but her first attempt at movement brought the memory of the incident with Mr. Burgess back with vivid clarity. She lay still a while longer before crawling with deliberate steps to her bed. Her head continued to throb with a dull ache, but at least the room had stopped spinning, she realized. She sat gazing about and wishing she could get a glimpse of her face before she left the solitude of the room, for she could see the dried blood on her hand and feel it on her forehead as well, and she didn't want to startle anyone with her appearance. She lingered in quiet contemplation for a time, until a light tap at the door stirred her to attention. Pushing herself to her feet with a grimace, she covered the short distance in a wary silence, wondering who would be calling on her here. She listened for a moment, until another hesitant knock sounded.

"Yes?" she called.

"It's Lieutenant Burgess," the officer stammered from the corridor.

Rebecca remained near the portal, bewildered by the unanticipated visit from the officer.

"Are you alright?" he asked, his voice muffled by the heavy, wooden door.

"Yes, I'm fine thank you," she murmured.

"Very well," he answered, relieved to discover that she still lived.

Rebecca stood listening to the sound of his footsteps as he retreated. How peculiar, she thought, that he should come to her quarters to inquire as to her welfare. It must be guilt, she reasoned, knowing full well the feeling herself after last night.

She opened the door and peered out into the hallway, hoping perhaps she could make it to the sick berth unnoticed to straighten her unkempt appearance before going to the galley. Seeing no one about, she took a tentative step through the portal, trying to keep her head from the throbbing with the pain that came from any sort of movement.

"Rebecca!" a voice called from behind her. She recognized it as Captain Jameson's voice, but did not turn around to face him.

"Sir?" she replied, hoping he would remain where he was.

"I'm sorry you missed Captain Stewart's departure last night...he enjoyed your company very much," he stated with exuberance, still walking toward her.

"I'm sorry as well, sir," she murmured.

"Is there something wrong?" he asked, wondering why she kept her face averted.

"No, Captain," she replied. "It's just that I'm a horrible mess and I had hoped to get to the sick berth to straighten myself up before anyone saw me."

He had sidled up next to her by now and could see the dried blood splattered on her tunic. "Good heavens!" he exclaimed, peering down at her in dismay. "What on earth happened?"

Rebecca kept her head lowered and said, "It's nothing, Captain. I fell...that's all. Now if you'll excuse me..."

She again began to walk towards the sick berth.

"Fell where?" he demanded, following behind her.

"In my quarters, sir…last night."

"Why didn't you call for me?"

"I didn't want to interrupt your time with Captain Stewart, sir. But don't concern yourself on my account, I truly am just fine. It looks much worse than it feels," she replied, continuing to meander through the narrow corridor.

He stepped in front of her then, and tilted her chin with the tip of his finger. A grim shadow of anger darkened his eyes and he demanded, "Who did this to you?"

"No one," she assured. "When I left the dinner party I wasn't feeling well, and I fell in my berth. I didn't think to light the lantern because I was going to go right to sleep. It was just a clumsy mistake, nothing more."

He followed her into the sick berth, where Dr. Ammons sat at a table poring over one of his many medical journals. He glanced up to greet them as they entered. "Finally had enough of her unruly manner, Captain?" he asked in a wry voice, instantly taking notice of the dark circle around her eye.

Rebecca giggled, and then grimaced as another stab of pain shot through her head. "Ooooh," she moaned. "Don't make me laugh, Dr. Ammons."

"Did you take a tumble out of your bed, Rebecca?" he asked.

"Yes, something like that," she answered. "Might I have a bit of water and your looking glass to wash up a bit?"

"Sit there," he told her, pointing to an examination table.

He stepped over to the basin resting on the counter to pour in a good amount of fresh water. With that done, he proceeded to gather clean cloths before moving to where she waited for him. With a gentle hand he dabbed at the gash above her eye, hoping to remove the crusted blood without causing her too much discomfort. He saw how still she held herself, unflinching even though he knew it must smart. "It's alright to cry, Rebecca," he teased.

"I did that last night, Dr. Ammons," she said through a quiet grin.

"You've got quite a bit of color around that eye...looks like you've been in one heck of a brawl..."

Captain Jameson watched with a suspicious scowl while they chatted. He didn't know if he should believe the girl's story or not, for she had been assaulted in a similar manner in the past. If someone had intentionally hurt her, he determined, there would be grave consequences to pay.

"Captain?" Rebecca called, glancing at him through her good eye. "May I speak with you in your quarters when you have a moment?"

"Yes, by all means," he replied in an exaggerated tone. "I will go there now to wait for you."

Dr. Ammons continued making progress revealing the girl's face from beneath the copious layers of dried blood, not bothering to look up as Captain Jameson left. "So what did happen, Rebecca?" he asked in a more serious tone.

"Just what I told the captain, sir, I fell."

He nodded his head, knowing the girl would not change her story. He only hoped she told the truth. "There! I can see you again," he said, leaning back to get a better look at her face. He offered Rebecca his mirror so that she could gaze at her reflection.

"Ugh!" she sighed. "That looks does look horrible, doesn't it," she groaned, seeing the purplish-blue color encircling her eye.

"It could have been worse, Rebecca," he replied, thinking someone may be harassing her. "If you really did fall, try to be more careful."

"Don't worry, Dr. Ammons," she stated. "I can assure you that it will not happen again."

Rebecca didn't want to be seen about on deck looking the way she did, so upon leaving the sick berth she made an attempt to pass unnoticed towards Captain Jameson's stateroom. When she arrived, she knocked with a hesitant hand, and entered when he called for her to do so. She saw that he sat at his table, watching her with a contemplative look on his face. "Captain," she said, "I want to apologize for my behavior last night."

"And what behavior would that be?" he asked.

"I was drinking wine, sir, and I have never taken a drop of alcohol before then. I'm afraid I was quite intoxicated, much as I'm ashamed to admit, but it won't happen again, I can assure you."

"There's nothing wrong with having a glass wine, Rebecca," he assured her.

"Sir, if I am to be an effective witness for the saving grace of God, I must guard my heart and present myself as a living sacrifice. What kind of a witness can I be if I'm in a drunken stupor?" she asked.

He gazed at her in wonder for a moment, again struck by the young lady's humble nature. "I should have been more aware of your intolerance to spirits, Rebecca. It is I who should apologize," he replied. "Is that what caused you to fall last night?"

Rebecca was relieved that she didn't have to lie in this matter, knowing that if she hadn't been intoxicated she wouldn't have stumbled, and Mr. Burgess wouldn't have reacted in the manner that he had. "Yes, Captain," she replied with all truthfulness, "that is precisely what caused me to fall, and I can assure you, sir, it won't happen again."

He gave her a wry smile and said, "I suppose it's a good thing Captain Stewart didn't insist on seeing you before taking his leave…I'd hate for him to remember you looking like this."

Rebecca laughed, and felt instant remorse as another stab of pain coursed through her head. "If it's alright with you, sir," she murmured through another grimace, "I think I'll take refuge in the galley for the next couple of days."

He nodded in understanding and watched her slow retreat into the corridor. He determined he would have to pay closer attention to the girl and those she came into contact with, knowing there were still some who resented her presence aboard the Redemption, and if any were harassing her, they would suffer for their infraction.

Chapter 11

The frigate was just two days sail from Bergen and the crew was growing restless with the anticipation of having a break from their rigorous activities at sea. Rebecca had no desire whatsoever to go ashore this trip, and would entertain herself instead she decided, with a good book. She had been making steady progress through the captain's vast selection of literature, and he teased that he would soon have to replenish his library for her.

Captain Jameson had been careful to keep a watchful eye on the men in their interactions with Rebecca, and had noticed that even Lieutenant Burgess seemed to have more tolerance for her since her accident. He still would not speak to her, but neither did he turn the other way when she approached. They maintained a careful distance but both seemed comfortable with it. As she had promised, there had not been a repeat of the incident that had occurred when Captain Stewart was aboard, and he was finally convinced that she had indeed fallen. Now, as they neared the port city of Bergen, he was planning to take the girl ashore himself, wanting to be the one to escort her to the sights she wished to see, while showing her one or two of his own favorites.

Rebecca was visiting with Dr. Ammons in the sick berth about his forthcoming trip to shore. "Do you know where to find our supplies, Dr. Ammons?" she quizzed.

"Yes, I've been there before, remember? You, my dear, haven't."

"And you have the list of what we need," she continued, her eyes bright with anticipation.

He smiled at her, wishing he could convince her to go ashore with him, but whatever it was that had happened on her last shore leave had obviously left an impression, for she was adamant in her decision to remain onboard the Redemption.

"Rebecca-" he began, only to be cut short by a firm rebuttal.

"Yes, I'm sure, and no, I won't go…I want to stay here," she affirmed, casting a winsome smile his way. "But take these," she urged, thrusting a fistful of coins towards him. "You'll need them at the apothecary shop."

His expression of mock consternation brought a delighted peal of laughter from Rebecca, and she gave him an affectionate pat on the shoulder as she made her way out into the afternoon sunlight, hoping to make it to the galley in time to help Eddy prepare a hearty supper for the crew.

The men were more jovial than usual that evening, aware that the frigate would be moored sometime within the next two days. Rebecca and Eddy laughed along with them as they served the dinner meal, and even sat for a time to dine with them. Petty Officer Andrews invited Rebecca to join him and his men in a card game after they had finished eating, but she declined, for she was in the middle of a good book and couldn't bear to put it off even one moment longer than was necessary. Instead, she remained behind to help Eddy with the last of the chores, listening as he spoke of his plans while on shore leave.

The wanton carnality which consumed his thoughts saddened her and Rebecca listened without speaking, troubled that he would seek entertainment of such a nature. Finally, she could be silent no more.

"There's more to life than women and drink you know," she reminded him in a gentle tone.

"Aye, for you maybe, Bec…but you'd speak differently if you were a man."

"Tell me, Eddy," she said. "What is it that truly makes you happy?"

His face took on a pensive expression as he contemplated her question for several moments and then answered, "I don't think I've ever been truly happy, Bec…until you came aboard." He gave her a fleeting glance, curious to ascertain if she was listening.

A warm flush rose to her face, and she felt both saddened and moved at the same time. "Oh, Eddy," she sighed, "I am *not* the source of joy that you should settle for…"

He studied her for several awkward moments, and then gave a quick shrug of his shoulders as if dismissing her comment. A tense silence hung in the air as the two returned to the chores at hand, working side by side without saying anything more. When they had finished, they sat back to gaze in satisfaction at the spotless galley. Eddy stood to his feet, offering his hand to Rebecca. With a large yawn she pulled herself up, hoping she could stay awake long enough to get through at least a few pages of the book that awaited her in her berth. Eddy grinned at her obvious expression of fatigue and took her by the arm to lead her to the deck.

"I think we can call it a night," he announced. He turned to proceed towards the crew's quarters below. Without looking back he said, "Sleep tight, Bec."

She watched him amble towards the darkened corridor for a moment, and then called out, "Eddy!"

He glanced over his shoulder to where she stood.

"Do you know that there is a God in Heaven who loves you very much?" she asked.

He seemed taken aback by the question, and mulled an appropriate answer over in his mind for a time while they stared at one another. "I suppose I never wondered about it before, Bec, and I've never really cared to wonder either. Never had need to I guess."

"But what if you died, Eddy?" she persisted. "Where do you suppose you would spend your eternity?"

"What difference would it make?" he scoffed. "I'd be dead."

"Oh, Eddy," she urged, "it makes a difference…a huge difference."

He pondered her words for a moment and then replied, "Not to me, Bec. I take care of myself…always have, always will. God was never there for me when I needed him before, so why should I think he'd come around now?"

"He will, Eddy…all you have to do is ask Him…"

"No, Bec," he replied. "I don't need to ask anyone for anything."

"But Eddy-" she urged, only to be silenced by a firm rebuke.

"Don't preach to me, Bec," he warned in a low tone, irritated by her persistence to conform him to her ways of thinking.

She saw that his gaze lingered on her for several terse seconds, as if daring her to continue, but Rebecca remained silent. A tender smile finally relaxed her apprehensive features, and she murmured through an acquiescent nod, "Goodnight, Eddy."

Only when he had disappeared into the corridor did she continue on to the comfort of her quarters, another yawn escaping her in her fatigue as she made her way down the narrow hallway that led to her berth. The deck was more quiet than usual on this night, for most of the crew was below partaking in the revelry of a night free from duties. Rebecca traipsed with a weary sigh into the shelter of her little room, lit the lantern, and crawled into bed. Knowing it wouldn't be long before she succumbed to sleep, she pulled herself from beneath the covers to the cold wooden floorboards, where she knelt to pray for the Lord to make Himself known to her friend. When she could no longer keep her eyes open, she slipped back into the warmth of her blankets, the book remaining untouched on the bedside table.

Chapter 12

Captain Jameson woke early on the day they would sail into port, wanting to be on the quarterdeck to guide the Redemption into her slip. He had not yet told the girl of his plans to take her ashore, but had hoped to surprise her instead. Gazing about, he watched for her to appear on deck.

Rebecca was awakened by the sound of the crew's activities as they scurried above in their haste to secure the riggings. She flew out of bed, anxious to observe the ship's mooring in Bergen, but first made her way to the sick berth to freshen up, as well as to remind Dr. Ammons to take the list they had prepared ashore with him. Before she could make it to the sick berth however, she saw the captain bidding her to the quarterdeck, and she pulled a handful of hair through her fingers as she turned to climb the stairs to join him there.

"Well, what do you think of Bergen so far?" he asked her in a cheerful voice, gesturing toward the shoreline.

"It looks like a beautiful place, Captain," she replied, her eyes bright as she gazed out over the water.

"Would you like to go ashore?"

"Oh no…not this time, sir," she smiled. "I'm afraid I've experienced enough of shore leave to last a lifetime."

"I would like to accompany you ashore myself, Rebecca," he said, watching her face in an attempt to catch a glimpse of her reaction.

She gazed at him with surprise, unsure of how to respond. She had determined never to set foot off the Redemption again until the sands of Portsmouth were beneath them.

"Please, let me show you the sights of the city. I assure you, no harm will come to you."

The confident assurance that lit his countenance made it difficult for Rebecca to deny him his request. She smiled at him warmly and nodded her head, saying, "Thank you, Captain. I would be honored to go ashore with you, sir."

Rebecca spent the next several minutes trying to make herself a bit more presentable. She slipped into her clean tunic and again pulled her fingers through her hair, wishing she could make herself appear more feminine for her visit to the city with Captain Jameson. She had never been one to fawn over fancy manners of dress, but she was growing somewhat weary of the drab tunics she had worn for the past several months, more so in moments like these when she would have liked to look like a girl again…especially in consideration of the one who would be accompanying her. She sighed in resignation at her grumbling, recalling all that she had to be thankful for, before returning to the deck to observe the activities.

The Redemption sailed into to port in regal splendor, while the crew lined the deck in anticipation of getting a spot on one of the many small dinghies approaching the frigate to carry them to shore. Eddy was among them she knew, but she did not seek him out. Rather, she was grateful that their paths did not cross, for she was still uncertain as to his frame of mind after their discussion the evening before. Instead, she stood on deck with the men who lingered, herself in no particular hurry to leave, for she knew that the captain would not disembark before the crew. She enjoyed watching the people bustling through the crowds, and noticed that the town of Bergen had many more merchants set up along the shoreline than did Gibraltar. In fact, she thought the whole waterfront appeared much cleaner and brighter, with children splashing about in the ocean waves while their parents bought produce from the many vendors lining the walkways. She found herself growing excited at the thought of venturing about in the quaint little town, and was relieved that it would be with Captain Jameson rather than Lieutenant Burgess.

Lieutenant Burgess observed the girl from his watch near Captain Jameson on the quarterdeck. She was leaning in a feminine fashion against the rail, where she observed the men who boarded the dinghies with a slight smile on her face. He wondered for a brief moment if she had plans to disembark, and was grateful the captain had not sought him out with a request that he escort the girl, having had his fill of her obstinate ways the last time. No doubt, he mused, after the horrendous situation she had managed to create in Gibraltar he expected she would remain on the Redemption, where she would be safely hidden away from Bergen, and all the threats that the city might pose to the faint-hearted, young girl.

"Have you got a full day planned, Mr. Burgess?" the captain asked from where he stood beside him, stirring him from his thoughts.

"Oh, a walk about town sir, and then perhaps a game or two of Whist..." he trailed, smiling at his commander.

Lieutenant Edwards approached the two officers on the quarterdeck, giving the captain a smart salute before he turned to join them in observing the activity on the deck below. It wasn't long until he caught sight of the girl lingering among the midshipmen, and he too was glad they were leaving her behind, having grown weary of her presence the last time they had gone ashore, and having no desire to see her flaunt her insolent manner yet again. He waited until the last of the men had departed before summoning Lieutenant Burgess, and then the two proceeded to make their way to the small dinghy bouncing on the waves, saluting the captain in farewell as they descended the rope ladder.

The Redemption had quieted after the departure of the crew, leaving Rebecca lingering in contented silence, still mesmerized by the beautiful display of the city. Captain Jameson, seeing she waited for him at the railing, hurried below to claim the last remaining dinghy.

"Are you ready to go, Rebecca?" he asked, moving up along side her.

Rebecca spun around in surprise, startled out of her daydream by the sound of the captain's voice. She peered at him through a timid grin and took hold of the arm he offered her.

Captain Jameson led her toward the bow of the ship, motioning for her to proceed ahead of him when they neared the side where they would disembark. As they approached the ladder that would lower them onto the bobbing dinghy below, he said, "This may be a bit tricky for you...perhaps I should go first."

"Oh no, Captain," she smiled, "I can climb up and down this ladder quite easily by now."

He looked at her with a surprised smile. "Oh really?"

Rebecca would have given herself a swift kick if he hadn't been standing there watching her. She thought in frantic haste, trying to change the subject. Unable to come up with an appropriate excuse, she gave him a winsome smile and crawled over the side, descending the ladder with ease while the captain watched on, amazed at her agility.

The trip to the landing walkway took just a few moments. Captain Jameson stepped out of the dinghy first, turning to offer his hand in assistance to Rebecca once he gained his footing on solid ground. She leapt out of the tiny boat with an air of eager enthusiasm on her face, and he laughed at her delightful manner, pleased that she had accepted his offer to come ashore with him.

They made their way along the waterfront where Rebecca gazed in wonder at the myriad of colors, people, buildings and animals. She was grateful that she had accepted the captain's offer to escort her ashore, for she was discovering Bergen was a much lovelier port when compared with that of Gibraltar. Everywhere she looked, merchants were attempting to draw her in to view their goods. She laughed and smiled, shaking her head politely, while she continued to maneuver the narrow walkway, being careful not to bump into anyone.

"Would you like to stop for a better look at anything?" Captain Jameson asked her.

"No, thank you, sir," she answered. "There is nothing that I am in need of."

"Well, perhaps there is something that you would *like?*" he grinned.

She smiled at him and continued to walk, wondering how she would ever be able to express to him her gratitude for all that he had already provided for her. Safety and security aboard the Redemption, his friendship, the promise of a safe return to her home...she continued to think on these things as they strolled through the town.

"Well?" he asked her once again.

She slowed and turned to face him. "Captain," she murmured, "I have been blessed beyond measure by your generosity these past few months. There is nothing I have lacked, nor had need of. Just being here and enjoying this day with you is a gift in itself, sir."

He regarded her with mock consternation, impervious to her reluctance to let him buy her anything. "Then I'm afraid there are some things I must insist upon," he said.

She smiled again before turning to continue her promenade past the vast selection of goods, wondering what it was that he spoke of.

They strolled the length of the waterfront and then chose to wander into the city itself, finding pubs, eating establishments, clothing shops and more. Her eyes could hardly take it all in and she remained speechless at the sight of it. She saw as women adorned in all manner of finery and lace strolled past her, eyeing first the captain and then herself, most likely, she realized with a wry grin, wondering what reason the captain had for consorting with the likes of a pauper. Paying them no mind, she continued on until her eyes fell on the apothecary shop, and she was quick to note the curious glance of Captain Jameson as he no doubt wondered what had caught her interest. Turning to him, she asked, "May I go in there for a moment, captain?"

He peered at the sign above the door and laughed, saying in a teasing tone, "I suppose, if you must!"

She had hoped to find Dr. Ammons still there, but the little shop was empty except for a clerk behind the counter.

"May I help you, miss?" he asked when she entered, eyeing her with a suspicious scowl.

Rebecca recognized the look of distrust that darkened the man's features, as did Captain Jameson.

"We'll manage on our own, thank you," he stated, taking Rebecca by the arm and hoping she hadn't seen the man's subtle grimace of scorn.

Captain Jameson studied Rebecca as she wandered with slow steps past the plethora of bottles and packages aligned on the shelves. She reminded him of a child in a candy store for a moment, and he enjoyed seeing the obvious joy that came to her through the most ordinary of things. For the first time since he had crossed paths with the girl he wondered about her parents... what they were like, and how they had reared this young lady to be so unlike any he had ever met before.

She glanced over her shoulder and saw he watched her from the corner of the small shop. "I'm sorry, Captain...I've stayed here longer than I should have," she apologized, certain he must be bored to death.

"No, take as much time as you like. I'm glad we've found something that you enjoy looking at! Would you like to purchase anything to take back to the Redemption?" he asked.

"Dr. Ammons has our supply list sir. He'll be coming here himself, if he hasn't already."

"I don't remember him asking for money to purchase supplies," he said. "I hope he has enough on hand until he can be reimbursed."

Rebecca giggled in a mischievous tone. "Oh, he has money, Captain."

Captain Jameson stared at her, wondering what it was that she found so humorous, and then a wry grin of recollection lit his eyes and he said, "Ah, yes. Your keen talent for Whist... let's hope the man is of sound character if it's *your* winnings he carries!"

When they left the apothecary shop, Captain Jameson steered Rebecca in a different direction than from which they had come. She followed without question as he led her to a clothing boutique, its windows full of lacy dresses and elaborate gowns. She slowed when she realized where he was leading her, and glanced up at him with a hint of sadness.

"I'm sorry, Captain," she apologized. "I'm afraid I gave all of the money to Dr. Ammons."

"You needn't worry about money today, Rebecca. I would like to buy you something as a gift."

He directed her into the shop before she could protest, and she stood astounded in the center of it all, staring at the vast number of selections on display.

"Pick out the ones that you prefer," he told her.

"I can't, sir," she stammered. "These are much too extravagant."

"Well if you don't make a selection, I fear I will be forced to make one for you," he teased.

Rebecca felt her face flush with humiliation. She had been taught as a child that wanton extravagance was disgraceful, and that it was selfish to take advantage of another's generosity. Now she found herself being told to spend the captain's money in a shop full of lavish dresses!

Captain Jameson was quick to note the color that rose to her cheeks and thought perhaps he had offended her somehow. "I only want you to have something that reminds you of the things you had at home, Rebecca," he said. "I had no intention of upsetting you."

She glanced at him for a moment before saying, "You haven't upset me, sir…it's just that… I didn't have dresses such as these at home."

"Well then!" he exclaimed, "Let's find some that are better suited to your preferences."

He led Rebecca to a shop clerk stacking fabric on a narrow shelf. "Excuse me, Madame," he stated. "Perhaps you could assist this young lady in making a selection…something a bit less extravagant, if you please?"

The clerk eyed Rebecca with a critical eye before smiling and saying in a bright tone, "I do believe I have just the dress you're looking for, Miss!"

Captain Jameson took a seat against the wall and watched the robust woman lead Rebecca away. He hoped she'd be able to find something the girl would feel more comfortable in, since he was certain Rebecca would've grown weary of the coarse, muslin tunics long ago.

Rebecca was deposited in a small changing room, and watched as the store clerk carried an armful of items in to her. She waited for the matron to leave, but instead she began to tug the tunic from Rebecca's shoulders. Realizing the woman wasn't about to depart, she allowed herself to be assisted into the items that had been delivered, but she did feel a bit silly trying on dress after dress with a complete stranger standing right there with her. It had been so long since she had been in the company of another woman that she found herself at a loss for words. No matter, she thought to herself with a wry grin, the woman is talking enough for the both of us. She smiled in appreciation when the lady voiced both her approval and disapproval of the dresses as she tried them on.

"Hmm, not your color..." she mused.

Rebecca began to disrobe, and slipped into another.

"Yes!" the woman exclaimed. "Come and have a look at this one, miss!" The matron took Rebecca by the arm and pulled her out to a large mirror.

Rebecca stood before the glass, staring at the strange reflection that gazed through curious eyes back at her. She had not stood before a mirror such as this since she had been away from Portsmouth, and she was stunned to see the changes that had happened so unexpectedly. She seemed taller than she remembered, and older somehow. Her hair, once a dark auburn, was lighter, and streaked with stands of honey colored gold. It fell in ample waves above her shoulders, curling in loose tendrils about her face and neck, for she had been in too much of a hurry to tie it back behind her head this morning. Her skin was tanned like that of the ship's crew, while her eyes reflected the emerald green hue of the dress she wore. Rebecca stood transfixed, wondering what had happened to the girl she once knew, and unsure of what to do about this new one who had taken her place.

The clerk went after Captain Jameson, a look of pert exultation on her face.

"C'mon, sir!" she called. "She's got a right lovely one on now!"

She led him to where Rebecca stood, still gazing with bewildered confusion at the figure staring back.

He stepped in behind her, seeing her for the first time as the young woman that she was, and he too, wondered at the change in her, while he stared at her enchanting reflection in the mirror. "Is this more like what you had at home?" he whispered.

She glanced at his reflection in the glass. "No, sir. I've never had anything as beautiful as this," she murmured.

Turning to the clerk, the captain said, "We'll take this one."

"Would you like to wear it today, Rebecca?" he asked her.

She nodded her head without speaking, overwhelmed by the captain's generosity.

"Perhaps you could find her some clothing that would be practical to wear on a ship, Madame?" he asked, turning back to the clerk, "and some comfortable shoes as well."

"Of course, sir!" she answered, scurrying off to gather another round of selections.

Rebecca remained silent, still staring at the strange reflection in the mirror. Captain Jameson found himself enchanted by her innocent loveliness, but confused by her silence.

"Is there something wrong?" he asked.

"Captain, this is just so extravagant...I can't possibly accept-"

"That will be enough of that!" he said. "It is by no means too extravagant, I assure you. It is the least I can do for you, Rebecca, and I enjoy doing it."

She gave him a shy smile as the clerk reappeared in the mirror's reflection, her arms heavy laden with dresses, shoes and petticoats, and when she had finished outfitting Rebecca, she had a plentiful supply of clothing to last her a good, long while. If there was any question amongst the men as to her gender before, there certainly wouldn't be now, the captain realized.

The two of them ventured out onto the street where Captain Jameson paused and said, "Why don't you wait here, Rebecca, while I return to the dinghy to have these packages stowed aboard the Redemption so we don't have to carry them with us."

She nodded her acquiescence and moved to sit in the shade of a fig tree as he departed, observing with a contented gaze the people passing by. In the distance, she saw a group of men ambling towards where she rested. She studied their faces with trepidation, hoping they were from the Redemption, but none of them were familiar to her. They continued to advance upon her and she soon became aware of their lewd glances. Her heart began to pound in her chest and she was quick to stand to her feet to escape their presence. With a determined step, she hurried to follow down the path the captain had gone on, hoping to catch up with him.

After walking several paces, she turned back to see if the men had followed her. Seeing no sign of them from where she had come, she slowed her pace a bit and peered about for a glimpse of Captain Jameson, not wanting to miss him when he returned to find her. The shops began to look unfamiliar as she continued on her way, and she thought it best to return to the place where he had left her, lest she worry him with her absence. Turning around in her confusion, she struggled to remember which direction she had come from.

Mr. Burgess and Mr. Edwards had been strolling about Bergen, enjoying the activities of the city since it was still too early for the dinner hour. They were attempting to negotiate a path through the throngs who lingered in the streets when they nearly collided with Rebecca, who was meandering around in circles hoping to spot a familiar landmark.

"Excuse me, miss," Lieutenant Burgess remarked with exasperation, not recognizing the girl at first.

"I'm sorry, sir," she replied, turning to offer an apology to the one who spoke, but her look of remorse was quick to change to surprise when she caught sight of the officer standing before her.

"What are you doing here?" Lieutenant Edwards demanded, while Lieutenant Burgess stared at her in an awkward silence, taken aback by the girl's changed appearance.

"I'm trying to remember where I came from," she replied with a thoughtful look on her face.

"Who accompanied you ashore?" he demanded.

"Captain Jameson."

"I don't see him anywhere."

Glancing about at the surrounding buildings, she soon saw the apothecary shop on the street corner just behind the lieutenants.

"There," she sighed in grateful recognition. She took a cautious step around the two men so as to return to where Captain Jameson would be expecting to find her, but Lieutenant Edwards grabbed a hold of her arm, preventing her from going any further. "I asked you a question!"

"You did?" she said with surprise. "What was it?"

"Where is the captain?" he repeated in a low voice.

"I don't know just now, but I'm on my way to find him." She waited for the irate Lieutenant Edwards to let go of her arm, but he held fast to her.

"I don't believe you," he remarked, a suspicious scowl on his face.

With an expression of bewildered confusion, she glanced at Lieutenant Burgess, unsure of how to respond to the man.

"Mr. Edwards, release her," the lieutenant mumbled at last.

The officer dropped his hand to his side, and both men stared after her as she hastened to make her way back towards the clothing shop she had come from. Glancing at one another, they fell into step and followed behind her, intent on discovering if she has spoken the truth or if she had once again managed to steal away from the escort who had accompanied her ashore.

Lieutenant Burgess found himself rendered speechless by the girl's striking appearance, and for a moment he wondered why he had never noticed the exquisite shade of her eyes before this day. He allowed his gaze to linger on the sun-glazed tendrils bouncing just below her shoulders, while the emerald-hued fabric clung graciously to her slender form.

Rebecca, oblivious to the men trailing behind her, continued to scrutinize the faces in the crowd for a sign of the captain.

Not seeing him she walked on, smiling in a polite manner at those who glanced her way. When she arrived back at the little shop, she was alarmed to find that Captain Jameson had not yet returned. She decided to sit beneath the fig tree and wait, knowing if he had come by already, he was sure to return to the place where he had last seen her.

The two officers slowed their steps when they saw the girl stop, and scrutinized her as she gazed around with calm assurance before sitting beneath a tree. With an air of feminine poise, they watched her tuck her knees beneath her, and she did in fact appear to be waiting for someone. They continued to observe her from a distance as she sat in a comfortable silence.

"Good afternoon, gentlemen," Captain Jameson greeted, approaching the men from the rear.

"Good afternoon, sir," they replied with a smart salute.

"I trust you are enjoying your time ashore?" he asked them.

"Yes, Captain," Lieutenant Burgess replied. "We saw the girl, sir," he added, nodding his head toward where Rebecca sat lingering.

"Oh, Rebecca you mean," he said, wishing his officer would stop referring to her as 'the girl'.

"Yes, her," he smiled. "We were concerned that she may be wandering about town unaccompanied, but I see that you have indeed returned as she said you would."

"Yes," he said. "Thank you for your attention to the matter, though. I would regret having to search for her again."

"It was not trouble, sir…no trouble at all. Good afternoon, sir," they said, turning to leave.

He nodded his farewell and returned to where Rebecca waited. He was again captivated by her attractive appearance as she rested with an innocent serenity, taking in her surroundings and casting infectious smiles at those who passed by. He stood at a distance and watched her for a time, not wanting to intrude on her solitude, until with a sigh he moved to where she waited for him and offered his hand to help her to her feet. "You look just lovely, Rebecca," he murmured.

Her face was radiant with joy as she replied, "Thank you, Captain."

"Would you like to find someplace where we can have something warm to drink?" he asked.

Rebecca nodded through a large smile, and followed him along a street filled with eating establishments and taverns. She basked in the warmth of the sun on her face, and felt like a young woman again for the first time in several, long months, and she found herself enjoying the complimentary glances she was seeing on the faces of those who passed by on the walkway. She caught sight of Dr. Ammons approaching from across the street, and pointed him out to Captain Jameson.

"Dr. Ammons," he called out over the throngs of people who ambled along the boardwalk.

Dr. Ammons turned toward the sound of the captain's voice, and a surprised expression of recognition lit upon his face when he caught sight of Rebecca adorned in her winsome finery. He wove his way through the crowd to where the two stood, and giving Rebecca a warm embrace he murmured, "My dear girl, I didn't think you could possibly get any lovelier, but look at you!"

Rebecca smiled her appreciation and cast a timid glance down at the dress, at a loss for words. Captain Jameson, noting her embarrassment, took her by the arm to direct her towards a quaint café on the corner saying, "Won't you join us for a cup of hot tea, Dr. Ammons?"

"I'd love to," he replied, falling into step beside them. "Oh, I have something for you, Rebecca," he said, reaching into the pocket of the trousers he wore.

Rebecca stared at him through a quizzical expression, watching him pull out a fistful of coins.

"I had more than enough money of my own to purchase what we wanted, so this belongs to you."

Rebecca took the coins and immediately turned to pass them on to Captain Jameson.

"Oh no," he reprimanded. "The clothes were a gift. Keep your money…I have no need of it."

She passed the money back to Dr. Ammons, who shook his head as well, saying, "Nor do I!"

Pocketing the coins, she gave a loud sigh of resignation, while the men chuckled at her mock disdain. They entered the eatery and proceeded to an outdoor patio filled with tables, where they chose one shaded by a canopy near the street.

"This will give us a good view of the local citizens," the captain said. "Bergen is filled with an assortment of colorful characters, and I'm certain you would enjoy watching them."

Their exchange was lighthearted and comfortable and they visited for well over two hours, sipping hot tea laced with sugar and cream. Rebecca remained rather quiet, finding herself more than entertained just by listening to Dr. Ammons and Captain Jameson, for she was seldom able to witness the simple camaraderie the two men shared.

"Tell me, Rebecca," Dr. Ammons asked, trying to entice her into conversation, "where did you grow up?"

Rebecca chuckled and replied, "I've lived in so many different places, Dr. Ammons, but I think I've done most of my 'growing up' on the Redemption!"

Both officers gave a hearty laugh at the girl's unexpected comment, and Dr. Ammons urged her to continue.

"I remember living in Africa, but I'm afraid that is my earliest recollection. I know we lived in Spain for several years when I was an infant…"

"Guinea, Africa," Captain Jameson commented. "I recall you speaking of that when Captain Stewart was with us."

"Do you remember much of Africa?" Dr. Ammons asked.

"Not too much," she murmured. "I see more in bits and pieces than full blown memories, but I do recall being hot most of the time…and sticky," she laughed. Her face took on a pensive expression and she quieted for a moment before adding, "My mother got very sick while we were in Guinea...we almost lost her. It was then that my father took us back to Portsmouth."

"How long had you been there?" the captain inquired.

"Three years."

"Did you stay in Portsmouth then?" the captain inquired.

"Only until my mother recovered. Then we went on to France."

"I didn't realize you had lived in France," he exclaimed. "Do you speak French?"

Rebecca cast an impish grin at him and said, "Mais oui, Monsieur." Seeing the curious grin Dr. Ammons gave her, she turned to translate for him, "But of course, sir."

Again, both men laughed at her quick wit and charming sense of humor. Captain Jameson found himself impressed by her vast travel experiences, as well as by her ability to converse so comfortably with the two of them. She seemed to him to be mature beyond her years, but then, he realized with an inward chuckle, he had none to compare her to save for the haughty wives of the various admirals and officers he came into contact with on occasion. Nevertheless, he remained intrigued by her keen sense of humor and her effervescent charm. When the conversation quieted for a moment, Captain Jameson took a small box from his breast pocket and held it towards the girl, while Dr. Ammons looked on with a smug grin as she glanced at his outstretched hand with a hint of curiosity.

"Merry Christmas, Rebecca," the captain said.

Rebecca's eyes widened in disbelief, and it took a moment for the significance of what he said to register. "Christmas?" she whispered.

"Well, not for a few day yet, but we wanted to give this to you today," Captain Jameson replied.

"How can it be?" she stammered, still stunned by their words. Her gaze grew distant as she realized that she had been missing from her home for well over nine months now...almost an entire year. Surely, she realized with dismay, her parents must think her dead and gone.

Dr. Ammons was quick to note the shadow of despair that crossed her features, and he asked, "What troubles you, Rebecca?"

"I hadn't realized how long I've been away..." she murmured. "My parents..."

She bit her lip to keep from crying and lowered her gaze to utter a prayer that God would somehow reassure her beloved mother and father that she still lived. She couldn't bear the thought of the grief that her disappearance must have caused them.

Captain Jameson reached across the table to cover her hand with his, both men acutely aware of the sorrow that had suddenly overcome her. "Rebecca," he declared, "I will do everything within my power to see you returned safely to Portsmouth one day, and your parents will rejoice at having you home again."

"Thank-you, sir," she whispered.

"Now, would you like to open your gift?"

Dr. Ammons gave her a smile of encouragement as she reached for the small box still lying on the outstretched hand of the captain, and she held it for several moments before lifting the lid to peek inside. With a sigh of delight she saw a delicate, woven chain on which hung a simple cross made of the purest gold.

"Refined by fire..." she murmured, fingering the beautiful emblem of the faith that had sustained her for as long as she could remember. Making a determined effort not to succumb to tears, she lifted the necklace to fasten the chain securely around her neck.

"I don't know how to thank you," she began, "not only for this beautiful gift, but for everything you've done for me. I hope you both know that I will carry the memories of our time together in my heart forever."

"Does that mean you like the gift?" Captain Jameson asked through a teasing grin.

"More than you'll ever realize," she whispered.

The three of them continued to sip their hot tea, unaware of the fading light of day as they reveled in the joy of simply being together. When they had finally exhausted themselves of words, they stood to stroll about the less populated sites of Bergen. Rebecca appreciated the solitude found on the back roads, away from the bustling activities of the waterfront. She was able to catch glimpses into the lives of the families who inhabited the city, where mothers strolled with their infants and children played on the street. Everywhere she looked she saw bright clothes hanging on lines strung out between trees, flapping lazily in the wind and scenting the air with a sweet fragrance.

"It reminds me so much of home," Rebecca mused.

They allowed her to lead them in the direction she preferred to go, and before they were aware of the distance they had traveled, they found themselves at the edge of the city, having walked as far as the roads permitted. They spoke for a time among themselves before deciding to meander back along the waterfront, in the hopes of watching the last of the suns rays as it slipped below the cloudless horizon.

The activities of the evening grew more boisterous as they approached Bergen from the outskirts, and Rebecca felt a twinge of fear flutter in her belly. Captain Jameson, oblivious to the girl's discomfort, pointed out the Redemption moored in the harbor and appearing as a fortress against the twilight hues of the evening sky. The three of them lingered for a time, admiring the frigate's regal splendor, and then proceeded to wind their way through the throngs of people milling about in the street.

Rebecca uttered a quick prayer, hoping that they would return to the ship straight away rather than venture into the city, but the captain seemed intent on a destination. The frenzy of activity was intensifying and Rebecca began to succumb to panic, for she had seen on more than one occasion the frightful things men were capable of when influenced by the effects of rum. She was huddled close to Captain Jameson when without warning she felt a hand reach out to grab her leg, and another pulling at the hem of her dress. She gasped in surprise and stumbled backward in fear, desperate to see who had taken hold of her. Together Captain Jameson and Dr. Ammons scanned the faces of the crowd with indignant agitation, intent on finding the culprit who had dared to touch the girl.

Rebecca peered around with a frightened expression, only to find a man crouched on the ground, his legs twisted in a cruel fashion beneath him. His eyes were glazed with the opaque color of blindness and his hair was matted in knots about his head. His face, unshaven and marred, was contorted in a pitiful representation of hopelessness and he begged wantonly for a morsel of food. He maintained his hold on Rebecca with dirty, claw-like hands, searching for something that would sustain him for another day. Captain Jameson stepped forward to strike the beggar's arms away from her, but Rebecca reached out in haste to restrain his angry blow, bringing a look of bewildered surprise to his face. No man had ever dared to touch him before, and he found he was unaccustomed to the girl's boldness. He glanced at her through narrowed eyes, intending to reprimand her, but instead was taken aback when he saw tears coursing over her cheeks, for he had never seen her cry before this night, despite the harsh treatment she had endured aboard the Redemption.

Rebecca remained frozen in place for several moments, her arm held over the captain's with guarded determination, while the man again reached to grasp whoever lingered within his reach. Bending down to look into his sightless eyes, she took hold of his hands and held them in her own. He raised his head in alarm, unaccustomed to the touch of humanity, as his empty gaze searched with desperation for that which he would never behold.

Rebecca lifted the vagrant's arms to her face. Her tears continued to flow unchecked while the calloused hands moved over her nose, her forehead, and through her hair, tracing her features so as to see her image as only he could perceive it. She lingered with the man in silence, praying for his deliverance from his earthly troubles, and when she felt his hands fall from her face she again took them in her own, hoping to convey to him her depth of compassion. Raising herself to her feet, she emptied her pockets of the money she carried and pushed it into his outstretched palms.

"No, Rebecca," Captain Jameson rebuked in a soft voice. "Someone will only take it from him."

The man held the coins in his hands, unaware of their significance, as Rebecca gazed up at the captain through her tears. "What can I do then?" she whispered.

"We'll purchase something for him to eat," he said.

She took the coins that fell from the calloused grip of the blind man and stood to her feet, hurrying toward the merchants selling food. Captain Jameson and Dr. Ammons followed close behind her, and she led them to a vendor near the water's edge who offered a variety of breads, vegetables and cheeses. She thrust a handful of the coins at him and began filling her arms with as much produce as she could carry. Dr. Ammons and Captain Jameson were quick to offer their assistance, and when they had collected as much as they could hold, the three of then made their way back to the beggar.

Rebecca lowered herself beside the man and placed the food in his hands, watching when he began to eat in a ravenous manner all that they gave him until the food had disappeared. When he had finished, he reached out to where Rebecca knelt before him and grasped her hands once more in his own. He squeezed them as if in a firm embrace and then released her. She stood to leave, glancing back at him one, last time as she walked away.

Captain Jameson took hold of her arm lest he lose her amongst the horde of people gathering in the street to solicit coins from those passing by. Rebecca followed without question, and he began to grow concerned by her listless manner as she trailed along behind him, an impenetrable expression hovering over her face. He continued to observe her peculiar behavior until they had arrived at the elite officer's club he had hoped to take her to, and he wondered for a moment if he should return with her to the Redemption and forgo the plans he had made for dinner. Rebecca broke free of her trance-like state when the captain slowed his steps, and she glanced around in disoriented confusion.

"They serve a wonderful fare here, Rebecca," Captain Jameson said. "I thought you might enjoy it."

A shadow of trepidation was quick to darken her features when she caught sight of the bustling tavern that loomed before her, and Rebecca felt as though she were caught between the hammer and the anvil, wanting to please Captain Jameson, but at the same time wanting to flee as fast as she was able to from the threat the establishment posed.

Dr. Ammons, sensing the girl's unease, assured her with a playful tug of her hair, "Everything will be just fine, Rebecca. There's no need to be alarmed."

Rebecca, realizing the captain's kind intentions, tipped her head to the side and offered him a polite nod of acquiescence. "I think I would enjoy it very much, Captain Jameson," she murmured.

"Wonderful!" the captain exclaimed, directing her toward the entrance.

Rebecca's thoughts lingered on the blind beggar left behind on the darkened streets of Bergen, and she was oblivious to the glances cast her way when she entered the room, nestled securely between Dr. Ammons and Captain Jameson. The trio proceeded to an unoccupied table near the center of the club, where Dr. Ammons was quick to withdraw a chair for her. Rebecca felt a sudden wave of panic threaten to overcome her when visions of being trapped on the floor of the tavern in Gibraltar pervaded her mind.

"Rebecca?"

Her head snapped up in alarm to find Dr. Ammons studying her with a perplexed expression, his hand still holding the chair for her.

Captain Jameson watched Rebecca for several moments, wondering what it was that troubled the girl, and he breathed a sigh of relief when she finally took a place at the table.

Smiling her thanks, she lowered herself into the seat Dr. Ammons offered, intent on dispelling the upsetting images from her consciousness. "Thank you," she murmured.

Captain Jameson caught Dr. Ammon's eye with a slight move of his head, but Rebecca didn't notice their silent exchange. Instead, she allowed her gaze to roam about the room, studying the faces of those who surrounded her. With an inward sigh of relief, she recognized that there were none present who appeared as if they would pose a threat, and she rested back in her chair, content to observe the activity in the club from where she sat.

Captain Jameson ordered beverages for three of them, and then commented in a light tone, "I see Lieutenants Burgess and Edwards have managed to find the finest eating establishment in town."

Rebecca peered over her shoulder to where the two officers were seated, and she could see that they were chatting amicably and sipping rum while they played Whist with two other gentlemen. She was amused by their pretense of civility when in the presence of other officers, and paused to consider what intolerable conduct of hers caused them to morph into the raging beasts she knew them to be. A befuddled grin tugged at the corner of her mouth, and she lowered her head lest anyone take notice.

The server appeared at the table with a tray of colorful drinks, placing one of them in front of Rebecca. She eyed the shimmering liquid with suspicion, while Captain Jameson chuckled and said, "Not to worry Rebecca...there are no spirits in yours!"

She smiled her relief and lifted the glass to her lips, tasting the fruity concoction that slid with ease down her throat. She relaxed some as the evening continued, and found the officer's club to be much quieter than the boisterous tavern she had been at in Gibraltar. She was amazed by the vast array of delectable food that was served to them, for it was unlike anything she had ever tasted. A delighted sigh of satisfaction escaped her and she sat back to make herself more comfortable in her chair.

"Is the meal to your liking, Rebecca?" Dr. Ammons asked.

"Oh yes," she breathed. "I have never tasted anything so wonderful."

Captain Jameson turned to her, saying with a smile, "Surely you've dined in many fine eating establishments...being the daughter of a medical doctor."

"My father was a doctor sir, but he devoted his talents to working among the poor. Unfortunately one can't live the lavish life on good will, nor do chickens make suitable currency," she smiled.

"Was it a difficult existence?" Dr. Ammons asked.

"For my mother, perhaps," she answered, contemplating her words with care. "But I was just a young child...I didn't know anything different than the life I had. Don't misunderstand me, Doctor Ammons..." she smiled. "What we lacked in financial assets was more than made up for with affection. I wouldn't change one, single moment of my childhood if given the chance."

The men regarded her with deference as the server brought each of them a cup of strong, black coffee. They savored the brew, enjoying the rich taste, when Rebecca caught sight of Lieutenant Burgess making his way toward their table.

"Good evening, Dr. Ammons, Captain," he began. Casting an awkward glance at Rebecca, he gave a slight nod of greeting and again found himself captivated by the girl's attractive appearance. "Lieutenant Edwards and I were wondering if either of you gentlemen would care to join us in a game of Whist."

Dr. Ammons and Captain Jameson eyed one another with amusement.

"Oh, I can think of one of us here who would give you a run for your money, Mr. Burgess," the captain laughed. "Are you certain you're up for it?"

"Yes," he smiled, "I believe we are this evening, sir."

Rebecca stole a glance at the young officer, enchanted by the courteous smile he offered his commander. She could recall the ready smiles that had brightened the features of the young officer in the past, when she had first come aboard, but ever since her identity had been revealed, he had remained sullen and morose when she was near. For a second time she found her self wondering what flaw in her character would cause him to despise her so vehemently.

Dr. Ammons stood and pulled Rebecca to her feet.

She glanced up in surprise and said, "Oh no…not me!"

"Yes, yes!" he exclaimed. "It will be wonderful! Think of all the money you could win." He gave her a sly wink, as if they share some great secret.

Rebecca stared at the man in utter confusion, wondering what it was that he hinted at, while Captain Jameson grinned in understanding.

"Rebecca," the captain began. "Do you recall that man on the waterfront? There are many more like him out there…and you did give all of your coins for the food you purchased…"

Rebecca's eyes lit up while a slow smile began to spread across her face, and she remembered how wonderful it had been to offer food to the hungry man. "Yes," she said, nodding her head in understanding. "I could win a lot of money!"

Taking their mugs of coffee along with them, the three cut a path through the crowded room to where Lieutenant Edwards waited. Lieutenant Burgess trailed behind them, wondering what mischievous scheme the girl had up her sleeve this time, for although he found himself attracted to her delicate features, he certainly didn't want her to join in on their game.

Rebecca took a seat beside Lieutenant Edwards, her features alight with an air of confidence. "Deal me in, please," she murmured.

The officer met her request with a calculated scowl, but at the sight of the captain lingering nearby, he began to shuffle the deck of cards.

Lieutenant Burgess placed himself on the other side of the table, intent on partnering with his friend rather than with the girl, while Rebecca turned to glance at the officers who remained behind her.

"I believe I need a partner," she smiled.

Captain Jameson stepped forward to say, "I will take on that challenge."

He took his position across from her while Lieutenant Edwards began to deal the cards. The table grew quiet when the round began, with Rebecca casting an occasional, covert glance at Captain Jameson. The game continued for several rounds before she and Captain Jameson called the trump, putting the jackpot in their favor. Rebecca, her face masked with delight, reached for the pile of coins, only to have Lieutenant Edwards stop her hand in midair.

"Not so fast," he admonished in a low voice. "We play best hand in two out of three."

"All right," she replied in an easy manner, lowering her arm.

Lieutenant Edwards passed the cards to Rebecca. She shuffled with an adept agility before dealing the new hand around the table, the captain looking on in amusement and enjoying the displeasure evident on the faces of his two, young lieutenants. It was obvious to him that his officers were uncomfortable in the presence of the girl, but she seemed unruffled by their hostility, as she turned the trump card with enthusiasm, signaling the beginning of the new game.

This round lasted several minutes longer than the last, for the two young officers were determined to gain control of the winnings. The tension around the table was thick, and it showed in the faces of the men. Rebecca however, had a peaceful optimism about her, knowing that she was playing this game for the poor and downtrodden outcasts of Bergen, and she had no doubt that they would be eating well this night.

When Captain Jameson turned the winning trick she beamed at him in triumph and again reached for the coins in the center of the table, only to have her hand restrained a second time by Lieutenant Edwards. "Mr. Edwards," she said in a calm voice, "we've won best hand in two out of two and we simply don't have time to see you through round three, as I'm afraid we must take our leave now. We have people to attend to," she added, casting a bright smile at Dr. Ammons and Captain Jameson.

She stood and filled her pockets with the mound of coins while the young officers peered at her with baffled agitation. "Thank you for a wonderful game, gentlemen," she grinned, glancing over her shoulder as she walked toward the door.

Captain Jameson and Dr. Ammons followed Rebecca out of the officer's club, leaving the disgruntled lieutenants grumbling in her wake.

Once outside, the threesome made their way to the waterfront, where throngs of people continued to linger. Rebecca was quick to seek out the paupers and the beggars standing on corners seeking alms from the more fortunate of stature. She approached each individual with a kind face and took their hands in her own, offering them words of hope and encouragement, and they listened with rapt attention to the message she shared with them, moved by her passionate testimony of God's love and saving grace. As she navigated her way through the crowd she left each person she spoke with a generous assortment of coins, and when she departed they peered after her, wondering if God had sent an angel to the streets of Bergen that night.

When Rebecca had at last dispensed her last remaining coin, she twirled around to see if the captain and Dr. Ammons were still within sight, and she was relieved to see that they had followed close behind her. Rebecca remained standing on the narrow walkway and waited for them to catch up to her.

"Are you finished?" Captain Jameson asked through a wry grin.

"Yes, captain," she murmured. "Let's go home."

He regarded her for a pensive moment, wondering if he had heard her correctly. "Home?" he asked, feeling a knot of emotion forming in his throat.

She nodded and tucked her arm into his, as Dr. Ammons joined them for the walk to the shoreline where they would board the dinghy that would return them to the Redemption. They proceeded down the craggy path together, laughing and retelling the memorable moments of their visit to Bergen. Rebecca was certain this day would live on in her memory forever, and she was thankful the captain had convinced her to venture into the city with him. For the first time since she had been abducted, she felt as if she was experiencing the life God had called her to, witnessing to the lost souls of this world and offering them some semblance of hope for their future.

Captain Jameson enjoyed hearing the sound of her animated chatter which was so full of life and breathless energy. Even in the darkness he could see that her face was flushed from the excitement and activity of their evening and her eyes shone bright, offering him a glimpse of a conviction he could not comprehend. In all of his seafaring years he had witnessed the passion men found in fighting, the passion they found in conquering, and even the passion many found in dying, but never before had he witnessed such a passion for living. He realized then that his most treasured enlightenment had come at the hand of an eighteen year old girl.

Dr. Ammons stepped into the awaiting dinghy and then turned to offer Rebecca his assistance. Captain Jameson, waiting until the girl had situated herself, climbed aboard and claimed a seat on the narrow bench beside her. The small boat began to scrape away from the sands of the shoreline, bobbing on the waves as it pressed on toward the Redemption, now brightly illuminated against the darkness of the night sky. Rebecca remained at rest, her gaze soft and distant, as the lights from the ship were reflected in the emerald hue of her eyes. It had been a full day in Bergen and all three of them were looking forward to being tucked away into the safe confines of the ship once more. When the dinghy neared the frigate, the shrill whistle sounded on board to announce the arrival of the captain. The long rope ladder was flung over the side and anxious heads appeared at the railing, waiting to offer their assistance if it was requested.

Dr. Ammons and Captain Jameson moved to help Rebecca in exiting the dinghy, both looking on in surprise when she reached out with a confident hand for the ladder to begin the long hike up the familiar rungs.

"How does she do that?" Dr. Ammons whispered.

Captain Jameson simply shook his head in bemused wonder, unable to explain anything at all about the girl who had graced their lives in such an unexpected manner.

Petty Officer Andrews stood at the rail, smiling down in wonder at Rebecca as she made the ascent to the deck. "Look at this! A new passenger has come aboard!" he teased.

"Don't get your hopes up, Mr. Andrews," she giggled. "It's just plain, old simple me."

"There's nothing plain or simple about you, Missy," he replied, catching her up in a firm embrace. He held her back at arms length to get a good look at her, having never seen her dressed in such a feminine fashion before tonight. "You look just lovely," he exclaimed in a tender voice, watching her lower her head to get a glimpse of the dress once again.

The crew lingering nearby cast approving glances over her lithe form, almost as if seeing her for the first time, but Rebecca remained unaware of their attention and said, "Thank you, Mr. Andrews," while trying to stifle a large yawn. "We had a wonderful time...and tomorrow I shall tell you all about our adventures in Bergen."

"I'll look forward to that, Missy," he smiled, patting her cheek with affection.

The men soon came to attention when Captain Jameson stepped aboard, followed closely by Dr. Ammons. Rebecca gazed at them with an expression of heartfelt gratitude, unsure of how to thank them for such a wonderful day.

"Would you like to join us for a cup of tea before turning in, Rebecca?" the captain asked.

She shook her head and smiled saying, "I'm afraid I couldn't stay awake long enough, sir. Instead, I will return to my quarters and savor every moment of this glorious day while I drift off to sleep. I can never thank you enough for these precious memories that I will carry with me forever."

Captain Jameson smiled at the girl's winsome expression and bid her a good night. Dr. Ammons stood beside him, and together they watched the girl stroll the expanse of the deck to slip into the corridor before they proceeded to the captain's stateroom to partake in a hot cup of tea.

Rebecca slept undisturbed until she was awakened just three hours later by a sharp rap at her door. She crawled from beneath her covers to see who knocked, only to find Mr. Andrews with a foreboding grimace upon his face.

"What is it Mr. Andrews?" she asked, feeling a knot of dread forming in the pit of her stomach.

"It's Eddy, Missy," he stammered. "He's been hurt real bad."

She stared in shocked silence, the words not registering in her mind. "Who?" she asked.

"Eddy…" he trailed.

A shadow of dismay cast itself over her face, as visions of her friend lying wounded and lifeless filled her mind. "Oh no," she murmured, while Mr. Andrews took her by the hand and led her toward the sick berth. Her eyes fell upon Dr. Ammons, who was leaning over the bloodied, limp body of the cook. Rebecca ran to his side, fearful of what he would tell her.

"He's in bad shape, Rebecca," he said, knowing there was little he would be able to do for the man.

Rebecca spun around on her heel, knowing there was only One truly capable of saving Eddy. She hurried to the rear of the frigate and fell to her knees, where she began to pray with unrestrained abandon, pleading with desperation for the Lord to spare the life of the injured sailor. She whispered in broken sentences interrupted by an occasional sob, her lips moving with the fervent passion of one who loves dearly. Rebecca wasn't in the habit of praying aloud, and so intent was she in interceding on behalf of her friend that she was unaware of the curious glances she was receiving from the crew who lingered nearby.

Captain Jameson was awakened by the sound of a sharp knock at his door. He stepped into his robe and strode across the floor of his cabin to peer into the corridor, where he found Lieutenant Burgess waited with an uneasy expression on his face.

"Captain, I'm sorry to wake you, sir," he said, "but there's been an incident in Bergen involving the cook."

"Is he still ashore?" Captain Jameson asked.

"No, sir, he has been brought aboard and he's in the sick berth with Dr. Ammons. He isn't expected to survive the night, sir," he added.

Captain Jameson was quick to don his clothing and proceeded to the sick berth with Lieutenant Burgess. They were intercepted by a young midshipman, his face contorted with apprehensive alarm.

"Excuse me, Captain," he said. "The girl, sir, I think there's something wrong with her!"

Captain Jameson groaned inwardly. Fear crept into his belly while he wondered what else could possibly go wrong that night. "Where is she?" he demanded.

"Over here, sir," the boy replied, leading the captain and the lieutenant to where Rebecca knelt in prayer.

The men slowed when they heard her voice carried on the breeze, reciting psalms of promise and of hope in soft tones, intermingled with impassioned pleas for mercy and an occasional sob, and when they rounded the corner they saw that she was on her knees, her face raised toward the heavens. The light of the moon was reflected off of the tears that slid from her eyes giving her a surreal, luminescent appearance, almost as if she were a phantom image of an angelic being.

Captain Jameson approached her with a hesitant step, not wanting to disturb her intercession but concerned that something may be wrong with the girl. "Rebecca," he called in a quiet voice.

Rebecca remained in the presence of God while she prayed and was oblivious to the quiet prodding of the men who tried to draw her out of her meditative state. Captain Jameson, hearing the voice of the midshipman on watch summoning him, was distracted for a moment.

"Captain, I'm sorry to interrupt, sir, but the doctor requests your presence in the sick berth immediately."

Captain Jameson shot a hard glance towards his lieutenant and said, "Stay with her."

Lieutenant Burgess remained near the girl, observing her from where he stood, while the captain hastened to the sick berth muttering under his breath about the fortuitous events of the evening. Dr. Ammons saw the captain coming and met him halfway across the broad expanse of deck, his elation evident in his countenance as well as in his tone.

"I don't understand it, Will," he began. "I was about to sew him into his burial bag when he just...woke up! He had no heart beat, no pulse...I checked him several times."

Captain Jameson ducked through the portal of the sick berth to see the battered face of the cook staring back at him.

He studied him with a hint of intrigue for several moments and finally asked, "How are you feeling, man?"

"Awful sore, sir. Where's Rebecca?" he answered in an unwavering voice.

Both Captain Jameson and Doctor Ammons stared at him with baffled disbelief. He'd been beaten senseless, left to die on the streets of Bergen, dragged back to the Redemption by his shipmates and declared dead, yet his first thought after his miraculous recovery was of Rebecca. Captain Jameson smiled to himself, somewhat confused by the incident, but accustomed to surreal things happening when Rebecca was in attendance. He was raised in the church, educated in a prominent religious institution, and yet, he realized, he knew nothing about this god of hers. He sighed in resignation and met the questioning gaze of Dr. Ammons.

"I'll bring her to you," he assured.

Dr. Ammons continued to peer at the young midshipman with amazed disbelief, while Captain Jameson went after Rebecca.

Lieutenant Burgess maintained his watchful gaze on the girl, listening as she sustained her fervent pleas for several more moments. He was caught off guard in his observation when she suddenly stood to her feet and turned around, and he was quick to take notice of the startled apprehension that shadowed her features when their eyes met.

"Excuse me," she murmured, taking a faltering step around his solemn form.

Rebecca was stunned to see the Lieutenant lingered nearby watching her and she wondered how long he had been there, but not wanting to waste time in meaningless deliberation, she hurried off towards the sick berth.

Captain Jameson saw Rebecca approach with an unwavering expression of resolve settled on her countenance. She lifted her gaze to meet his and he was again taken aback by the unnatural appearance of her eyes, while her face looked ghostly pale in the light of the moon. "There is a certain patient requesting your presence," he commented with a wry grin, relieved to see that she was alright.

"Yes," she smiled. "And I'll not keep him waiting."

Eddy made a feeble attempt to prop himself upright on the table, watching the door with an anxious scowl until he saw Rebecca enter. When she caught a glimpse of his pitiful appearance she began to laugh, grateful the Lord had spared his life, and she rushed to wrap him in a tender embrace.

He pushed her back to hold her at arms length, eyeing her with an intensity she was unaccustomed to. "I saw you, Bec!" he exclaimed. "I saw you down on your knees at the stern. I was with someone but I couldn't see his face..." His rapt gaze was fixed on Rebecca while he continued to ramble. "It was so bright my eyes could hardly stand it-but I saw you! Down on your knees praying for me..." he trailed, his voice breaking with emotion.

She nodded her understanding, hoping to calm the man a bit. She knew the elation he was experiencing at the moment would put undue strain on his already broken body, and with a gentle pressure she attempted to coax him back down onto the table.

"He told me I needed to stay with you...that you would need my help before too long. I'd do anything for you, Bec, you know that don't you?"

"Yes, Eddy," she murmured in a calm tone. "I'm so glad you stayed for me."

He continued to stare at her, as if making sure she wasn't an apparition.

Rebecca again tried to persuade him to lie down saying, "You need to rest, Eddy. Your body needs to recover from your injuries."

"Don't leave me, Bec," he implored, his eyes glued to her face. "Please don't leave me..."

"I won't, Eddy. I'll stay right here with you," she promised.

Dr. Ammons instructed the young man to take a sip of the opiate tonic he offered to help ease his pain and allow him to rest, while Rebecca lingered nearby, her hand still enfolded in Eddy's grasp as he slipped into a peaceful slumber.

"How long do you intend to stay, Rebecca?" Dr. Ammons asked, once the boy had drifted off.

"I'll stay until daylight," she replied. "I'll have to prepare the morning meal for the crew then…hopefully he'll understand," she smiled, tilting her head at the cook.

"Why don't you try to get some sleep," Captain Jameson suggested, wishing she would return to her quarters. "I can stay with him."

"He won't be waking before morning, Rebecca," Dr. Ammons added.

"It's alright," she said. "I've given him my word, so I'll just stay here for the remainder of the night. It won't be long before sun up, so I ought to manage just fine."

Captain Jameson returned to his stateroom but found sleep slow in coming. He lay in bed for a long while pondering the events that had transpired that evening, and made a note in his mind to speak to the girl about the cook's miraculous recovery. After two hours of floating on the brink of sleep he found his thoughts still remained on Rebecca, and he wondered with restless contemplation how she was faring in the sick berth. With an exasperated sigh, he finally drug himself out of bed and went to check on her.

Rebecca was growing more tired with each second that passed and she yawned as she made an attempt to get more comfortable in the unyielding chair she rested in. Dr. Ammons had been right about Eddy sleeping through the night, she realized. He had not stirred even once since she had been there, and several times she hovered over him to make certain he was still breathing. She filled the quiet moments by offering words of praise and thanksgiving to God for hearing her pleas and sparing the life of her friend.

Captain Jameson entered the sick berth just in time to see Rebecca in the midst of a large yawn, and she giggled when she realized that he had seen her. He cast a tender smile at her in return, surprised to find that she was still awake.

"How is the patient?" he whispered.

"Hasn't even stirred, Captain."

Captain Jameson stepped over to where Eddy lay and gazed down at the bruised and torn flesh that covered his body. He was relieved to see that the boy rested in a peaceful slumber, in spite of his brutal brush with death. With a heavy sigh he glanced over his shoulder to peer at Rebecca, and saw that she was gazing back at him with a sweet sensitivity, her legs tucked beneath her and her head resting against the wall.

"You're tired, Rebecca," he commented. "Why don't you try to get some rest? I'll stay here with him."

"It's just about time to attend to the breakfast meal, sir. I'm afraid I wouldn't be able to sleep much at this point," she smiled.

"I'll have some of the midshipmen to see to the meal. You've dealt with enough for one day."

"It's alright, sir…the morning chores are the easiest. It'll just take me an hour or two, and then I'll lie down for a bit."

He looked at her in consternation. "I won't have you fall ill, Rebecca."

"Just breakfast, sir, and then I'll go straight to my quarters."

Before breakfast had even begun, Rebecca regretted not allowing the captain to follow through with his offer of turning over the task to someone else. She was exhausted before the men had finished, and was relieved when Mr. Andrews offered to stay and help her in the galley. She moved about slowly in weary fatigue, oblivious to his grimace of concern as he watched her.

"I can finish this up, Missy…you'd best run off to get some sleep," he admonished.

A tired sigh escaped her when she lifted her head to say, "Let's just leave the rest of this until the noon meal, Mr. Andrews. I'll be able to manage things better then, and you won't have to wonder where to put everything."

He nodded in agreement, and walked with her to her cabin, assuring her he would wake her before the noon meal.

Rebecca slept undisturbed for just two hours when a tap at her door brought her out of her slumber. She stumbled out of bed to see who called, and found Petty Officer Andrews pacing with restless steps in the hallway. "What is it, Mr. Andrews?" she mumbled.

He gave her an apologetic look and said, "I'm sorry to wake you, Missy... I thought I could handle the noon meal on my own, but I'm having a hard time of it. Do you think you could help just for a bit?"

She offered a willing nod when she saw the troubled expression on his face. "Of course, Mr. Andrews," she smiled. "Just give me a few moments to get myself ready."

He returned to the galley and peered with a helpless scowl at the chaotic mess, while he made a second attempt to light the stove.

Rebecca pulled her fingers through her hair and hurried off to help the petty officer. As she meandered through the men working on deck she slipped into the sick berth to have a look at Eddy, who was lying on the table where she'd last seen him, his eyes closed in a contented slumber. A grateful smile lit her features and she continued on her way, confident that the man would be back on his feet in no time at all.

Rebecca gasped when she saw the horrendous mayhem in the galley. Mr. Andrews had recruited two of the crew to help him, and the men now stood in the center of the room glancing at one another in confusion. Flour dusted most of the exposed surfaces and utensils were scattered throughout the small area. It appeared to Rebecca, who stood staring in a shocked silence, that a battle had occurred and the men had been miserably defeated.

She tried to stifle the giggle she felt rising in her throat, while the men gazed at her with helpless looks upon their faces. Unable to restrain her laughter any longer, she leaned against the wall as it burst forth from her. The men watched on with curious glances before they too, began to chuckle at the precarious situation they had found themselves in.

Up on deck, Mr. Edwards and Mr. Burgess heard the commotion in the galley from their position near the stern. Descending the narrow stairwell, they stepped through the doorway to determine the cause for the upheaval, and their expressions darkened with irritation at the sight that greeted them.

"What the devil is going on here?" Lieutenant Edwards demanded, glowering at Rebecca.

Rebecca continued to lean lackadaisically against the wall, a feigned expression of innocence lingering on her face, while she made a desperate attempt to stifle her laughter.

"We were just working on the noon meal, sir," Mr. Andrews tried to explain, hoping to draw the officer's attention away from the girl, who was quite giddy by now from lack of sleep.

"Well who's in charge?" he roared.

The flour-coated crew turned their hopeless eyes toward Rebecca.

"I suppose I am," she said, still trying to quell the laughter that quivered in her throat.

"You will get this mess cleaned up immediately," he shouted, slamming his fist on the table in anger.

A large cloud of flour erupted into the air when his hand dispelled it from where it had settled, sending Rebecca into a new fit of giggles. Mr. Andrews watched in dismay as Lieutenant Edward's stormed toward the girl, his eyes filled with rage. Without thought to his own safety, the petty officer leapt in front of her to protect her from the fury of the man's wrath, but the officer raised his hand in a menacing gesture of warning.

"Please, sir," the petty officer implored, maintaining his stance to prevent the man from laying hold of Rebecca, "you don't understand...she hasn't slept more than a couple of hours and she's not herself!"

"Get out of my way," he growled.

Lieutenant Burgess hurried to place himself between the two men in the hopes of diffusing Mr. Edward's anger. Rebecca, in turn, tried to move in front of Mr. Andrews, not wanting him to suffer a beating at the hands of the officer on her account, while the Petty Officer struggled to hold the girl behind him with the intention of protecting her. Rebecca again burst into a fit of uncontrolled laughter while they tussled, the helpless, flour-coated crew looking on in disbelief.

Lieutenant Burgess drug Lieutenant Edwards away from the precarious situation in haste and instructed him to return to the deck, knowing the emotional fuse of the exasperated officer was growing quite short by this time. He then returned to take a firm hold of Rebecca's arm. "If you value your life," he hissed, "you will refrain from this nonsense and clean this mess up!"

Rebecca nodded in understanding, while she covered her mouth to stifle yet another fit of giggles with her free hand, the other still in the grip of the irate lieutenant. Mr. Burgess, subduing an intense desire to trounce the girl, released his grip on her and stormed from the galley.

Rebecca collapsed into the arms of the petty officer, still chuckling in her giddy mirth, and he made a desperate attempt to quiet the girl lest the men return a second time. The two crew members in attendance breathed a grateful sigh and set about to reassemble the disordered room to its original state. Rebecca remained in the galley straight through the dinner hour, and when the last of the chaos had finally been cleared away, she drug herself to the sick berth to check on her friend. Eddy saw her as she entered and gave her a winsome smile, and she, in her great relief, grinned back at him in mock consternation while offering an inward prayer that he would be back on his feet again soon.

"I don't know how you ever managed without me, Eddy," she sighed, sinking down into the chair.

"I don't know how either, Bec," he replied.

They sat in together in the dim shadow of evening, both comfortable in one another's presence, until without warning Rebecca began to drift off to sleep.

"Go to your cabin, Bec," Eddy urged in a quiet tone. "You'll be more comfortable there."

Rebecca pulled herself to her feet, too exhausted to argue, and made her way to her quarters. She heard the sound of boisterous singing coming from the men below deck, and she giggled at the festive sound of men well fed. With a contented smile still lingering on her face, she slipped into her tiny berth and crawled beneath the blankets. She made a sincere attempt to thank the Lord for his protection on that day, but her eyes drifted shut even before her head landed on the pillow, her dreams shrouded by the deep cloud of slumber that enveloped her.

Chapter 13

THE REDEMPTION HAD set a course for Scotland, sailing for Glasgow. The seas had been churning in agitation for several days, and the sky was a deep, brooding gray. The foul weather had engulfed the frigate, leaving the captain as ill tempered as the weather, and the crew was growing weary of the tension on deck, as well as of the brittle drops of rain that lashed their faces while they worked. They struggled to keep their wits about them as the waves tossed the ship to and fro on the rolling crests, while the midshipman on watch peered through the telescope, unable to see much of anything beyond the huge walls of water. Eddy had recovered well from his injuries, and this night found he and Rebecca huddled in the confines of the galley intent on staying dry. They sipped hot tea while the chatted near the stove, hoping to draw the lingering chill from their bones.

"Honestly, Eddy," Rebecca told him, "I feel as if I've been waterlogged for the past three weeks!"

They had long ago finished with their chores, the men retreating to the warmth below rather than lingering in the galley, and now their free time allowed them to engage in an unusual game of Whist, alternating hands as if to simulate a foursome. She giggled when she raised the stakes against herself by two pounds, boasting of her good fortune to Eddy for the past several minutes, while he looked on in amusement, charmed by her childlike manner.

They were startled out of their comfortable camaraderie by the sound of the watchman's shrill whistle announcing an unfamiliar ship on the horizon. Their attention was distracted from their game for a moment as they glanced at one another, but both remained confident that whoever it was sailing toward them wouldn't pose much of a threat in this inclement weather, and so they remained at the table, determining that it wasn't worth getting drenched over at this point in time. Rebecca felt a twinge of empathy for the captain, who would most likely be summoned to the quarterdeck to stand in the cold rain while hoping to catch a distant glimpse of the vessel on the water through his telescope.

"Trump!" Eddy called with gusto.

"Drat," she replied, looking at the cards in her left hand. "Hooray," she called again, lifting the cards in her right.

Eddy met her gaze her and they both burst into delighted peals of laughter. "You know, it's not so bad losing to myself, Bec!" he stated.

"Yes, it's quite enjoyable isn't it Eddy? Shall we split the winnings now, or play another round?" she grinned.

They again laughed together while they sipped their tea, no longer warm due to the pervading chill in the air.

Up above, Captain Jameson stood on the quarterdeck surrounded by his officers, the rain pelting them without ceasing.

"It looks like a Spanish supply ship, sir," Lieutenant Burgess commented, peering through the telescope, "although their sails seem somewhat awry."

The captain took the scope his lieutenant offered, and looked again through the small hole. "We'll steer toward her," he said. "She certainly isn't making any progress towards us," he added, regretting that he had left the comfort of his quarters for such a minimal threat as this.

"Aye-aye, sir," Lieutenant Burgess replied. "I will notify you when we draw closer to her captain."

Pausing to think for a moment, Captain Jameson glanced at his officer. "While you're waiting, prepare a team to board her, Mr. Burgess."

Lieutenant Burgess nodded his head in acknowledgement of the captain's order and set out to gather a group of men to accompany him aboard the Spanish vessel. Petty Officer Andrews was below deck trying to stay dry when Lieutenant Burgess finally located him. "Mr. Andrews, I'd like you and some of your men to accompany me aboard a Spanish supply ship. Can you assemble a crew within the hour?" he asked.

"Yes, sir. How many of us would you like, sir?"

"Ten more besides the two of us," he replied. "And tell them to come armed. We can't be sure of what we'll find." Lieutenant Burgess returned to the quarterdeck to monitor the activities aboard the small ship as they advanced.

Petty Officer Andrews gathered a group of his shipmates together and began to prepare for a probable battle. The men, restless from being cooped up below deck to stay out of the rain, appeared eager at the prospect of a good brawl, even if it was just with the Spanish fleet, and they laughed and jostled one another while they readied themselves to disembark.

Rebecca and Eddy, having nothing better to do, began to shuffle the deck of cards for another round of Whist. They were momentarily distracted by the sound of the shuffle of activity below and wondered as to the cause of the activity, but neither of them wanted to venture into the wall of rain to find out. Instead, they remained where they were, hoping to catch a glimpse of someone passing by who might know what was going on. Within no time at all Mr. Andrews hurried past the portal, his gait purposeful and sure.

"Mr. Andrews!" Rebecca called out to him.

The petty officer stepped back to peer into the room before ducking through the narrow doorway, grateful for the momentary shelter from the frigid rain.

"What's happening?" she asked with a curious look, frowning at the unfamiliar sight of the sword strapped to his hip.

"There's a Spanish supply ship we're heading towards, Missy. Captain Jameson wants a group of us to board her."

It took a moment for Rebecca to digest what the petty officer had said, while a dark foreboding began to descend on her features. "Are there men aboard the ship?" she asked.

Mr. Andrews smiled at her in a teasing manner. "I'd hope there are, Missy...ships don't usually sail themselves."

"Well what will you do with them?" she asked, growing alarmed.

"Well, we'll try to take the ship as a prize of war, and we'll take the crew as prisoners."

Rebecca stared back in a pensive silence, not fully comprehending this whole business of warfare.

"There's money in ships taken as prizes of war, Bec," Eddy explained.

"And that leaves one less supply ship in the Spanish fleet," added Mr. Andrews, nodding a curt farewell as he retreated into the corridor.

Eddy grabbed Rebecca by the arm and said, "Come on, Bec. We don't want to miss this!" He too had grown weary of past several weeks of uneventful monotony, and the prospect of a sure battle offered a welcome distraction from the boredom he had been feeling. Rebecca cast a wary glance at him and he was quick to assure, "Trust me...this is worth getting drenched over."

She was startled by the wind which lashed her face when she left the safety of the galley, and she hurried to the rail, where she had a difficult time locating the ship the men spoke of. It wasn't until the Redemption rose on the crest of a wave that she was able to see the full sail billowing on the small vessel, and she watched while it reeled dangerously in the churning water. They were drawing nearer to the supply ship, and for a moment Rebecca expected it to be engulfed by the huge waves crashing over it. She watched the group of men who had appeared from below, dressed as if expecting a fierce encounter, while they lowered themselves with vigilance onto the small dinghy that would take them out to the supply ship. With anxious eyes she peered through the darkness to the deck of the strange vessel, searching for signs of life.

Lieutenant Burgess and the men struggled to row against the angry waves toward the listing ship. He could see the name painted on the bow as it lifted, and then dropped again. The Pepita. He thought it odd that no one was on deck, appearing almost as if the vessel had been deserted. His men were alert to the danger at hand, and adrenaline coursed through their veins in anticipation of their approach. When they arrived at the side of the Spanish vessel, they clung with a firm grip to the slick railing and struggled to climb aboard. They were quick to move into position after gaining their footing, crouching low outside the doorways and spreading out along the deck.

Rebecca watched as Lieutenant Burgess, the only officer among the crew who had departed, began to kick at a portal near the bow, while the others swarmed into place behind him. Still there were no signs of life, and Rebecca felt her fingernails piercing the flesh of her palms while she watched with fearful eyes from the safety of the Redemption.

Captain Jameson stood observing his crew from the quarterdeck, accompanied by Lieutenant Edwards and several other officers. None spoke as they waited, ready to assist the crew on the Pepita if need be, while Dr. Ammons was on guard in the sick berth waiting for report of the first casualty. It seemed like hours had passed before Rebecca saw any sign of the men again, and she breathed a deep sigh of relief when Lieutenant Burgess exited a doorway, a solemn look upon his face. He walked slowly across the deck, appearing as if he were deep in thought, before raising his head to glance across the swells at Captain Jameson.

"Mr. Burgess!" the captain called. "Are there any men on board?"

"Yes, captain," he shouted back, "but only two still live, sir."

The captain stared at him, waiting to hear the worst of the news.

"It appears they succumbed to small pox, sir," Lieutenant Burgess called over the waves. "The remaining two are barely alive."

"Good heavens!" Captain Jameson gasped aloud, certain that the men had been exposed to the dreaded disease by now.

Lieutenant Edwards and the other officers present on the quarterdeck shifted on their feet with nervous glances upon realizing the severity of the circumstance their shipmates had found themselves in. They knew without a doubt that the fate of the away crew would be a slow and agonizing death on a foreign vessel, and each one breathed a quiet sigh of relief at not having been chosen to lead the mission.

Rebecca's face paled when she heard the words that Lieutenant Burgess spoke, and she turned to peer up at the captain who stood on the quarterdeck, a grim expression of dismay contorting his features. She hurried to cut a line through the throngs of men to where he lingered, the tension in the night air thick enough to slice with a dull knife.

"Get Dr. Ammons," Captain Jameson barked at Lieutenant Edwards.

Lieutenant Edwards retreated toward the stairwell, only to find Rebecca attempting to make her way up. "Get out of my way!" he ordered.

Rebecca stood frozen on the top step, her gaze warily moving from Lieutenant Edwards, and then back again to Captain Jameson. "Captain," she called around the disgruntled officer. "May I speak with you for a moment?"

"Not now, Rebecca," he growled.

"Please, sir," she begged, "it's very important."

"No!" Captain Jameson stated in a resolute tone. "Now is not the time."

Lieutenant Edwards continued to stalk towards her, glaring at her from beneath the rim of his rain drenched hat, while Rebecca observed his approach with a cautious, but determined expression.

"I must sail with the men on the Pepita, Captain!"

Captain Jameson spun around to give her an enraged look of disbelief. "Mr. Edwards, remove her from my quarterdeck this instant!" he shouted in agitation, waving his hand as if she were an insect he wished to fling away.

Rebecca anchored herself with her arms to the rail where she stood, pleading for the captain to hear her. "Please, sir, the survival of your men may depend on this..."

The young lieutenant took hold of her in an attempt to loose her from the unyielding banister to which she clung.

"Captain, please..." she begged, "Don't let your anger cloud your good judgment now!"

Captain Jameson fixed a fierce scowl upon the girl while she struggled against the grip of the irate officer. "You would be wise to mind your tongue, Rebecca Halloway," he warned in a low voice, in no mood to argue with the obstinate girl any further.

Lieutenant Edwards continued to wrestle against her strength, the crew peering at them through curious glances from the deck, while Dr. Ammons attempted to make his way through the throngs of men to where the captain stood, having caught wind of the predicament the away team had found themselves in.

"Please, Captain," Rebecca begged, "listen to me, if only for a moment."

He stormed toward Rebecca then, disturbed by his inclination to strike her. "Release her," he commanded to Lieutenant Edwards, tired of watching the struggle between the two of them.

She stood to her feet on shaky legs, aware of the hostility she had invoked in both men. Speaking in haste, she said, "Captain, I've had the small pox…in Africa. It's unlikely that I would be infected a second time. Please, let me sail with the men…their chances of survival would be much greater if there were someone to tend to them should they fall ill with the disease."

Captain Jameson glowered down at her as she maintained her pleading gaze on his face, while she hoped he was considering her offer. "No," he growled, spinning on his heel to return to the railing.

"Please," Rebecca begged, her eyes clouded with desperation, "I can help-"

"I SAID NO!" he bellowed, glaring at her over his shoulder.

Rebecca met his gaze with stoic determination, their eyes locked in a battle of wills, and after several terse moments she implored in a hushed tone, "Don't make me disobey your order, sir..."

He spun around in his fury to face her. "I will have you flogged, Rebecca Halloway, if you so much as *dare* to disobey me!" he stated in a cold and threatening voice.

"Captain," she continued, "The risk of losing my one life is minimal when compared with the risk of losing twelve!"

"Thirteen!" he shouted, growing weary of her persistence.

"I'm prepared to take that risk, sir," she replied. "The others have no choice in the matter."

He turned away from her in exasperation as Dr. Ammons made his way up the stairs to join them on the quarterdeck, his expression grim. "If its small pox, Captain, I'm afraid we cannot let them return for at least four weeks," he remarked. "If they should've contracted the disease, it will have run its course within that time, but we simply mustn't risk contagion to the fleet by allowing them to return before then."

"Dr. Ammons," Rebecca began anew, "I've had the small pox while in Africa. I can go aboard with the men and care for them if they should become ill."

Dr. Ammons stared at her through a shroud of disbelief and said, "You survived the small pox?"

She nodded, and again said, "I can look after them..."

Dr. Ammons eyed Captain Jameson. "Their chances of surviving this would be greatly increased if she were with them, Captain," he said.

Captain Jameson breathed a heavy sigh and moved to brace his hands against the rail, a deep weariness etched in his features. Rebecca felt terrible at having pushed him so, but Mr. Andrews was aboard the Pepita and she wasn't about to see him die. She hesitated before stepping across the short expanse to where the captain stood, and placed a light hand on his arm.

"I'm sorry, sir," she began. "I had no intention of upsetting you, but please, trust me in this. I promise you...I will return unharmed."

"Don't make promises you can't keep, Miss Halloway," he snapped. "How can you say you'll return unharmed when it is in all certainty that you won't?"

She pulled her hand away at his fierce rebuttal, but stood her ground in the defense of her argument. "Please, sir, I'll be alright...if only I-"

He raised his hand to silence her, having grown weary of the argument. "Just leave, Rebecca. Do what you will."

"Captain..." she murmured again, desperate to make amends before departing.

"GO!" he shouted, not bothering to look at her. Turning to Lieutenant Edwards, he growled, "Get her off my quarterdeck."

She stepped back, startled by his angry words, and then turned to Dr. Ammons, wanting only to escape lest the captain see the tears which threatened to spill from her eyes. "I'll need to gather some supplies," she choked through a sob catching in her throat.

Lieutenant Edwards took an angry step towards the girl, but seeing she was leaving on her own volition, he slowed for a moment to await further instruction from the captain.

Dr. Ammons called out over the waves to Lieutenant Burgess, who was watching the exchange from the deck of the Pepita. "Prepare to take on a passenger, Mr. Burgess."

"Sir?" he called, unsure he had heard the man correctly.

"The girl is coming aboard. She will sail with you for the next four weeks until you are declared to be free of disease."

"We have no need of the girl here, sir. May I request she stay on the Redemption?"

"No, Mr. Burgess, the matter has already been decided upon," Captain Jameson barked. "Prepare to take on the passenger!"

The lieutenant gave his commander a curt nod and moved to instruct Mr. Andrews to prepare for the girl's arrival, while Captain Jameson glowered in silence from rail of the quarterdeck.

Lieutenant Edwards decided to follow Rebecca below to the sick berth after all. He was incensed by her insubordination towards the captain, as well as towards Lieutenant Burgess. Just a few steps behind her, he entered the portal to find her stuffing a canvas bag full of various items she was pulling from the cupboards. She remained unaware of his presence while he watched her in silent agitation, until she turned to leave the room and proceeded to walk straight into him, her face registering guarded surprise.

"Why are you doing this?" he hissed.

"Because they need my help," she answered.

"They don't want your help," he said.

"They'll want it when they're lying near death."

"Well Lieutenant Burgess doesn't want you there!"

She gave him a fleeting glance before walking out the door. "This has nothing to do with what Lieutenant Burgess wants, sir," she said, stepping through the narrow doorway.

He stared after her when she departed, seething in his anger.

Rebecca made her way to the rear of the ship to descend the rope ladder which would put her aboard the dinghy bobbing up and down on the churning waves. She peered over the side of the frigate and saw that two midshipmen were already there, prepared to row her out to the Pepita. She turned back to where Captain Jameson and Dr. Ammons stood, observing her with somber faces. She lifted her hand in a solemn farewell and tossed the canvas bag down to the men who waited for her, before slinging herself with lithe grace over the side to climb down to the little boat. The Captain and Dr. Ammons watched her until she had been safely stowed aboard the small Spanish ship, and then turned their attention to the young officer peering back at them from the deck of the Pepita.

Rebecca crawled across the deck of the Pepita to lean against the wall before trying to gain her footing; her legs shook and her stomach churned from the waves that had tossed the little dinghy about like a leaf on the wind. Petty Officer Andrews towered over her in anger, his eyes livid as they bore down on her frail frame huddled in the rain.

"What a stupid thing to do!" he shouted, intent on being heard above the din of the storm. "Why in tarnation would you come aboard a vessel full of dead men?" he demanded. "You stubborn little fool!"

Rebecca kept her eyes closed against the onslaught, having too recently had words with Captain Jameson to care about further arguments at this time. Her only thoughts were of quelling the nausea she felt stirring in her belly before she lost the contents of her dinner right there on the deck. The petty officer continued to rage on, while she made a feeble attempt to stand to her feet.

"I can't believe the captain let you come aboard…and after hearing of our predicament even. What was he thi-"

"Mr. Andrews, please!" Rebecca said, unaccustomed to such heated discord. "I came here to help you."

"I don't need your help!" he shouted.

"Well you might not, but somebody else may."

She began to move toward the stairwell, hoping to find the crew and warn them not to touch the bodies of the infected. Mr. Andrews followed along, incensed that she continued to ignore his chastising, until he finally took hold of her arm and spun her around to face him.

"Do you hear me? You're going to die here with the rest of us!"

Rebecca remained silent, still fighting the urge to vomit, while she listened to him as he continued to voice his opinion about her presence aboard the Pepita. After putting up with enough of his tirade, she shook loose of his grasp and again set out to have a look about. She remembered Mr. Burgess saying that two men were still alive, which left her to assume that there were several other infected bodies aboard. She turned into the first doorway that she came to and saw several of the men from the Redemption huddled together in confusion and unsure of what to do. Mr. Andrews stepped in front of Rebecca in an attempt to keep her from going any further, while he continued to admonish her for venturing aboard the disease laden ship.

"You think you can handle anything, but you can't," he muttered. "You're just a girl who's a little too sure of herself, I think. Captain ought to have delivered that lashing long ago…"

"Mr. Andrews," she sighed, "I came aboard to tend to you men should you become infected with small pox…if that upsets you then I'm sorry, but you needn't continue to scold me. What's done is done."

He followed after her cursing under his breath, while she made her way through the cabins, intent on locating those who had perished as well as the two who remained living. She had hoped to find Lieutenant Burgess, having last seen him on the deck shouting something over to Captain Jameson.

"We'll need to dispose of their dead as soon as possible, without touching the bodies," she said, turning to glance over her shoulder at the irate petty officer. He was watching her through eyes contorted with agitation.

"Where is Lieutenant Burgess?" she asked.

"You'd best stay away from him," he growled. "He's as fit to be tied at your coming aboard as the rest of us."

Rebecca shook her head in wonder at the disposition of these men. Deciding to take matters into her own hands, she returned to where the crew from the Redemption was lingering. She approached them with bold self-assurance, while they eyed her with aloof indifference.

"We need to bring all of the deceased together to dispose of the corpses as quickly as possible," she informed them, "but it is critical that you not touch the bodies directly."

The men stared at her dumbfounded, never before having taken orders from a woman, and not appearing as though they were about to now. Rebecca waited for some hint of a response, but getting none, she asked, "Does anyone even *know* where the bodies are?"

The men continued to stare at her with blatant resentment. In her frustration, Rebecca hurried toward the corridor, determined to find the misfortunate crew of the Pepita on her own. As she neared the doorway, she nearly collided with Lieutenant Burgess who had just stepped through the tiny portal. When he caught a glimpse of her standing before him, his eyes blazed with fury and he snarled, "You!"

She stepped back in alarm, aware for the first time since her arrival on the Pepita that Captain Jameson was not present to protect her from the wrath of the officer, nor the men who accompanied him. Glancing over her shoulder at those who lingered behind her, she suddenly felt as though she were a lamb in the midst of an angry den of lions, and her heart began to pound in her chest at the sight of the seething eyes which bore down on her. She returned her gaze to Mr. Burgess, expecting to feel the cold blade of his sword penetrate her flesh right then and there, but instead he looked past her to his crew and barked, "You men! Gather the dead and throw them into the sea!"

The men scurried to obey his order while Rebecca shouted after them, "Don't touch them!"

Mr. Burgess took hold of Rebecca by the arm and drug her across the short expanse of the room to back her into a corner. He had never struck a woman in his lifetime, nor had he been tempted to before now, however his temper was running quite short by this time and had she been a man he would have delivered a fierce blow to the side of her head. Instead, as fate would have it, she was not a man but a woman, and so instead of striking her he towered over her and challenged in an ominous tone, "You would dare tell my men to disobey my order?"

Rebecca was confused for a moment by his query, but then realized he must have misunderstood the meaning of her words. Knowing well that she was on turbulent ground with the young officer she responded in a meek whisper, "No, sir…I only felt the need to remind them that they mustn't touch the bodies directly…it's thought to be the method of transmission."

"The what?" he demanded.

"The way the disease is passed from one person to another," she continued. Adding as a measure of safety, she murmured, "I apologize if I spoke out of turn, sir."

He released her in an abrupt move, troubled by his desire to shake the life right out of her in spite of her quiet response, but he continued to tower over her and said in a clear and calculated manner, "You will go below and remain there for the duration of this quarantine. If I so much as see you set foot on deck, you will regret it. Do I make myself clear?"

Rebecca was aware that his breathing had become irregular and his features were dark with fury, a sure sign that she had pushed him far too near the limits of his self control. She nodded, lowering her gaze to display an attitude of complete submission. Holding her breath in nervous anticipation, she waited for him to step aside and allow her to pass, but instead he remained where he was, looming over her while he continued to speak in a low voice.

"I am the captain of this vessel now, and what I say goes. You do not have the benefit of Captain Jameson coming to your aid every time you make some foolish mistake, like coming aboard a vessel full of diseased men," he spat.

She continued to stare at his feet, wanting only to escape to the safety below deck and far away from him, while Mr. Burgess, finding himself growing incensed by her seemingly indifferent attitude, slammed his fist against the wall behind her head.

"Look at me when I'm speaking to you!" he shouted.

Rebecca raised her eyes in perplexed confusion, willing herself not to cry lest he find some perverse satisfaction in knowing that he had scared her senseless.

Mr. Burgess was startled by the blatant fear darkening the girl's eyes and he felt a sudden twinge of remorse at having spoken to her in such a harsh manner. Once again he was struck by the emerald green hue of her eyes, and the sudden awareness of her femininity overcame him. He saw that her gaze remained transfixed on his features, no doubt, he considered, while she waited with expectation for his verbal onslaught to continue. Growing agitated by his conflicting emotions, he pointed to the stairwell and growled, "Go on then…and stay out of my sight."

Rebecca, needing no further prompting, hurried toward the stairwell. Her eyes had a difficult time adjusting to the darkness below and she was uncertain as to what she would find there.

Upon reaching the last step, her gaze fell upon several of the crew attempting to light lanterns as they wound their way through the few remaining bodies strewn across the wooden planks. She saw one man wrapping the corpse of a young, dark skinned sailor into canvas hammock. She crept around him in silence, taking care not to step on anyone, while she searched for a quiet spot away from the activity in which to hide herself from the irate crew of the Redemption.

Lieutenant Burgess stormed out into the daylight, his conflicting emotions still wreaking havoc on his conscience. He approached the bow of the ship where he saw Captain Jameson, waiting and watching for him from the quarterdeck of the Redemption.

"Is everything under control, Mr. Burgess?" he called out.

"Yes, Captain," the young officer replied, "although we are still securing the ship, sir."

"I will await your report then," he replied, his face grim.

Rebecca had been away from the Redemption for less than an hour, yet Captain Jameson was already acutely aware of her absence. He regretted having spoken to her in such a harsh manner before she left, and he wished now for an opportunity to make amends for their altercation. He resisted asking his lieutenant about her, knowing the man had been upset at having to take her aboard in the first place, so instead, he peered about for a glimpse of her on the small ship when the men began to appear on deck, dragging with them the bodies of the stricken crew. Seeing no sign of the girl, he remained at his post to await the forthcoming report from Lieutenant Burgess.

Rebecca hovered in the darkness until the last of the crew had made their way above deck. Reaching for the solitary lantern left behind, she peered about in the dim light trying to see into the penetrating darkness. Holding the lamp before her, she set out to explore what would be her home for the next several weeks. She took along with her the canvas bag she had brought from the Redemption, hoping to find an area large enough to hold several of the crew should they become infected with small pox. Rebecca smiled to herself, unexpectedly struck by the Lord's mercy, when she realized that they were to be quarantined on a supply ship loaded with both food and fresh water. If need be, they could manage very well for quite some time. With her eyes finally adjusted to the dim light, she began to search each room with careful attention in order to find the perfect spot to set up a sick berth, finding what she had been hoping for at the front of the ship. It was a broad, open area with six port holes, allowing for plenty of natural light as well as fresh sea air. The room was void of furnishings except for several large barrels, which upon closer examination Rebecca found to be empty. She began taking them apart and moving the slats of wood to a narrow closet next to the berth she had claimed. She transferred the few supplies she had brought with her from the Redemption into the small closet as well, while giving thanks to the Lord for providing such a perfect place in which to store them. She then set out to gather any rags, cloths and buckets she could find in the dimly lit rooms scattered below the deck of the Pepita.

Lieutenant Burgess remained above with the rest of the crew, offering words for the deceased who were being released into the sea one by one. The men on the Redemption observed in respectful silence, with Captain Jameson keeping a watchful eye out for Rebecca. When the last of the bodies had been delivered into the watery grave, Lieutenant Burgess went forward to deliver his report to Captain Jameson.

"Thirty-four dead and buried, sir," he remarked.

"Any survivors, Mr. Burgess?" the captain called out over the waves.

"None, sir," he replied without emotion.

"And Miss Halloway?" he asked, unable to wait any longer for news of her whereabouts.

"She is below, Captain."

Captain Jameson nodded his head in a curt fashion, deciding to lay the matter to rest rather than test the patience of his young lieutenant, especially seeing as how he wasn't there to deflect the young man's wrath from the girl. A troubled thought passed through his mind when he realized that she had been rendered defenseless in the midst of the crew who had boarded the Pepita, as she had never been away from his protective presence before now. Stirred from his thoughts by the voice of his officer, he glanced up to listen to what the young man had to say.

"On a more positive note, Captain," Lieutenant Burgess continued, "the larders are full and we have no need of supplies. I have examined the ship and have found it to be sound, and the sails are in good repair as well."

Captain Jameson nodded his head in acknowledgement, relieved to hear an optimistic report after the strain of past two hours. He continued to peer across the turbulent swells at the Lieutenant, desperate to pass a message of apology onto Rebecca, but hesitant to do so under the present circumstances.

"Do you have plans for our course of sail, sir?" Lieutenant Burgess called out, breaking him from his thoughts.

"Yes, Mr. Burgess," he replied. "We will sail toward the Shetland Islands. They lie in neutral territory and will provide us some measure of protection in which we can wait out this quarantine of yours. We shall remain nearby in the instance that one of us should come under any difficulties. My plan is to sail during the daylight hours, and anchor at sundown until we arrive at our destination. For the remainder of today however, we will drop anchor here to allow you time to get settled in your new surroundings. We'll sail at first light on the morrow."

Lieutenant Burgess nodded his understanding as the two men looked at one another one last time.

"Do you have need of anything, Mr. Burgess?" the captain asked his young officer.

"No, sir, I believe we will manage without too much difficulty," he answered, giving him a respectful smile.

"Very well then," the captain replied. "We will sail on the morrow. I wish you the best of luck, Mr. Burgess," he added, his heart heavy with the knowledge that neither the confident lieutenant, nor those who had accompanied him onboard the disease laden ship, were likely to survive their maiden voyage. In his dismay, he muttered under his breath, "Pray, Miss Halloway… pray, because your life depends on it."

"Thank you, sir," the officer replied, bidding Captain Jameson a solemn farewell.

Chapter 14

The Pepita had set sail with the Redemption on the morning after that fateful day. Now, three days into their maiden voyage toward the tiny islands in the North Sea, Rebecca was keeping herself busy organizing the sick berth. She had battled a brief bout of despondency over the blatant rebuttals of the men, but not one to wallow in self pity, she soon found there were more important tasks at hand. She continued to be troubled by the fact that she had so greatly upset Captain Jameson with her insistence on accompanying the crew aboard the Pepita, but she was at a loss at to how to mend things from so great a distance. Instead of wallowing any longer, she focused her attentions on locating and arranging the supplies on hand and was astonished to come across an impressive stash of medical tinctures, as well as blankets, towels, and even excess clothing in a plethora of sizes. She had been quick to offer these to the men on board, who had brought nothing with them from the Redemption other than the clothes they wore, however, they remained distant and aloof, making it clear that they wanted nothing to do with her. She had even volunteered herself for kitchen duties, assuming that they would have at least deemed her worthy to serve their needs by cooking for them, but Mr. Andrews coolly informed her that Lieutenant Burgess had assigned the task to another more capable than she. She determined in her heart at that moment that she would harbor no resentment toward Mr. Andrews and the crew, but neither would she subject herself to their cruel comments and behavior for the duration of their quarantine. With a firm resolve she tucked herself away in the safe confines of her sick berth, where none endeavored to harass her.

The days passed with agonizing monotony for Rebecca, having no chores to attend to and no one to visit with, so it came as quite a surprise on the fourth day to hear a soft knock at her door, and for several moments Rebecca waited, certain that it must have been her imagination playing tricks on her, but again she heard the sound of light tapping. Standing to her feet, she crossed the broad expanse of the berth and lifted the latch to see who might be calling on her. "Mr. Andrews?" she mused, more in surprise than in greeting. Taking note of his troubled features, she was quick to ask, "What is it? What's wrong?"

"Nothing's wrong," he said. "I've just been worried about you. Have you been eating? No one's seen you moving about..."

A tender smile crossed Rebecca's face. "This is a supply ship, Mr. Andrews. I've had no trouble finding food to eat."

"All right, then," he said, turning as if to leave.

Rebecca, recognizing the old man's attempt at reconciliation, called out, "Mr. Andrews...thank you for thinking about me."

He glanced over his shoulder at the sound of her voice. "You don't have to hide yourself away in here day in and day out, you know," he said.

"I think everyone made it clear that this is where I belong," she remarked in a soft voice. "Especially Mr. Burgess."

"Oh, he never comes below deck...takes all his meals in his stateroom. If you'd like, you can come down to the galley with me...it'd get you out of this hole for a while."

Rebecca was surprised by his invitation but hesitant to accept, as she was unsure of the feelings of the other men who may be in the galley. The thought of escaping the oppressive confines of the sick berth she had hidden away in was appealing though, and a pensive deliberation lit upon her features.

Mr. Andrews was quick to note the hint of ambivalence in her eyes and he said, "Come on, Missy. If the others give you any trouble, I'll deal with the likes of them."

Rebecca took a tentative step through the doorway and followed the petty officer when he beckoned to her. The two walked side by side down the narrow corridor toward the galley, the sounds of the crew's boisterous bantering echoing off the wooden walls. Rebecca's stomach began to knot in apprehension as they drew near, but Mr. Andrews, sensing her hesitation, took her by the elbow to gently pull her along. When they stepped through the narrow portal, Rebecca was quick to note the eerie silence that fell over the room.

"Hey," one of the men grumbled. "What's she doing here?"

The others looked on in an obligatory indifference, waiting for an explanation.

"She's with me," Petty Officer Andrews replied. "Any of you have a problem with that?"

One by one the men shook their heads, in no position to argue with the man, for even though his title did not outrank them, his history of service on the Redemption did, as well as his position of loyalty in the eyes of Lieutenant Burgess. Many knew that the young officer would side with the old man, even in matters pertaining to the girl. Never-the-less a fight was averted that night, and Rebecca sat at the end of a long table, away from the leery glances of the crew. Mr. Andrews disappeared into the kitchen for a short time, and returned to place a hot cup of tea and a biscuit in front of her. Taking a seat nearby he said, "That's quite a sick berth you've fixed up, Missy."

She smiled her appreciation at both the compliment as well as at the presentation of food, but before she could offer her thanks she saw Pete Jones approaching from behind Mr. Andrews. Her dim recollection of the beating he had suffered on account of the incident with the pewter mug resurfaced in her mind, and she waited with baited breath for him to provoke an argument with her.

"So what *are* you doing here?" he demanded.

Mr. Andrews twisted around to face him. "I don't want you giving her no trouble, Jones," he warned.

"No trouble intended now…I'm just curious as to why she'd want to come aboard a ship full of dead men."

His piercing gaze bore into hers as he slouched against a wall, but if his intention was to intimidate, Rebecca remained unaffected. Instead, she met his gaze, the biscuit held in mid air between the table and her mouth. Without hesitating, she lowered it back onto the plate and said, "I came here for you, Mr. Jones…and for Mr. Andrews, Lieutenant Burgess, and any other man who may or may not have contracted the small pox."

"Well we didn't ask you to come…" a man called Sims muttered.

"And why do you suppose we'd want you around even if we do get the small pox?" Pete Jones scoffed.

Rebecca held the man's gaze, and in a quiet voice replied, "Ask me that when your body burns near death with fever and the pustules that cover your skin rupture, spilling an infectious pus all over your flesh…when your mind is lost to delirium, and you know neither to eat nor drink…"

Several of the men grimaced in disgust at her blatant description of a body stricken by a horrendous disease, while Mr. Andrew's face took on a smug grin of satisfaction at her ability to withstand the harassment of the crew.

"What makes you think you won't get it first?" Sims retorted, his face paled by the mention of the word pus.

"I've had the small pox…in Africa, and I survived only because of the swift interventions of my mother and father. Now that I've been exposed to the disease it's unlikely that I'll become infected a second time."

The small room remained deathly still for a time while all eyes focused their gaze on the young girl who sat in complacent solitude, her stomach beginning to prod her for a taste of the biscuit that had been placed before her.

"So you came here…just to take care of *us*?" Pete Jones finally asked, a look of guilty disbelief settling on his face.

Rebecca gave a curt nod and picked up her biscuit. The men glanced at one another in an uncomfortable silence, while the measure of the girl's sacrifice weighed heavily on their minds. Rebecca, appearing somewhat clueless as to their silent suffering, devoured the biscuit with ravenous intent and then asked for another.

"I thought you said you'd been eating," Mr. Andrews teased.

"I said I had no trouble finding food, Mr. Andrews," she replied. "But I didn't say I'd been eating it. For some odd reason, I found my appetite lacking until this evening."

Mr. Andrews was pierced by an unexpected stab of guilt, and he wondered if the girl's diminished appetite was perhaps due to the hostile reception she had received upon her arrival onboard the Pepita. With a shadow of remorse weighing heavy on his features he replied, "I'm sorry we made things so hard for you, Missy. I should've known you had a plan and all…"

Pete Jones, almost as if in an act of repentance, had gone to retrieve another biscuit for Rebecca and a bowl of mutton stew as well. Rebecca eyed him with cautious suspicion when he neared the table where she sat, but when she saw his hands were full of food she considered it an acceptable peace offering and gave him a gracious smile of appreciation. The other men, while not so exuberant in manner, remained pensive and quiet, but all save for Lieutenant Burgess were aware of the sacrifice the girl had made on their behalf.

Rebecca continued to eat with hearty gusto, oblivious to the thoughts and speculations of the men around her. When she could eat no more she glanced up, only to find all eyes in the room watching her. She felt a crimson heat spreading over her face, and stood to make a hasty retreat to her sick berth.

"You don't need to go yet, Missy..." Mr. Andrews said. "We usually end the night with a game of Whist or two. Why don't you sit in on a hand?"

The men waited with expectant faces for her reply when Pete Jones piped up, "You can be my partner for the first round if you like."

Rebecca was taken aback by his unexpected change of disposition, but accepting the man's generous offer, she took the seat he gestured her to. Pete Jones produced a stack of playing cards from his pocket and began to deal the hands. The game continued well into the evening and Rebecca found herself enjoying the company of the men, even though most remained pensive and quiet in her presence. Only when her eyes grew heavy with fatigue did she excuse herself to retire to her berth, bidding the men a timid goodnight.

Mr. Andrews was quick to jump to his feet, and gesturing toward the corridor said, "I'll walk with you, Missy."

A light giggle bubbled out of Rebecca and she murmured, "I think I can manage, Mr. Andrews. It's not *too* far to travel..."

"I insist," he smiled.

They strolled along the length of the hallway without speaking until a tired yawn escaped the girl. Petty Officer Andrews, in an unexpected display of emotion, gathered her in a firm embrace and said, "I'm glad you're here with us, Missy. I hope we don't fall ill, but if we do, I'm awfully glad you're here..."

Rebecca simply smiled through a nod and entered the sick berth, grateful that the lingering contention had dissipated. She knelt to offer heartfelt thanks to the Lord before slipping into a restful slumber, her dreams of home fading as swiftly as the evening sun.

Rebecca's newfound camaraderie with the crew alleviated her restless boredom, and on many occasions in the early evening she would join the men in their quarters for a game of Whist or an hour or two of boisterous singing. On other nights, long after the men had retired to their cabins, she would slip into the cold waters of the North Sea, swimming with long strokes along the length of the ship in the hopes of coaxing her body to life with a good workout. She missed the physical activity that had kept her in top form on the Redemption, and she did not want to lose her stamina for the hard work once they had returned. During the daytime hours she was confined to the sick berth, as the men were needed to work on deck, and so on this day she was rearranging her supplies for the hundredth time when she caught a glimpse of Mr. Andrew's head jutting through the door.

"Why don't you come down to eat in the galley tonight, Missy," he said. "Lieutenant Burgess will be taking his dinner in his quarters again."

He knew the girl wouldn't go near the dining hall if the lieutenant was there, and although he didn't think the man would refuse to eat in the galley if she was present, he knew she preferred not to test him, wanting to abide by his request that she keep her distance. Still, he hated to see her shut up in that room she spent all of her time in and he took it upon himself to see that she ate with the other men whenever the opportunity presented itself. Fortunately, Lieutenant Burgess preferred to remain in his quarters in the evenings, allowing the girl to move about below deck at least part of the day.

"I'd love to, Mr. Andrews!" she exclaimed with a winsome smile. "I'll be down presently."

He retreated into the corridor while Rebecca tidied up her quarters, wanting to finish the task she had started. She chuckled to herself with delight, certain she must have the most organized shelves on the sea.

Rebecca left the safety of her berth to attend to the festivities in the galley, bringing a shout of welcome from the men seated at the narrow tables. They enjoyed her companionship and found her to be a worthy opponent in their card games, as well as a good sport when they teased her, which most often occurred when she was winning. Rebecca in turn, appreciated being welcomed into their circle and expressed her appreciation often.

Rebecca claimed a seat near Mr. Andrews, and relished in the lighthearted bantering of the crew during the dinner meal. She often felt lonely tucked away in her sick berth, but looked forward to nights like these when she could laugh and visit with the group in casual conversation. She thought of Eddy most every day, and realized tonight how much she missed his friendship and his easy manner, until she was startled out of her thoughts by one of the men speaking to her.

"Are you up for a game of Whist tonight, Rebecca?"

She turned her face toward the man who had spoken and saw that it was George Robbins, a man well seasoned from a life spent at sea. "Only if you're up for losing," she teased with a mischievous smile.

He laughed at her show of confidence and replied with enthusiasm, "You're on then!"

Up on deck Lieutenant Burgess reclined at a small table in the solitude of his berth, savoring the food and the respite from the demands of being in command. He missed having the other officers present to consort with, as well as to partake in a card game or two. Since he had taken command of the Pepita, he felt it his duty to maintain a formidable distance from his crew. Consequently, much of his free time was spent alone in his quarters, allowing ample time to for random thoughts to accumulate in his mind. On this night he found his thoughts turning to the girl, and he realized he hadn't seen her since the day they had come aboard. He had assumed the petty officer would alert him to any potential problems if they arose, but as of yet, he had not had word of her from any of the men, nor had he seen her wandering about the Pepita. He considered for a moment inquiring about her but decided against it, well aware that no news was good news. Now, while he relaxed in his berth, he could only hope that the worst was behind them, for he was anxious to return to the Redemption and his less demanding duties as a lieutenant.

Down below Rebecca played several hands of Whist with the men before declaring herself too exhausted to continue. She had hoped to go for a brisk swim before she retired, with the intent of easing the ache in her muscles which had grown stiff from sitting so long in the galley. Standing to her feet, she bid the crew goodnight and made her way down the corridor towards her berth, but instead of proceeding into the room she slipped up to the deck of the Pepita. The night sky was lit up with thousands of twinkling stars, while a full moon cast a luminescent glow on the waves. She could see the Redemption in the distance brightly illuminated against the darkness, and she envisioned the captain in his stateroom, lounging in comfort with a good book. A wave of homesickness struck with unexpected force, and she smiled when she realized it was homesickness for the Redemption, and not for England.

Rebecca stepped to the edge of the small vessel and crawled up onto the railing to dive deeply into the beckoning sea, where she swam below the waves for several moments before surfacing to gasp for a breath of air. How she relished the quiet solitude beneath the water, where her thoughts were clear and her body weightless. She dove under again and again, each time staying just a moment longer than the last. She recalled a story she had heard long ago, of men who could be submerged beneath the great waters and not drown, and she wondered as to their thoughts...and of what it must have taken to coax them back into the harsh, noisy reality of this world. If it had been her, she knew, she gladly would have remained beneath the waters forever, safe in the blanketing cocoon of the tide.

She broke the surface with a clean stroke, opening her arms in great strides and gliding through the waves with ease. She swam around the Pepita, enjoying the easy laughter of the men coming from below deck and giving thought to the whereabouts of Lieutenant Burgess. The waters were calm, offering her an edge to her speed, and she swam straight out beyond the bow of the ship for several moments, not looking back but imagining instead that she was swimming to the Redemption. She prayed for the men on the distant frigate, as well as for the crew on the Pepita. How she longed to see the saving grace of Christ made real to them!

Pausing for a moment to catch her breath, she let herself be carried on the waves, lifted high and then dipped down low. She felt as if she was in a dance with the universe and she reveled at the orchestration of it all. With a sigh of contentment, she took a deep breath and disappeared again into the murky depths of the sea.

Lieutenant Burgess lay in bed, his many thoughts thwarting all attempts for slumber, and he wondered if his restlessness was due to his recently acquired duties of taking command or if they were common to one acting as captain. If the latter were the case he determined, he might have to rethink his lofty ambitions as a lieutenant, not wanting to assume the responsibilities of commander after all.

Thinking perhaps a breath of fresh air would induce sleep, he crawled from his hammock and made his way to the deck. He knew none would bother him there, for the entire crew was most likely below immersed in a card game or two. The cool breeze greeted his face with a soft caress and he took deep breaths of the salt laden air, while wondering how the landlubbers could live without the fresh scent of the sea and the rolling waves lulling them to sleep at night. He cut a path to the bow of the ship and rested his arms on the railing. The brilliance of the moonlight caught his attention and he tried to recall a night sky so full of stars as this. Gazing into the heavens with wonder, his eyes caught a glimpse of the Redemption, and he stared at the massive frigate that was listing about on the water. How he longed to be back onboard with his friends and fellow officers he realized, while he wondered how the captain was faring without him.

He saw her then, being pushed and pulled by the waves. At first he feared she was attempting to swim back to the Redemption and he considered diving in after her, but instead, he continued to gaze at her, waiting for her to make a move. After several, long moments she began to swim again, her agility in the waves making it appear as though she was a creature of the sea. He found himself mesmerized by her grace in moving through the water, and he found it difficult to take his eyes from the sight of her lithe form.

In an abrupt move she disappeared beneath the waves and his heart began to pound as he felt his breath catch in his throat. He peered with keen eyes over the surface of the water, watching for her to reappear. After several moments had passed he began to grow frantic, certain she must be in some dangerous predicament. He started to climb over the railing in an effort to rescue her, but before he was able to jump from the deck, he heard her gasp for air, her face breaking free of the murky depths. He slipped back into the shadows lest she see him and waited for her desperate cries for help, but instead of flailing about as he had expected, she began to swim with effortless strokes toward the Pepita. He stepped back towards the railing and onto the deck, where he remained in the shadows of the bow to observe her until she had climbed safely aboard.

Rebecca floated with lazy strokes in the water for several moments, not wanting the peaceful interlude to end, but her arms were tired from her vigorous swim and her body was numb from the chill of the water. She pulled herself with deliberate ease toward the rear of the ship where she grasped the short rope that would return her to the deck. Standing upright, she took a moment to reorient herself to the unmoving planks of the Pepita, and then tread with soft steps to her berth.

Lieutenant Burgess nearly stepped out from the shadows to chastise the girl for her foolishness of swimming unattended in the darkness, but decided instead to deal with the matter later, when he was in a less distracted frame of mind. He watched her make her way below, and then turned to retreat to his own quarters in the hopes that sleep would come more easily this time around, but instead he found his thoughts drifting to the girl and her serene presence in the cold waters of the sea. She was unlike any person he had ever known he realized, both man and woman alike. He knew the captain and Dr. Ammons had grown quite fond of her, as had other members of the crew, yet he preferred to maintain his distance, for her feigned innocence disturbed him. He had been impressed however by her calm reserve when faced with the many trials that had come to her during her time aboard the Redemption, as well as by her tenacity in her dealings with the captain. Few men would have been as brave in withstanding his wrath and scrutiny.

Enough about her, he determined, struggling to turn his mind to other matters. He tossed about in frustration for several minutes more before slipping into a fitful sleep, but instead of escaping his thoughts of Rebecca, he found himself in the midst of a disturbing dream involving the girl. They were aboard the Redemption and the sky was dark. The crew was bustling about in a panic, almost as if in the midst of some great catastrophe, when he caught sight of her face from a distance. Although he could not see where it was that he stood, he knew it was on the quarterdeck, and even from so great a distance he could see the frightened confusion etched on her features. A sense of dread filled his mind as he watched her being pushed about by the men she was in the midst of. Suddenly a shot rang out and she turned her startled face toward him, gazing at him in shocked sadness for just a moment before she began to drop listlessly to the hard, unyielding planks of the deck. He watched in horror as the men gathered around her on deck, until in his confusion he glanced down to find a smoldering pistol in his hand.

He awoke in a cold sweat, his heart pounding in his chest. Pushing himself upright, he struggled to slow his breathing as he again heard the sound of a single gunshot. He stood and moved to the door of his berth to fling it open in a swift motion, wondering if it hadn't been a dream at all but a hostile attack on the Pepita. He was relieved to find an empty deck, still cloaked in the dusky light of the approaching sunrise. Retreating to his cot, he crawled again beneath the cotton covers, but sleep would not come.

Rebecca slept undisturbed after her relaxing swim in the cool water until she woke with an abrupt start. She stared out into the early morning light, listening for a clue as to why she had awakened, but hearing nothing, she turned over with a sigh and slipped back into a deep slumber.

The Pepita had been trailing the Redemption for eight days now, and they were finally nearing the Shetland Islands where they would moor for the duration of their quarantine. Lieutenant Burgess felt certain that he and his crew had escaped contracting the dreaded disease, for all of the men appeared to be well, and seeing as how he had not received word on the girl, he assumed she had remained unaffected as well. He was relieved to find that she had complied with his order to remain below deck, yet still he saw her face each day as he recalled with vivid clarity the horrible dream. He resisted asking his petty officer about her and chose instead to watch for her on occasion in the evenings, in the hopes of seeing her moving about. It troubled him to realize that he yearned to catch a glimpse of her, and with exasperation he pushed the thought away, directing his attention instead on locating the Redemption over the waves. He lifted a gold plated scope to his eye and peered at the vast horizon, sliding his arm in a graceful arc until the frigate came into view. He was distracted from his search by the voice of his petty officer.

"Sir," he began, "I'm sorry to trouble you, but Harry Sims isn't feeling well."

A knot of dread began to form in the officer's belly as he asked, "Where is he Mr. Andrews?"

"He's below, sir, in his hammock."

Lieutenant Burgess gripped the railing, contemplating for several moments the best course of action. Motioning to his petty officer, they proceeded below to determine what sickness ailed the midshipman. He entered the crew's quarters through a small doorway, but was stopped short when Petty Officer Andrews offered him a respectful warning.

"You don't want to get too close to him, sir. I know I'm no doctor, but I'm pretty certain it's the small pox that ails him."

"Well what am I supposed to do, Mr. Andrews?" he snapped. "I can't just leave him here!"

"We could get the girl…she's had the small pox and says she won't catch it a second time."

"She lies," he muttered. "She couldn't have survived the disease."

"But, sir," he protested, knowing Rebecca would not have told him a falsehood, "that's why she came aboard."

"Alright, Mr. Andrews," he barked. "Get the girl and bring her to the deck."

"Aye-aye, sir," he said.

"And tell the men to stay away from Mr. Sims," he shouted, irate at having to get the girl involved in the situation.

Rebecca had stolen away from the sick berth to help Ron Peters with the morning meal, knowing Lieutenant Burgess usually took his breakfast in his quarters, but still she remained alert to the sound of his footsteps in the corridor. Hearing someone approach, she watched the doorway with a guarded expression until she saw the troubled face of Petty Officer Andrews peering into the galley.

"What is it, Mr. Andrews," she asked, a hint of concern in her voice.

"Lieutenant Burgess wants to see you on deck, Missy. I'm afraid the news isn't good."

Rebecca followed the petty officer up the narrow stairwell in a wary silence, wondering what sort of trouble she had gotten herself into now, but before she stepped foot onto the deck, she wondered if this was some cruel trick to test her. Sensing her hesitation, Petty Officer Andrews took her by the arm and pulled her out into the bright sunlight, where she could see Lieutenant Burgess at the rail, his face a grim contortion of dismay.

Lieutenant Burgess glanced at Rebecca when he saw her slip from the stairwell, and even from a distance he was aware of the fear that shadowed her features. He turned away from her when she met his gaze, disconcerted at the prospect of speaking with her.

"Sir," Petty Officer Andrews began, "she's here, sir."

"Yes, I can see that, Mr. Andrews," he replied with irritation, turning to face them both.

Rebecca remained in quiet contemplation, waiting for the officer to speak. She had never been summoned by the man before now, and the thought had crossed her mind on more than one occasion that Captain Jameson was not there to protect her from his wrath.

Lieutenant Burgess studied the girl's wary expression while she waited with expectation for him to speak. He couldn't help but wonder what thoughts must be coursing through her mind, for he had never offered her a kind word in the past and he doubted she expected to hear one now. Still, he was impressed by her ability to refrain from speaking, in spite of the anxiety he was certain she must be feeling. "It has been brought to my attention that one of the crew has taken ill," he informed her.

"Which one?" she whispered, a dark foreboding taking root in her belly.

"Harry Sims."

"Is he still below?" she asked in a soft voice.

Mr. Burgess gave a curt nod in answer to her question, and was taken by surprise when he saw her turn as if to depart. "Where are you going?" he demanded.

"To Mr. Sim's berth, sir," she said, surprised to see him glaring at her with a hostile scowl.

"Well what is your intention for handling the matter?" he demanded, growing irritated by her simple acceptance of the situation. He had expected tears, gnashing of teeth, and even outright panic, but she did none of these and that frustrated him.

She turned back to face him with an apologetic look. "I'm sorry, Mr. Burgess," she sighed. She was unsure of how to speak to this man without invoking his contention, and now she struggled to find the words that would convey her thoughts without annoying him further. "He needs to be quarantined from the rest of the men."

"You don't even know what ails him," the officer retorted.

"No, but we can assume it's small pox," she murmured.

"And if it is?"

"I need to move him, but the rest of the crew should maintain a safe distance, not only from him, but from all who should fall ill."

"You can't move him by yourself," he scoffed.

"Then I'll get Mr. Andrews to help me," she replied, trying to maintain some semblance of composure under his scrutinizing glare.

"And just where do you plan on moving him to?" he continued.

"I have a sick berth prepared."

"A what?" he asked, looking incredulous.

"A sick berth."

"And where, might I be so bold as to ask, is this sick berth of yours?"

"Down below, at the front of the ship," she said.

"The bow," he corrected, giving her a condescending look.

"Mr. Burgess," she sighed, "I really should tend to Mr. Sims... before the rest of the crew realize he has taken ill," she said, too weary to spend one minute longer arguing with the man than she had to. She remained on deck waiting for him to dismiss her, but when he said nothing she turned to hurry below, wanting to get the sick man away from the others as quickly as possible. Much to her chagrin, Lieutenant Burgess followed close behind her until they came to the doorway of the crew's quarters, and she stepped in front of him to say in a quiet tone, "You might want to return to the deck, Mr. Burgess. I wouldn't want you to risk becoming infected."

"I will return to the deck when I am ready," he replied, determined to see this sick berth she spoke of.

Rebecca stepped into the room and approached the hammock slung near the wall, its canvas bulging from the weight of the man still lying in it. She saw that the midshipman kept his eyes closed but mumbled a greeting when she spoke to him, and lifting his tunic to peer at his torso she began to search for the telltale rash of small pox on his body. Seeing nothing, she placed her hand with a light touch on his forehead and gave an inward groan when she felt the man's flesh burning with fever beneath her fingertips. She glanced over her shoulder to where Mr. Burgess waited with an irritated air about him, and saw Mr. Andrews shifting on his feet beside him. "Mr. Andrews," she said, "would you help me move him?"

The petty officer took a cautious step around Lieutenant Burgess, well aware of the man's hostile resentment towards the girl, and moved to stand beside her to await her instruction.

"We'll cut him down in his hammock," she began. "That will prevent you from having any direct contact with his skin.

Whatever you do Mr. Andrews, don't touch the men who are infected," she said, a grave look upon her face.

He nodded his understanding and pulled a short knife from the sheath on his hip to cut the rope supporting the side of the canvas sling nearest him before reaching over to cut Rebecca's side, hoping to bear the brunt of the man's weight before she had to.

She faltered for a moment when the hammock was cut from the rafters, stunned by the heaviness of the man. They struggled to maneuver his body between the empty beds while Lieutenant Burgess continued to scrutinize them from the doorway. He stepped back to allow them to pass and then proceeded to follow them down the narrow corridor that took them to the bow of the ship, where Rebecca had been meticulous in preparing the sick berth.

When they entered the brightly lit room Rebecca led Mr. Andrews to a spot near the wall. They laid the bulking form of Harry Sims there, still tucked inside his canvas hammock, while Rebecca set out to gather the supplies she would need. Lieutenant Burgess glanced around the tidy berth with an aggravated grimace upon his face before following Rebecca out to the hall, where he found her loading her arms with stacks of cloths and clean blankets. With her arms full she twirled around to return to the sick berth, only to find Lieutenant Burgess blocking her path. "Excuse me, sir," she said, surprised to see he still lingered.

Giving her an infuriated look he snapped, "When you have finished here, you will report to the deck immediately."`

With that said, he stormed off, leaving Rebecca near tears. She sought refuge in the solitude of the sick berth, taking her time arranging the supplies in an orderly fashion near her first patient. After a time, she realized Mr. Andrews had remained and was hovering in the doorway, watching her through a troubled expression.

"Are we all going to die, Missy?"

She took a deep breath and stepped over to where he stood. Moving in close while being careful not to touch him, she said, "I came here for one reason only, Mr. Andrews, and it's this…to care for you and the men if you should become ill with small pox. I promise you…I will do my best to ensure that we all return to the Redemption alive."

He smiled at her consoling words and wished Lieutenant Burgess would not treat her with such harsh reproach. Reaching out to pat her cheek, he said, "You know, he's not so bad once you get to know him."

She rolled her eyes at the man, but managed a weak laugh before venturing up to the deck to speak with the lieutenant. Rebecca could see him pacing in agitation when she approached, and her apprehension only increased with each step she took. Before she had even drawn near to where he stood he spun on his heel, his rebuke coming swift and sure.

"Who is the commander onboard this vessel?"

"You are, sir," she replied, stopping short lest he attempt to strike her.

"Then why was I not informed of your plans before now?"

He stood glaring at her, waiting for an explanation, and Rebecca knew that whatever she said at this point would only infuriate him further. She took a deep breath and began to speak, while praying that her soft tone would deflect his obvious resentment. "I apologize, Mr. Burgess," she said. "I was only trying to stay out of your way as you had requested."

He expected to see a tearful outburst at any moment but it did not come. Instead she continued to watch him with a guarded expression, and he was struck by an overwhelming sense of guilt as visions of her falling listlessly to the deck replayed themselves in his mind, just as it had on the night of his horrible dream. Unable to hold her gaze any longer, he turned his back and said, "What's done is done, but from this point forward you are to inform me of any course of action you might take that involves my ship and my men, is that clear?"

"Yes, sir," she murmured in a contrite tone.

Lieutenant Burgess stalked towards his berth to escape the awkward tension he felt in the girl's presence. He had been so infuriated when Captain Jameson insisted she accompany them, that he never paused to consider why she had wanted to in the first place. The words his petty officer spoke only brought him further confusion. How could she have possibly survived small pox, he wondered. And why did she choose to accompany a mission that was doomed from the start? He retreated into the darkness of his berth, determined to have answers to his questions before nightfall.

Rebecca stood fast until the lieutenant was out of sight before hurrying back to the sick berth, where she saw Mr. Andrews watching the unmoving body of Harry Sims from safety of the corridor.

"Is everything alright, Missy?" he asked in a low whisper.

"Yes, Mr. Andrews," she sighed, choosing to keep the officer's harsh reprimand to herself while she set about tending to her patient.

"Do you think he'll survive?" the petty officer asked, gesturing to where Mr. Sims lay.

"I hope so, Mr. Andrews," she said, "but please, take care not to touch any of those who become ill...the disease is thought to be spread through skin contact and I don't want you to risk contagion."

"Oh, don't worry about me, Missy," he assured her, "this tough, old skin won't let anything through!"

She put on a brave façade while trying to dispel the tears that welled in her eyes, her heart heavy with the knowledge that a sure battle for the lives of the crew had begun. Needing a purposeful distraction, she directed her attention to the sick man lying on the floor of the sick berth. His skin was flushed and warm and Rebecca's first thought was to gather fresh water to cool him. Taking one of the buckets from the closet, she hurried to the galley to gather a good supply that would last throughout the night. She then returned to the sick berth and began to lay the wet cloths on the man's face. She removed his tunic to sponge his arms, neck and chest, hoping the fever would soon break. She tried to stir him to wakefulness, but he mumbled incoherent words and refused to open his eyes.

Rebecca stayed with her patient throughout the day. Mr. Andrews brought her a bowl of mutton stew in the early evening and made an attempt to coax her from Mr. Sims for a time. She refused, not wanting to leave his side, for she had been unable to control the rise and fall of his feverish state. She soon lost track of time, and was surprised when the room began to grow dim in the twilight of evening. Standing to light the lanterns she had set about she felt the stiff pull of her muscles, and she longed for a brisk swim to relieve the aching in her limbs. Instead, she returned to the sick midshipman and attempted to coax him into drinking some water.

"Missy?"

Turning her attention to the sound of Mr. Andrews shouting to her from the other side of the door, she hurried to answer his call, not wanting him to enter the room where the infected man lay.

"Yes, Mr. Andrews, what is it?" she asked, tilting her head into the corridor.

"Johnny isn't feeling too well," he said, his eyes filled with dread.

She held his gaze and said in a low voice, "Have him come here straight away, Mr. Andrews, and tell him to bring his bed linens."

She watched him turn to do as she asked and called out in haste, "Mr. Andrews!"

He stopped when he heard her voice, and looked back at her with a fleeting glance.

"Don't touch him..." she whispered.

The second patient joined Rebecca and Harry Sims in the sick berth within minutes, and she felt compassion for the boy when she saw the worried expression darkening his features. He couldn't have been more than seventeen years old, but still he made a desperate attempt to put on a brave face when he entered the warmly lit berth, trailing behind him the coverings from his hammock.

"You can come over here, Johnny," she told him, beckoning him to the floor near where Mr. Sims lay.

He followed her instructions without argument and laid his coverings on the stark, wooden planks. Rebecca asked him a myriad of questions relating to the symptoms he was experiencing, and he answered them in a quiet voice while he sat propped against the wall of the Pepita, but before night had fallen his face was flushed with fever, and he lay shivering beneath the thin, cotton blanket that would be his bed for the next several days.

Mr. Andrews appeared that evening with a fresh supply of water and Rebecca had a strong desire to give him a firm embrace, but knowing she could infect him with her touch, she remained well within the confines of the room, thanking him in a grateful tone instead. Before he departed for the night she said, "Mr. Andrews, would you please tell Lieutenant Burgess that Johnny has joined us here? He'll want to be kept abreast of the situation." He smiled through a short nod and went directly to the officer's berth as the girl had asked, happy to oblige her this one, small request and wishing he could do more to help ease her burden.

Lieutenant Burgess lingered in his berth, still deliberating over the peculiar presence of the girl aboard the Pepita. A light knock at the door offered him welcome distraction and he called out, "Come!"

The petty officer slipped through the portal and stood with an apologetic expression of penitence. "I'm sorry to disturb you, sir, but I'm here to inform you that Johnny Giles has taken ill and has joined Mr. Sims in the sick berth."

"When?" he asked.

"Earlier today."

"Why didn't the girl tell me herself?" he demanded, his resentment welling.

"She won't leave the room, sir...thinks she's infectious now too."

The lieutenant shot a hard glance at the petty officer and demanded, "Why is she even here, Mr. Andrews? Why did she come aboard?"

"She said she came to help us through the sickness, sir."

"And if she gets sick along with the rest of us?"

"She had the small pox once before and says she won't get sick a second time."

"I don't believe her..." the officer grumbled, having never heard of any who had survived the dreaded disease.

"Well if it's not true, sir, then I suppose she's every bit the conniving liar you think her to be, isn't she now?"

The petty officer's contrite statement stunned him into a melancholy silence, and with great conviction he dismissed the man, wanting to digest the words that assaulted his conscience in the solitude of his quarters, away from the prying glances of the crew.

Rebecca was afforded little opportunity for sleep that night and remained diligent to divide her time between Mr. Peters and her newest patient, Johnny Giles, in a fervent attempt to cool their feverish bodies. She yawned when the first rays of the sun's light streaked through the portholes and found herself amazed that morning had come so quickly. Lowering herself to her knees in prayer, she thanked the Lord for sustaining them all through the night, while she prayed for the perseverance to see her friends through the difficult time that lay ahead. When she had finished she stood to coax her body back to life with a good stretch, and was alarmed when the voice of Petty Officer Andrews summoned her from the corridor once again. She hurried to the portal, anxious to hear what news he came to deliver, but when she peered through the door she found a steaming bowl of porridge extended towards her.

"Oh, Mr. Andrews," she murmured, the smile that lit upon her face communicating more heartfelt thanks than mere words were capable of. "You are so very kind, and I am so very grateful."

"Do you think your patients are up to a bowl of gruel yet?" he queried in a hushed tone.

"I'm afraid not, Mr. Andrews," she answered, stifling a yawn. "How are the other men feeling this morning?"

"So far, so good," he assured, concerned at the fatigue which shadowed her features.

"I'm glad to hear that," she sighed.

"Are you getting enough rest, Missy?"

"Some, Mr. Andrews, but don't worry about me…I'll manage well enough," she answered. "Does Mr. Burgess know that Johnny is sick?" she asked, wanting to keep the officer well informed on the activity in the sick berth so as to avoid another confrontation with him.

"Aye," he replied, "I told him last night, after I spoke with you."

"Thank you, Mr. Andrews," she said, offering a generous smile of relief.

Rebecca remained in the sick berth with the men for the entire day. She ventured out only once to replenish her water supply and to ask the petty officer if he would prepare some warm broth for the men, in the hopes that she could persuade them to take sips of the liquid nourishment to soothe their parched throats. Upon returning to the sick berth, she saw another one of the crew, Anthony Porter, propped in a miserable fashion against the door.

"Tony!" she exclaimed with surprise, hurrying to where he stood.

"I'm not feeling too good, Miss Halloway," he proclaimed in a weary voice.

Rebecca pushed open the door to the sick berth and led him to an unoccupied spot in the center of the room, offering a steady arm while he lowered himself to the floor. She gathered clean blankets to place over him, certain his skin would be flushed and burning before long, and within the hour he erupted into spasms when his shivering limbs succumbed to the fever that took hold of his body at last, while his mind drifted into the diseased and unresponsive stage of small pox.

Chapter 15

The days began to blend into nights for Rebecca as she worked with relentless determination taking care of the diseased men who filled her sick berth. They had finally reached the Shetland Islands where the Pepita would moor for the duration of their quarantine, and the Redemption dropped anchor at a safe distance on the horizon. It was fortunate for them all that they had finally arrived at their destination, for the crew had been reduced to just four men...Petty Officer Andrews, George Robbins, Pete Jones and Lieutenant Burgess himself, all of whom had thus far remained unaffected by the disease that had engulfed the rest of the crew. Rebecca continued to make every effort to keep the healthy men away from those stricken with small pox, and rarely left the sick berth for anything other than fresh water. Mr. Andrews had been a great source of comfort and support to her, bringing hot food for both herself and for the men that were well enough to eat. He was careful to place whatever he delivered just outside the door, knowing Rebecca would not let him enter into the sick berth itself. He remained diligent to deliver frequent reports to Lieutenant Burgess as well, keeping the acting captain abreast on the status of the men who had fallen ill.

The afternoon sun cast its rays over the deck of the Pepita, blinding Lieutenant Burgess for a moment as he stood peering through his telescope. Averting his gaze from the discomfort, he caught a glimpse of Petty Officer Andrews scrubbing the wooden floorboards near the stern. George Robbins, he knew, had taken up residence in the nearly deserted crew's quarters, hoping to clear the room of the diseased air that had consumed the small supply ship, while Pete Jones remained below, working in the galley to prepare another batch of mutton stew for the men confined to the sick berth.

Pete Jones was slicing through a generous shank of mutton when he cringed from the grip of a painful spasm in his belly, and he felt an unexpected wave of nausea come over him. Dropping the knife onto the counter, he was quick to stumble up the narrow stairwell to the deck where he leaned over the railing and heaved up the contents of his lunch. Mr. Andrews and Lieutenant Burgess looked on in surprise, while the man's body was wracked by the spasms that had taken hold of him.

"Stay with him, Mr. Andrews," the officer ordered, turning to make his way down to the sick berth in search of the girl.

Rebecca was sitting on the floor of the brightly lit room, bathed in sunlight and surrounded by her patients. Her legs were tucked up beneath her in a feminine fashion and she was spooning broth into the mouth of Johnny Giles, who was finally feeling well enough to eat. She heard the latch of the door disengage and turned in surprise to see who had entered, knowing it wouldn't be Petty Officer Andrews, for he knew better than to enter the room directly. A shocked grimace of dismay sprang to her face when she saw it was Lieutenant Burgess who had stepped through the portal, and she jumped to her feet to coax him back into the corridor. "You shouldn't come in here, sir," she cautioned.

Retreating into the hallway, the officer stared at the girl through an expression of irate disbelief when he saw her pull the door shut with a resounding slam behind her.

"What can I do for you, Mr. Burgess?" she asked, making a conscious to appear unruffled, in spite of the nervous trembling in her limbs.

They were distracted for a brief moment when Mr. Andrews arrived, stumbling down the last of the steps with a fraught Pete Jones trailing behind him. Rebecca stepped back and opened the door to the sick berth, taking her most recent patient's arm and leading him inside. She was quick to return to the corridor, but remained standing in front of the foreboding door and peering up at the hostile Lieutenant Burgess towering over her in firm rebuke.

"Step aside," he ordered in a terse voice.

She shook her head saying, "I can't let you go in there, Mr. Burgess."

His hands curled into angry fists as he continued to scowl down at the girl, irate that she would have the audacity to rebuff his authority. "I'll go anywhere I please on this ship," he snapped.

"But not in here, sir," she said in a soft voice, aware that she was tempting fate.

"Mr. Andrews," the officer said, his eyes fixed on Rebecca, "please inform the girl that she will step aside, or I will remove her by force."

Petty Officer Andrews glanced with nervous apprehension between the officer and the girl, knowing full well that he would be unable to convince Rebecca to allow the lieutenant to enter the sick berth.

"Mr. Burgess," she reminded, "this room is full of sick men and I will not let you pass. Small Pox is extremely contagious."

Rebecca had wondered on several occasions how she would ever manage to provide care for the officer if he were to become ill, but now, as the angry lieutenant stood towering over her, she determined that death would be preferable to taking him in as a patient. So rather than stand down she maintained her obstinate stance in the doorway of the sick berth, where she gazed with surprising calm into his livid eyes.

Lieutenant Burgess had never laid a hand on any woman in anger, nor had he been tempted to before the girl's untimely intrusion into his world, but in his fury he felt his resolve waning, and uncurling his fingers he took a knife from a sheath at his hip solely with the intention of frightening her into submission lest he strike out at her in her rebellion.

"Sir!" Mr. Andrews exclaimed in astonishment.

"Step aside!" he said again, an ominous threat hovering in his voice.

Rebecca stood firm, waiting for the blade to pierce her flesh as she repeated with deliberate clarity, "I will not let you pass, sir."

The two kept their eyes locked in a battle of wills, while Petty Officer Andrews paced about in nervous trepidation wondering who to reprimand first, the officer who could invoke his death, or the girl who could save his life.

Rebecca was first to breach the silence in an attempt to diffuse the tense situation when she reminded the officer in a gentle manner, never averting her gaze from his, "Mr. Burgess… you are in command of this ship. You, of all people, must not fall ill."

He studied her obstinate form for several moments through narrowed eyes and then turned on his heel to retreat to the solitude of the deck, where he pounded his fist on the rail in his frustration, incensed that the woman could drive him to such madness. He stared out over the waves, intent on dispelling the anger that lingered, until a quiet voice distracted him from his tortured thoughts.

"She's just tired, sir," Petty Officer Andrews commented, sidling up beside him. "She hasn't been sleeping much you know, what with all the men needing her attention."

"She infuriates me, Mr. Andrews," he replied, grateful for the man's listening ear.

"Oh, I know she does now, sir, but she's not so bad once you get to know her."

"Well I certainly don't intend to do that, Mr. Andrews," he growled, spinning on his heel to storm off to his quarters.

Petty Officer Andrews tarried for a time on deck, wondering what it was about the girl that evoked such relentless exasperation in the officer. He had never known anyone so sweet natured and accepting of her circumstance, regardless of how difficult it might be. The girl had demonstrated a vast capacity for selfless servitude, and exuded a sense of peace and joy, in spite of the crew's frequent harassment. Glancing at the portal of the lieutenant's cabin, he gave a weary shake of his head and proceeded below to deliver an encouraging word and a warm bowl of stew to the sick berth, knowing the girl would need a bit of solace after the fierce confrontation with the officer.

Rebecca retreated to the safety of the sick berth on unsteady legs, relieved to live another day. She was astounded by her behavior in standing up to the man the way she had, and it occurred to her that being away from the Redemption and the protection of Captain Jameson was giving her a surprising boldness. Either that, she reasoned with an infectious giggle, or she was simply delusional with fatigue. She hurried to attend to Pete Jones, the newest patient in the berth. He was looking quite miserable by this time, and she wondered how the male gender had ever survived for so long without women to care for them.

Back on the Redemption, Captain Jameson relaxed in his stateroom, his thoughts lingering on his crew, his lieutenant, but even more so the girl onboard the Pepita. He maintained a continual watch of the small ship moored in the distance, and he was consumed with worry for the well being of those who had ventured aboard the diseased vessel. How he wished there were some way he could communicate with them, so he could at least be assured that they still lived. Instead he was left pacing the floor of his stateroom late into the night, overwhelmed by his darkest fears. Dr. Ammons made every attempt to put the captain's worries to rest, assuring him that Rebecca was more than competent when it came to her skills at doctoring her patients, but still, the thought of losing her was more than Captain Jameson could bear, especially in consideration of the circumstances in which they had parted. He had noticed that the movement on the deck of the small ship had decreased noticeably over the past several days, but the British flag continued to be raised at sunrise and lowered at sunset, giving him the assurance that at least one still lived.

Chapter 16

When the days of their confinement moved into weeks, Rebecca was able to release more and more of the men from the sick berth. Their pustules had dried up, leaving pitted scars as the only reminder that they had visited death's door. She continued to give careful attention to the men who remained, the fatigue beginning to take its toll on her. She was physically, mentally and emotionally depleted, and Petty Officer Andrews was growing more and more concerned with each passing day. Rebecca offered frequent assurance that she was managing just fine, but in the darkness of night she would weep in weary despair, begging the Lord for the strength to continue on for just one more day.

Lieutenant Burgess maintained a safe distance from the sick berth after his tenuous altercation with the girl and he hadn't seen her since, nor had he inquired about her wellbeing. He was grateful that his men were surviving their brush with death and he only hoped they would soon be able to return to the Redemption. He was growing weary of the responsibilities of being in command, and he found that he missed the company of the other officers, as well as the consistent direction of Captain Jameson. Hoping to clear his jumbled thoughts, he left the stuffy confines of his berth to collect a breath of fresh air on deck. The evening sun was slipping below the horizon and he could see the multitudes of twinkling stars positioned in the cloudless sky. He moved to the railing to gaze out over the smooth, glass-like waters of the North Sea, feeling for the first time since they had come aboard confident that life would soon return to normal.

Rebecca had been below, telling tales of her adventures to the patients who remained in the sick berth, while they hung with rapt attention on every word that proceeded from her mouth. She had hoped to quell the boredom that always seemed to come after the novelty of idle dawdling had worn off. From the corner of the room, she heard Ron Peters, the most recent of the men to have fallen ill, call out to her.

"Rebecca? Is there anything left from the evening meal that I might eat?"

Rebecca breathed a quiet sigh of relief at hearing his voice. He had been burning with fever and unresponsive for the past three days and she hadn't been able to stir him awake long enough to eat or drink anything since that time.

"Yes, Mr. Peters," she smiled, grateful to hear that his appetite had returned. "I would be happy to get you something to eat, sir."

She excused herself from the group and made her way down the darkly lit corridor to the galley. She was surprise to see that it was quiet and empty of men at this early hour. Yawning, she entered the room and began to search for something of sustenance that she could take back to the sick berth with her. No one had been doing much food preparation in the weeks since the men had taken ill with small pox, and the galley was bare of any food this night as well. She sighed in resignation and set about to boil a chunk of meat with some shriveled potatoes, reaching for a small pot buried behind a stack of large kettles.

When she tried to tug it free the entire heap fell with a crash onto the floor, leaving Rebecca aghast with surprise at the chaos settling at her feet with a deafening clatter.

Lieutenant Burgess heard the commotion from where he lounged on deck. He hurried below and made his way to the galley where he found the girl sitting amidst a mound of pots and pans, a tired expression etched on her features and dark shadows encircling her eyes.

"What's going on down here?" he asked, his gaze taking in the clutter strewn about the room.

Rebecca glanced at the officer with an inward groan. The last thing she had anticipated on this night was another confrontation with the lieutenant. "Nothing," she sighed, having little energy left to explain the situation.

"Well it certainly doesn't look like nothing," he snapped, irritated by her casual air of indifference.

Another yawn escaped her as she gazed at the disarray which surrounded her. "One of the men requested a bite to eat…" she began. "I was just hoping to boil a bit of mutton for him."

His eyes narrowed with suspicion. "Why didn't he eat earlier, with the rest of the men?" he asked.

"I don't know," she murmured.

He continued to stare at her, feeling the familiar root of agitation beginning to take hold. "Well, what do you know?" he scoffed.

"I know I am going to feed the man," she answered, finally locating the small pot amidst the pile of kettles.

"My men are not afforded the luxury of dining when they feel like it. He will eat with the rest of the crew, and not before then." He gave her a look of admonition, his silent warning not to pursue the matter further.

Rebecca began to fill the pot with water and attempted to bring a flame from wood inside the stove. "He hasn't eaten for the past three days, Mr. Burgess, but he will eat tonight," she said, not about to relent on the matter, for she knew the man was in dire need of nourishment.

Their eyes locked in a silent battle of wills and they remained intractable in spirit, both determined to win the battle. Rebecca held the small pot in her hand, appearing as if it were a weapon she intended to use if the situation warranted it.

Lieutenant Burgess broke the silence first by growling in a low voice, "Why are you so obstinate?"

Rebecca's gaze never faltered as she whispered in return, "Why are you so ignorant?"

It took the officer a moment for the words she had spoken to register in his mind and when he became aware of her blatant impertinence he warned in a threatening tone, his eyes narrowed and calculating, "You are walking a fine line of insubordination, Rebecca Halloway."

She was taken aback for a moment when she heard him call her by her given name, for he had never done so before this night. Maintaining her gaze along with her composure she replied, "I will not return to the sick berth empty handed, Lieutenant Burgess."

"Do you recall the punishment for disobeying a superior officer?" he asked.

"Yes I do, sir, but need I remind you that I am not one of your enlisted," she stated, growing angry at his harassment. "I have not, nor do I intend to, join the royal forces!"

"Then get off my ship," he ordered in a terse voice.

Rebecca considered his words for a moment before taking a quick turn on her heel and marching up to the deck, realizing full well that she should have left this blasted vessel long before now. "That I can do, sir," she declared, not bothering to turn around.

He stared after her in a confounded silence as she stormed from the galley and wondered what scheme the girl had connived this time. Sighing in his exasperation, he followed her out into the night air where he watched her climb with a cautious step over the railing to perch at the edge of the deck. With a meticulous demonstration of showmanship she lifted her arms over her head and dove in a graceful arc into the murky waters below. Lieutenant Burgess cursed forcefully under his breath and dashed to the railing to see her swimming with long, full strides away from the Pepita.

"Where on earth do you think you're going?" he shouted, knowing it had better not be to the Redemption because they were still under quarantine.

She paused mid-stride for a moment to yell over her shoulder. "I'm going home to England!"

"Well you're going the wrong way!"

She stopped swimming in order to turn herself around, hoping to make the impact of her words as fierce as she felt at the moment. "Then I'll stop to ask for directions later!" she screamed, becoming even more incensed that the only time the man bothered to show any whit of concern for her wellbeing was when she was fleeing his presence.

The officer peered into the darkness in bewildered agitation, realizing that it was doubtful she would return on her own volition. Another angry curse escaped him as he peeled off his uniform and kicked his shoes from his feet, diving into the frigid water to make an attempt to retrieve the ill-mannered girl. By the time he had oriented himself in the darkness she was well on her way to wherever it was she intended to go, and he thought in desperation for a way to convince her to return. Knowing her penchant for saving people, he dove beneath the waves, surfacing only when he was too far away from the Pepita for the crew to come to his aid. Resurfacing, he began to thrash about wildly in the hopes of attracting her attention. "Help me!" he cried out, knowing his plan had better work before she swam much further from the small vessel. He knew without a doubt that her chances of survival in the frigid waters were frighteningly slim.

Rebecca heard the splash when his body hit the water and she glanced over her shoulder, wondering what underhanded ploy the horrid man was attempting to initiate. It took her a few moments before she caught sight of him and when she did he was flailing about in the waves several yards from the Pepita. She watched for a short time, trying to persuade herself to keep on swimming, but instead she found herself eyeing the situation with wary suspicion, lest she be lured into a trap.

Lieutenant Burgess was aware that he had caught the girl's attention, though he noticed she was taking her time in coming to his aid. Never-the-less, he continued his dramatic performance, hoping she was convinced by it, while the men within hearing distance began to filter to the deck in their curiosity, lured by the commotion at sea.

"Sir!" he heard Petty Officer Andrews call. "Do you need a rope?"

"No!" he hissed over the waves.

Rebecca began a slow crawl back to where the lieutenant flailed, her eyes watching him intently while she swam. An internal conflict was taking place as she drew near, with her rational mind wanting only to escape and her willful mind needing to save the drowning man. While she wrestled with her conscience she continued to swim with slow strokes toward the officer, intending to move in to rescue him only when he went under the water and did not resurface. She stopped just short of where he was thrashing about, watching and waiting for him to tire of his struggle. In an unexpected move of force she saw him spring into action, swimming toward her with powerful strokes. She turned and dove beneath the waves, aware that speed was crucial at this point, but when she could no longer ignore her lung's burning hunger for air she surfaced, and with a startled cry of defeat felt herself being caught up in the lieutenant's sinewy grasp.

Lieutenant Burgess was amazed that the girl had fallen for his trick, but he was tremendously relieved as well. He knew the captain would string him up by the neck if he were to return without her. Now, as she struggled in vain to escape his hold, he was amazed at how frail she felt within his firm embrace. He fought to maintain his grip on her but was fearful of crushing her with his strength, and in an attempt to calm her he began to speak in a quiet tone. "Stop fighting me...I'm just going to return you to the Pepita."

"I will not go back to that ship!" she shouted, continuing in her efforts to escape while he struggled to keep his hold on her.

"You can't swim to England! You'll drown before you ever see sight of land," he shouted, still holding her to him in an unyielding embrace.

"Well I'd rather die than get back on that ship with you!" she screamed, as she began to weep in her frustration of being caught up in his clutches.

The men on deck began to chuckle in their discomfort at the exchange taking place between the two, while keeping a keen eye on Rebecca. She had been the one who had seen them through their bout with small pox, and none of them were about to see any harm come to her.

"Please," Lieutenant Burgess said, "just come aboard and we'll discuss the matter there."

"No!" she cried, thrusting her head back with violent force into his face.

Lieutenant Burgess gasped from the stinging blow of the impact and his grip loosened for a moment, allowing her to slip from his arms. He watched her claw at the water in her desperation to get away from him, but a second time he overtook her, and he fought to catch his breath amid the struggle with the girl and the pain coursing through his head.

"Let me go!" she screamed again, choking on the salty water coursing down her throat.

"I will not release you until you agree to return to the ship," he said, fighting to maintain his hold on her while the waves crashed over them.

"You are a cruel and despicable man," she sobbed. "I've done nothing to warrant your disdain yet you've treated me with nothing but contempt..." she snarled through her tears. "I will not go back to that ship...I hate you!"

Rebecca was beside herself with rage, fear and frustration. She had never been driven to this point of utter despair before, and now her only thought was of escaping this man and the powerful hold he had on her.

Lieutenant Burgess was at a loss for words. He debated forcing the girl to return to the Pepita, but knew that it would be futile since she would only try to escape again. Instead, he struggled to hold her in his grasp as she again put forth a fight to break free of his embrace. He was aware that she was tiring and he remained quiet for a moment, contemplating what he might say that would persuade her to return to the ship. The force of her sobs shook her body and he was struck by the sudden realization that he had never seen the girl cry before tonight.

"Listen to me...there are sick men onboard who still need you. Come back and I will not harass you again...you won't even see me... I give you my word."

She became motionless and quiet when he finished speaking and he hoped she was giving careful consideration to his words. He could feel when the sobs that shook her gave way to the uncontrollable spasms of shivering brought on by the cold water, and he realized he must act quickly in order to save her before her body succumbed to hypothermia. He loosened his grip to allow her to put some distance between them, prepared to catch her up again if she attempted to flee. Instead, she moved away from him and toward the Pepita, never once looking back.

Petty Officer Andrews waited for the girl on deck, his arms full of dry blankets, and when he saw Rebecca approaching he lowered the rope for her to climb up. He stood waiting for her, his arms opened wide to embrace her cold, quivering body.

Rebecca was stunned by the words that had come from her mouth. The instant she said them she was overcome with guilt and remorse. Never had she felt hatred towards anybody or anything, and now after having spoken the words aloud, she felt vile and filthy for having uttered them. She glanced at the face of Mr. Andrews peering down at her and wondered if he had heard the confrontation between herself and the lieutenant, praying that he hadn't. A soft groan of despair escaped her when she fell into his arms, exhausted from the battle, and he wrapped the blankets around her and led her below to the galley where he held her in a soothing embrace while she wept.

Lieutenant Burgess climbed aboard the Pepita after Rebecca had retreated below, and he breathed a heavy sigh of relief. He was grateful to see that the petty officer attended to the girl, especially since it took her off the deck and away from the temptation to flee again. She had given him a good fight and he doubted he would have had the strength to subdue her a third time. He glanced over at the men who were eyeing him with curious faces and waved them away with a fierce scowl before heading towards his berth, where he peeled off the remainder of his wet clothing and collapsed with weary exhaustion onto his hammock.

Rebecca sat wrapped up in the arms of Mr. Andrews for some time before she had quieted her sobs enough to speak with coherence. The petty officer made soft, comforting sounds while he held her and it brought to mind memories of her mother, who had calmed her tears in much the same way when she was a child. She would have given most anything just then to be back in the presence of her family, desperate to seek the counsel of her father as to how to make amends to the lieutenant for the horrible thing she had said to him. Rebecca remained nestled in the safe embrace of Mr. Andrews for nearly an hour before she pulled herself away from him, covering her mouth to stifle a large yawn. The petty officer gave her an encouraging smile and patted her cheek with tender affection.

"I'm sorry you had to go through that, Missy," he said.

A tired grin tugged at the corners of Rebecca's mouth and she reached out to embrace him, grateful for his kindness. One, final sob shook her frame and she sighed in her fatigue. Pushing herself to her feet she murmured, "I'd best return to my patients, Mr. Andrews."

He followed her to the sick berth and remained at the door for a moment after she had entered. "Try to get some sleep," he urged. "I don't want to see you get sick."

She nodded before shutting the door with a light hand behind her, being careful not to wake the men who slept.

Lieutenant Burgess lay in his hammock, finally warm and dry but troubled by his feelings of remorse. He pondered the things the girl had said and realized that even though they had been uttered in anger, she spoke the truth. She had never done anything with the intention of being malicious to any member of the Redemption's crew, yet he, as well as several of the others, continued to harass and ridicule her at every opportunity that presented itself. He contemplated his motives for bullying her with such vehemence, but could think of none save for the fact that she was a woman, and women had always proven themselves to be vain and unpredictable. He tried to recall an instance when the girl had exhibited that sort of immature behavior, but could think of none. Never-the-less he determined in his great irritation, he had little inclination to bend to her wanton insubordination, and with fitful reluctance he tossed himself over in his hammock and hoped sleep would come quickly, for he knew only in slumber would his guilt be alleviated.

Rebecca was relieved to see that all of the men were resting when she returned, as she had neither the spirit nor the stamina to tend to them. Slipping without a sound across the broad expanse of the room, she lowered herself onto the unyielding planks of the floor where she had slept since coming aboard, and tried to warm herself beneath the weight of her blankets. She closed her eyes in an attitude of reverent prayer but found to her dismay that no words would come. Instead, the malicious comment she had spoken to Lieutenant Burgess replayed itself in her mind, and she wished with all that was within her that she could take it back. A heavy sigh escaped her and she reached out to pull the cotton covering tighter against her chilled body, while she began to utter the verses of scripture that she hoped would bring her comfort. *"Create in me a clean heart, O God, and renew a steadfast spirit within me. Do not cast me from your presence, or take your Holy Spirit from me. Restore to me the joy of your salvation and grant me a willing spirit, to sustain me."*

She repeated the words over and over a in a fervent whisper, fresh tears flowing from her eyes as she prayed with desperation for the presence of God to comfort and quiet her inconsolable spirit. She continued her conciliation long into the night before falling into a fitful slumber, her pillow dampened by the tears that continued to flow without restraint.

Chapter 17

THREE FULL DAYS had past with no sign of Lieutenant Burgess. Even the midshipmen and the petty officer were hesitant to call on him after his angry confrontation with Rebecca, thinking he would still be in a foul mood. So for fear of upsetting the calm that had settled over the Pepita, none dared report to his berth. All of the men except for George Robbins had been discharged from the sick berth, and even he was making a hasty recovery, allowing Rebecca some much needed rest. On this particular day, she lingered about in casual conversation with the midshipman until she was distracted by a light tap at the door. Peering into the corridor, she saw Petty Officer Andrews waited with an indecipherable expression on his features. Rebecca cast a warm smile at him and said, "Hello, Mr. Andrews."

"Missy, we may have a situation on our hands," he began, forgoing all pleasantries. "Do you think you can you come to the deck?"

She excused herself from her patient and followed the petty officer into the bright sunlight, where he glanced at her through an apprehensive grimace.

"We haven't seen Lieutenant Burgess about and we're getting a bit concerned. Pete's been knocking at his door since I went to call on you but he still hasn't appeared. We figure he's either left the ship or something's wrong in there. I thought you ought to be the one to check on him..."

He and the other men on deck waited with wary anticipation for her response while Rebecca paused to contemplate the best course of action. Her heart began to pound in her chest at the thought of entering the man's room and she took a deep breath in an attempt to calm herself. "You're right, Mr. Andrews," she murmured at last. "He may have succumbed to the small pox. I'll go in..." she trailed, casting a hesitant look at the door of his berth.

She knocked with a light hand at first, but then began to pound more loudly when she heard no response from inside. Opening the door with a reluctant hesitance, she peered into the room which was darkened by heavy curtains hung over the windows. Even from where she stood she could see his still body lying in his hammock and she wondered for a moment if he was dead. A knot of fear crept into her belly as she began to make her way with deliberate steps to where he rested, silent and unmoving.

"Mr. Burgess?" she called out, praying he would answer her, but hearing nothing she continued on to where his weight bulged from beneath the cotton sling. She peered down into his face, terrified of what she might find. She saw his eyes were closed and his skin was flushed with color, while his breaths came in ragged, sporadic gasps. She laid a tentative hand on his face, pulling it back in alarm when she felt the feverish heat that penetrated her skin. Glancing over her shoulder she spoke to the men clustered around the portal of the officer's cabin. "He has taken ill but he still lives, thank the Lord."

She heard their well orchestrated sigh of relief well before she caught a glimpse of their faces. "Tony," she called to the midshipman beyond the doorway. "Will you help me move him? Now that you've recovered we needn't put Mr. Andrews at risk of contagion any longer."

"Why don't you just tend to him in here, Missy?" the petty officer asked.

"George Robbins is still recovering in the sick berth, Mr. Andrews," she reminded in a soft tone. "He won't be ready to leave for at least two more days. It will be easier to keep them together."

Anthony Porter moved along side Rebecca, who had remained near the hammock which held the young officer. Giving him gentle instruction, he assisted in supporting the canvas sling when it was cut from the wall, and the rest of the crew watched on in silence as their acting captain's body was carried to the sick berth, all hoping it was not too late to save him.

Rebecca was stunned by the innocuous appearance of Lieutenant Burgess at rest and wondered how he had ever aroused such fear in her. In his slumber she found him to be rather harmless, and on his features she could trace the lines that were cut into his face from his ready smiles. She studied him now with a curious intrigue rather than a wary hesitance and realized the man was one whom she would have found attractive if she hadn't been aware of his ill tempered nature. The voice of Petty Officer Andrews stirred her from her musing and she peered over her shoulder to give ear to his muttering.

"All this time he was in there alone…I shouldn't have waited for so long…"

Rebecca eyed him with consolation, knowing all to well the feelings of guilt he must be grappling with. "You can't blame yourself for this Mr. Andrews…just be thankful you've remained uninfected."

"Is it too late to save him?" he asked.

"It may be too late for me to save him, but it's never too late to ask the Lord for a miracle," she sighed, thinking that now might be her redeeming moment for the horrible thing she had said to the officer.

They laid his body near the wall of the sick berth, where the very first patient, Mr. Sims, had lain. Rebecca went after fresh water and linens for Lieutenant Burgess, while Mr. Andrews watched on from the corridor.

"A new patient?" George Robbins asked, knowing that all of the men had been through the sick berth except for two, and he could see Mr. Andrews lingering in the doorway looking quite well.

"I'm afraid it's Mr. Burgess," Rebecca replied, returning from the closet with her arms full. She stood in the middle of the sick berth for a moment, wanting to give an encouraging embrace to the forlorn Petty Officer, but instead she gave him a reassuring smile over the stack of linens she held. "I think this leaves you in charge, Mr. Andrews," she said with a soft voice. "Perhaps you ought to speak with the men."

He nodded his understanding and turned to leave, a grim expression etched on his face.

Rebecca returned to the stricken lieutenant and knelt beside him to lay cool, wet cloths on his feverish body. She began to pray for him, interceding on his behalf as she petitioned the Lord to spare his life, while he lay silent and unmoving beneath her gentle touch. She maintained a silent vigil at his bedside throughout the night, determined to see him return alive and well with the rest of them to the Redemption.

The activities onboard the Pepita continued with all sense of normalcy with Petty Officer Andrews in charge, and there was a sense of camaraderie about the small ship, the men making an earnest effort to see to their safe return to the Redemption. The crew had begun their fifth week of quarantine, and Rebecca wondered if any on the Redemption still concerned themselves with their welfare, not having heard anything from the captain, nor the crew, since they had disembarked.

Lieutenant Burgess had been in the sick berth for just two days, and he continued to toss about in restless discomfort but rarely woke from his feverish state, even when Rebecca attempted to coax water down his throat. She was diligent in her prayer vigil over him and was surprised when Charlie Robbins asked if he could join in her intercession for the officer. Together they plead for God's healing touch to fall upon the young lieutenant, and gave thanks to Him who had brought the rest of the crew through their harrowing ordeal.

Mr. Robbins dozed frequently throughout the daytime hours, allowing Rebecca the opportunity to sit and gaze upon the handsome face of Lieutenant Burgess without constraint. Again she found herself mesmerized by the man's kind and genteel features and thought it unfortunate that such a peaceful countenance could transform into such a vengeful one when stirred to wrath, yet she maintained her watchful care of the sick man in spite of her feelings of ambivalence. The passage of time slipped without a care from her mind as she studied the placid face for hours on end, until late one evening the voice of George Robbins stirred her from her pensive musing.

"Miss Halloway? Is Lieutenant Burgess alright?" He had been watching the girl, and was aware of her steadfast gaze lingering on the lieutenant as she hovered over his unresponsive form.

"Yes, Mr. Robbins," she assured, slipping over to sit near the man. "I think he'll be just fine."

The sun was setting low in the sky while Rebecca and George conversed with quiet voices. Mr. Andrews brought them steaming bowls of potato stew, but Mr. Burgess' sat untouched near where he lay. She had tried for several minutes to get him to take some of the thick broth with no success, and so she left it resting near him, intent on trying again before too much time had passed.

Rebecca was happy to listen to Mr. Robbins cheerful banter, thankful he was feeling almost back to his old self again. They chuckled in soft tones at the pleasant memories of their adventure aboard the Pepita, as the fading light of day cast the room into a shadowy darkness. It seemed to her as if they had been afloat on the small vessel for a lifetime already, and she wondered if she would miss the solitude when the time came for them to leave.

Lieutenant Burgess lay unmoving on the floor of the sick berth listening to the soft hum of voices that lulled him into a pleasant stupor. His body ached with the disease that had afflicted him and he shivered now beneath the thin, cotton covering that had been placed over him. Opening his eyes, he turned his face to see who it was that spoke. He was unsure of where he lay and could not recall anything that had happened since his confrontation with the girl. Peering around the room, he recognized it as the bow of the ship, the light casting a warm glow over the curvature of the walls. His eyes continued to roam with curious intrigue until they fell on Rebecca, reclined on the floor next to one of the crew. Her legs were tucked beneath her while she propped herself on one arm, the other resting lightly in her lap. She covered her mouth as if to stifle the giggle that erupted at the words the man had spoken, and then began to respond to him in a quiet tone. He strained to hear the thoughts she conveyed but her voice was too soft, so instead he gazed at her unnoticed while she continued in her dialogue. He was struck by her tranquil and unpretentious manner, even in the company of one of the ship hands. He found he enjoyed listening to the melodic rise and fall of her voice while she conversed with effortless elegance in a manner lacking haughty conceit or condescension, but full of the comfortable camaraderie common among a close knit group of friends. Still staring at her, he slipped back into a restful slumber, lured into sleep by the one who spoke with such beautiful eloquence.

Rebecca was unaware that Lieutenant Burgess had awakened and grew frustrated when she could not stir him to consciousness a short time later, when she again made an attempt to coax food down his throat. Sighing in resignation, she lay down near him in the hopes of resting her eyes for a bit.

Two hours passed unnoticed while Rebecca slept soundly. Lieutenant Burgess again stirred, and peered through the dim light to see her lying very near to him. He was charmed to find the peaceful smile had remained on her features, even in rest, and he found that he could not take his gaze from the sight of her. He studied her face for several moments more, until the voice of George Robbins drew the girl from her rest. Closing his eyes in haste, he remained unmoving, not wanting her to know that he had been watching her.

Rebecca crawled over to where Charlie lay and gazed down to whisper, "What is it, Charlie?"

He looked at her with a hopeful expression and asked, "Do you think you might have a bit of that stew left?"

She smiled and stood to her feet, longing for a night of uninterrupted sleep, but knowing too that her time aboard the Pepita would soon come to an end and she would be afforded the luxury of rest once she was back onboard the Redemption. "I'm sure I can find some," she grinned, hurrying to galley to warm a bowl of the leftover stew from the evening meal.

She returned with a generous serving of mutton stew, and found Mr. Robbins propped against the wall with a large grin of appreciation beaming at her from across the sick berth. She slipped through the room to take a seat next to him, placing the steaming bowl into his outstretched hands. It was fortunate for her, she realized, that the lieutenant remained in a careless slumber, for she recalled with vivid clarity the last time she had gone after food for a hungry patient.

"Tell me again how you happened aboard the Redemption, would you?" Charlie asked through a mouth full of mutton.

Rebecca hesitated before speaking, wanting only to crawl back under her warm covers, but instead she launched into her tale of capture and abduction, sparing most of the more intimate details, and embellishing the grandiose. She enjoyed the enraptured look on his face while she spoke, and didn't even grow weary when he interrupted her with a question or a comment.

She paused for a moment in the midst of her account to glance over at Lieutenant Burgess, only to find him staring back at her. Thinking he was in some sort of feverish hallucination, she turned her gaze back to Mr. Robbins and continued telling her story. A few moments later she glanced again at the officer, and still his eyes remained fixed on her. She stared at him for several moments, trying to determine whether or not he was in a conscious frame of mind. She smiled at bit, and gasped with surprise when he gave her a slight smile in return. "Mr. Burgess?" she whispered, still thinking she was imagining things.

"Yes?" he answered.

"You're awake," she commented, beginning to feel the familiar flutter of nerves for the first time since he had been carried to the sick berth.

He grimaced through a low groan and shifted his body beneath the blanket in an attempt to find a more comfortable position. "Have I been out of commission for very long?" he asked, a hint of a tired smile on his face.

"Three days now," she told him, knowing he must be worried about the crew aboard the Pepita. "Mr. Andrews has been in charge since you fell ill, sir," she informed him, "and he has been managing very well. You needn't be concerned about anything at this point."

He regarded her with a curious look and nodded his head, wondering who had put the Petty Officer in charge.

"Can you take a few swallows of this broth, Mr. Burgess?"

He watched her raise the spoon to his lips and opened his mouth with willing anticipation. The warm liquid felt soothing on his parched throat and he eagerly swallowed all that she offered. When he had devoured the last of the stew, she set the bowl aside and removed the damp cloth from his forehead. He continued to observe her as she dipped the rag into a bucket, wrung it out, and laid it back on his face, its cool moisture soothing his feverish skin. She took his arm then and held it in her hands, giving it close examination for the telltale signs of smallpox.

"You have officially been declared contagious," she said with a timid smile, raising his limb high to show him the bright pustules scattered about. "But consider yourself fortunate," she added. "You're case is mild in comparison to Mr. Robbins."

He continued to watch her, struck by her winsome manner. "How long until I am to be declared uncontagious?" he asked with a grimace.

"Anywhere from five to ten days now," she said, hearing his inward groan.

"We are well beyond our four weeks," he sighed. "The captain will not want to tarry any longer."

"Don't despair, Mr. Burgess," she murmured. "I'm certain the captain considers you one worth tarrying for."

He stared at her face for some time, humbled by the look of compassion it held. "Did you really contract the small pox in Africa?" he asked.

"I did," she replied, sponging the cool water over his feverish skin.

"I don't understand…how is it you survived?"

"I had a wonderful doctor," she smiled, gazing down into his face, "and the prayers of many lifted up for me as well."

He continued to watch her, mesmerized by her lovely features, and he wondered how he had never taken notice of them before now. "Why did you come here," he asked, "when you knew we were as good as dead?"

Rebecca paused for a moment, her expression filled with humble conviction as she answered, "Oh, Mr. Burgess, God is not willing that any should perish, and neither am I."

The two of them remained quiet for a time as she continued to sponge cool water over his blistered skin, bringing soothing relief to the uncomfortable burning of his flesh. When she had finished she stood and moved to the door, giving him a reassuring smile over her shoulder before she retreated into the darkness of the corridor. He was suddenly overcome with an incomprehensible remorse for all of the unspeakable difficulties he had plagued her with since she had come aboard the Redemption, and he thought desperately for a way to make amends.

Rebecca walked to the deck to empty the bucket of water over the side of the ship. Several of the men were moving about the Pepita and all eyes lit up when they saw her. She took a deep breath of the salty sea air, offering a silent prayer of thanksgiving when she gazed upon the faces of those who had survived their brush with death.

"How's Lieutenant Burgess coming along, Missy?" Mr. Andrews asked.

"Very well," she smiled. "As a matter of fact, he woke for the first time today, his appetite intact!"

Mr. Andrews seemed relieved to hear the news, but then gazed at her through a shadow of concern and said, "How are you managing?"

"As well as I could hope, Mr. Andrews."

She lingered on deck for a few moments more, wishing she could take a quick swim in the beckoning waves, but instead she bid a quiet goodnight to the men and returned below to the sick berth, where she found Lieutenant Burgess sleeping once more, his countenance a relaxed expression of contentment.

The remainder of the week passed quickly for Rebecca, for she was down to her last patient. Charlie Robbins had since returned to mingle among the rest of the crew, leaving

Lieutenant Burgess as the only one who remained in the sick berth. His recovery was slow, allowing the two of them to engage in long, comfortable hours of conversation during his time of convalescence. It seemed he couldn't hear enough about her travels with her father and her mother, and one evening he suggested she write her adventures and experiences down on paper, lest she forget them one day.

"I'll never forget the moments I've lived, Mr. Burgess," she explained to him. "They're what make me who I am." She gazed at him with an air of passionate conviction, hoping he could comprehend the words she spoke from her heart.

"Well if that's the case," he remarked in a dark tone of remorse, "then I fear for what lies beneath that calm exterior of yours as a result of your time aboard the Pepita."

She held his gaze, her face masked in confusion.

"I've treated you despicably, Rebecca," he sighed, "and I wish I could retract all of the cruel things I've ever said or done to you."

She averted her gaze then, uncomfortable with the contrition conveyed in his tone.

"I'm terribly sorry for what I've put you through during our confinement here," he continued, "and I know your time aboard the Redemption hasn't been easy either..."

They remained silent for some time, he overcome with a tremendous sense of guilt, and she struggling to find the words to express her forgiveness towards him.

"Mr. Burgess," she whispered, "I don't hate you."

"Well that's encouraging, isn't it?" he sighed through a wry grin.

She looked at him then with a solemn expression. "I've never hated anybody, not even you...what I said that night I said out of anger and frustration, and I too wish I could take it back."

He glanced at her when he heard the passionate conviction that filled her voice and was surprised to see tears welling in her eyes. He tried to sit up, feeling terrible that he had brought her to tears yet again. "Please, don't cry…" he said, watching as she allowed the tears to flow, unashamed by her display of emotion.

"Don't you see, Mr. Burgess?" she continued, her piercing gaze steadfast and confident. "We can never take away the condemnation of our transgressions, but we can be certain that there is hope for forgiveness. It's our redemption."

"Our what?" he asked her, a quizzical look on his face.

"Our redemption," she said with a breathless sigh, as if someone had just given her a priceless gift. "Our chance to be redeemed for our sinful nature…I said something horrible to you, for which I am terribly sorry, and I beg you now for your forgiveness."

"What you have said to me pales in comparison to what I have done to you," he murmured.

"But you see, even if you were to bear a grudge against me for the rest of my life, I have already taken the matter before God. I have been forgiven, so I need not carry the guilt of my transgression any longer. I could never take back what I said to you, but Christ, our Redeemer, has paid the price for our corrupt nature, and he has taken that burden of condemnation from me. You needn't carry any guilt for what has passed between us, and you needn't harbor any regret either. I have forgiven you, just as Christ will do if you but ask…"

There was an urgency in her tone, and he was transfixed by the profound sincerity with which she spoke.

"Remember this, Mr. Burgess," she said. "Life is not about the mistakes we make, but it's about who we turn to when we make them."

He studied her thoughtful features for several moments, his heart consumed by her presence. Rebecca suddenly felt overwhelmed by his piercing gaze, and she stood and moved to the door, needing to escape the emotions coursing through the small berth. She cast a quick glance over her shoulder and said,

"If you'll excuse me, I think I'll go on deck to catch a breath of fresh air."

He stared after her retreating form, watching as she pulled the door tightly shut behind her, and he paused to consider the words she had spoken. He lay back down with a sigh, thankful for the first time since she had come aboard the Redemption, for her humble intrusion into his life.

Rebecca stood gazing over the waves from the deck of the Pepita for several long minutes, hoping to understand the unexpected pounding of her heart. She was confused by the emotions coursing through her and could not recall having ever felt quite this way before. She began to pray for understanding, confident even now in the Lord's divine hand of providence. Murmuring a final amen, she slid over the edge of the railing and dove deep into the darkness below. She realized that her time aboard the small ship was nearing an end and she wanted to take advantage of every moment of solitude that she had left. She swam for nearly thirty minutes before the chill of the water brought her back to the Pepita. Crawling over the railing, she tiptoed down to the supply closet to retrieve a dry blanket, and then returned to the deck where she wrapped herself in a tight cocoon and lay down to gaze into the fathomless night sky. She drifted off beneath the warmth of her covering, and was awakened two hours later by Mr. Andrews, the watchman on duty, who stared down at her through a mask of concern.

"Are you alright, Missy?" he asked, thinking that Lieutenant Burgess must have rattled the girl's nerves again.

She glanced around in confusion until she remembered where she was. Offering a sheepish grin she said, "I'm fine, Mr. Andrews...I must have fallen asleep."

"Well aren't you going to go back to your berth?" he asked.

"No," she replied through a yawn. "I think I'll stay right here."

"You'll catch your death of a cold if you stay out here!"

"Mr. Andrews," she laughed, "I have yet to catch my death of a cold so you needn't concern yourself over it any longer!"

"There's always a first time, Missy," he admonished through a scowl.

"I won't stay long, Mr. Andrews," she assured with an impish grin.

He shook his head in an irate manner as he returned to his post, certain the girl would just go right back to sleep again.

Rebecca grinned at the petty officer's admonition while she watched him depart, and then burrowed down deeper into the folds of the cotton blanket, relishing the feel of the cold air on her face and the warmth of her body beneath the thick covering. A soft sigh of contentment rose as her eyes turned toward the heavens, and she tried to recall the constellations in the night sky. She named their positions aloud using the language common in seamanship, in the hopes of bringing to mind some of what Mr. Andrews had taught her about the various locations used aboard a frigate. Pointing to random stars she recited in an eloquent whisper, "Larboard, aft, forward, port..."

Lieutenant Burgess had awakened in the middle of the night and tried to determine Rebecca's whereabouts in the sick berth. He called out to her in the darkness, but when no answer came he grew concerned by her absence. Stumbling to his feet, he made his way to the door and stepped out into the corridor, where he glanced about hoping to catch a glimpse of her. Seeing no sign of her through the dim light, he made his way up the stairwell toward the deck thinking that would be the next most likely place to find her. He did not see her at first, but rather he heard her, murmuring words he could not make sense of. Turning his face toward the sound of her voice, he saw her resting on the deck, one leg crossed over the other and swinging in a relaxed manner while she nestled the rest of her body beneath a heavy blanket. He studied her from afar, enjoying the carefree nature which radiated from her countenance, and he was hesitant to disturb her contented solitude. After several moments had passed, he determined he would leave her to her musing rather than disturb her, while he returned unnoticed below to the sick berth.

Rebecca, sensing someone was near, tilted her head back to see who it might be. She was certain Mr. Andrews had returned to chastise her once again, but in her confusion she stared for several moments at Lieutenant Burgess, her face registering surprise at the curious expression smiling down at her. A quick gasp of embarrassment escaped her and she struggled to stand to her feet when she realized it was the lieutenant who stood before her and not the petty officer.

"Please…don't get up," he urged, beckoning with his hands for her to remain where she was.

She lay back down with a cautious glance, a vulnerable air of timidity overcoming her.

"Are you reciting poetry to the stars?" he asked through a wry grin.

"No," she murmured, "just trying to recall the commands of your officers before we return to the Redemption. I'm afraid I've forgotten most of what Mr. Andrews has taught me."

He smiled at her as he rested his gaze on her delicate features. "Man the sails," he whispered elaborately.

She shook her head, casting him a look of confusion.

"Well, that's alright," he assured. "I suppose you wouldn't be doing that anyway." He stroked his chin with his hand and tried to think of another command she might recognize. "Secure those riggings!" he shouted in a low voice.

She smiled, her eyes lighting up, and said, "I'd coil the ropes!"

"Yes!" he said, nodding his encouragement.

"Ship to larboard…" he commanded.

Rebecca thought for a moment, and then raised her arm to make a smooth, slicing maneuver through the air, while casting a hesitant glance up at the young officer. Lieutenant Burgess smiled in affirmation of her correct gesture of response, again overcome by her captivating mannerisms. His gaze lingered on her face for a moment, while Rebecca waited expectantly for another request.

"Lay aft here!" he stated with a mock scowl of consternation.

She erupted into a fit giggles at the odd look he gave her, and a sheepish grin lit upon his face. "I think I'd run away as fast as I could," she teased.

"Yes, that would be very wise," he laughed, having heard the command on more occasions than he cared to remember.

Rebecca was unexpectedly captivated by the resonant sound of the officer's laughter and realized that she had never before seen him in such an affable frame of mind. She felt at ease with him for the first time since their paths had crossed and she found herself wishing that their time aboard the Pepita was not drawing to so close an end. They remained in a comfortable silence for several moments, both of them peering overhead into the night sky.

Lieutenant Burgess felt as though he could remain in the tranquility of the girl's presence for as long as time would allow, yet he was hesitant to intrude on her peaceful solitude. "Will you stay out here for the remainder of the night?" he asked.

"No," she assured, "just a little while longer."

"Very well, then I suppose I shall return below," he said, his piercing gaze focused with intent on Rebecca.

"Thank you for your help, Mr. Burgess," she murmured, peering at him through the darkness.

Giving a slight nod of his head he replied in a soft tone, "Thank you for coming aboard, Miss Halloway."

Rebecca's face warmed with the words he spoke, and although he had insinuated nothing more than grateful appreciation, she felt a peculiar tingle coursing through her. She studied his retreating form until he had disappeared into the corridor, and wondered for the first time in her young, adult years what her life would be like had she allowed herself to fall in love.

Back on the Redemption, Captain Jameson stood on the quarterdeck, eyeing the Pepita through the lens of his telescope. The small vessel had been moored for well over five weeks now, much longer than they had anticipated. He found himself growing irritated by their delay, and contemplated sending one of his men over to where the supply ship tarried so as to determine the status of the crew. Unwilling to risk another contagion, he resisted, and instead took up an hourly vigil in the hopes that the vessel would soon set sail and return to the Redemption.

Chapter 18

THE DAY OF their return dawned sunny and bright, the cloudless sky a sure promise of the warm day ahead. The prospect of a brisk, morning swim stirred Rebecca from her slumber and she crawled from beneath the warmth of her covers to hurry to up the narrow stairwell. Much to her chagrin, she saw that most of the crew mingled about on deck, thrilled to be returning to the Redemption at last. Rebecca slowed her step for a moment to enjoy the warmth of the sunlight on her face, and heard a voice calling out to her.

"Good morning, Miss Halloway!"

Glancing through the reflective glare of the wooden floorboards, she saw Pete Jones reclined against the rail at the bow of the Pepita. She offered him a friendly wave and meandered across the expanse of deck to join him.

"Bet you're glad to be leaving..." he mused.

Rebecca nodded through a tight smile but said nothing as she wrestled with her befuddled emotions. She was torn between her longing to return to the Redemption to mend the lingering contention with Captain Jameson, and her desire to remain aboard the Pepita to pursue the budding friendship with Lieutenant Burgess.

Lieutenant Burgess appeared from his cabin dressed smartly in his uniform. He walked with a purposeful step to where his crew lounged and began to shout orders to hoist sail, signaling his intent to rejoin the rest of their comrades onboard the Redemption. The men were quick to respond to his directive, happy to have their acting captain alive and well and back in command once again.

The anchor was hoisted from the water, setting the ship in motion after having lain still for several weeks, and the men lifted a chorus of shouts when the lieutenant called out, "Lay a course for the Redemption!"

A soft smile lit Rebecca's face at the sight of the lieutenant, and she gazed at him in a passive silence, enjoying his confident air of authority. She studied his features while he assisted the crew in securing the sails to the plethora of masts that jutted up from the deck, and for a moment he appeared as he had the first time she had ever set eyes upon him. Her heart quickened when he caught her eye with a slight move of his head, and shifting on her feet she watched him negotiate a path through the men who worked to hoist the sails.

"Hello, Miss Halloway," he smiled.

For the first time in her brief eighteen years of life Rebecca Halloway was rendered speechless, captivated by the young man's winsome charm and gentle manner.

"I trust you are ready to take your leave?" he remarked through a wry grin.

Rebecca could only smile and nod while he continued to gaze at her.

"Is everything all right, Miss Halloway?" he asked in a low tone, somewhat concerned by her silence.

"Yes," she murmured. "But please, it's Rebecca...you can call me Rebecca."

His eyes glinted with a curious hint of amusement and he said, "Rebecca, then."

She nodded, a warm flush staining her face. "I think I'll go below one last time," she whispered, certain he could hear the erratic pounding of her heart.

Lieutenant Burgess stared after the girl, taken aback by her peculiar behavior and even more so by her hasty retreat. He considered the emotional upheaval she must be experiencing at their impending departure from the Pepita, and wished he had given more thought to the matter before now. Realizing there was little he could do at this point in time, he turned his attention to the crew who waited for his instruction, while he determined in his mind to speak with the girl later.

Rebecca sought refuge in the darkened corridor below deck. Her heart continued to pound in her chest and she was confused by the unfamiliar sensation coursing through her. Although it wasn't an unpleasant feeling, it created a deep sense of restless tension, and she struggled against the frailty of her emotions lest she succumb to the panic that threatened to overwhelm her. Hearing a commotion coming from the galley, she walked the length of the corridor to discover who it was that lingered there. Peering through the portal, she caught sight of the petty officer making a hasty attempt to straighten the disarray in the small room.

"Hello, Mr. Andrews," she sighed, grateful for the ready distraction. "Would you like some help in here?"

He nodded at her generous offer and handed her a dry cloth so she could blot the water off of the dishes he was scrubbing.

"How long until we arrive at the Redemption?" she asked.

"Not too long," he replied. "Shouldn't be more than a half an hour in this wind."

Rebecca felt a flutter of nerves take flight at the thought of their imminent homecoming. While she was eager to see Eddy and Dr. Ammons again, the thought of facing Captain Jameson and Lieutenant Edwards left her with an inexplicable fear.

"What're you going to do when you get back, Missy?" he asked, stirring her from her troubled thoughts.

She offered a tired grin and said, "I'm going to take a long nap."

"Well you of all people deserve that," he replied. He was well aware of the sacrifice she had made on their behalf, and knew that the past several weeks had been especially trying on her.

"This is about as good as it's going to get, I'm afraid," Petty Officer Andrews grumbled, his critical gaze roving about the small confines of the galley. He motioned for Rebecca to proceed into the corridor, but seeing her hesitate he said, "Come on, then…it's time to go."

Rebecca shook her head and murmured, "You go on ahead. I'd like to stay down here for a bit." She had hoped for a moment of solitude to sort through her conflicting emotions.

The petty officer gave her an affectionate pat on the cheek and said, "I'll see you on deck, Missy."

Rebecca wandered through the humble confines of the room, tracing a finger along the scars cut into the worn slats of wood and recalling the many hours spent in the easy mannered company of the crew. How she would miss the inexorable games of Whist and the relaxed conversation among those whom she had come to consider her friends, and she paused to wonder how their demeanor would change toward her after they had returned to the Redemption. More than anything though, she realized she would miss being needed by the men she had cared for. A dismal sigh of uncertainty escaped her, and she ducked through the portal to meander toward the sick berth, wanting to see it just one last time.

The early morning sun's rays bathed the room in a warm glow and Rebecca was cheered simply by the sight of it. Standing in the center of the cabin, she peered around at what had been her home for the past several weeks, and her throat tightened at the thought of leaving the Pepita and the solace that had finally come to her here. She slipped to her knees in humble reverence, thanking the Lord for sparing the lives of the men she had come to adore, as well as for His gracious provision during the time of their confinement. A sob broke free at last and she fought to quell the overwhelming jumble of emotions wrestling within her as she lowered her head in confusion, willing herself not to break down.

The men lingering on the deck of the Pepita gathered at the railing to watch the approach of the small dinghy that would carry them back to the Redemption. They laughed and jostled one another about in feigned argument of who would disembark first as the long, rope ladder was flung over the side. The crew onboard the Redemption watched on with amused expressions of relief, thrilled to see that their shipmates were alive and well after their brush with death. Captain Jameson stood near Dr. Ammons, both of them peering out over the waves for a glimpse of Rebecca, who had remained below, unaware that the men were preparing to disembark.

Lieutenant Burgess mingled among his crew, enjoying their mischievous carousing. He peered about for a glimpse of the girl and was surprised to find that she was not among the group. Thinking perhaps she was taking one of her customary swims, he cast a fleeting glance over the side of the Pepita, but seeing no sign of her there he cut a path toward the stairwell to see if she had remained below. The darkness of the corridor slowed his steps and he called out, "Rebecca?"

Rebecca's heart quickened at the sound of the officer's voice and she stood to her feet when she heard his approaching footsteps.

"Ah! There you are," he smiled. "The men are preparing to disembark..."

His lingering gaze caught sight of the tears that glistened in her eyes and he could sense the emotionally charged tension in the room even from where he stood. Stepping closer to her he asked, "Are you sure everything's alright?"

Rebecca nodded through a soft smile, touched by his expression of concern. "I suppose I'm just a little nervous at the thought of our return," she murmured.

He gave her a look of bewildered confusion. "Why would returning to the Redemption make you uneasy?" he asked, certain she would have been eager to be taking her leave of the Pepita by now.

"Captain Jameson and I had words before I left. He was upset by my insistence to sail with you and your crew, and I fear he continues to resent me for my impertinence."

"*You* had words with Captain Jameson?" he asked.

Rebecca nodded through a weary grimace and murmured, "He refused to let me accompany your crew on the Pepita."

"But you're here..." he commented through a quizzical grin.

"I threatened to leave on my own volition," she whispered.

He erupted into a hearty laugh at the thought of the girl and the captain in a verbal standoff. "I would like to have been there to see that, Miss Halloway," he exclaimed, struck by the girl's winsome tenacity. He saw her expression remained hesitant, in spite of his lighthearted response, and he stepped closer. "Rebecca," he assured, speaking in a soft tone, "Captain Jameson could never resent you for what you've done...you've saved the lives of twelve people by your selfless determination."

Rebecca mulled over the officer's words for a time before she received the solace that was intended by his reassurance, and with a timid smile she said, "Then I suppose we should take our leave."

"Only when you're ready to do so," he affirmed.

A confident grin brightened her features and she nodded, finally feeling a tug of excitement at the thought of seeing Eddy again. She slipped into the corridor when he gestured her ahead of him and together they climbed the steps to the deck one, final time. Stepping into the bright sunlight side by side, a chorus of glad shouts arose, as the crew of the Redemption paid homage to the one who had saved their shipmates from certain death. The men waiting to depart on the dinghy below stood to join in on the accolades as well, and Rebecca glanced up at Lieutenant Burgess with a curious expression, wondering what all of the excitement was about.

"That's for you, you know," he whispered in her ear.

"No," she trailed, giving him an impish smile before throwing herself on the rope ladder. "I'm certain that's for you!"

Captain Jameson's heart hammered in his chest when he saw Rebecca emerge with the lieutenant. The harsh words he had spoken to her before her hasty departure had left him with a tremendous sense of guilt and remorse for the past several weeks, and now he couldn't help but wonder if she continued to begrudge him for the cruel things he had uttered in anger.

Dr. Ammons moved along side Captain Jameson, and the two officers breathed a collective sigh of relief when they saw the girl had remained safe from harm. "I'm glad you allowed her to sail with the men, Will," he commented, aware that all aboard the Pepita would have perished if Rebecca had not been there to attend to them.

Captain Jameson gave a curt nod and studied Rebecca as she flung herself over the side of the Pepita to descend the sinewy rungs of the rope ladder. Willing arms reached out to steady her when she neared the dinghy bobbing on the waves, and drew her into the center of the boat.

"How does she do that?" Dr. Ammons mused again through a wry grin.

The return to the Redemption took less than ten minutes, and when the little dinghy had finally been secured to the massive frigate the crew prepared for the long climb to the deck. Rebecca was instructed to ascend first, and when she cleared the railing the men took hold of her arms and pulled her aboard, offering shouts of welcome and gentle pats on the back. She peered into the sea of faces with eager anticipation, hoping to catch a glimpse of Eddy among them, and she was stunned by the kind expressions that beamed from the faces of men she recognized, but who had in the past, been distant and aloof in her presence. She felt herself being pulled into the crowd and felt a momentary wave of panic, but before she could succumb to it she saw Eddy peering at her through eyes heavy laden with emotion. A thoughtful grin tugged at the corners of his mouth and Rebecca knew she couldn't have felt more welcome had she just returned to her family in Portsmouth. The two of them observed one another in a complacent silence for a time before coming together in a firm embrace.

Lieutenant Edwards descended from the quarterdeck to greet Lieutenant Burgess who had just come aboard. "It's good to have you back, Paul!" he exclaimed, taking his friend's hand in a firm grasp.

"It's good to be back, James," the officer replied through a genuine smile of gratitude.

The two cut a path through the throngs of men to climb the steps to the quarterdeck where Captain Jameson stood observing the activities below.

"Mr. Burgess!" he shouted. "I see all have returned in good health?"

"Yes, Captain," he answered. "All but Petty Officer Andrews and Miss Halloway became ill with the small pox, sir."

Captain Jameson glanced at the lieutenant in surprise when he heard him refer to the girl by name, as did Dr. Ammons and Lieutenant Edwards.

"She has saved us all from certain death, Captain," he said, while the officers looked on with intrigue at his obvious display of admiration for the girl.

"Well then," Captain Jameson remarked, "we'll have to show her our gratitude, won't we?"

Eddy, who had gone much too long without the endearing company of his friend, drug Rebecca to the galley where Mr. Andrews and several of the midshipmen joined them to tell of their activities while quarantined aboard the Pepita. George

Robbins gathered several decks of cards, and the men set about dealing a hand of Whist while they conversed. Rebecca observed their activity from the corner of the room through a tired smile, delighted to be back onboard the Redemption and among the crew she had grown to love.

"C'mon Bec," Eddy called. "I have your hand over here by me." He pointed to a pile of cards stacked in careful order next to him.

"Eddy," she murmured, "I don't think I could stay awake long enough to get through even one hand…I'll just look on for now."

She pulled her chair near the table where she contented herself to watch the men begin their game. She was grateful for the opportunity to be included in their assembly without having to make conversation, for her lack of sleep during the past seven weeks, coupled with the uncertainty at being back onboard the frigate, were playing havoc with her emotions.

Eddy continued to peer over at her from where he sat, as if she were an apparition that might disappear at any moment. Rebecca met his gaze and gave him a reassuring smile. He was suddenly overcome with an intense feeling of reverent adulation, and he wondered why her God had ever deemed him worthy to receive the unconditional friendship she had offered him. He stared at her through a contemplative grin and saw the tired yawn that she attempted to hide behind her hand.

"Go on, Bec," he said. "Go get some sleep."

She gave him an apologetic look, trying to stifle a second large yawn.

"Go on," he urged. "We'll still be here when you wake up."

Needing no further prompting she stood to her feet, wondering if she could even make it to her berth before falling fast asleep. She meandered across the galley to the doorway, and collided with Lieutenant Burgess who had just stepped into the room. The collision sent her reeling backwards and he reached out to steady her with a firm hand. The tension in the room was thick as the men gathered around the table observed the incident with wary glances.

"I'm sorry, Miss Halloway," he said. "Are you alright?"

Rebecca nodded, and felt the familiar pounding in her chest start up again. The officer's hand remained on her arm, and his touch sent a pleasant, tingling sensation along her spine. She righted herself and murmured, "I'm fine, Mr. Burgess."

"Well then," he smiled, "your presence is requested in the captain's quarters."

The others in the room stared on with incredulous faces at the lieutenant's kind manner towards the girl, and watched as he directed her through the doorway.

Rebecca began to shudder when the lieutenant stated that the captain wished to speak with her, and she stood paralyzed with trepidation in the middle of the corridor. She had anticipated this moment for the past several weeks and now that the time had come to face the man, she found herself wishing she was back onboard the Pepita. Her last interaction with the commander had not been a pleasant one, and she feared he would continue to bear a grudge stemming from her all too recent insubordination.

Lieutenant Burgess was unsure of why Rebecca tarried, nor why her face held such a look of alarm, and had the men not been gawking at him with such flagrant disbelief at his manner of addressing the girl, he would have offered her soothing words of encouragement, but instead he simply asked, "You're not still upset over the confrontation with Captain Jameson, are you?"

Rebecca, realizing that she couldn't hide herself away from Captain Jameson for ever, nodded through a weary sigh before continuing on to his stateroom, the young officer following close behind her.

"Why does that continue to trouble you?"

She didn't risk turning around to speak with the officer, for her emotions hovered too near the surface. Instead, she murmured over her shoulder while continuing on towards the captain's berth. "I've seen the captain's wrath before, Mr. Burgess, but never as unforgiving as the night I left. I doubt this reunion will be a pleasant one."

He was stunned by the fact that she believed the captain continued to be angry with her and contemplated assuring her otherwise, but he determined instead that she would soon discover for herself just how grateful the captain had been with her courageous resolve to join the crew aboard the disease stricken vessel.

Arriving at Captain Jameson's stateroom, Rebecca paused for a moment, hoping to slow the pounding of her heart before entering. Her legs felt like limp pieces of rigging and her only hope was that she could make it through the next few moments without upsetting the captain further. She watched Lieutenant Burgess reach around her to open the door, and before she had even taken one step, she caught sight of the officers that filled the cabin, Lieutenant Edwards among them. Rebecca could feel their curious glances upon her when she slipped to the center of their circle, her mind intent only on finding Captain Jameson, and with a heavy heart she saw that he stood with his back towards the group, while he stared through a solemn gaze out the window, his customary stance when he was angry. Rebecca felt the tears that formed in her eyes and she prayed this meeting would come to a quick end.

Making an abrupt spin on his heel, Captain Jameson turned to confront the girl, and he was unexpectedly taken aback by the pallor in her features, in spite of her tanned skin. He began to pace around her with slow, deliberate steps, unaware of the shudder that coursed through her small frame. "Well, what do you have to say for yourself, Rebecca Halloway?" he teased with a serious face, the other officers watching on with amused grins as he continued to saunter about the room. "When you left you were threatening a serious act of insubordination...mutiny even! I hate to think of what must have transpired once you arrive onboard the Pepita."

Rebecca remained frozen in a stoic silence listening to the words the captain spoke. She was aware of the glances of those in the room lingering on her forlorn face, while a thousand thoughts tumbled through her mind. The tears began to spill from her eyes at the captain's grim rebuke, and in her weary exhaustion her reserves had been depleted, allowing the flood of pent up emotions to drain from her unchecked. She wanted nothing more than to flee this congregation of men, slip off by herself and escape into the seclusion of her cabin, away from the oppressive atmosphere of this room. She found the attention of the crew overwhelming, and she longed to be an insignificant face in the crowd once again. A soft sigh of despair welled within her, bringing an expression of startled confusion from both Captain Jameson and Lieutenant Burgess.

The officers present shifted in an uncomfortable silence when they realized that the girl was weeping, and Captain Jameson seemed stunned as well. He stepped in close, speaking to her in a gentle voice, "What is it, Rebecca? Surely you know I was speaking in jest?"

Lieutenant Burgess watched on, desperate to shield the girl from the scrutinizing glances of the others present in the room. He heard her offer a soft response and strained to hear the words she spoke.

"I'm sorry," she whispered, a sob catching in her throat. "It's just that I'm tired...I'm so tired... and I never meant to upset you, sir..." Her voice faltered with the humiliation of her emotional breakdown in the presence of his officers. "I'm so sorry, Captain..."

Dr. Ammons motioned to the officers and they began to file out into the corridor, Lieutenant Burgess lingering for a moment before joining them, while Rebecca stood silent, her gaze cast down toward the floor in shame. When everyone had departed, Captain Jameson took her with a gentle hand by the arm and led her to the lounge where he lowered himself to sit beside her.

"Rebecca," he murmured, "how could I possibly be angry with you…especially in light of what you've done?"

"I shouldn't have argued with you, Captain…and in front of your officers, too," she asserted. "You have every right to be angry with me, sir, it's just that…I can't bear the thought of lingering contention between us…I didn't think you'd let me come back…"

He studied her woeful countenance as she gave voice to her darkest fears, and his heart ached with compassion for the girl. He edged in next to her and wrapped his arm in a reassuring embrace around her shoulder, glancing down in surprise when she rested her head against chest. Another weary sigh escape her and he patted her arm in a sympathetic gesture of understanding. "I've never had a family, Rebecca… until you came along. You are like a daughter to me, and I'm afraid at times I may be overly concerned for your safety. I am fortunate you pursued the matter of the Pepita, and I am grateful for the care you provided to the men while aboard. They are alive only because of your selfless determination, and the entire crew of the Redemption is aware of that. You should be proud of yourself."

She peered up through her tear rimmed eyes and said, "Thank you, sir. I was more than happy to be of assistance."

He burst into laughter at the formality of her speech, happy to see a hint of a smile light her face. "And I do believe you've even won over Lieutenant Burgess!" he exclaimed.

"Oh, Captain," she began, sounding like herself again for the first time since she had returned, "it was so wonderful being there with them. The men were so kind to me."

"Even Lieutenant Burgess?" he asked, wondering what magic she had worked on the young officer to bring about his change of heart.

She gave a short nod, deciding not to complicate matters by elaborating on their tumultuous start.

An unexpected knock at the door interrupted their exchange, and Dr. Ammons took a tentative step into the room at the captain's call to enter. "Oh good," he said. "You're still here." A hint of relief softened his features when he saw the girl. "I'd like to have a look at you, Rebecca, before you go off to sleep for the next few days," he stated, concerned by the lack of color in her face.

Rebecca stood to her feet, much too tired to remain in the soothing embrace of Captain Jameson any longer. "I truly am sorry for upsetting you, sir."

"That will be enough of that, Miss Halloway," he chided. Slipping her arm through his, he walked her to the door and said, "I'd like to have a celebratory dinner in your honor when you've rested, Rebecca, would that be alright?"

"I'll look forward to that, sir," she smiled, retreating into the dim light of the corridor.

"Rebecca!" he called.

She glanced around in surprise at the sharp sound of his voice.

"It's good to have you back," he affirmed.

"Thank you, Captain," she whispered.

Dr. Ammons led Rebecca to the sick berth, where he adamantly declared her to be suffering from a bout of exhaustion and tried to convince her to take a dose of Laudanum to help her sleep. She refused, assuring him she needed nothing to encourage rest, it would no doubt come on its own volition.

"You may have been the acting doctor for the past few weeks, young lady," he admonished in a stern voice, "but now I fill that role."

She continued to refuse the opiate tonic he offered, and instead patted his shoulder with affection as she bid him goodnight.

"It's wonderful to have you back, Rebecca," he said through eyes filled with tenderness. "This frigate just wasn't the same without you."

"It's wonderful to be back, Dr. Ammons," she replied, bidding him goodnight with a wave over her shoulder. She made her way to her small quarters, relieved to see that all was just as she had left it. In her darkest of dreams she had imagined Captain Jameson tossing everything overboard in an angry rage, but now, she realized, her fears had been proven unfounded. She crawled beneath the heavy blankets, sighing in contentment at the feel of the old, familiar room, but before her head was on the pillow long enough to even warm it, her eyes closed in a heavy slumber, and she remained in a dreamless sleep for the next several hours.

Lieutenants Burgess and Edwards made their way towards the officer's quarters after leaving the captain's stateroom.

"What was that all about?" Mr. Edwards scoffed.

Lieutenant Burgess was just as surprised by the girl's tearful outburst and wondered what had happened to upset her.

"I'm sure she's just tired, James," he replied. "She's toiled nonstop since she arrived aboard the Pepita and has had little rest to speak of since then."

"You're beginning to sound sympathetic toward the girl," he remarked with a probing glance. "Did something happen that I should be aware of?"

"No, no…I just don't like to see her so discouraged after her determined efforts to see the crew through their quarantine."

They continued on to the officer's quarters, Lieutenant Edwards eyeing his friend with suspicion, while he wondered what had transpired over the course of the past seven weeks to change the man's attitude toward the girl. Both officers remained in a contemplative silence for the remainder of the night, for neither wanted to broach the matter of Rebecca Halloway, even though both harbored unspoken thoughts of her in their mind.

Chapter 19

Captain Jameson had planned Rebecca's dinner party for the evening after their return, hoping she would have had sufficient time to rest by then, but much to his surprise he saw her moving about on deck later that afternoon. He studied her from the quarterdeck as she stopped to speak with the petty officer for several moments before meandering toward the galley, no doubt he considered, to resume her tasks along side the cook. Breaching all standards of protocol, he had invited the petty officer and the galley cook to join in the commemoration, where he hoped to acknowledge the girl's heroic efforts at saving the lives of his crew. He knew Rebecca cherished the close relationship she had forged with the two men, and he thought having them in attendance might make the celebration more memorable for her. With a sudden realization, he remembered that Rebecca had never intended to remain aboard the Redemption indefinitely, and he pondered the impact her imminent departure would have on the crew who had come to enjoy her captivating presence. His heart was grieved by the knowledge that he would eventually lose her, and he cast his eyes over the distant horizon to quell the anguish that wrenched at his soul. When he had regained some semblance of composure, he turned back to observe his enchanting stowaway, only to find that she had disappeared from sight.

Eddy grinned in delight when Rebecca stepped through the portal, thrilled to find that she was looking almost like her old self again. He hadn't anticipated seeing her cheerful countenance for at least another day or two, and with a glad shout he said, "Welcome back!"

A bubble of laughter escaped her when she caught a glimpse of the charming expression on the cook's face, and she threw her arms up in the air, as if overjoyed to be working in the galley again and cleaning up after hundreds of men.

"Did you get enough rest?" he admonished through a teasing scowl. "I don't want you drifting off over a kettle of boiling stew."

"I'll manage..." she murmured. "I suppose my body has finally adjusted to functioning on little to no sleep."

He stared at her, his gaze distant and soft. "I missed you, Bec," he said in a low tone.

"I missed you too, Eddy," she murmured, pulling a stool from beneath the counter to perch herself on while she set about peeling a mound of potatoes.

"I hear you're invited to a special dinner in the captain's quarters," he remarked.

She nodded, feeling the familiar root of trepidation taking hold when she recalled the horrific experiences of the last two dinner parties in the captain's quarters. "I just don't know about that, Eddy," she sighed. "Both times I've been asked to join the captain at his social affairs something dreadful has happened. And besides that, the last thing I want to do is eat dinner with a roomful of arrogant officers," she pronounced through a grimace. "I'd rather scrub the galley."

He laughed at the forlorn expression that shadowed her features and said, "Don't worry, Bec…I think you'll enjoy yourself this time."

❧

The evening of the imposing celebration came much too soon as far as Rebecca was concerned, and she remained in a brooding silence for most of the day. She had grown accustomed to the lazy, unstructured days aboard the Pepita, and she found herself missing the ready seclusion to be found in the secure confines of the small ship. Eddy, disgruntled by her sulking manner, sent her off to her cabin well before the afternoon chores had been completed, and Rebecca grumbled at the audacity of the young cook. A wry grin tugged at the corners of her mouth when she thought of her father, and the firm chastising he would deliver upon hearing of her ingratitude, so instead of protesting further she began to rifle through the dresses Captain Jameson had purchased for her in Bergen. The lovely, emerald gown caught her attention and she held it against her with a happy sigh, grateful for the opportunity to dress like a young woman again after having to wear the stiff tunics that had been her only option aboard the Pepita.

Eddy trailed behind Petty Officer Andrews along the length of the corridor towards the captain's stateroom. Both men were apprehensive at the thought of socializing with the officers whom they were accustomed to taking orders from, and they stood for several terse moments before the portal, eyeing one another with wary caution. Their hesitant knock brought Lieutenant Burgess to the door, and smiling a warm greeting, he invited them to enter with a gracious wave of his arm. Captain Jameson stood to welcome the midshipmen as well, and offered the pair a portion of rum from his decanter resting on a side table. Rebecca appeared soon after, and those present were enchanted by her smile of delight when she spotted the unexpected guests mingling among the group of officers. Lieutenant Edwards was the last to arrive, and lingered in the corner for a time to observe the activities from a distance.

The group circulated about the room exchanging casual pleasantries until the captain's steward arrived to serve the first course, and all took a place at the table to partake in the aromatic food that had been brought to them. Lieutenant Burgess cut a path across the room to claim a seat near Rebecca, hoping he would once again have the opportunity to spend some time conversing with her. He found himself missing the amicable intimacy of her friendship, which he had grown quite fond of during their final two weeks of their confinement aboard the Pepita.

Rebecca glanced up in surprise when Lieutenant Burgess took the seat across from her, thinking he would have much preferred the company of Lieutenant Edwards, especially after having been away from the officer for so long. Nevertheless, she gave him an engaging smile and the two slipped into a comfortable conversation, leaving the others in the room looking on with expressions of inquisitive speculation.

"Did you manage to get caught up on your rest?" he asked.

A mock grimace sprang to Rebecca's face and she said, "I think I've put an end to a good night's rest with my sleeping habits of late!"

"No, I suppose waking every hour is not conducive to slumber," he laughed. "I do hope you know how much the crew… and myself, appreciate your sacrifice, Miss Hal…Rebecca."

A lovely shade of crimson stained Rebecca's face and she cast her gaze down in humble appreciation of the officer's generous compliment. Her heart began to pound through the sheer fabric of the satin gown she wore, and she felt certain all seated near her could hear it.

Lieutenant Edwards studied the exchange between his friend and the girl with a piqued curiosity, and wondered anew if something hadn't transpired between the two of them while they were detained on the supply ship. Even Captain Jameson was struck with intrigue, for he clearly recalled how adamant his officer was to maintain a cautious distance from Rebecca before they had been forced together in quarantine. Now they appeared as though they had been lifelong friends who had never shared a harsh word.

Rebecca enjoyed herself throughout the entire dinner affair and was amazed at how quickly the time passed. She realized that she hadn't enjoyed herself quite as much at such an event since her evening in Bergen with Captain Jameson and Dr. Ammons, and with contented smile splayed across her face, she gazed around the room at all those she considered dear to her heart. She was pleased to see that even Mr. Andrews and Eddy appeared to be having a wonderful time, in spite of the officers that surrounded them.

When at last the steward had collected the remainder of the food from the table, the guests began to stroll about the room, mingling with one another in relaxed conversation. Eddy and Mr. Andrews stayed late into the night, enjoying Rebecca's cheerful company, and they, as well as those who lingered in the captain's stateroom, were quick to note how diligent Lieutenant Burgess was to hover near the girl for the duration of the evening, all except for Rebecca that is. She remained oblivious to the young man's attention, as well as to the snickers interspersed among the officers teasing comments.

Lieutenant Edwards was determined to discover what had transpired between the two and made a move to draw Lieutenant Burgess off by himself for a moment. "What's happened, man?" he asked in a whispered hush. "You haven't taken yourself away from the girl all night!"

"What?" Lieutenant Burgess questioned with a look of innocence. "I don't know what you're talking about, James."

"The girl, Paul…she's been throwing her affections at you since you've arrived here…and you seem intent on returning them. What's happened to you?"

"Nonsense," he retorted. "I've just been making conversation...this dinner party is in her honor, after all." Lieutenant Burgess was disconcerted by the accusations of his fellow officer, and strode to the quarterdeck to clear his thoughts with a breath of fresh air.

Lieutenant Edwards followed behind him hoping to make amends and said, "I apologize," he began. "It's apparent to me that I spoke out of turn."

"No, no...you're right. I suppose I've grown accustomed to the girl's company. After all, I've been confined with her for the past several weeks you know," Lieutenant Burgess asserted, wondering why he felt the need to explain his conduct and his desire to consort with the girl.

"Yes...perhaps," Lieutenant Edwards mused. "I hate to think of what *that* must have been like," he added with a hint of sarcasm.

Lieutenant Burgess stared at the man for several terse moments, wanting to inform his fellow officer that it was rather pleasant once he had taken his haughty nose out of the air, but he thought better of it and remained silent, nodding instead in agreement.

Within the confines of the captain's quarters, Rebecca and Captain Jameson attempted to coax Eddy and Petty Officer Andrews into a game of Whist. The two men finally relented after she accused them of being afraid of losing to a girl. Gathering around the table, Rebecca dealt the cards, and the foursome grew quiet with the competition at hand. Dr. Ammons and the other officers present watched on with high spirited enthusiasm, while Rebecca and Captain Jameson took the winning trick again and again. Those who had remained unaware of the girl's penchant for the game chuckled in their amusement at Rebecca's uncanny luck, while the two crewmen began to empty their pockets and hand over their loose coins.

"You're going to win it all anyway, Missy," the petty officer remarked through a wry grin. "Why don't you just take it now, and spare us all the humiliation."

The voices of the men who lingered nearby erupted into peals of laughter, just as the two lieutenants stepped into the stateroom. Rebecca, unaware that they had been absent for a time, cast a gracious smile over her shoulder and invited them in on a round.

"Would you like to join us?" she asked, watching the petty officer and the cook step away from the table in feigned defeat.

"No, thank you," Lieutenant Burgess replied, his voice distant and aloof. Perhaps Mr. Edwards was right, he thought to himself. He had made the decision long ago to remain unencumbered by a family, preferring instead his solitary life at sea to one bound by responsibility to a woman and children, and while he felt an intense attraction to the girl after returning from their time together aboard the Pepita, he attributed it to the emotional tension of being forced into such close proximity for the past several weeks. He *had* noticed the girl had been particularly attentive to him that evening...perhaps she did have her sights set on something other than just casual association. He tried to push the thought from of his mind while eying her with suspicion, watching as she and Captain Jameson continued their game with the two officers who were willing to accept their challenge.

Rebecca, hearing the curt tone of the officer's reply, raised her eyes to peer at the young lieutenant, and even from across the room she could sense the change in his demeanor. She hoped she hadn't offended him somehow but couldn't excuse herself without drawing the attention of everyone present, so she returned her gaze to the cards displayed before her, in no mood to approach the surly officer while he remained near Lieutenant Edwards. She and Captain Jameson played Whist well into the early hours of morning, and she didn't slip away until she saw Lieutenant Burgess taking his leave from the captain's quarters, unattended by other officers. Jumping to her feet, she assured the men that she would return momentarily, while she hurried to follow the lieutenant into the corridor. "Mr. Burgess," she called, "may I speak with you for a moment?"

He spun about to face her with an abrupt move, sending her reeling back to avoid slamming into him, and she found herself lost in his piercing gaze, uncomprehending of the change that had come over him during the course of the evening.

"What is it?" he snapped in a terse voice.

Rebecca felt a twinge of alarm when she heard his tone, and took a precautionary step towards the captain's stateroom. "It's just that…you seem upset, sir, and I'm can't help but wonder if I've offended you somehow," she remarked, her solemn gaze filled with apprehension.

"No, you haven't," he replied through an audible air of indifference.

He made a motion to leave and Rebecca called out once again, "Mr. Burgess, wait…"

The lieutenant paused in mid-step, wavering between his conflicting emotions, and an internal struggle ensued as he willed away the desire to take the girl in his arms and pledge his undying devotion to her, while at the same time he wanted nothing more than to escape her suffocating presence. He stood for a moment in brooding silence, never bothering to turn around, before muttering, "What is it?"

Rebecca felt her heart being ripped apart over the impending loss of what was to her such a new, but precious friendship, and she willed herself not to break down in front of him as she whispered, "It's nothing, sir…nothing at all."

Lieutenant Burgess continued down the corridor without looking back. His shoulders were squared in resolute determination, and though he had hoped to feel a tremendous release at his quick dismissal of the girl, all he was left with was an incredible yearning for what would never be.

Rebecca stood in dejected silence watching him go, puzzled by the officer's brusque manner. After several moments she breathed a heavy sigh and made her way back to the captain's stateroom to bid all who remained a quiet goodnight. She didn't know what to make of the officer's strange behavior, but it left her feeling perplexed. A shadow of sadness darkened her features as she returned to her quarters and burrowed deep beneath the comforting blankets, where she began to pray for the Lord to give her insight into the mind of the young man whom she had finally come to consider a friend.

Chapter 20

LIEUTENANT BURGESS HAD determined in his mind to avoid the girl after that night, but Rebecca remained clueless as to his new resolve. She was unaccustomed to seeing him during the course of her day unless he had some sort of altercation to discuss with her, and so life, as she knew it, resumed with the only normalcy she had ever known since stowing away on the Redemption. Her routine settled comfortably into place once more, and she found herself thinking about her time aboard the Pepita less and less with each passing day.

Captain Jameson was grateful to see Rebecca's safe return to the Redemption, and he reveled in her presence in the evenings as they read together, played Whist, or simply spent time conversing with one another. He took the opportunity to teach her several new card games when she felt up to the challenge, and he was relieved to find that her luck came to an end when she was not playing something so familiar to her as her beloved Whist. On this particular night, they relaxed on the sofa sipping hot tea, and Rebecca was content to listen and observe while Captain Jameson read to her from the bible she had given him, choosing a passage from the book of Philippians.

"Be anxious for nothing, but in everything by prayer and supplication give thanks, letting your requests be made known to God," he murmured, casting a quick glance at the girl. Seeing the distant gaze that lingered on her features, he asked, "Are you anxious about anything, Rebecca?"

Rebecca was stirred from her pensive musing by the mention of her name and she glanced up to ask, "What did you say, sir?"

"I asked if you were anxious about anything," he said through a tender smile, aware of the change in the girl since the night of his dinner party. Until now she had remained unwilling to volunteer any details as to her time spent with the crew in their confinement, but he was aware that something had transpired between his lieutenant and Rebecca aboard the Spanish vessel, as well as after they had returned.

Seeing the hesitant expression that shadowed her eyes, he asked, "Why is it you never speak of your time away during the quarantine?"

"Oh, I don't know, sir..." she murmured, wondering why the captain had broached the subject when she wanted only to forget about it.

"Mr. Burgess," he said, "he was quite upset when I ordered him to take you on as a passenger, was he not?"

She lowered her gaze to contemplate his words, knowing that anger did not even come close to describing the emotions of the young lieutenant at the time, but she was unsure as to how much information she should divulge to the captain.

"Did he make things difficult for you?" he continued, wanting to understand the relationship that had begun to develop between the two while they were away.

"You might say we had a difficult start," she grinned, "but it wasn't long before we settled on an agreement...he would stay above deck and I would stay below, well out of his sight."

"Oh? And how long did that continue?"

"A while," she said, evading the question.

"How long of a while?" he persisted.

Rebecca eyed Captain Jameson skeptically for a moment and said, "I'm not sure I should be telling you this, sir..."

She was unsure as to why he was prodding her for the information, and did not want to stir contention between himself and Lieutenant Burgess over something that was over and done with.

"No, please, go on," he said. "I will not speak of it after this evening."

"Well, we were able to avoid one another for the first few weeks," she continued, "except on the occasions when he found me doing something that he considered inappropriate."

"And what, perhaps, might that have been?" he asked, an incredulous hint of amusement on his face, for he was well aware that his officer had, in the past, considered everything the girl did inappropriate.

Rebecca paused for a moment, realizing how trivial it all sounded now, when at the time Mr. Burgess had posed a very real threat to her. "Well, to begin with, he was upset when he discovered that I had prepared a sick berth without first asking his permission to do so," she began.

"You managed to set up a sick berth?"

Rebecca gave an emphatic nod and said, "Yes, and when the men began to succumb to small pox, he tried to come in there to chastise me for something I can't even recall anymore."

"Oh my," he murmured. "Whatever did you do?"

"I told him he wasn't allowed in the sick berth...that I wouldn't let him pass. After all, I couldn't let him enter a room full of infectious men!"

Captain Jameson's face took on a grim appearance, for he knew that surely would have infuriated his young officer. "And how did he take that?"

"He threatened to kill me," she giggled, retelling the incident in a lighthearted manner. Rebecca felt a warm sensation stirring within her at the recollection of the memory, and continued to ramble on. "But he didn't kill me, sir," she assured with a smile.

Captain Jameson stared at the young woman, stunned by what she was revealing, but even more so by what she had kept to herself until now. "How long did you have to suffer with his contention?"

"Until I decided I was going to leave," she replied.

Captain Jameson was rendered speechless, his dumbfounded silence filling the space between them. Rebecca gave him a nervous glance then, aware that what she was divulging was making him very uncomfortable, and she wondered once more if she should continue sharing the information with him. His probing gaze encouraged her to continue, in spite of her hesitance to do so.

"One of the men had been delirious with fever for almost three days, and no matter what I did, I couldn't coax him eat or drink anything. When his mind finally cleared, his only request was for food. Well, in my great relief I hurried to the galley to make him a bit of stew, but ended up making a horrible racket instead. That, of course, caught the attention of Mr. Burgess," she sighed, "and when he found out what I was trying to do, he ordered me to return to the sick berth and tell the man he would eat with the rest of the crew and not before then."

"Go on..." he urged.

"Well," she elaborated with an exaggerated sigh, "I told him I would not return empty handed when I had a hungry patient in my sick berth, which prompted him to remind me once again that I was being insubordinate. So I just reminded *him* that I was not one of his midshipmen that he could order about." Her thoughts lingered on the distant memory before continuing her story. "It was then that he ordered me to leave the Pepita."

"He didn't!"

Rebecca smiled. "He did."

"Well what did you do?"

"I left," she said simply.

His eyes narrowed. "What do you mean you left?"

"I walked up to the deck, crawled over the railing and jumped into the ocean. I figured I might as well just swim home to England and be done with the lot of you." She was laughing now, but saw that Captain Jameson remained quiet, his grim expression speaking louder than mere words ever could have. "Captain," she assured with a light touch on his arm, "this story has a happy ending...there's no need to be upset."

"You could have been killed," he growled.

"No," she declared. "He jumped right in after me! Well, I wasn't about to stop swimming long enough for him to catch up, but he eventually convinced me that he was drowning. Part of me wanted to let him, but then my conscience got the better of me and I swam back to save him, only he didn't need saving...but by the time I realized that he was only trying to lure me within his reach, he had a hold of me, and I couldn't get away no matter how hard I tried."

She paused for a moment to catch her breath and breathed a contented sigh, recalling the memory with a strange sense of longing for those final days of peaceful friendship aboard the Pepita. Captain Jameson was quick to note the distant yearning in her eyes and he wondered what else might have transpired between his officer and the young woman. He allowed her to remain immersed in her thoughts for as long as she wished, and after several moments she began to speak again, but instead of continuing with the tale of Mr. Burgess, she spoke only of the sick berth, and of the solitude she felt when tucked away in there with the afflicted men. She told him also of the camaraderie that was so apparent among the crew, and even of her late night interludes in the sea, bringing another stern look of admonition. Finally, she spoke of the comfortable friendship that had finally developed between herself and the young officer, ending the story with a heavy sigh.

"Why does that upset you, Rebecca?" he asked. "I thought the two of you were getting along splendidly since your return."

"So did I, Captain," she murmured, "but something happened the night of your dinner party...I don't know what... but he hasn't been the same since..."

He studied her through sympathetic eyes, aware that even the thought of anyone being upset with her troubled her a great deal. "Would you like me to speak with him?" he asked.

She shook her head in a resounding no and said, "There's no need to, Captain. I hardly ever see him about the ship, but I can't help but wonder if I've done something to offend him."

"You can't make amends if you aren't aware of the infraction that was committed, Rebecca," he reminded.

She made an attempt to stifle a yawn and nodded in agreement. "I know, sir, and someday I will pursue the matter further. But...not tonight," she pronounced, standing to her feet. "And now, I will go and speak with God. He has a peculiar way of telling me things I don't necessarily like to hear," she added, an impish grin spreading over her cherubic face.

He laughed at her endearing manner, and stood to walk with her to the door. "Goodnight, Rebecca," he said in a quiet voice.

"Goodnight, Captain Jameson," she murmured.

Before returning to her quarters, she decided to meander up to the deck, hoping to slip into the beckoning waves for a quick swim. She hadn't had an opportunity to stretch her limbs in the ocean since they had returned from the Pepita, and she was desperate for the solitude of a nighttime plunge in the cool water. Stepping out into the starlit night, she lingered at the bow for a time, enjoying both the solitude and the peaceful quiet of nightfall. A full moon was hovering overhead, casting its sheen of yellow light over the gentle ripples, and Rebecca began to contemplate the events that had come to pass since their return from the Pepita, trying with desperation to recall what might have caused the abrupt change in Lieutenant Burgess.

She lowered her head, her eyes drifting shut, as she began to seek divine guidance on how to pray for the young man. How she yearned for reconciliation before taking her leave from the Redemption, but she knew that any efforts made on her part might only push him further away. With a determined sigh, she continued in pleading her cause before the Lord, her eyes shut tight against the darkened sky.

Lieutenants Burgess and Edwards left the confines of the officer's quarters hoping to get a breath of fresh air. Climbing the steps to the quarterdeck, Lieutenant Burgess spotted Rebecca standing near the bow of the frigate. He was hesitant to reveal her presence to his fellow officer, and tried to distract the man's attention away from where she lingered lest he try to provoke an argument with her. "You know, James, it's a bit chilly…let's go back inside, shall we?"

Lieutenant Edwards glanced at his friend and said, "What're you talking about? It's perfectly fine." He continued on toward the railing, his gaze at last falling upon the girl. "What the devil is she doing out here?" he muttered.

"Probably in need of a bit of fresh air, just like us," Mr. Burgess replied with a casual glance. "There's no need to disturb her."

The officers observed Rebecca from the quarterdeck, both curious as to why she stood with her eyes closed against the luminescent hue of the moonlight, while Lieutenant Burgess was again captivated by the girl's enchanting appearance. Rebecca, sensing someone was near, twirled around, and a slight gasp of surprise escaped her at the sight of the two men staring down at her. Realizing she had lingered too long in the evening air, she hurried to the corridor that would return her to her berth, but a sudden shout stopped her in mid-step.

"You there! Lay aft here!"

The officer's words snapped through the silence of the night, bringing Rebecca about on her heel. With a hesitant eye she glanced up to meet Lieutenant Burgess' gaze, unaware of who had called out the command, but thinking surely it had to have been him, acting in a simple gesture of good humor. Lieutenant Edwards watched on in arrogant indignation, waiting for the girl to respond to the order.

After several tense moments, a slight grin began to tug at Rebecca's features. She gazed up at the one whom she had come to consider a friend, while the memory of their last night aboard the Pepita sprang to mind with vivid clarity, and she was hopeful that perhaps he wasn't as disgruntled with her as she had previously thought him to be. Not wanting to broach the subject in the presence of Lieutenant Edwards however, she lifted her hand in a slight wave and again began to walk toward the corridor.

Without warning, Lieutenant Edwards clamored down the narrow steps, lunging at her with a grimace of rage splayed across his face. "You do not scoff at the orders of a superior officer!" he spat, taking hold of her arm to pin her small frame against the unyielding wall of the frigate.

Rebecca was stunned, too frightened to speak, while the angry officer towered over her. Lieutenant Burgess raced down in a desperate attempt to subdue him, leaving Rebecca glancing from one man to the other in perplexed confusion.

"I'm sorry!" she stammered. "I thought Mr. Burgess was…I didn't know-"

Lieutenant Edwards interrupted her frantic explanation. "I don't care what you thought!" he shouted in her face, glaring at her through stormy eyes. "You do not turn your back on the orders of an officer!"

"Stop, James," Lieutenant Burgess urged with desperation, "She thought I was speaking in jest!"

"So now you feel the need to defend her insolence?" he growled, never loosening his grip on Rebecca as his anger turned towards his fellow officer.

"No," he insisted, "I'm not defending her actions, but you must release her! If Captain Jameson hears of this you'll see a flogging for sure."

Lieutenant Edwards spun back to glare at Rebecca, giving her a resounding shake as he grumbled, "I ought to flog you right here and now to teach you a good lesson about subordination!"

Rebecca glanced through panicked eyes at Mr. Burgess, pleading for help as she struggled to break free of the wrenching grip on her arm. Lieutenant Burgess continued in his efforts to deflect the rage of the incensed officer away from the girl so she could escape, and taking a firm hold of Lieutenant Edwards, he forced the man's arms to release her from their angry grasp, causing Rebecca to stumble backwards in surprise. Her wary gaze remained fixed on Lieutenant Burgess, and he frowned down at her as she struggled to regain her footing to shout, "Go on! Get out of here!"

Lieutenant Edwards lunged at Rebecca once again, but she jumped to her feet and ran toward the safety of the corridor, descending with haste the steps that led to her quarters. Stumbling into the small berth, she slammed the door behind her and leaned back on shaky limbs, her breath catching in ragged gasps. The officer's assault had left her hurt and confused, and she listened with an ear to the door, hoping they hadn't followed her below. She heard nothing, but remained propped against the wall for several moments, trying to still her trembling legs before crawling into her bed. She lay down with an anguished sigh, her heart aching with sadness at the betrayal of one she had only too recently considered a friend. It was in moments like these that she wanted nothing more than to be safe at home in England in the presence of those who loved her without condition. She closed her eyes, hoping to still her pounding heart, but visions of the angry lieutenant continued to replay themselves over and over again in her mind, only heightening the fear that consumed her.

Lieutenant Burgess returned to his quarters after escorting Lieutenant Edwards to his berth. He had been sickened by the confrontation that had occurred, for he knew that Rebecca thought the order had been spoken by him, and in jest. Had he known of the intentions of Lieutenant Edwards, he certainly would have dissuaded him from harassing the girl, but now it was too late to prevent what had already happened, and the weight of her anguish weighed heavily on his mind. He recalled her selfless determination to risk her very life for the men onboard the Pepita, and the compassionate words she had spoken to him while he lay feverish and ill, and he realized just then that he would have given most anything to be back onboard the small vessel and alone in her peaceful presence once again, rather than here with the crew he had subjected her to.

Rebecca slept fitfully that night, and never mentioned the incident to anyone lest they harbor malicious intentions towards the officers, but she made every effort to avoid the two men and spent most of her time below, where she was sheltered from their harassment. On rare occasions in the early mornings she would sneak above to the deck and slip into the cool waters for an indulgent swim, as evenings, she had discovered, were no longer safe. It grieved Rebecca to think about it, but she realized her time aboard the Redemption must soon come to an end.

Lieutenant Burgess knew that Rebecca was avoiding him, and he was grateful for her discretion in the matter. He was well aware that Lieutenant Edwards harbored an intense resentment for the girl, although he had no ideas as to why, but his primary concern was keeping protected from the officer's wrath until she was safely returned to her home and her family. By keeping herself hidden away he determined, it helped to avoid further confrontations from arising. He regretted not having taken more of a stand in her defense on the night of the incident, and he continued to carry the guilt for his lack of recourse, remembering with vivid clarity her bewildered despair at his apparent betrayal.

Captain Jameson had sensed something was amiss, for Rebecca seemed guarded and aloof and not as quick to mingle with the rest of the crew as she had enjoyed doing so many times before. Seeing his young officer returning to his quarters one evening, he called out to him in a casual voice, "Mr. Burgess!"

"Yes, Captain," the Lieutenant answered, turning to approach his commander.

"I wondered if you might like to join me for a cup of tea."

Lieutenant Burgess smiled, giving a polite nod to the captain, and said, "Yes, sir, I would enjoy that very much."

He entered the captain's stateroom, and took a seat on the lounge when the captain motioned for him to do so. Pouring two steaming cups of tea, Captain Jameson handed one to his officer before taking a seat across from him.

"Things are going well for you, I take it?" he inquired.

"Yes, sir," Lieutenant Burgess replied, wondering where the conversation was headed.

"Tell me about your time aboard the Pepita," he suggested. "We haven't spoken of it since your return."

Lieutenant Burgess studied the man with a slight smile on his face, realizing what it was the captain hinted at. "It was fortunate she came aboard, sir," he said, "although I wouldn't admit it until the very end."

He grinned at his officer's keen sense of intuition. "She's very much like you, Mr. Burgess," he remarked, standing to his feet to pace about the room. "Bright, intellectual, courageous… assertive in nature when the situation warrants it…"

He turned to look back at his officer, pausing to let his words take hold before he continued. "Perhaps that is why you feel threatened by her presence aboard the Redemption."

Lieutenant Burgess glanced up in surprise at his words. "I do not believe I have ever felt threatened by her presence, sir," he replied with indifference.

Captain Jameson eyed him a wry glance, disbelief showing on his face. "Did she ever tell you how she came to be aboard the Redemption, Mr. Burgess?"

"No, sir, she hasn't," he replied, realizing that he had never bothered to ask, nor had he wondered. Instead, he had simply assumed she was seeking an inconspicuous escape from something, or someone.

"She was taken by force," Captain Jameson began. "Stolen away from her family, her home, and all she held dear...and by our very own British sailors no less!"

"By some of *our* men, Captain?" he asked through a skeptical grimace.

"No, she was abducted by some of Charles Cromwell's men and taken aboard the Defiance. For three months she managed to conceal her identity from them..."

The young lieutenant sat in silent contemplation, stunned by the girl's tenacity at surviving three, long months onboard the Defiance.

"She escaped when the Defiance moored in Cadiz, and managed to steal her way onto the Redemption."

The young officer was taken aback by the captain's words. The resentment he had felt when he discovered that there was a woman onboard the frigate was a memory still fresh in his mind, and the guilt he had experienced as a result resurfaced once again. "I...I didn't know that, Captain," he stammered.

"Oh," the captain smiled, "I'm certain there is much you don't know about her, Mr. Burgess. Much she would willingly share if given the opportunity."

"Sir, I mean no disrespect," he began, "but I choose to consort with my fellow officers. I've never felt comfortable in the presence of women," he added, trying to defend himself against the subtle innuendo of his commander.

The young lieutenant thought just then of the easy manner in which he and Rebecca had conversed aboard the Pepita after he had fallen ill, realizing unexpectedly that he had never felt quite as comfortable in the presence of anyone else before then. He recalled the selfless care she had provided to the crew since she had stowed away on both the Redemption and the Pepita. He also remembered her fierce determination to protect the one who had released her from the hold, even when threatened with the prospect of death, knowing that none of the men on board would have been as brave under the same circumstances.

Captain Jameson's voice stirred him from his thoughts when he chose with careful consideration the words he spoke next. "The life of a seaman is a lonely one, Mr. Burgess. I made the decision many years ago to forgo a family, choosing instead an unhindered life at sea." Captain Jameson paused for a moment, hoping Mr. Burgess was listening, while he continued to walk about the room casting an occasional glance at his young officer.

Lieutenant Burgess remained silent in his discomfort, wondering for a moment if Rebecca had asked the captain to speak to him. He felt resentment welling at the thought, but it dissipated just as quickly as it had begun when he realized that she would never even consider doing such a thing. He hesitated to speak while he pondered the sentiments Captain Jameson shared with him. "Do you regret that decision, Captain?" he finally asked.

"I do now, Mr. Burgess," the captain replied. "I've been greatly affected by the girl's presence aboard the Redemption… it has made me realize what I've forfeited in the ignorance of my youth."

The two men regarded one another in silence for a time, thinking on the words that had been spoken. Hoping to put his officer at ease, Captain Jameson said, "How about a game of Whist?"

Lieutenant Burgess paused to consider the offer for a moment, but then shook his head in resignation, still perplexed by their conversation. "If you'll excuse me, sir…" he said, wanting to return to the privacy of his own quarters where he could think more clearly.

"Of course," Captain Jameson replied.

When Lieutenant Burgess left the captain's stateroom, he was confused by the conflicting emotions coursing through him. He had a strong desire to see the girl, to speak with her again, and to tell her how much he longed to spend time with her in uninterrupted conversation, yet the thought of doing so terrified him. After much deliberation, he diverted his course away from his berth to slip below to the crew's quarters, where the men partook in their evening activities. He cast a cautious glance through the dim light in the hopes of catching just a glimpse of the girl, and it didn't take long for him to locate Rebecca, for her presence alone brightened the room.

He stood unnoticed, hidden behind a rafter at the edge of the crew's quarters watching her while she sat near a foursome playing Whist. She appeared to be sharing with them her precocious talent for winning, laughing with a radiant smile while she spoke with the men. He had never seen a game of Whist played among his crew when the tension of the competition hadn't been intense, and now, they acted as if it were some sort of great, entertaining performance, with none giving a care as to who would turn the winning trick. He wanted to join them, if only to hear the melodic rise and fall of her voice once again, but instead he retreated into the darkness of the corridor and made his way back to his quarters, where he lay awake in his bed for what seemed to him like hours, unable to sleep due to images of the girl's features lingering in his thoughts, and the sound of her laughter ringing in his ears.

Chapter 21

THE WEATHER HAD turned noticeably warmer as the Redemption sailed south towards Ireland. It had been several weeks now since the crew had seen land and the men were growing restless in the monotony of their daily activities aboard ship. Rebecca had maintained her vigilant watch for both Lieutenant Burgess and Lieutenant Edwards, and had thus far been successful at avoiding another confrontation. Lieutenant Burgess however, made every attempt possible to study Rebecca from afar, stealing into the crew's quarters in the evenings to observe her while she sat conversing with the midshipmen, or watching for her from the quarterdeck when she swam with graceful strokes through the waves in the early mornings. She remained oblivious to his attention and he preferred it that way, the guilt of his betrayal still weighing heavily on his conscience. Captain Jameson was aware of Lieutenant Burgess' ardent eye toward Rebecca, and he debated on whether or not to tell the girl. After much consideration, he decided to let fate take its own course, knowing that if he intervened he may very well drive the two of them even further apart. Instead, he observed their interactions from a distance, enjoying the innocent naivety of the girl, while he hoped his officer had nerve enough to make his intentions known before her return to Portsmouth.

A bout of cold, brittle rain had dampened the crew's mood, and Rebecca sat near Eddy in a comfortable silence below deck, enjoying the warmth of the fire and the respite from the chill of the air. She had long ago finished with the dinner clean up, but remained to linger in the peace and solitude that she had always found in the small confines of the galley. The men were becoming increasingly boisterous as the evening progressed, for the captain had allowed them all an extra portion of rum to lift their spirits during the period of inclement weather they had found themselves in, and now their revelry carried over into the galley, where the noise was rising to a deafening pitch.

"There'll be at least one bloody fight tonight, Bec, mark my word!" Eddy exclaimed with a grimace. She nodded in agreement, having seen firsthand the effects of overindulgence when the rum flowed too freely among the men.

A fierce gale had been blowing all day and showed no sign of relenting for some time. The frigate rolled with a frightening pitch on the waves, tossed by the ferocious blasts of wind, and Rebecca was beginning to feel bouts of nausea with each rising swell. From where they rested they could hear the sound of the sails, slapping with fierce determination in the storm. "Eddy," she breathed through pursed lips, "I need to go on deck for some fresh air..."

She hurried into the corridor, covering her mouth with her hand in an attempt to quell the vomit rising in her throat, and ran to the deck where she flung her head over the side of the frigate. She took deep gulps of the sea air, oblivious to the salty spray that pelted her face.

Eddy followed after Rebecca in concern, determined to remain with her lest she be swept overboard into the churning waters. She stood at the rail for several minutes before he spoke to her, his features darkened by a shadow of foreboding.

"Are you going to be alright, Bec?"

"Yes," she answered, keeping her head averted. "But I think I'll stay here a while. The cold air is soothing to my stomach."

He stared at her pale form gazing out at the horizon, the wind whipping her curls about her face. "Well then...I'll be staying here with you," he replied, turning his back to the blustery gales while keeping a watchful eye on the girl.

Lieutenant Burgess happened to be the officer on watch that evening, and he caught sight of Rebecca the moment she appeared on deck. Even from where he stood he could see the pallor of her skin, and he became troubled by the absence of her usual cheery countenance. Seeing the galley cook trailing behind her, he wondered if perhaps they had had an altercation. He continued to glance towards where they lingered in case she needed someone to intervene, while the cook remained nearby in a brooding silence. His apprehension was evident even through the darkness, as he watched the girl gaze out over the turbulent waves.

From below deck, Rebecca and Eddy heard the sound of a scuffle break out, and they turned to see one of the ship's crew stumbling blindly towards them, his eyes masked by blood streaming from a deep gash on his head. Eddy grimaced when he saw the man and muttered, "Looks like Tony'll be the one taking the brunt of the fighting tonight."

Rebecca was horrified by the gruesome display and made an immediate attempt to attend to the injured man, while Eddy grabbed her by the arm to restrain her. His eyes widened in alarm when he saw another crew member who wielded a bloodied knife storm to the deck, his face contorted with hateful malice.

"Bec!" he shouted, pulling her close, "stay here!"

Lieutenant Burgess watched on in dismay at the scene playing out before him. He drew his pistol from his hip when he saw the angry sailor advancing upon the helpless Tony Porter, the bloody knife poised high in the air. He tried in desperation to get Rebecca's attention, to warn her to step away from the deadly confrontation, but she could not hear him over the din of the storm. He stared on in dismay as the cook struggled to detain her in his grasp, but in her determination to assist the injured man, she continued to pull away from him.

"Rebecca!" he screamed across the wind, "Stand away there!" He lifted the pistol in his hand to train it on the crazed, knife-wielding midshipman, and waited for the girl to move out of the path of the bullet.

Rebecca, unaware of the danger she had placed herself in, struggled to calm the injured crewman, while the advancing menace stalked up behind her. Rebecca struggled with desperation to suppress the blood streaming from the gaping wound, while she knelt over the man's writhing body, still unaware of the officer and the cook who tried to distract her. Eddy again moved in to take hold of her, while in a last, frantic attempt to catch the girl's attention, Lieutenant Burgess shouted out, "You there!"

Rebecca glanced up sharply to locate the voice, thinking it was Lieutenant Edwards shouting down at her, but instead she was startled to find the agitated form of Lieutenant Burgess standing on the quarterdeck. She was stunned when she saw he held a pistol in his hand with the barrel trained on her, and she gasped in shock, her eyes moving to his face in utter confusion.

"Step away!" he screamed, flailing his arm in a wild motion toward the railing of the ship, as he watched the livid midshipman raise the knife up over his head in an attempt to land another blow to the already fallen Mr. Peters.

Eddy dashed in to grab Rebecca by the arm, pulling her away from the melee just as Lieutenant Burgess released the hammer on the gun. Their world began to move in slow motion then, as a forceful wave rocked the Redemption at the precise moment that the pistol was fired. The unexpected pitch sent Rebecca reeling into the path of the oncoming bullet, while Lieutenant

Burgess watched on in horror. Eddy reached out to steady her, feeling her body recoil against him when the bullet tore through her flesh. The men stood in stunned silence as Rebecca wavered for a moment, unable to breathe. She kept her eyes locked on Mr. Burgess, gazing at him in bewildered disbelief before falling listlessly to the deck.

Lieutenant Burgess was paralyzed with fear when he realized that his dream of this night had relived itself in stark reality. He watched as a group of men swarmed from the stairwell at the sound of the gun's blast, and seeing Rebecca, they hurried to the girl's side, crouching low to assist her where she lay.

Captain Jameson heard the brawl from his stateroom and he stood in agitation at having had his quiet evening interrupted. Slipping into his overcoat, he hastened to the deck to assure the situation was brought under control in a timely manner. When he arrived, he was startled to see a cluster of men huddled over someone lying on the wooden planks, and he proceeded to the quarterdeck where Lieutenant Burgess stood in an eerie silence, his face drained of all color. "What is it, Mr. Burgess?" the captain shouted over the noise of the slapping sails. "You look as if you've seen a ghost."

The young officer was speechless, as visions of his dream in which he held the pistol that had mortally wounded Rebecca Halloway continued on with relentless clarity in his mind. An unexpected wave of nausea came over him, and he turned his face to retch violently over the railing.

Captain Jameson, repulsed by the sight, diverted his attention from the lieutenant to glance down at the chaotic scene below, hoping to discover what it was that had so distressed his officer. He was quick to locate Dr. Ammons among the crowd, and was relieved to see that he was already attending to the injured sailor. He kept his eyes fixed on him, waiting for some clue as to what was happening beneath the horde of men, and his stomach began to clench in knots of dread when he saw the piercing gaze of Dr. Ammons peering up at him through a grim expression of dismay.

Rebecca writhed in agony while the features of the worried crew hovered over her. It felt as though someone had kicked her with a powerful force in the stomach and she struggled to catch her breath. She wished the men would move away so she could get some air, but she couldn't seem to make any sound come from her mouth. Her eyes darted anxiously from face to face, while Dr. Ammons spoke in a soothing voice to her, trying to keep her calm while he applied a firm pressure over her heart in an attempt to suppress the flow of blood.

Lieutenant Burgess had finally collected himself and sprinted down the steps of the quarterdeck to see if the girl still lived. Captain Jameson followed close behind him, unaware that it was Rebecca who had been injured.

When the two officers neared the circle of men, Rebecca's eyes fell on Lieutenant Burgess, her face a contortion of pain and sadness. Her only thought was of escape, for she was certain the officer had arrived to finish the task of killing her. She made a desperate attempt to flee, in spite of the excruciating spasms that coursed through her body, until the firm hands of the crew hovering over her restrained her at the doctor's sharp request.

Lieutenant Burgess was taken aback by the sheer terror that darkened the girl's eyes, as if she believed the bullet had been intended for her all along. He saw that her gaze never wavered from his, but her eyes remained filled with terror as she struggled beneath the hands of Dr. Ammons.

Dr. Ammons was bewildered by the girl's thrashing about and glanced behind him to discover what it was that held her in such a distraught frame of mind. Seeing only the young lieutenant, he again turned his attention to Rebecca, urging her to lie still while they attempted to move her to the sick berth. She continued to struggle against the men that held her, desperate to protect herself from further injury at the hands of the officer, while she maintained her fearful gaze upon him.

Captain Jameson approached the circle of men from the rear, making an attempt to peer over their shoulders to see who lay wounded. When his eyes fell upon Rebecca lying on the deck, blood staining her light cotton tunic and pooling beneath her, he stared in bewildered silence, unable to speak.

❧ ❧

Hundreds of miles away, Dr. Colin Halloway woke with a start in his bed, his brow breaking into a cold sweat and his heart pounding. He immediately woke his wife Katherine who had been resting in a deep slumber beside him, as he heard the voice of the Lord urgently calling him to pray for his daughter. Rebecca had been missing for almost two years now, yet in his heart he knew she still lived. He had been faithful to pray for her with diligence since she had disappeared, occasionally feeling it was more imperative at some times than others, but now the call to pray was stronger than it had ever been before. His wife peered through the darkness to gaze at her husband, knowing without even asking what was required of them, and together they moved from their bed onto their knees, where they began to intercede with passionate pleas for the life of their beloved child.

❧ ❧

Dr. Ammons and several of the crew hurried to carry Rebecca, who had already slipped into an unconscious state, to the sick berth. As they laid her on the table, she stirred with a slight moan but did not awaken. Dr. Ammons dismissed the men who lingered when he began to make an attempt to retrieve the bullet lodged within her chest. Captain Jameson remained in the room for a time, refusing to leave the girl's side. She had already lost a substantial amount of blood, and when the captain and Dr. Ammons gazed upon her pale face, they feared her days aboard the Redemption were drawing to an abrupt end.

Lieutenant Burgess stood on the quarterdeck, cursing himself for all of the incidents that had occurred since the girl had come aboard, but especially for what had taken place that night. He wished with his very soul that he could reclaim the moment that had shattered their world, and he would have been willing to give his very life to do so. Now, as he stood in a tortured silence staring out at the waves, he was aware that Captain Jameson had moved to the quarterdeck to stand beside him.

"Are you alright, Mr. Burgess?" the captain asked, already knowing in his heart that his officer had been responsible for Rebecca's injury.

Lieutenant Burgess glanced at his commander, his eyes filled with anguish. He returned his gaze to the water and began to weep bitter tears of regret. Captain Jameson looked on without speaking, at a loss as to how to console the man when he, himself, felt as if his heart had been ripped from his body.

Eddy and Mr. Andrews maintained a silent vigil outside Dr. Ammon's sick berth waiting for word of Rebecca's condition. Over an hour had passed, and yet they had not received news on whether she was still alive, or if she had succumbed to death. As they paced the wooden planks of the deck in nervous anticipation, they wished with all that was within them that the girl would survive the night.

Eddy stopped pacing long enough to glance at the petty officer. "Did you ever hear her pray?" he queried.

Petty Officer Andrews mulled over the words for several, tortured moments before nodding in affirmation, recalling how every time he had come across the girl it appeared as though she was uttering a prayer of some sort.

"Do you think we could pray for her now?"

Again, he nodded, while he struggled to keep his emotions as bay. Lowering his head in reverent submission, he joined the young midshipman, and the two began to utter pleading words of desperation to the God she had forever entrusted her life to.

Inside the walls of the sick berth, Dr. Ammons worked with fervent desperation to save Rebecca's life. He had retrieved the bullet from where it had lodged, deep within her sternum near her heart, and now he struggled to suppress the flow of blood that streamed from the wound while she lay still and silent, her face deathly pale against the dim light of the room. Never having uttered a prayer in his life, he was unsure of how to begin, but he made a feeble attempt on behalf of the girl, knowing that if her God could bring the cook back to life, He would surely have the ability to save Rebecca.

Captain Jameson remained on the quarterdeck with Lieutenant Burgess for several minutes, waiting for him to regain his composure. He regarded the troubled, young man with a sympathetic gaze, for he had borne witness to the officer's obvious affection for Rebecca and there was no doubt in his mind that the injury inflicted upon the girl was the result of a dreadful accident. "Come now, Lieutenant Burgess," he stated, placing a reassuring hand on his shoulder. "What happened tonight was a terrible mishap and I regret that it involved you. Were it anybody else, I know the guilt would not weigh as heavily on their conscience as it weighs upon yours."

Lieutenant Burgess made an attempt to accept Captain Jameson's words of consolation, but his conscience was overwhelmed with the guilt of what had happened to Rebecca, and he feared that if she did not survive the mishap, he would not be able to bear the burden of having brought her death upon her. He knew that Captain Jameson remained near him, and felt certain the man must despise him for what had occurred that night. Turning to glance at his commander, he saw that Captain Jameson peered through a forlorn grimace at the waves breaking against the side of the Redemption. "I'm so sorry, Captain Jameson," he uttered, knowing there were no words that would be adequate in conveying his feelings of remorse.

The two men gazed at one another in a grim silence for a moment before Captain Jameson spoke again.

"Would you like to see her?"

Lieutenant Burgess shook his head, despair etched deep in his brow, and he answered, "I couldn't possibly face her now, Captain. It was obvious that my presence terrified her."

"I don't think she is conscious, Mr. Burgess," he stated. "She will not know you are there."

Lieutenant Burgess stared at Captain Jameson, while he wrestled with his desire to see the girl, and his fear of losing all control of his emotions when he did come face to face with her.

Captain Jameson, sensing the young man's ambivalence, took him by the arm and led him toward the sick berth. When they approached the door behind which Rebecca lay, Lieutenant Burgess began to draw back in apprehension, recalling the look of terror in the girl's eyes when he was near her.

"I'm not going to force you to see her, Mr. Burgess," the captain said, wanting the man to come to terms with what had happened on his own accord, "but I think it's important that you do."

Lieutenant Burgess gave the captain a weary look, his face pale. "I can't go in there, sir," he stammered.

Captain Jameson nodded in understanding and said, "Try to get some sleep, Mr. Burgess."

Dr. Ammons sat near Rebecca in quiet regard, amazed at her peaceful countenance, even when so near death. He glanced toward the door when he heard someone enter, and saw that it was Captain Jameson. Motioning him to a chair near where he sat, he took note of the captain's diffidence. The officer appeared hesitant to move, almost as if he were afraid of waking the girl, and the two men stared at one another without speaking for several moments, neither of them knowing what to say. Finally, Captain Jameson took the seat Dr. Ammons had offered.

"Will she survive the injury?" he asked, his voice grave.

Dr. Ammons observed the captain with solemn eyes, deliberating the man's question. He had seen many injuries similar to Rebecca's in which none had lived, but then again, he realized, Rebecca was unlike anyone he had ever known. He wondered if her determined spirit would see her through this tragic accident, as it had seen so many of the crew through their own brush with death.

"I cannot say," Dr. Ammons replied. "I think we should consider returning her to Portsmouth, Will. If she does not survive this, we at least owe her the courtesy of returning her to her family."

Captain Jameson regarded Dr. Ammons through a contortion of dismay, the thought of losing Rebecca incomprehensible. "Very well," he pronounced. "We will set sail for England."

Chapter 22

THE DAYS ABOARD the Redemption were empty of the spontaneous energy that Rebecca seemed to exude. Many of the crew were affected by her absence, but none more than Lieutenant Burgess. He had not yet visited the sick berth where she lay feverish and hallucinating. Instead, he monitored her status through the reports of his petty officer, Mr. Andrews.

The Redemption had been sailing toward Portsmouth for the past seven days in a desperate attempt to return Rebecca to her homeland before she died. Her closest friends alternated shifts in the sick berth, where they maintained a vigil by her bedside, never leaving her alone for even a moment. The infection which had begun when the bullet pierced her body was taking its toll on her, and she had not returned to consciousness since the night she had been wounded.

Captain Jameson sat with her every evening, reading to her, speaking to her, or just sitting in quiet contemplation watching her. He was amazed by her radiant countenance, even in the face of death, and he cherished his moments alone with her, grieving the hour when they would come to an end.

At times he would recall memories of her early days aboard the frigate, and of how infuriated he had become when he had discovered there was a woman aboard his ship. He recalled too, the day she was found wandering about on deck, refusing to disclose the name of the one who had opened the door of the hold to let her out, not even wavering under his threat of punishment. He regretted the instances he had treated her with harsh consternation, and was grateful those times had been few, for it had not taken long for her winsome manner to win him over to complete adoration.

With a heavy sigh he broke free of his melancholy musings to glance at Rebecca, only to see her gazing with keen awareness back at him. Thinking she was in some sort of fever induced hallucination, he continued to stare at her, waiting until she again closed her eyes. To his utter amazement, a gentle smile lit her features and she held out a tentative hand.

"Captain Jameson," she breathed.

He moved to stand next to her, taking her feverish hand in his.

"Rebecca," he said, faltering for words, "I've missed you."

"I'm so sorry, Captain," she replied in a whisper, as tears began to run from her eyes. "I don't want to leave you in this manner, but my soul is hearing the call of my Savior."

He collapsed with a despairing heart into a chair, his grief washing over him, and he buried his face in his arms, ashamed of the tears that brimmed in his eyes.

"Do not weep for me, sir," she plead. "This has been my goal all along…to receive the inheritance of my faith…a house not made with human hands, but an eternal kingdom prepared for me by God…"

He continued to gaze at her as a tortured moan escaped his throat. "You mustn't leave us yet, Rebecca," he urged with desperation. "You have experienced so little of this world…your days have been too few on this earth."

Her eyes softened and she sighed, giving careful consideration to her words as she began to speak once again. "Captain, the bible says that *all* of my days were ordained for me, and written in God's book before even one of them came to be. My life has always been in His hands, and I must trust Him even in this. God's ways are so much higher than my own, sir, and if I were to be granted one final prayer, it would be that you would find His peace and His wisdom which surpasses all understanding." Her eyes were bright and clear and she spoke with a passionate conviction, in spite of the severity of her injuries.

Captain Jameson stared at her in silence, too distraught for words. He hung his head to lower his gaze, hoping she would not catch a glimpse the pain in his eyes, while he clung to her in a desperate attempt to hold her captive among the living, knowing she would soon slip away from him forever.

Rebecca watched as a brilliant light descended upon Captain Jameson, leaving her transfixed by its luminescent glow. In the midst of the magnificent vision, a scene played out before her in which Captain Jameson stood among thousands of men, his head bowed in prayer. She saw Eddy, Mr. Andrews, Lieutenants Burgess and Edwards, and several of the other crew members from the Redemption. They were on their knees praying along with the captain, and she gasped in the revelation of what the Lord had shown her.

Captain Jameson glanced up sharply when he heard Rebecca's quick intake of air, fearful she might be taking her last breath, but he saw that her eyes remained clear and bright, and her face was tinted with color.

"Captain," she whispered. "God brought me here for you!"

He stared at her in confusion, unsure of what it was that she spoke of, and wondering if perhaps it wasn't just feverish delirium.

"To the Redemption…it was for you, sir, that God brought me here! Oh, Captain, you are a leader of men and commander of thousands…you have the ability to change your world, sir… to make known the saving grace of God to the multitudes of lost souls…"

Her face shown with a triumphant peace at the revelation that had finally come to her, and she whispered again in her amazement, "It was for you…you were my mission all along…"

He continued to stare at her, waiting for the words she spoke to sink into his consciousness.

"You were worth every moment of my being here, Captain," she sighed, "and I'm so glad He brought me to you. I have no regrets, sir."

The flood gates of his emotional reserve burst open, and he fell to his knees before her. "Tell me what I must do Rebecca, to share in your eternity with you," he begged, tears of anguish coursing down his face.

Rebecca began to speak in humble reverence to the Lord, her hand resting with tenderness upon Captain Jameson's shoulder. She soon asked him to join her as she led him in prayer, asking for God's gracious mercy and forgiveness to descend upon his soul. When they had finished, he grew silent, while Rebecca continued to utter the life giving words of scripture from deep within her heart.

"Remember always, Captain, the words of the faithful written in the book of Hebrews…*God is not unjust; He will not forget your work and the love you show Him as you help His people and continue to help them…show this same diligence to the very end, in order to make your hope sure."*

She sighed then, her voice breaking with great passion in her intense love for this man whom the Lord had entrusted to her. "The Lord bless you, and keep you; the Lord make His face to shine upon you and be gracious to you; the Lord lift up His countenance upon you, and give you peace, Captain Jameson."

He waited for several moments before raising his head to look at her, allowing the Lord's benevolent grace that washed over him to settle in his soul.

Rebecca gazed at him and whispered, "Tell Mr. Burgess I forgive him, Captain."

Her eyes closed then, as she slipped into her unwaking slumber once again. As he knelt on the floor beside her bed, he wondered if he had dreamed the whole scene, but her pillow was wet with tears, and his heart was full of the grace and peace of God. Standing to his feet, he tucked the covers around her shoulders and sat once again, praying for just one more moment with her before she was taken to the heavenly realms.

Rebecca remained in her unconscious state for the duration of the journey to Portsmouth, the fever of infection continuing to push her ever nearer towards death. Captain Jameson maintained his nightly vigil with her, only now he prayed for the Lord's healing touch to fall upon her feverish body.

Lieutenant Burgess had not been in to see Rebecca as of yet, and Captain Jameson feared for the emotional wellbeing of his young officer. Rather than force the lieutenant to confront his guilt, the captain determined he would enlist the officer to assist them in transporting Rebecca to her family's home once they reached Portsmouth. He hoped that would help to alleviate the burden weighing heavily on the young man's conscience, while offering him some semblance of closure.

The Redemption neared the coast of England on the evening of the ninth day, and Captain Jameson peered over the shoreline of the city in an attempt to identify the locations of the places Rebecca had spoken of so many times. From the quarterdeck, he was able to find with ease the small, white church on the west edge of the city, and he tried to imagine her there, vibrant and alive. Sensing the heart wrenching anguish rising within him, he turned his thoughts toward other matters, while his crew prepared for their mooring, lest they see their commander lose all control of his emotional reserve.

Dr. Ammons approached Captain Jameson from the stern and moved to stand beside him at the railing of the quarterdeck, while they observed the men guiding the frigate into port.

"How is she?" Captain Jameson asked, not having seen Rebecca since early that afternoon.

"To be honest, Will," Dr. Ammons replied, "I believe she is holding on just long enough to be in the presence of her family before she passes."

Captain Jameson nodded his understanding, unable to speak any further. After several, terse moments Lieutenant Burgess approached with a solemn look on his face.

"Excuse me, Captain, Dr. Ammons," he called.

The men turned to glance at the officer standing behind them.

"Shall I prepare the men to disembark, sir?" he asked, looking at Captain Jameson.

"Yes, Mr. Burgess," he stated, "and I would like you to accompany us ashore as well."

It appeared for a moment as if the young officer would refuse, but then thinking better of it, nodded his acquiescence and waited for the captain to dismiss him.

"And gather the petty officer and the cook…they will want to attend as well," he added, his gaze distant and impenetrable.

Lieutenant Burgess retreated to crew's quarters where he found Eddy and Petty Officer Andrews lingering in a melancholy state near the doorway, well away from the men who engaged in card games and casual conversation. He caught their attention with a slight nod of his head, and was relieved when they followed after him without question.

Dr. Ammons had wrapped Rebecca in a thick, cotton blanket and the men lowered her to the awaiting dinghy with reverent caution. As soon as she was secured, Captain Jameson and Dr. Ammons joined the rest of the crew who were already aboard, and the small boat began to move toward the bustling shoreline of Portsmouth.

Captain Jameson kept his eyes fixed on the distant horizon, his heart breaking with an inexplicable sadness. When the sands of the shoreline finally scraped against the hull of the dinghy, he stepped onto dry land and led the men to the small, white church building he had seen from the deck of the Redemption, praying that someone would be there to assist them in finding Rebecca's family home. Her limp body was strapped to a board which had been prepared for this sole purpose only, and the men carried her with delicate prudence, as if she were a fragile treasure that might break with a careless step. In essence, she was, and each of the men who had been chosen for this task held different aspects of whom she had been close to their hearts, while all were honored to accept the responsibility of seeing her safely home.

Moira Bronlee had been the caretaker of the little church since it had been built well over fifty years ago. She had seen many things come to pass during her time at the Church by the Sea, but none so disheartening as the unexplained disappearance of Rebecca Halloway. None in the church's congregation spoke of the incident, for the girl's father refused to believe her dead, and when the matter of her vanishing was mentioned, he spoke with a wistful voice of when she would return, leaving the others glancing about in an awkward silence. The most difficult aspect of the bizarre incident was in not knowing what had happened to the girl. Had she been murdered and then buried in a haphazard grave, or had she left willingly, unconcerned with the heartache of those she had left behind? The latter was too difficult for most in the congregation to comprehend, for she was held in high esteem, loved and cherished by all who knew her. So, life had gone on without her, and though none spoke of that terrible night, the memory of it never lingered far from the minds of those who had adored her.

Moira was resting on a bench near the quaint, little church, enjoying the rare treat of a starry night in Portsmouth. The evening service had continued on well past her bedtime hour, and she figured since she had already strayed from habit, she may as well enjoy it. She was unaware of the men who approached, and glanced up in startled apprehension when she heard the voice of the captain speaking to her.

"Excuse me, madam," he said. "Can you tell me where I might find the home of Dr. Colin Halloway?"

Moira studied the sullen faced group of men, all handsomely dressed in smart uniforms, and stood to her feet, making an attempt to straighten her clothing. It wasn't long before she caught sight of the stretcher carrying a limp body swaddled in a cocoon of blankets. Not realizing who it was that lay there, she assumed it was an injured sailor, and she hurried to give the men clear instruction on where to find the doctor, before offering to lead the men there herself.

Captain Jameson accepted the woman's gracious offer with an inward sigh of gratitude, knowing that the time of Rebecca's death was drawing near. He watched as she stepped to the front of the group to lead them, not even bothering to introduce herself. He offered a silent prayer of thanks to the Lord for providing this woman in their time of need, and he hastened the men in following behind her.

Lieutenant Burgess was stunned when he saw Rebecca being lowered onto the dinghy and now, he continued to stare at her with a mixture of sadness and guilt. Her face was the color of death and void of all expression, and he realized he had never before seen her without some sort of emotion in clear display on her face, most often of which was joy, as evidenced by her easy smile. The grip of sorrow clenched at his heart when he realized that the only time she had appeared guarded and distraught was when he was reproaching her for one thing or another. He ambled along with trepidation, desperate to avoid speaking with her father lest the man discover that it was he who had led her to this demise. He averted his gaze to stare in remorse at the ground, no longer able to gaze upon the still form of the one who had with such selfless abandon impacted the lives of all who served aboard the Redemption.

Moira pointed out the home of Dr. Halloway through the trees, almost as if urging the men to hurry. Captain Jameson studied with heartrending intrigue the humble dwelling Rebecca had considered her home, and imagined her sitting on the porch swing perched near the bubbling brook flowing through the yard. In a matter of seconds he saw the shadowed form of a tall man striding with great lengths of limb to meet them. He soon became aware of the man's strong resemblance to Rebecca, even from a distance, and he knew with certainty that this was the father of the one who had changed his destiny. He struggled to suppress the emotions that were threatening to overwhelm him.

"Katherine!" the man shouted in exultation. "Rebecca has come home!"

Eddy broke down then in great, heaving sobs at hearing the man rejoicing over his daughter's return, certain he knew not of the precarious situation she was in. Dr. Halloway regarded the men with a curious glance and softly caressed Rebecca's face. He motioned them to follow him to a small structure beside his home, urging them along to hurry. Katherine, Rebecca's mother, joined the group there.

The men stood about in an awkward silence, watching Dr. Halloway lift Rebecca's lifeless body from the wooden stretcher to lay her on a table. Katherine spoke gentle words of appreciation to the men, and gathered them together with urgent determination in an attempt to move them toward the house, knowing that time was crucial in the task required of her husband and herself.

"I can never thank you enough for returning her to us, gentlemen," she murmured, turning to leave.

Captain Jameson stared at the woman with a brusque expression, wondering why she hadn't even inquired as to where her daughter had been for the past nineteen months. "Madame," he snapped, irate at her rudeness and thinking she was not at all like her daughter, "would you not even like to know of your daughter's whereabouts since she disappeared?"

Katherine Halloway gazed with compassionate patience at the smartly dressed officer, for it was obvious to her that Rebecca had won his heart, just as she had won the hearts of all who knew her. "I apologize, gentlemen," she stated with polite humility, glancing at the disheartened group standing before her. "But I am desperately needed by my daughter for reasons you might not understand, and I am truly sorry for having to leave you in this manner. You are all welcome to wait in the cottage for us, and we can speak more later perhaps?"

For a brief moment, Captain Jameson thought he was looking into the face of Rebecca...the expression on the woman's features being very similar to the girl's. He wanted nothing more than to embrace her... to beg her to bid her daughter a final farewell, but he knew it would not be appropriate. Instead, a broken sigh escaped him and he turned to face his men. "We will return to the Redemption," he said, his voice laden with despair.

They nodded at him with solemn faces, all bearing the burden of grief that weighed heavily upon their hearts.

Turning back to Mrs. Halloway, Captain Jameson remarked, "If she stirs, please bid her our farewell."

Katherine Halloway wished she could have taken the time to lay hands on each of the men to pray for them, aware of their tremendous sense of loss, but instead she nodded and said, "I will tell her. God be with you all." She again turned to hurry to her daughter's side without waiting for the men to leave, while the crew of the Redemption stood watching her until she had disappeared from sight, knowing that their last earthly bond to Rebecca had departed for evermore.

Captain Jameson began to retrace the steps they had taken to the cottage, the crew following along behind him in silence. None spoke for the remainder of the evening, each bound up in a personal anguish that was incomprehensible to all aboard the frigate. Katherine Halloway hurried to kneel beside her husband, who was already deep in prayer, his hands lying with a light touch on Rebecca's head. She fell to her knees beside him, and joined him in the vigil to bring their daughter home.

End of part one.

LaVergne, TN USA
26 August 2009
155932LV00001B/26/P